DYING BY DEGREES

DYING BY DEGREES

An Emily Goodstriker Mystery

EILEEN COUGHLAN

RaveN
STONE

Dying by Degrees
copyright © 2000 Eileen Coughlan

published by Ravenstone
an imprint of Turnstone Press
607 –100 Arthur Street
Artspace Building
Winnipeg,Manitoba
R3B 1H3 Canada
www.TurnstonePress.com

Turnstone Press gratefully acknowledges the assistance of the Canada Council for the Arts, the Manitoba Arts Council and the Government of Canada through the Book Publishing Industry Development Program for our publishing activities.

Canada

Cover design and artwork: Doowah Design

Interior design: Manuela Dias

This book was printed and bound in Canada
by Friesens for Turnstone Press.

Canadian Cataloguing in Publication Data

Coughlan, Eileen Patricia.

Dying by degrees

ISBN 0-88801-247-0

I. Title.

PS8555.082282 D95 2000   C813'.6   C00-920102-5
PR9199.3.C6577 D95 2000

For
Don, Mom, Eve

Acknowledgements

I gratefully acknowledge Dr. Stanley Milgram for his brilliant research and the inspiration it gave me for this book.

A special thank you to Manuela Dias, Patrick Gunter and Marijke Friesen of Turnstone Press. Much appreciation goes to my editor, Jennifer Glossop, for helping me make the book much better. Thanks also to Pat Sanders for her copy-editing skills. I extend a gracious thank you to Dr. Connie Varnhagen and Dr. Lahoucine Ouzgane, two outstanding professors who made a difference in my life. Thanks also to Brenda Tink and Debbie Dollimount for reading the manuscript and making insightful suggestions. Todd Hill I thank for his sound advice, wit, and inspirational thoughts. I am indebted to Gail Bowen for her sage advice that made me stop reading "How to Write" books and actually get down to writing one. Many thanks to the Johners, Elizabeth J. Owens, Patti, Tim, Jocelyn, and David for their enthusiastic book promotion. Michelle Leoppky I thank for her love of words, all the great pixs, and for the hours of reading and constant supply of kind words and encouragement. Much thanks to T. Chops for being a quiet, loyal friend. My sisters Colleen and Catherine, brother Sean, and their spouses, I thank for their support and interest. My father, John C. Coughlan, I thank for teaching me the value of truth and every human life. I gratefully acknowledge my mother, M. Patricia Coughlan, who has championed everything I have ever aspired to. I thank her for her love of the English language and for editing almost every word I have ever written. I thank Evelyn Carignan for her friendship and wisdom, and for all the hours she listened and knew.

Most of all, my deepest thanks and love go to Don Gee, my husband and best friend, who believes in me and makes it possible for me to achieve my dreams.

"This is perhaps the most fundamental lesson of our study ... ordinary people, simply doing their jobs, and without any particular hostility on their part, can become agents in a terrible destructive process...."
— Stanley Milgram

Chapter 1

MY DAY STARTED WITH what should have been a routine run through the procedure. It was December 17th, the day before the long-awaited Christmas holidays and a much-needed break from the University of Southwestern Alberta. As always, I arrived at the lab early to make sure everything was in order. I went through the list twice, and it all seemed fine, but I couldn't shake the feeling I had forgotten something. I started at the top again and said each item aloud, dutifully ticking them off as I went.

"Paper sheet on bed." Check. "Pillow in place." Check. "Hose connected from face mask to carbon dioxide tank." Check. "Hose connected to oxygen tank." Check. I walked over to a small desk in the corner and leafed through the forms I had placed there earlier.

"Debriefing and questionnaire." Check and check. I filled the water glass and placed it back on the desk. Next to it was an envelope. I picked it up and looked inside to make sure the twenty-dollar bill I had stuck in there five minutes earlier was still there. Sure enough, it was.

My hands were stiff with cold. I rubbed them together and felt my back tighten against a shiver that ran up my spine. I was never sure whether it was the actual temperature of the place that caused this, or just my nerves. Whatever the reason, I knew that within a few minutes of getting started, I'd be warm enough to want to take off my lab coat. I stared at the list again and was about to go over it a fourth time when mercifully, my friend and lab partner, Zac Farnham, came bounding in.

"Hey, Em, Jerry Booth's in the waiting room, you know."

"Hi, Zac. Yes, I know. I told him we'd be with him just as soon as Beth and Mullarcant get here. Do me a favor." I passed him the clipboard. "Go over this one more time. I'm pretty sure I've forgotten something."

"You always think you've forgotten something, and the Emily Goodstriker I know never does. It's just your little way of acting out your anxieties over whether you really want to be doing this to people, or if you'd rather be at home sipping hundred-year-old cognac in your solarium."

I gave him a pained look. "Thanks, Doctor Zac."

"Any time, that's what I'm here for," he said with an impish grin.

"And it's not my solarium. But I could use a shot of cognac if you've got one, and I don't care if it's one week, one year, or one millennium old."

He laughed. And for a moment I was envious of his calm demeanor.

Zac and I met a year and half earlier when we both arrived at the university, full of enthusiasm and egos the size of a Longview ranch. Zac came from Montreal and I from Edmonton. The first time we spoke was during a "welcome to the department talk," where faculty pump up new graduate students by telling us how we are the "chosen ones" and all that.

When Doctor Byron Sanders, weekend cowboy extraordinaire and born-again health nut, referred to us as the "cream of the wheat," Zac leaned over to me and said, "That must be the western equivalent of the *crème de la crème*." I liked him immediately.

We were both starting our master's degrees in psychology. And at the time, I drank in every word Byron Sanders and his cohorts said about us, and so did Zac. We truly believed we were a cut above the rest. In a way, it was understandable, and I've since learned to forgive myself for it. Moving from undergraduate to graduate school is much like leaving kindergarten and becoming a full-fledged "grade oner." But reality eventually set in, and four months into our second year, all that unbridled enthusiasm had been beaten out of us and replaced with a dogged determination to see the finish. By the time we had finally picked a thesis topic, found an interim supervisor who would deign to speak to us, and then lived through the experience of being a teaching assistant to students who were barely a year behind us, our egos had shrunk to the equivalent of little more than insy-sized belly buttons. And we were considered the lucky ones! Zac and I had been chosen by the great man himself—Doctor Martin Mullarcant—to work on the Aspen Projects.

"So where's Beth?" Zac asked.

"I was just about to ask you the same thing. Did you tell Mullarcant we were running the subject at four instead of five?"

Zac hopped up on the bed and let his long legs dangle over the side. "I slipped a note under his door earlier. And I just went by there on my way down here, but the door was closed."

"Had the 'Do Not Disturb' sign up, did he?"

"You bet, but he's revised it. Looks all professional now, done up in big block letters that say"—Zac made quotation marks in the air—"Conference in Progress."

"Nice touch."

"Indeed. And I'll tell you, he was having one hell of a conference with someone. I could hear him yelling all the way down the hall."

I shook my head and started to back away toward the door that led down the hall to the other rooms. "The man's a maniac," I said. "He's got absolutely no conception of what a conversation is."

"Oh, he does. But it's usually one way. His way."

"I think you're right. I'm just going to run down to Beth's office and see if she's there," I said over my shoulder.

Since the entire lab, along with its adjoining rooms, took up the better part of the science building's west corner wing, it was possible to be in the main part of the lab and not know if someone else was down the hall in another room. Doctor Martin Mullarcant's world was like a mega-corporation that continued to expand as he absorbed more and more space, faculty, and students. His growing empire tended to be a sore spot with other faculty members and departments, who were themselves working with limited budgets and even more limited space and people power.

Mullarcant's lab was separated from the main part of the building by solid, locking doors that we were allowed to prop open in order to get some heat circulating, but only if one of us was in the lab. Zac and I hid a key in the assignments mailbox because we were forever forgetting ours.

Inside the doors was a reception area just large enough to hold a pine table and two chairs, nothing fancy—strictly IKEA. A few steps around the corner and you were in the main part of the lab, two spacious rooms that could be separated with the aid of a folding divider. On the right side was the conference or work area with a table and enough chairs to accommodate eight people. Along the back wall, two brand-new iMac computers and two G3 Macs, with enough power to run even the most sophisticated statistics, were grouped into a pod. Next to the computers was a couch that looked as new as the computers, but apparently had been there for a number of years. The pristine condition of the couch was my first indication that people didn't typically relax in Mullarcant's lab.

The other half of the room housed the experimental lab, which looked much like a hospital emergency room, with its chrome-sided bed, metal desk, and CO_2 and oxygen tanks.

A little further down the hall was the library—a small room, but one that was almost as well-stocked in psychology literature as the main university library. Mullarcant made certain that we had all the most recent periodicals and up-to-date texts. And with Internet access at four of the computer terminals we shared among three of us, Zac, Beth, and I rarely had to venture outside the building to do any research. The door was open and I could see that no one was in there.

Across the hall from the library, a second experimental room held audiovisual equipment, a desk, table, and chairs. That too was open and there was no sign Beth had been there, either. The file room next to it held all our subjects' demographic information and study results. The door was locked, but there was a little window on the door and the lights were out. Across from it was Mullarcant's lab office—another bone of contention among the faculty, since Mullarcant also had a faculty office in the main part of the building.

At the very end of the hall was Beth's office. The door was closed. I gave it a quick rap before I opened it and poked my head in. It was a long, narrow room with a desk pushed up against the window. Even Mullarcant's office, across the hall, didn't have a window. Earning a window at the university was akin to acquiring wall-to-wall carpeting, an oil painting, and a window with a view in a large law firm. But I didn't begrudge Beth her office. Beth Wong worked harder than anyone I had ever known. The lights were on and files were open on Beth's desk. Her coat was hanging on the coat rack, signs that she had been there and would be returning.

Back in the experimental room, Zac glanced at his watch. "So what do you think, should we just go ahead without them? Ol' Jerry's looking kinda pale out there."

"I'm sure Jerry always looks pale."

"You know what I mean, paler than usual."

"Yeah, yeah, I know, but I'm not going to do anything until at least one of them gets here."

"Come on, Em, I think it's cruel to leave him sitting out there."

"I think it's crueler to bring him in. Zac, every time I have to do this, it gets worse. He's letting them go longer and longer each time. Have you noticed that?"

"I know, I've been thinking about that myself. But remember, ours is not to question, it is to listen and learn and above all"— he thrust his index finger into the air—"to obey."

"Yeah, well, I'm marking the days off."

"Look on the bright side. After today we get three long weeks of relaxation, fun, and sun."

"And just where are you going to find all this sun in Montreal? You'd get a better tan staying right here in good ol' Cowtown. At least we still have blue skies."

"Oh, please," he said, moving across the room toward the main doors. "I'd go mad if I had to stay in these cultural badlands for the holidays."

I rolled my eyes. "Okay, go bring him in, and we'll get him set up. Maybe by then Mullarcant or Beth will have shown up."

When Jerry Booth walked in, his eyes darted around the room like a frightened bird. His file indicated he was a forty-eight-year-old, five-foot-seven, Caucasian male. What the file didn't say was that from years of abusing his body with alcohol and other toxic substances, along with sleeping on the streets and in shelters, he was an emaciated figure of weathered skin and bones who looked closer to seventy.

"Hi, Mr. Booth, back again, are you?" I said in that professionally cheery tone people like gynecologists use just before they do some unspeakable thing to you.

Jerry returned my nicety with a weak smile. "Yup, back again." He fixed his gaze on the bar that hung over the bed, with all its tubes, wires, and gauges. "So, uh, do you think it's going to be as bad as last time, or do you think maybe a person gets used to it?"

"That's a good question," Zac said, leading him to the bed. "I guess we'll find out, since you're the only one who's ever done it twice."

"Oh," was all Jerry Booth said before he stretched his 135-pound frame stiffly out on the bed. The paper sheet under him made scrunching noises as he tried unsuccessfully to rearrange himself into a comfortable position.

Zac checked the connections on the mask. "Since you know the routine, Mr. Booth—"

"You just call me Jerry."

"Okay, Jerry," Zac said, as he fitted the mask over Jerry's nose and mouth. "Since you've been through this before, we'll skip all the preamble and get right to it just as soon as Doctor Mullarcant and Beth get here."

"Maybe we should talk Jerry through the procedure again," I interrupted. "Just so we're sure we all know what we're doing."

Jerry lifted the mask from his face. "Yeah, that's good with me. Tell me again how I can stop it if it gets too bad, and all that. Sometimes I don't remember too good." He replaced the mask over his mouth and nose.

Zac and I looked at each other, and I knew we were both thinking the same thing. I went over to the bed and sat beside our subject, then pulled the mask gently off Jerry's face.

"Listen, Jerry," I said quietly, "if you don't feel comfortable about doing this, that's fine. You're under no obligation to continue. I just want to make sure you understand that."

Before Jerry Booth could respond, Beth Wong and Martin Mullarcant bustled in.

"Sorry I'm late," Beth said in an almost inaudible voice. I jumped down off the bed as Mullarcant came over to take the clipboard from my hand.

"Doctor Mullarcant," I said, "we were just explaining to the subject that if he wasn't feeling comfortable about going through the procedure, that was—"

"Of course he doesn't have to proceed with the session," Mullarcant said, cutting me off. "Is there a problem, Mr. Booth?"

Jerry looked pensively from the door to the gas tanks, and then back to the door. A small bead of perspiration formed on his upper lip. "No, no problem," he said, licking his lips. His eyes shot to Mullarcant, who was staring at him intently. "I didn't say nothin'. I was jus'—"

"Good, then," Mullarcant said and turned to me. "Emily, you and Zacarie may start the procedure."

Zac and I looked at Beth, who was standing on the other side of the room, staring out the window. It was obvious something was wrong because Beth was usually all business in the lab—personal issues were left at the door.

"Beth, we're ready when you are," I said.

"Elizabeth will be observing today," Mullarcant said brusquely. "You will operate the gas flow, and Zacarie will monitor the subject's responses."

I did as I was told and took my place up on the stool at the end of the bed, next to the tanks. Then I checked the gauges and lines running to Jerry's mask. Our subject was wringing his hands and his face was a shade of gray I thought one could attain only posthumously. I listened while Zac completed the procedure protocol.

"Okay, Jerry," Zac said. "It's going to be just like last time. When we turn on the CO_2 you will experience a feeling of oxygen deprivation. You can stop the procedure at any time by taking off the mask or by raising your hand for one of us to do it. But, as you know, the longer you are able to keep the mask on, the better it is for the study."

Jerry lifted the mask from his face. "But even if I only go a little bit, I still get the money, right?"

"Yes, of course, but I will stress again that the longer you can keep the mask on, the better it will be for the project." Mullarcant was standing on the other side of the bed, nodding his head in approval. "Do you understand everything I've just said, Mr. Booth? And if so, are you ready to begin?" When Jerry gave two tight little nods, Zac pointed a finger at me. "All set, Em."

"Emily, what is your mixture percentages?" Mullarcant asked suddenly. I wondered if he was testing me because our ratio had always been the same.

"Uh, it's thirty-five percent CO_2 and sixty-five percent O_2. Same as always."

Mullarcant came up behind me and reset the gauge on the carbon dioxide tank to forty percent. "Please make sure you indicate in the log that we have increased the carbon dioxide to a forty-sixty ratio," he said.

I looked at Zac, who shrugged.

"You may proceed, Emily," Mullarcant said.

I stared at the gauge. All the other panic studies I had reviewed used a maximum thirty-five percent CO_2 concentration, and I had no idea if anything higher was dangerous.

"Emily, please begin," Mullarcant said firmly but not unkindly.

I took a deep breath. "Uh, Doctor Mullarcant, are you sure you want forty percent?" As I watched his face take on a pinkish hue that was quickly moving up the color wheel toward fuchsia, I wished with all my heart I could have stuffed those words right back in my mouth. I had never been on the receiving end of one of Doctor Martin Mullarcant's famous tirades, but I was getting a sinking feeling that my time had come.

He managed to control himself until we were out in the hall, which was more than I could say he had been able to do with other people.

"How dare you question my judgment and authority?" he said. "Particularly in front of a subject."

"I just wanted to make sure it was safe, that's all."

"I don't give a damn what you want. I am in charge. This is my lab, my project. Do you understand that?"

I felt my eyes well and my throat tighten, partly out of fear, but mostly out of anger. He was close to screaming and I knew everyone in the lab, as well as all the people who were poking their heads out of their offices to see what all the commotion was about, could hear everything.

"I want you to apologize to me, Emily, and assure me that this type of insubordination will never happen again."

I thought I might try reasoning with him. Explain where I was coming from. "Doctor Mullarcant—"

"Apologize!" he screamed.

At that moment I wanted nothing more than to oblige him and say I was sorry. But I couldn't because I wasn't.

He was leaning in closer now. "Who do you think you are?"

I thought I was doing pretty well holding my own, but when his breath and a little spittle hit my face, I knew I had to say something. "Okay, I'm sorry I brought it up in front of the subject. It won't happen again." Ha! but I didn't say I was sorry for saying it.

"Thank you, Emily, and I'm glad we've cleared this up. I think we should go back in now." It was as though someone flipped a switch. He was suddenly as calm as he had been five minutes earlier. Oddly, I found this change to be more unnerving than his temper tantrum.

When we walked back into the lab, it was pretty clear by the look on Zac's face and Jerry's face that they had heard the whole thing. They tried to look away, but there really wasn't anywhere else for them to look.

"Sorry for the interruption," Mullarcant said. "We will proceed now."

I sat back up on the stool and tried to regain my composure. After a minute or two of fiddling with the tanks and anything else I could get my hands on, I was as ready as I'd ever be.

"Okay, Jerry, I'm going to start the gas now." I turned both gauges to the appropriate settings. I held my breath and got that same feeling I get when I'm in a plane that's about to take off.

For the first five seconds after the gas hit Jerry Booth's face, he breathed in and out normally. At eight seconds, his eyes bulged, his breathing became rapid, and his hands came up to the mask over and over again, but he didn't tear it off.

Zac looked at our subject, then back at the stopwatch he was holding tightly in his left hand. At the half-minute point, he began calling off the seconds. "Thirty, thirty-one, thirty-two, thirty-three, thirty-four, thirty-five, thirty-six, thirty-seven, thirty-eight." Zac shot Mullarcant a look and when he didn't get a response, he looked at me for help. Jerry Booth's face was now mauve-gray, his feet were kicking, and his eyes were wild with panic. "Thirty-nine, forty seconds." I glared at Mullarcant, who was leaning passively against the wall, giving no indication he would end the session.

"I'm cutting the gas," I said, and with vibrating hands, turned the dials to the off position. I felt moisture beading under my arms, and my heart beating in my throat. Zac took a deep breath and swallowed hard as he lifted the mask from Jerry's face.

"Holy . . . Hannah," Jerry said in a halting voice. He wiped a sleeve across his sweating forehead. "That . . . that . . . was a real doozy."

"Just lay back and relax, Jerry," Zac said. "Boy, you really went for the gold this time, didn't you?"

"Thought my head was gonna explode there for a minute."

I tried to record the level of carbon dioxide in the logbook, but my hands were shaking too badly. I looked up toward the window. Beth still hadn't moved.

"Good work," Mullarcant said. He picked up the questionnaire and debriefing forms from the desk and handed them to Beth. She barely looked up when she accepted them.

"Elizabeth will do the debriefing and the questionnaire, and I will run Mr. Booth through the second phase," Mullarcant said to no one in particular.

On his way out, he stopped briefly beside Jerry, who was now sitting up, sipping the water Zac had given him. "Thank you, Mr. Booth, for your cooperation. I'll be waiting for you in my office. Be sure to collect your remuneration before you leave."

Jerry gave him a puzzled look. "He means your money," I said quickly.

"Oh, don't worry, I wouldn't forget that."

I went over to Beth. She was hugging a file folder and the forms Mullarcant had given her against her chest, and rocking slightly from side to side.

"Uh, I'll just get Jerry settled over here for you, okay?" Zac said to Beth as he helped Jerry off the bed and led him past us to the desk.

"Zac, why don't you take Jerry into the library?" I said. "It's more comfortable there." He got the message and led Jerry down the hall.

I turned to Beth. Tears were streaming down her face. This

was a side of Elizabeth May Wong I had never seen before. In the year and a half I had known her, I had rarely seen her get flustered, let alone cry.

"Beth, what is it?"

"I'm sorry," she whispered between sobs. "He had no right to do that to you." She turned away to brush the tears from her cheeks.

"Why are you sorry? God knows you've put up with your fair share of it. Besides, it really didn't get to me," I lied.

"You shouldn't have to put up with that, none of us should."

"I know," I said and followed Beth's gaze out the window. She was watching a blond, preppy-looking guy in a double-breasted, navy duffel coat, who was standing in the middle of the commons area. He clapped his gloved hands and a black and white border collie came barreling around a stand of trees and skidded to a stop at his master's feet. The guy took a neon-pink Frisbee from the hound's mouth and threw it high in the air. The dog charged after it and made a graceful pirouette in the sky before snatching the toy between its teeth. The air was thick with ice fog and the dog's breath came out in solid puffs that stayed suspended in the air. The sun was already setting and the lights from the lamps that lined the sidewalk cast a hazy glow over the snow-covered grounds.

"He goes out there and plays with that dog every day." The tone of her voice made it sound as if the guy was doing something offensive.

"Do you know him? Who is he?" She didn't answer. Beth Wong was miles away, lost in her thoughts. "Beth? What's going on?"

She shook herself back to the moment. "I'm okay. I'm just tired or something."

"No kidding, you've been working like crazy for the past month. We've hardly seen you."

She tried to smile. "I'm fine, it's okay. I've been spending a lot of time down at the center. And working at home. At my parents'," she added quickly.

"Hey, no offense, but you don't look so fine." Her face was drawn and her usually bright, black eyes were dull and blood-shot. I put my hand on her shoulder. "Why don't you go and get some rest?" I said. "Zac and I'll finish up here."

She glanced toward the doors where Mullarcant had just left through. "Thanks, but I should do this. You have enough to do yourself. And besides, I have to run down to the drop-in center with a few hampers and clothes." Beth had been organizing a Christmas drive for New Beginnings, a drop-in center for street people.

I took the forms from her. "Good, all the more reason you should get a little rest. So how about I come by your dorm in an hour or so and we can go down there together? I've got a couple of hampers and some other stuff in my car I was going to give you anyway."

She glanced at the doors again.

"Maybe we could grab a coffee or something after." I took her arm and led her to the door. She left, albeit reluctantly.

Zac had a lot to do for the Christmas party coming up the next night, so I sent him on his way too. After I shooed him out the door, I flipped through the questionnaire forms and noticed I had also taken a blue file folder from Beth. I slipped the folder into a back pocket of my pack, where it wouldn't get mixed in with my things, and made a mental note to return it to Beth later.

I finished up with Jerry Booth, gave him his well-deserved twenty dollars, and then led him down to Mullarcant's office.

Chapter 2

WE PARKED OUR CARS at a couple of meters in front of the old, two-storey cinder-block building that was once home to a paint and hardware supplier. The building was located on the south-eastern edge of the downtown core, next to the rail tracks, which made it close enough to the center of town to be accessible to its patrons, but far enough from business owners, shoppers, and tourists so as not to be offensive. Calgary is noted for being a friendly city, but like most other large metropolitan centers, pan-handling and homelessness are discouraged in the highly visible, economically viable downtown core.

Since working with Beth in Mullarcant's lab, I had met a number of the study participants Beth had recruited from New Beginnings. But I had never been to the center myself. It was just after six-thirty when we started unloading the hampers.

When we walked through the front doors of New Beginnings, we entered a thick fog. A couple of dozen tables were set up in the foyer. Around each table, three or four people sat talking, playing cards or checkers, and smoking cigarettes. The room had high ceilings with ineffectual fans that rotated at glacial speed. The air was so thick with smoke my eyes were tearing by the time I made it to the reception desk, where Beth and I piled the hampers.

A number of the people knew Beth and either waved or came over to say hello. We had stopped at Tim Horton's on the way over and picked up four dozen donuts. Beth gave the boxes to a couple of the center's clients and asked them to pass them out.

"I'll just be another minute," Beth said to me. "I need to find Carmen."

Carmen was one of our study participants. I had met her a few times in the lab. She was a pleasant, frail woman in her mid to late fifties with a a history of drug and alcohol abuse. However, she was well on the road to recovery, and Beth had been taking a personal interest in helping her along.

I felt conspicuous standing alone in the middle of the room, so I moved over to a wall and read the billboard posters that advertised everything from safe needle and condom use to job opportunities and rental properties. Just as I was considering an ad for a volunteer position, a very good-looking man with lustrous black hair that fell just below his shoulders stuck his head out a door next to the billboard.

"Hi, I'm Tom," he said, extending a hand. He was wearing a name tag that said he was a social worker. "You waiting for me?" I said no, then introduced myself and explained that I was from the university and that I was with Beth.

"Oh, so you run those experiments." He didn't say it unkindly, but the emphasis on the word "those" indicated he probably took issue with what we were doing.

I nodded and then tried to skirt the issue and gain a few brownie points. "We just brought down some hampers," I said.

He glanced over at the offerings. He nodded and said, "So, I suppose you've heard the bad news?"

"Uh, I don't think so. What's that?"

"One of your study participants passed away last night."

"Oh, no. I'm so sorry. Who?"

"Carmen."

It hit me like a slap. "Oh God." I looked around the room for

Beth. She was nowhere in sight. My mind went immediately back to the lab. Had Beth known then? Was that why she was so upset? But why wouldn't she have told me?

Just then, Beth came around the corner and from the look on her face, I knew that she too had just received the terrible news.

Tom led us into his office and introduced us to another social worker named Leslie, a wholesome-looking woman who no doubt ate a lot of granola and little meat.

"I'm sorry, Beth," Leslie said. "Carmen's body was found close to an abandoned warehouse near the old stockyards and packing plant." Leslie turned to me. "It's a common hangout for some of our clients and other street people."

"What happened to her?"Beth asked.

Tom and Leslie exchanged a look. "She was burned, with gasoline," Tom finally said.

Beth and I both gasped.

Knowing what we were thinking, Leslie quickly added, "Most likely, she did it to herself."

Beth was incredulous. "Carmen had been sober for over four months. And she was in a good frame of mind. She wouldn't commit suicide, if that's what you're saying."

"I agree," Leslie said. "It was probably an accident. This is the third time it's happened this winter at the same place. Remember last month, those two bodies that were found burned?"

Beth nodded. I remembered reading something about it in the paper.

"They were next to an open firepit," Leslie said. "It looked as though they were trying to keep warm. They'd used gasoline to get the fire going."

"It's common," Tom added. "They siphon gas out of cars and then use it to get the wood going. The fire inspectors figured those two other victims passed out too close to the fire. They had the gas can sitting between them, probably so no one would steal it. The can got too hot and, bam. It exploded. Their clothes probably had gas on them too. They wouldn't have had a chance. It was like a bomb."

"Or maybe someone poured gas on them," I said. "It certainly isn't unheard of for inhuman idiots to go around doing that sort of thing, even in Calgary."

"We thought of that too," Leslie said. "But the fire guys think it was just an accident."

"Did you ever find out who the other two were?" Beth asked.

"Still no word. They couldn't identify them."

"Well, surely someone noticed they were missing," I said.

"Not in our business," Leslie said. "Our people move around a lot. They usually don't have anyone to miss them."

I felt my throat tighten. "Well, then, how do you know this one was Carmen?" I could see that Beth was having a hard time keeping the tears back. She was taking this hard.

Beth looked up at Leslie. "Carmen wouldn't go down there. She, she was staying at the Mission Shelter," Beth said.

"Jerry Booth said he'd seen her down there a few times over the past month."

"I thought she was doing okay," Beth said. "Maybe it's not her."

"The dental records matched," Tom said gently. "Carmen was having work done here."

BETH WAS VISIBLY SHAKEN when we left New Beginnings. As we headed to our cars, I asked her to come and have a coffee with me.

"I think I'm just going to go home," Beth replied.

After how upset she had been in the lab and now with this blow about Carmen, I didn't want her to be alone all night in her residence room.

"Beth, why don't you stay with me tonight at Rusty's, instead of driving all the way back to the university?"

"Thanks, but I'm going to stay at my parents'," she said.

"Do you want me to drive you? We could pick up your car tomorrow."

She shook her head. I could see that she was close to breaking down, and I could also see that she wanted to do it alone. Beth unlocked her car door and got in. I said good night and told her I'd call her in the morning. I closed the driver's-side door and watched her pull away.

EARLY THE NEXT MORNING, I called Beth at her parents' house, but her mother told me she had already left.

"She's working too hard, Emily," Mrs. Wong said in her soft, sweet voice. "Her father and I are worried. We want her to take it easy over Christmas. Maybe make some changes. Until last night, we hadn't seen her in weeks, you know. We live in the same city, but we hardly ever see her."

Beth told me she had been working at her parents'. Why had she lied? It suddenly occurred to me that I might know the answer. Beth had been acting a little strange lately, coming into the lab late, never in her residence room.... Zac said he suspected she was seeing someone—someone whose identity she wanted to keep to herself. Perhaps he was right. It might explain why she had been so upset in the lab yesterday and why she lied about working at her parents'. She had been "working" at the boy-friend's place. Okay, mystery solved. Man troubles! I couldn't help but feel a little hurt that she hadn't confided in me.

"I'll tell her, Mrs. Wong." I said. She thanked me and we rang off. I headed off to the university and stopped in at the residence to see if Beth was in her room. She wasn't. By noon she still hadn't come in and I was worried. I tried her room a couple more times that afternoon. I didn't want to call her folks again because I knew it would only worry them.

At three that afternoon the lab phone rang. It was Beth. She had been running around doing errands, organizing hampers and the like, and was now at New Beginnings. She said she would see me at the Christmas party that night. I asked her if she was okay. She said yes. But I didn't believe her.

Chapter 3

BY THE TIME I DROVE HOME, changed, and made it back to the university, it was nearly half-past eight. I checked Beth's room. She wasn't around so I started across campus. Up ahead, Danmoth Hall loomed in the dim evening light, casting a soft, hazy emerald glow through its glassed walls. I looked up to the tenth-floor windows where Christmas lights, obviously tacked up in haste, blinked out their irregular Morse messages in tiny bursts of festive color.

There are only two buildings on campus I like, and Danmoth Hall is one of them. The other is the administration building—a handsome, sandstone structure built in the late twenties as part of the original campus. The rest were constructed during the sixties and seventies, when Alberta was flush with oil money and architects lost their minds and found their passion for square, windowless, industrial ugliness. Consequently, our library looks like a huge, white ice-cube tray; the sports complex is referred to as the Loaf Dome, and the others boast an early bunker style.

Danmoth Hall, however, was built in the late eighties when architects reclaimed their minds and a sense of style. The result is an attractive building with green glass exterior and an open floor plan. With its ten floors, Danmoth Hall is the tallest building on campus and looks like a small, chic office tower the football team stole on a whim from downtown and relocated on campus. The top floor, or "boardroom," as we students liked to call it, is home to the coveted graduate students' lounge.

As I trudged up the snow-packed path toward the main entrance of Danmoth Hall, big, wet snowflakes the size of ostrich feathers were falling from the sky. I looked back at my fresh tracks and was reminded of those nature shows where only the bravest of Canadian men, women, and caribou break virgin trail to leave their mark. And then I felt my toes curl against the cold in my new black-patent leather shoes. Why didn't I wear boots? Because you're conceited, that's why, I reminded myself.

I passed a clump of spruce trees with branches so laden with snow they bowed to the ground. A banner done in red, white, and blue was strung between two trees: "USA's Department of Psychology Welcomes You To The Annual Graduate Christmas Party." I was peeved at whoever made up the sign. Why they couldn't have used Christmas colors and avoided the tiresome joke, just this once, was beyond me.

The University of Southwestern Alberta, or USA as it has come to be known, had its beginnings in the late twenties when it was started as an agricultural research center. Apparently, back then, no one considered the inevitability of the acronym, and perhaps no one much cared. Over the years, however, as the center grew into a bona fide university, people started to care. So much so, in fact, that each spring a committee is struck for the sole purpose of finding a new, more culturally palatable name and acronym. And each spring someone cleverly suggests simply changing the order of the name to Southwestern Alberta University. And at the end of each spring, the same dog in the manger writes a thirty-thousand-word dissertation about how it's not that simple, and how it simply can't be done. So the name sticks, as does the acronym, along with the sweatshirts some industrious students print up each year that have an American flag in green, gold, and white (our school colors), and a bold "USA" stamped above it. Needless to say, the faculty is not amused.

USA's main campus sits on about 200 acres of prairie land in the far southwest corner of Calgary. Originally, it was outside the city limits and surrounded by miles and miles of wheat and oat fields. But financial needs and urban sprawl eventually claimed much of it, and today USA is surrounded by miles and miles of subdivisions and strip malls. Notwithstanding the urban encroachment, USA's campus still maintains a rural feel. In many ways, Calgary as a whole has a rural feel, sustained by its strong sense of its heritage. One would be hard-pressed to go anywhere in Calgary and not be reminded that this city grew out of ranching, oil, and the railroad. And USA's campus is no exception.

I smiled when I passed the bronze replicas of the oil derrick and the pump jack (that actually moves up and down). Both sculptures were created by an Alberta artist and given to the university as gifts from a local oil company. I always smiled when I passed those sculptures. I liked Calgary's spirit. And you have only to be in the city a few hours to feel and see it. Cowtown's cultural heritage shows up everywhere. It's in the pictures of CPR trains, winding their way through the snowy Rocky Mountains, that hang on corporate walls. You see it in the outdoor murals of cowboys, cowgals, and cattle, and in the sculptures of bison and First Nations People that decorate the city sidewalks and parks.

But like any other big, metropolitan center, Calgary has its dark side. What had happened to Carmen, and to the other two unidentified people who were burned, was a poignant reminder of it.

I breathed in the crisp air and gazed up at the sky, letting the heavy flakes splat on my face and run down my cheeks. The halide lights that lined the path cast delicate pink pools in the snow. It was a silent night, as the song goes; there wasn't another soul around, and the only sound I could hear was the crunching and squeak of my shoes on the cold, packed snow. Suddenly, a male voice broke the silence and gave me a start.

"You're late."

I spun around to see Mark Gunn, my thesis supervisor, coming up behind me. "Wow, you startled me. Where did you come from?"

"Same place as you, I expect," he said.

I looked back at the single set of footprints leading from the parking lot up the path. "Don't think so, unless you wear size six and a half pumps."

"It's a little thing I do to impress the students."

"Neat trick."

"Actually, I was tying my shoe back there by the trees, and you walked right past me."

"What you mean is that you were hiding back there in those trees, waiting to scare the pants off some unsuspecting student."

He laughed, but it was a nervous laugh, and there was just enough light to show me he was blushing.

He glanced at his watch. "Gee, it's already after eight."

"I guess that means we're both late, then, doesn't it?"

"Yes, it does," he said with a bright smile. "And it also means people will talk when they see us come in together."

Now I was blushing. "I doubt it. They'll think we're just coming from the lab."

"You're probably right." He chuckled. "We do have a bit of a reputation for burning the midnight oil."

The word "we" made me smile. Mark Gunn certainly showed his face around the lab from time to time and seemed genuinely interested in helping students, but I doubted anyone ever accused him of being a workaholic. In fact, I often wondered how he got anything done at all, since most of his days were spent either counseling students in his office, or having coffee with them in the graduate lounge. But he must have been doing something; he had a stack of research publications to his credit, and he had just received tenure. Which meant Mark Gunn was guaranteed a job for the rest of his natural-born life.

"Did you and Doctor Mullarcant get that paper wrapped up?" I asked. He had told me earlier in the week he wouldn't be around much because he was working at home on a co-authored paper.

"Yes, but we sure cut it close. The deadline was today."

I shook my head. "You know, Mark, I just can't figure out how you do it."

"What's that?"

"What you do. How many publications do you have now?"

"Oh, a few, I guess."

"A few? I've counted over a dozen just on the panic stuff alone."

"Well, I have to give Martin a lot of the credit, he's the power-house. I just do a little fiddling here and there." We walked into the deserted foyer of Danmoth Hall.

"I'd say it must be a little more than fiddling to get first author on over half of them," I said. My voice echoed in the cavernous room.

"Boy, this place is like a morgue," he said, changing the subject.

"I know. It's such a madhouse during the week. I never come here at noon."

"Neither do I," Mark said as we made our way past empty tables and darkened food kiosks to the elevators. "Ever try that little Italian place over in Eastbridge Mall?"

I shook my head.

"Oh, then I'll have to take you there sometime," he said.

It was common knowledge around the department that Mark Gunn was married but separated, and that he was in his mid to late forties; however, his blond hair and boyish good looks easily put him in the thirty- to thirty-five-year range.

When the elevator doors opened on the "boardroom" floor, the sound of Leonard Cohen singing or talking, I can never decide which it is, "First We Take Manhattan," drifted down the hall to meet us.

"Ah, the sounds of Zac," I said.

"Should be a good party," Mark said.

23

"I hope so, Zac's been organizing this for weeks." We picked up our pace and headed down the hall toward the graduate lounge to join Leonard and Zac in the festivities. But when we reached the entrance, we both stopped short.

Across the room Zac was standing by the stereo system, organizing his CDs. Near the middle, Martin Mullarcant was at the "faculty members only" table wearing his usual clean, white, starched shirt, a nondescript, conservative, blue and red tie, and a black suit jacket. The man was no fashion plate, but his dress code was like everything else about him: meticulous. Next to him was his wife, a woman I had seen only once or twice before, when she showed up on the occasional Friday night to join her husband for a quiet dinner in the faculty club. A small, dark-haired woman, she was at least ten years Mullarcant's junior, putting her somewhere around forty. Her name was Pauline: she was a Russian immigrant who spent the majority of her days at home alone. She spoke little English. And according to Beth, Pauline Mullarcant was absolutely dedicated to her man.

Seated across from Pauline was Sandra Penny, who was swilling herbal tea and looking bored. Next to her, John Summers, professor emeritus, was making little napkin fans and strategically arranging them around his drink glass. John, as he liked students to call him, was wearing his circa 1967 brown cords and matching brown tweed sports jacket. The ensemble should have passed for the rumpled professor look, but he missed the mark and ended up with a rumpled skid-row look instead.

Now Mark Gunn, on the other hand, had the more carefully practiced, rumbled professor look that came right out of an L.L. Bean catalogue. John Summers was about eighty-five years old, and as professor emeritus, he occupied an office but didn't really do anything other than show up once in a while to stir things up with the students. Across from him, Colleen Dresser, who specialized in dream psychology and who, in my opinion, was one of the few normal faculty members, was sipping a glass of red liquid, which I assumed was Zac's famous Montreal Redeye punch. Zac makes the stuff with cranberry juice, ginger ale, black tea, and three kinds of rum. The tea part sounds disgusting, but it's surprisingly good—too good, in fact, as I learned the previous Christmas, when I drank enough of the stuff to produce a two-day hangover.

Next to the faculty table, a few PhD students were milling around, looking at their watches and sipping punch. Over to the right, another group of three or four people I didn't recognize, but assumed were alumni, hung around the hors d'oeuvre table, snuffling down everything in sight.

And that was it.

In a room that could hold over three hundred people, there was a grand total of fifteen. I scanned the room again, looking for Beth, and in the process caught Colleen Dresser's eye. She waved me over.

"We're being paged," I said to Mark.

Before Colleen Dresser could get a hello out, Mullarcant jumped to his feet to greet us. "I'm so glad you were able to come, Emily," he said effusively. After his performance in the lab the previous day, I wondered if he had been into the Redeye, but the only thing in front of him was a cup of black coffee.

"Uh, thanks. I, uh, wouldn't miss it. Last year's was great."

"Yes, and you were the life of the party," he said.

I felt my cheeks heat up as I vaguely remembered dancing on the table with—who was that? Oh, God, I couldn't even remember his name.

"Now that you are here, things will surely liven up," Mullarcant said. My face was warming to the point of combusting. Everyone at the table was smiling up at me. Then, like the touch of an angel, Mark's hand came down on my shoulder and I heard his voice say, "Emily, why don't we go try some of Zac's punch?"

"Excellent idea." Mullarcant said. "Let the party begin." Then I could have sworn he winked at me.

I think I smiled and said something like, "Nice talking to you," before I made a dash for the punch.

"So what's up with him?" I said as I ladled the Redeye into two plastic cups.

"You mean Martin?" Mark asked.

"He showing his human face?"

"Come on, he's not that bad, is he?"

"If you would have asked me that on Wednesday, I might have said no. But after yesterday, I'm not so sure."

"What happened?"

I didn't feel like re-living the experience, so I said I'd tell him later. "But I will tell you this much, I think his behavior tonight is weird."

"Take it as a compliment. I think he's just trying to get to know you. He's impressed with your work, you know."

"No, I didn't."

Zac joined us at the punch bowl. "Hey, you two, make sure you leave some for the crowd."

"It is pretty quiet," I said.

"Don't worry," Mark said. "Things will pick up later."

"Well, if they don't, Em here has one hell of a lot of punch to drink, don't ya, Em?" he said and slapped me on the back.

I gave him what I hoped was a withering look. Mark laughed, then excused himself to go join the faculty table again.

"Thanks, you made me sound like a lush."

"I was just kidding. What's with you? A little sensitive, aren't we?"

"Yeah, maybe," I said, fingering the silky, cherry-red fabric of his vest. "Nice touch for Christmas."

"Thanks. My mom sent it from Montreal."

"Ah yes, the fashion capital of Canada."

"I just thank God she still lives there. What am I going to do if she moves to Florida?"

"Oh no, Zac, you'd be forced to shop right here in Calgary, where—"I pointed a finger at him to finish my sentence.

"Where the people have the fashion sense of John Wayne, and that's just the women."

We always went through this routine and I have no idea why. "Listen, buster." I poked his Calvin Klein T-shirt. "I'll remind you just one more time that this here university grew out of the labors of rig hands and ranchers, and we Albertans are damn proud of it, and not afraid to show it."

"Hey, I'm the first one to say celebrate your history, but for God's sake do it with a little fashion sense. And speaking of clothing, where is our other fashion-conscious friend?"

"I was hoping you'd seen her."

He shook his head. "She seemed pretty messed up yesterday. She tell you why?"

"Just that she was tired."

Zac pulled a face. "Looked more like mystery dude problems to me."

"My thoughts exactly. If she is seeing someone, Zac, I can't figure out why the big secret." He shrugged. "Anyway, to make matters worse, she got some really bad news last night. Did you hear about Carmen?" He hadn't, so I filled him in on the tragedy.

"Poor Beth."

"Poor Carmen."

"Yeah, poor Carmen. Beth was spending a lot of time with her. Is Beth okay?"

"I think so. She said she'd be here tonight."

"I better save some Redeye for her. Sounds like she'll need it." Zac took a drink of his punch and let out a hoot. "Yow! This one's even smoother than last year's. You might want to watch it there, Em. We wouldn't want you to miss out on the next couple of days of your life again."

"Very funny. I wasn't aware I made such a lasting impression on everyone."

"Oh, come on, I was just teasing. Everyone else was drunk too, and no one remembers."

"You do, and apparently Mullarcant does too."

"I doubt it, I don't think he hung around very long last year."

"He just said I was the life of the party, and then I think he winked at me."

"Really? Maybe he has a crush on you," Zac said as he licked some yellow matter off a Ritz cracker.

"Don't be disgusting."

"Sorry, but I don't like the cracker part."

"I was talking about what you said."

"Oh. So maybe he had something in his eye."

"Let's hope so." A couple of students came by the punch bowl for refills, and one of them already seemed to have a good glow on as he sloshed punch in his glass. When they were gone, Zac took a bottle of ginger ale from under the table and dumped it into the bowl.

"That guy's only had two or three glasses. Think maybe I better tone it down a bit."

"Zac, I know I was pretty smashed last year toward the end there," I said as I watched him dilute his poison hooch. "But I don't remember seeing any faculty."

"You forgot Mark. He stayed till the bitter end."

"Did I hear my name being used in vain?" Mark said, appearing beside us.

"We were just reminiscing about last year's Christmas party."

I shot Zac a look that said, shut up. In the background, Leonard was crooning out "Tower of Song."

"Hey, I like this song," I said. But they ignored me.

"What a hoot that was. I don't think it wrapped up until three or four. Must have been your punch, Zac," Mark said.

Zac beamed. "And the music."

"Yes, and the music. But I seem to remember you played a lot more Stones last year," Mark said.

"I did, toward the end. That's the way I work it. See, I start out with the get-everyone-comfortable stuff like Van Morrison, Leonard Cohen, and maybe a little Sting, if the crowd's right. Then I get people walking around and talking a little louder with some good ol' blues boys like Muddy Waters, John Lee Hooker, and T-Bone. And then, when everyone is starting to get real thirsty I give 'em the Doors, Springsteen, and Mick. And I'll tell ya, 'Paint it Black' is always a real house burner."

"A house burner?" I said with a smirk. "Careful, Zac, you're beginning to sound like an Albertan. But I think the expression is 'barn burner'." I turned to Mark. "Zac used to be a deejay in his Montreal days. Now, was that before or after your ballet days?" I said to Zac flashing him a triumphant smile.

"Pardon?" Mark said. "Your what days?"

Zac gave me a look that said, I'm going to get you for this. "I was a ballet dancer in Montreal."

I love telling people this because with Zac's six-foot-four, 195-pound frame, all supported on size twelve feet, the image of him flying around in a pair tights allows your imagination a lot of latitude.

"It was a small dance troupe. We did a lot of experimental stuff."

Mark nodded his head thoughtfully. "That's really neat."

"I think so too," I said, and meant it. Zac and I loved to rib each other, but the truth was I was very impressed with him and his accomplishments. He had had to overcome a number of personal, not to mention financial, obstacles to get to where he was.

His mother had been a fashion model and his father was a banker of some sort. For the first seven years of Zac's life, the Farnham family lived in Montreal in the prestigious Westmount area. Zac and his brothers went to private schools and vacationed in Florida and Martha's Vineyard. However, shortly after Zac's eighth birthday, Zacarie senior took off with his secretary and drank himself into oblivion, losing everything in the process, including the secretary. By the time Zac was nine, he and his two brothers and his mother were living in a one-bedroom apartment farther down the mountain, in the inner city, where for five years they shared their new neighborhood with drug addicts, drunks, and prostitutes.

Mrs. Farnham worked as a department store clerk until she remarried a decent, but, according to Zac, not a particularly interesting or generous, man who owned a chain of high-end furniture stores. For two years after the blessed event, Zac and his brothers lived like unwelcome guests in "that man's" house, which, ironically, was back in the Farnhams' old stomping grounds of Westmount. When he moved out at seventeen, Zac vowed he would get an education and earn something that no one could ever take away. The ballet thing was apparently a short-lived segue on his way to the halls of higher learning.

From his eclectic background, Zac developed an attitude and personality that were a curious mix of street-wise common sense, ivy-league snobbishness, and artsy individualism. And I adored him for it.

"So you were a dancer, a deejay, and now?" Mark said.

"And now I spend my days gassing people in Mullarcant's little lab of horrors. Who woulda thunk it?"

"That's quite a resume."

Leonard was coming to the end of his song, so Zac excused himself and went to start phase two of his musical extravaganza.

"What about you, Mark? What's your resume look like?" I asked.

"I'm afraid mine would sound pretty boring next to Zac's," he said. "So where's Beth?"

"I was just wondering the same thing," I said. "I think I'll slip over to residence and see what she's up to."

"Good idea. We could use another body around here."

I grabbed my coat as John Lee Hooker was singing about his desire for a bourbon, a scotch, and a beer. Yeah, well, John, maybe I'll just stick to the one drink tonight, I thought as I headed for the elevators. A few more students and faculty were drifting in and the room was starting to fill up. Maybe the night was going to be all right after all.

The corridors, TV room, and cafeteria of Browning Hall were as silent and empty as the rest of the campus. The majority of the students had gone for the holiday season—either spending it at home with their families or with their friends on the ski slopes of Banff and Lake Louise.

Beth's room was on the fourth floor. I took the stairs because I have a thing about elevators at night in deserted buildings. I gave her door a quick couple of raps, and waited. The door next to Beth's room opened a crack and a young woman with sleepy, bloodshot eyes poked her head out.

"Hi. I was looking for Beth Wong," I said.

"You just missed her. She was heading over to the Christmas party."

I thanked her and hurried back across campus. The temperature had dropped and the snow was falling steadily. On my way down the hall back to the graduate lounge, I stopped in at the ladies' room. It was down a long corridor outside and around the corner from the graduate lounge. If you didn't know where it was, you'd never be able to find it. And that was the very reason Beth and I used it—it was always empty and always clean.

It was a long, narrow room with at least ten or twelve stalls and as many sinks. At the end was a tall, frosted-glass window that started about three feet from the floor. When I pushed through the door, Beth was stepping out from the end stall.

"Hey there, I was just at residence looking for you. So how are you doing?" I needn't have asked, because even though she was dressed to the nines and had on make-up, Beth looked even more wan and tired than the day before. She moved beside me and turned on the water to wash her hands.

"I'm okay," she said. "Thanks again for everything yesterday."

"I really didn't do much, Beth. Did you find out anything else about Carmen?" She shook her head. "No. But oh, well, these things happen."

"It's really terrible, though," I said. "Sure is. Let's talk about something else," she said. This was odd. This was not Beth.

"Okay," I said slowly and tried to think of something to say. "I love your outfit," I said. She had on a plain black dress with spaghetti straps and a thin strand of pearls, which no doubt were real. Her long black hair was swept up loosely on her head. And she looked absolutely stunning. Beth was about five-foot-five, but most of that was legs. Everything, including jeans, hung on her as elegantly as dewdrops on a willow tree.

Beth and I were about the same height, but that's where the similarities ended. Next to her, I too looked like a willow, but one that hadn't wintered too well. I'm thin, but not that model

31

kind of thin; mine's more of a long-distance runner thin. In other words, I have a body like a guy: no hips, no boobs, and a lot of legs. And my hair, oh God yes. My hair is actually more like a shrub that grows out, not down, in this wild mess of sandy blond curls. Every three or four weeks I have to go through the misery of having it pruned back.

Next to Beth, I always felt underdressed and severely out of style. I hate wearing tight-fitting clothing and opt for comfort over fashion. If I have to get dressed up, I make sure whatever I'm wearing has no waist and is long enough so that I don't have to wear pantyhose. But that night I didn't feel too bad about what I was wearing. It was a Laura Ashley, black wool crepe jumper number that I put a nice, high-collared white blouse with. The shoes I wasn't too comfortable with, though, because they reminded me of when I was a kid and my mother always insisted on buying me black patent-leather dress-up shoes. Black always makes your feet look bigger. Ever since then, I've had this obsession about buying black shoes that are at least a half-size too small.

"Thanks, you look great yourself," Beth said. "That dress is perfect on you. And the purse is great too."

"Thanks. It's Rusty's." I searched for something else to say. She seemed so distant at that moment, and I felt vaguely uncomfortable talking with her. It was as though we were casual acquaintances trying to make small talk. "Beth, would you rather just skip the party? We could go someplace else. Grab a bite to eat, just talk."

She stared at me a moment as if she was carefully weighing what I had asked her. Then she said no a little too quickly and a little too harshly, as though I had offended her. Just as suddenly, her tone softened. "I'm all dressed up." She looked down at her shoes. "Do you think these are okay with my dress? Grandma brought them back for me, and I promised I'd wear them tonight."

"From Hong Kong?"

She nodded, and I couldn't help but notice that she was wringing her hands. "I think the heel's too chunky."

I agreed, but said, "No, they're perfect."

"Liar," she said with a nervous smile.

"Okay, they're a little big but you still look great."

"I'm telling Grandma you lied, and just you wait and see what she brews up for you next time you're sick."

I laughed. Beth's family was from Hong Kong, but she was born in Canada. Her father was an engineer at one of the big oil companies in town, and her mother, like mine, had always been at home. I loved hearing about her family's stories and customs, and especially about her grandmother, who ran a herb shop in Chinatown. Every time Zac or I came down with an ailment, Beth would show up with a little packet of some foul-smelling cure-all Grandma Wong had whipped up.

"Grandma Wong would never believe you, anyway," I said. Beth laughed, but it was a forced laugh. She was obviously struggling with something and I wished she'd just come out and tell me what it was. I was certain Carmen's death was only part of it.

"Why don't I meet you out there, Emily?" Beth said. "I just have to touch up my make-up."

"Me too," I said and leaned toward the mirror to apply my lipstick. "So what do you say, Beth? Why don't we just forget about everything and go have ourselves a great time tonight?"

"Sounds good," she said. "I think I could do with a little unwinding."

Mullarcant's words suddenly came to mind. "Uh, on second thought, maybe we should watch the unwinding part, since everyone seems to remember how completely unwound I got last year."

She cocked her head.

"Oh, it's nothing, really. Mullarcant said something about me being the life of the party last year. I must have been the talk of the department because I don't remember even seeing him. And I think he winked at me, if you can believe that. Oh, and I also think Mark Gunn is flirting with me. Which, I might add, is far better than having Mullarcant do it."

Beth stared at me in disbelief, and her already pale face grew paler.

"I had the same reaction," I said. "It's no big deal. Mark said I should take it as a compliment. That Mullarcant's just trying to get to know me. Well, if he's right," I continued, "I think maybe I'll try to behave myself this year. I wouldn't want to find myself chatting up Mullarcant by the end of the night." I laughed. Beth didn't.

"No. You wouldn't want that, Emily." Beth said in a low voice. She looked very fragile at that moment, and I wanted to give her a hug. But I didn't. I walked down the length of the room and went to open the door to one of the end stalls (a practice my mother taught me—fewer people take the time to go all the way to end, she had reasoned), but Beth stopped me.

"Don't use that one," she said. "There isn't any toilet paper down there."

"Thanks," I said and headed to one of the closer stalls.

"Can I borrow your lipstick?" Beth asked. "I forgot mine."

I left my purse on the counter and entered the stall. While I was lining the toilet seat with tissue (another of my mother's tricks), Beth said, "I'll put it back in your purse, okay?"

"Sure. So are you going to stay at your folks for Christmas?" I said through the door. "Because I should tell you that I talked to your mother this morning and—"

Beth said something, but I couldn't quite hear her. Her voice sounded as though it was coming from the far end of the room. I heard a tap run and then the loud hum of a hand dryer as I strategically placed the last square of paper on the toilet seat.

"Sorry, Beth, what did you say?" I called out over the din of the machine.

Then suddenly, there was a loud crack as though someone opened a door or window that had been sealed shut by frost. A blast of cold air rushed across my feet and up my legs.

"Hey, Beth, did you open a window or something?"

Nothing.

Then I heard it—a distant, piercing scream that paralyzed every cell in my body. I stood there in that stall, staring blindly at the green tiled wall.

"Beth, you hear that?" I said in a raspy whisper.

The hand dryer shut off. A silence enveloped the room like nightfall. I knew instinctively what had just happened, but my mind would not let me believe it.

I turned slowly, as if moving through water, and unlatched the door. I looked down the room to the window. It was pushed open. Fluffy bits of snow floated in and wafted down into the sink. My legs felt leaden as I ran the length of the room. I grabbed hold of the sill to steady myself and peered down to where a small, dark form was sprawled in the snow. It looked like a doll some child had carelessly tossed out the window. But I knew it wasn't a doll.

It was Beth.

Chapter 4

THE TERRIBLE SOUND OF A woman's screams broke the night's silence. For a moment, I thought they were coming from the broken figure in the snow. Then I realized it was the woman standing next to Beth's body. I don't remember doing this, but apparently I yelled down that I would call an ambulance. After that, Mark Gunn said, I ran out into the party, yelling for someone to call 911.

And someone did. But, of course, it was too late.

The police came with the ambulance. They took our statements. Beth's parents were notified and her body was taken away. A coroner's investigation was conducted, but mostly as a matter of policy and routine; there was no doubt Beth jumped. I had been there. I was a witness.

There was a funeral.

And that was it.

Life was supposed to go on as usual.

I stayed in Calgary for the holidays with my landlord, friend, and sometimes surrogate mother, Rusty Monaghan. My father flew in from Victoria, where he had been living since retiring.

Zac went to Montreal, and I went through the motions of Christmas. Zac called a few times from Montreal, and sounded as though he wasn't doing any better than I was.

I had planned to catch up on some schoolwork over the holidays, but the thought of going to the campus was too much for me. At times I felt restless and busied myself with important tasks like cleaning out the myriad bird feeders in Rusty's expansive backyard. I went for long runs, and on good days I was nearing fifteen miles. At other times, I felt too depressed to move. During those times, all I could do was sit in the living room and stare out the window at the black-capped chickadees happily dancing about, singing their little chickadee, dee, dee, dee song, while they filled their sweet little beaks with suet and sunflower seeds. Those birds were the only things that brought me any joy during that long Christmas break.

When I went to bed at night, I had terrible nightmares in which I was talking and laughing with Beth one minute, and the next she was climbing up onto a windowsill, waving and smiling. I'd try to grab her, but I'd always miss by a fraction of an inch, and then I'd have to watch in horror as her body whirled down to the ground like a paper cut-out doll.

By January I wasn't sure I could go back to the university, and I was seriously considering taking a leave to go live in Banff for a few months. I had friends I knew I could stay with. Maybe I'd start back again the next fall. One thing, however, kept me from packing—my father. Over the holidays he had told me about a hundred times how proud he was of me. And even at twenty-five years old, I still couldn't bear the thought of disappointing him, again. When I couldn't stand it any longer, I went to talk it out with Rusty.

I found her in the living room sitting on the couch and nibbling a chocolate bar. As always, she listened to my every word.

"Well, dear, it sounds to me that one part of you wants, and possibly needs, to go back. But the other part needs an escape route, just in case. Why don't you go back for one month, and if at the end of that time you still feel you need a break, take your leave and go work things out on the ski slopes."

A sense of relief flooded me, and two thoughts came to mind. The first was that I couldn't believe I hadn't come up with this solution myself. And the second was how lucky I was to have a friend like Rusty.

Since moving to Calgary a year and a half earlier, I had been renting a room—actually it was more like a suite—in Rusty's six-thousand-square-foot, Mount Royal house. I had known the Monaghans for years because my father did legal work for Mr. Monaghan. Once or twice a year, when I was a kid, he would plan his work around a weekend so that my mother and I would get a little holiday out of it. For me, staying at the Monaghan house was like a trip to Disneyland. The first time we drove through those big, wrought-iron gates and up the curvy drive to the front door, I thought we were going to a castle. The house was a turn-of-the-century sandstone beauty, with huge pillars and two stone lions that stood watch on the front steps.

Rusty's father-in-law, Jerald Monaghan II, built it after he came west from England in 1914 to exploit the abundant Alberta gas reserves for the Canadian Pacific Railway. He brought with him the plans for the house, and succeeded in re-creating a piece of grand European architecture on seven sweeping acres in the middle of Calgary, Alberta. Many after him followed suit and built similarly grand, gabled and turreted homes, thus creating the very posh Mount Royal district. Today, the area is still inhabited by top Canadian Pacific Rail officials and their families, who live alongside oil company executives and software developers.

The front hallway of the Monaghan house was like a small ballroom, with a domed, stained-glass ceiling that fascinated me to the point of obsession. The floors were slippery, variegated gray and black marble, and in sock feet I could slide from the door to the foot of the oak staircase in seven pushes. From there, another eight and a half pushes took me to the immense living room—a spooky room done in heavy, dark sixteenth-century furniture, with lots of green and black needlepoint hunting scenes, and pictures of little boys in weird blue velvet outfits. Five more pushes and slides took me as close as I was allowed to get near the center of the room, which was reserved for Mr. Monaghan's pride and joy—the ebony Steinway grand piano, complete with two silver candelabras.

I remembered Mr. and Mrs. Monaghan as very polite, formal people. And my role as the child was definitely to be seen and not heard. After dinner we would sit in that big living room and listen to Mr. Monaghan play Chopin, Bach, and Beethoven, for what seemed like hours. Those were the worst times for me, and I would squirm on the sofa until Mrs. Monaghan finally came to my rescue and whispered in my ear that the dogs needed walking or that Mrs. Zelinski, the cook, needed my help in the kitchen.

Three weeks after my sixteenth birthday, my mother died. Two months later, Mr. Monaghan died, and our trips to Calgary ended. The first time I saw Rachel Monaghan again was nine years later, when I moved to Calgary to attend the University of Southwestern Alberta. My plan was to stay with her for a day or two until I found a place of my own. My father's plan was to have me stay with her indefinitely. In the end, he won out, but only by default.

The day I arrived, a woman I didn't recognize flounced out the front door and across the green expanse of lawn to my car. I knew it couldn't possibly be Rachel Monaghan because the Mrs. Monaghan I remembered had mousy brown hair pulled back so severely in a bun it made me wince. Her basic, neutral clothes matched the hair, and her shoes were obviously expensive, but definitely sensible.

The woman coming toward me that day with outstretched arms had a wild mess of silver-white hair, shockingly bright orange lipstick, and a Hawaiian print kimono to match. And whoever she was, she looked absolutely wonderful. When she was a little closer, I realized it was indeed the new Rachel Monaghan.

"Emily," she said, throwing her arms around me. "I'm thrilled you're here. It's just been years and years, hasn't it?"

I was so taken aback by her appearance, I found it difficult to respond. For lack of anything more original, I said, "It's very nice of you to let me stay, Mrs. Monaghan. It will probably only—"

"Nonsense, my dear, I'm delighted to have you. Stay as long as you like. And please call me Rusty."

"Rusty?"

She flashed a mischievous smile. "I changed it after Jerald died. In fact, as you will see, I've changed just about everything else too. Now, where are your bags?" she said, sweeping past me to the trunk of my old car.

Rusty led the way into the house, and then showed me around the new Monaghan digs. We started in the living room, which had undergone such a complete transformation, it bore almost no resemblance to its former self. All the dark brocade had given way to bright chintzes, creams, and pastels. The once somber hardwood floors were now glistening white and gray granite tiles. Greco-Roman pillars were added, with flowing fabrics of complementing whites and golds. The only thing that remained untouched was the Steinway. Rusty followed my gaze and ran her hand over the shiny black surface.

"I had thought about painting it orchid, but I didn't think poor Jerald could take much more."

I was still getting used to the new Mrs. Monaghan and wasn't sure whether I should laugh or say I was sorry.

She sensed my discomfort. "I know I must sound terrible, but life with Jerald Alexander Monaghan The Third wasn't exactly what one would call light, if you get my meaning." I nodded, remembering the stiff man who wore dark suits even in summer.

"But enough about that. Your father tells me you're going to do your master's. Well, that's just wonderful. I'll want to hear all about it. And by the way, I'm on their board of something or other over there, so if I can be of any assistance, you just say the word."

"Thanks, I'll keep that in mind."

That night we drank brandy, ate crepes for dinner, and had Camembert cheese and grapes for dessert. We talked about everything from the arts and university politics to psychics and spirituality. By the end of the evening, I felt as though I had been reunited with a very old and dear friend. After that, one day just seemed to pour into the next, and I never got around to moving out, and Rusty never got around to asking me.

"Thanks, Rust," I said, giving her a hug. "I don't know what I'd do without you."

"My dear, you were the one who came to the decision, I merely repeated it back to you."

I eyed her suspiciously. "You know, this reminds me of when I was a little kid and I told my mother I was running away. She said it was okay with her, but that I should wait until the morning, since I wasn't allowed out alone after five."

Rusty laughed. "And wasn't that good advice?" We both laughed, and it felt good. "It's nice to see you smile again, Emily."

I heaved a sign. "It feels good too." Until that day, I hadn't really talked to Rusty or anyone else, for that matter, about Beth or school.

The night it happened, Rusty stayed up with me, but after that, I couldn't even bring myself to mention Beth's name. Now Rusty was studying me and appeared to be weighing what she was about to say.

"Emily, I was going to wait until you were ready to talk about Beth," she said, measuring her words, "but I feel I need to say something." The mere mention of Beth's name made me feel weak and I sat down on the edge of the couch to listen. "What happened to Beth was not your fault. And there was nothing you or anyone else could have done to help her."

Tears welled up in my eyes, and Rusty put her arms around me and held me. "That's right, Em, you just let it all out," she said softly.

I told her about the nightmares and all the feelings of guilt. By the time I was through, I was exhausted. But it felt good. It was a purging. And I knew I was ready to go back.

Chapter 5

THAT NIGHT, FOR THE FIRST TIME in weeks, I slept without having the terrible scene play over and over again in my dreams. When I woke the next morning, I wasn't exactly ready to take on the world, but I felt I could at least give it a try.

The sun was shining brilliantly as I made my way across the university commons, and the warmth on my face was rejuvenating. The air was crisp but not as dramatically cold as it can be when it's that clear in January. The new snow that had fallen in the night gave everything a fresh, pure look. I've always liked Alberta winters, even when it's minus twenty. I couldn't imagine living anywhere else that didn't have this time of rest and purification. The freezing Alberta winters bring with them a hardship, but they also bring a cleansing. Each spring, when the snow melts, it's as if we all get a second chance to start afresh. Diamonds in the snowy duvet that covered the ground and trees winked and flashed as the sun caught the crystals and set them alight. Each twinkle made me feel more optimistic as I approached the front doors of our building, and I thought maybe I would be able to get through the next four months.

I was hoping Zac would be in, but when I reached our office I was disappointed. There was no sign of him. I use the term "office" loosely, because the space Zac and I shared amounted to little more than an over-sized storage closet. Two desks, a bookcase, a filing cabinet, and an old battered coat rack completely filled the room. We didn't even have a phone because there were no jacks, which I took as direct evidence to support my theory that the room was originally intended to house custodial implements.

Classes hadn't begun yet, and the department halls had an eerie silence. While I leafed through my in-basket, I heard footsteps down the hall. I knew they didn't belong to Zac because he usually wore soft-soled shoes. In the empty halls, each step made a hollow, ominous sound. When Martin Mullarcant poked his head in, I jumped.

"I'm sorry, Emily, I didn't mean to surprise you. I saw you come in and wanted to say hello and welcome you back. If you have a moment, I'd like to speak to you about a few matters."

"Sure, I'm free now," I said, even though I had wanted to get started on my own things. I followed him down the hall past his faculty office and waited until he unlocked the main lab doors. He led me to his office and closed the door, which I thought was a little odd, since it appeared that no one else was around.

"Can I get you something to drink? There's pop or juice in the fridge."

"Uh, no thanks, I'm fine," I said, shifting in my chair.

He sat down behind his desk and positioned a pad of paper directly in front of him. He was an exacting kind of man. Everything he did, including the simple placement of a pad of paper, was thought out carefully first, then executed with a kind of precision. He also had a little ritual he went through every so often. When he began it now, all I could do was watch in mute fascination. First, he ran his right hand across the three or four strands of dark hair that clung to his skull. He smoothed them down, then gave them a little swoop at the end as though trying to effect a wave. He took the same hand and found the cuff of his left shirt sleeve and pulled it down to the exact place where it met the cuff of his lab coat. He did the same with the other sleeve. Following this, he leaned down and took hold of his pant cuffs and drew them down to the tops of his shoes, after which he cleared his throat and began. We students shared some rather colorful theories about this ritual, such as that he suffered from obsessive-compulsiveness, triggered by his anxieties over his psycho-sexual dysfunctions and authoritarian personality disorder. When he was done, I had the overwhelming desire to give him a round of applause. I held myself back, of course.

"Emily, I would like to know how you are managing, what with everything that has happened."

"Do you mean my work?" I asked, confused.

He cleared his throat again. "Of course, I am interested in your work, but I am also speaking about you."

"Oh."

"Losing Elizabeth as we did was very shocking. It has been trying for everyone. She will be greatly missed."

"Yes, she will," I said quietly.

"What has happened is a terrible tragedy, and we will all be living with its burden for some time, and that is the reality."

I let a long sigh escape. "It's hard to imagine that she's really gone."

He nodded. "But we also have a great deal of work to do. That too is a reality. So my question to you, Emily, is, do you feel you will be able to function adequately here?"

"Sorry?"

"I'll get right to the point. If you feel that you are up to it, I'd like you to take over some of Elizabeth's work."

My jaw dropped and I felt two things almost simultaneously: anger at his complete and total lack of sensitivity toward Beth, and a rush of adrenaline. I had assumed this man thought I was an insignificant speck of a graduate student—an insubordinate speck, at that. But here he was giving me what I considered the biggest academic compliment I had ever received.

"This will be of great benefit to you, Emily. Firstly," he said, holding up his right hand and counting off each item on the fingers with his left, "the work will aid you in completing your master's thesis. Secondly, it will almost certainly guarantee you admission to the doctoral program. And thirdly, you will be released from your teaching assistant duties, although you will still be paid as a research assistant. All your time, therefore, can and will be spent on your research. This, in turn, will ensure the completion of your program no later than April fifteenth. I trust this arrangement is acceptable to you."

"I'll have to give it some thought," I said. Which I knew sounded idiotic because it was pretty clear he wasn't asking me.

"Emily, I really don't see what there is to think about. Either you are capable of doing the work, or you aren't. I believe you are, and since you have given me no evidence to the contrary, I will proceed as planned. You may go now."

I nodded and left, feeling like Anna after the King dismissed her. I wandered back to our office in a daze, where I found Zac sitting with his feet up on the desk, reading a Far Side cartoon book.

"Hey, Em, I've been waiting for you."

"Zac, you're back." I gave him a hug. "Feel like a coffee break?" I said.

"Why not? I've just put in a good hard fifteen minutes here."

We both grabbed our coats and headed over to Danmoth Hall. When we reached the front doors, we both stopped and looked up to the tenth floor.

"Do you want to go somewhere else?" Zac said.

I thought for a moment. "No, we have to go in sometime, might as well be now. If you're okay with it."

He shrugged and said, "I guess, as long as we avoid the grad lounge." We agreed to stay on the main floor.

While we were standing in line at Ziggy's Koffee Kiosk, I thought about the last time I had walked through this foyer. It had been so dark and quiet when Mark and I strolled toward the elevators that our shoes echoed with each step we took. Now it was alive with people. Although it was nowhere near as busy as it would be in a day or two, it was nonetheless bustling with students and faculty milling around and exchanging holiday stories and the dread of having to "get back at it."

Except for the "did you hear"and "wasn't it awful" talk, life at the University of Southwestern Alberta would go on as always, and Beth Wong's death would be nothing more than a footnote by spring convocation. My eyes traced the path Mark and I had taken to the elevator: past the French pastry counter, past Taco Lane, alongside Donut Delights, neither one of us ever imagining what was about to transpire. I remembered the kiosks as being dark and lifeless; now they were bright and inviting. But everything associated with that night seemed dark; darker, I'm sure, than was actually the case.

When it was my turn to step up to the counter and place my order under the sign that read "Brew It, and They Will Come!," Zac had to give me a gentle nudge in the back to bring me back to the moment.

We found a quiet table by the windows. "So I take it your Christmas wasn't any better than mine," Zac said, adding a second package of sugar to his double espresso.

I looked down at my small, peach-flavored coffee. I used to drink large lattes with Beth. "I miss her, Zac," I said. "And I really want some answers. I need to know what went so terribly wrong."

"I've been going over and over it, and you know, Em, maybe there aren't any answers. Maybe she was just too hard on herself, nothing more than that. Remember that study we looked at in Sandra Penny's seminar?"

"The one about student suicides?"

"Yeah, remember the one where they found that most of the students who killed themselves were doing fine in school? What sent them over the top was their perception that they weren't doing well enough. Not one of those kids was failing."

"But Beth wasn't doing just fine; she was doing great and everyone knew it. No matter how hard she was on herself, she couldn't possibly have imagined she wasn't doing well."

"True. Everyone knew she was Mullarcant's star student, including her. And once she graduated, she would have been set."

Zac's words made the full impact of Mullarcant's offer hit home. Of course, I wouldn't be doing exactly what Beth had been doing, since I was just a lowly MA student, but it did sound as if I would be following in at least some of her footsteps.

"Earth to Em."

"Sorry, Zac, I need to talk to you about something." I told him about my conversation with Mullarcant.

"Em, that's great. This is a huge compliment. I can't believe you waited to tell me. Congratulations. You can't lose. You'll get published and everything."

"Yes, I know, but it's hard to feel good about it. One half is pleased, but the other half feels guilty as hell, knowing the only reason this came my way is Beth's death. Then another half—"

"How many halves do you have?"

"Three, I'm a very complex person. And that third half is wondering about the prospect of having to work more closely with Mullarcant. I like the way things are now."

"Why? Did he say Mark couldn't be your supervisor any more?"

"No."

"Well, then, what's the problem?"

"The biggest thing is Beth. I don't know if I'd feel right about it."

"You're not thinking of turning this down, are you?"

"I don't know. I can't talk to Mark about it because he's still away and I have no idea when he's going to be back."

"I'll tell you right now you'd be crazy to say no. Especially if it's out of some sense of misplaced loyalty to Beth."

"I don't think it's misplaced, Zac. I just think it's a little soon to be taking her place, don't you?"

"Em, you're not taking her place, you're just going to carry on her work. Think about it reasonably. How is not continuing the work going to make any difference? Whether it's now, or in six months from now, isn't going to change anything. Besides, you're doing some of the work now, anyway. Things have to get done."

"Careful. You're starting to sound like Mullarcant."

"Thanks."

"Just kidding."

"Look, I can't see that much will change, except that you'll get to concentrate on your research more and be done faster."

Everything Zac said made perfect sense. Especially the part about things not changing. I'd still be working on the same projects and no one said anything about changing supervisors.

"Em, you won't be doing Beth a disservice. In fact, maybe you'll even be doing something for her."

"Like what?"

"Like carrying on her research. And who knows, maybe even dedicate it to her or something."

"Hmm, maybe I could do that. You know, Zac, you're going to make a brilliant psychologist one day."

"Hey, what can I say, it's a gift."

I threw a balled-up napkin at him.

I felt grateful for our friendship. Jealousy and competition among students are two of the more unpleasant facts of graduate life. With Zac, it was never an issue because we were headed in two very different directions. Zac was in the clinical program, which meant he would eventually become a chartered psychologist, and I was in the experimental stream, which meant I had absolutely no idea what I would become. Zac and I ended up doing the same research, because part of his program was to write a thesis based on experimental data. For Zac, the research was just another requirement. But he knew his chances of gaining acceptance into the PhD program would be enhanced significantly if he had the backing of someone like Martin Mullarcant.

"So it's settled, then," Zac said clearing our cups. "You're going to tell Mullarcant yes, right?"

"I guess so."

"I'll take that as a yes."

I narrowed my eyes at him and then smiled. "Well, who

knows, Zac, maybe you're right. Maybe I can do something for Beth along the way."

On our way out, we passed a group of students and caught snatches of their conversation.

"She just jumped," one of them said. "Maybe she was pushed," someone else added, savoring the thought.

"No. She jumped. It was something about her grades she was failing."

"I thought she was . . ."

Zac and I exchanged a look. "By the end of the week the official story will be that her boyfriend dumped her after he found out she was gay and having an affair," I said.

"Yeah, and that's when she lit herself on fire, slit her wrists and then jumped," Zac said, a bitter note in his voice.

It saddened me to know that within a couple days, once classes started, hundreds and possibly even thousands of people would be talking about Beth as if they had known her.

Chapter 6

MARK GUNN'S ASSURANCES that little would change for me under Mullarcant's new plan, and the fact that Mullarcant himself went ahead and dealt with the administrative work that changed my status from teaching assistant to research assistant, made up my mind for me about accepting Mullarcant's offer.

On January 13, I officially took over a number of Beth's roles. But aside from a few new responsibilities, little did change. For the first couple of weeks, things went along pretty much as they had before Beth's death. The only major difference, of course, was the huge void Beth had left in our lives.

Most of my new tasks were pretty straightforward, like compiling data and writing reports. However, there was one job I had inherited from my predecessor that I wasn't looking forward to, and that was recruiting subjects from New Beginnings.

THE MAIN FOYER and meeting area were filled with the same soupy fog of cigarette smoke, body odor, and damp clothes it had been the last time I'd been there with Beth. On my way to the reception desk, I passed the tables where some of the same people were playing cards or checkers—as if these particular tables were specially reserved for them. Maybe they were, I thought, as I stepped up to the reception desk.

A woman in her mid-twenties was sitting behind the desk. She wore a lime-green T-shirt with a bright sun and a royal blue door superimposed over it. The message "We All Deserve New Beginnings" was printed in aquamarine lettering. Pinned just above the sun, a name tag read, "Hi! I'm Heidi."

"Hi, Heidi. I'm Emily Goodstriker. I have an appointment with—"

"Marjorie," she said. Heidi had a bright, warm face and an attitude that clearly said: I like my job. "I'll take you right back."

"Thanks."

On our way, she offered to give me a mini-tour. "This is our needle exchange program," she said, indicating a door that was open at the top but not at the bottom. A sign tacked on the wall next to it advertised the times the service was open and information about safe needle use.

"We have volunteer health workers who come in every Monday and Saturday," Heidi said. I shifted my gaze away from hers when guilt made me search my memory banks for the last time I had done any volunteer work.

Farther down the hall, we passed a flight of stairs and I heard children's voices coming from above. Heidi explained that the center also ran a family day program that instructed parents on things like proper hygiene, good nutrition, and appropriate discipline techniques.

"Sounds like a good idea."

"Oh, it is," she said brightly and then frowned. "We're really going to miss Beth. She donated a lot of stuff to this place." She shook her head. "It was such a shame. Were you friends with her?"

I said I was.

"You know, I saw her that last day. And do you know what she said? She said she had just hooked up with some people at a baby food company she was sure would sponsor us. She was planning to get it all arranged in the New Year."

"Really."

"When I was talking to her, I thought she looked tired, I remember that. But she sure didn't look like someone who was planning to commit suicide in a few hours."

"Maybe she wasn't."

"I'll never get my head around it."

"Beth's death?"

"Yes, that, of course. But suicide in general. You just never know. Do you?"

I was suddenly lost in my own thoughts. Why would someone who was about to kill herself make promises she knew she couldn't keep? Beth would never do that. She obviously wasn't planning to kill herself when she was here. So what happened between then and when she arrived at the party?

". . . if you know anyone who can donate some diapers, baby food, and kids' books, we're always grateful," Heidi was saying.

"I think I might," I said, bringing myself back to the moment. I made a mental note to mention it to Rusty, and to buy some diapers and books myself. Just then, a teenager on crutches, with a cast up to his thigh, came toward us. Heidi said hi, and asked what happened to his leg.

"Aw, it's nothin'," he said. He was a good-looking kid with chestnut hair cut in the latest style.

"Some puke jumped me. Me and some others guys were catching a few Zs under the bridge."

Heidi gave him a motherly hug and told him to try the youth emergency shelter next time.

"Not as much fun there," he said and flashed a perfect smile before he limped off down the hall.

"That kid sleeps on the streets? He dresses better than I do," I said.

"He should. His father is one of the most successful oil executives in the city. A lot of people would be surprised to find out that the kids on the street don't all come from poor homes. Many of them are from Mount Royal and Scarborough, where their parents are too busy making money and having cocktail parties to care about what their kids are up to or where they sleep."

We came to the end of the hall and stopped at an office door. "I'll give you the rest of the tour later if you like. I know Marjorie is waiting, so I'll leave you here."

"Thanks, Heidi," I said. "

"Sure, any time." She rapped on Marjorie's door and then pushed it open. "Just go on in. She's expecting you."

Marjorie Chaperell was sitting at her desk, and talking on the phone. She was in her late thirties or early forties, I guessed, and she was the antithesis of Heidi's wholesomeness and natural beauty. Whereas Heidi's hair was a long, wavy, natural burnt umber, Marjorie's was short, frosted, and sprayed into a stiff helmet a tsunami couldn't move. Her tailored red wool jacket and high-necked white blouse looked more suited to an oil company boardroom than to a drop-in center.

She waved me in and motioned toward a chair. "Yes, she's right here now," Marjorie said into the receiver. "Yes, I will certainly do that. I'm sure we can work something out. Thanks for calling." She said good-bye and replaced the receiver.

I leaned across her desk and extended my hand. "Hi, I'm Emily Goodstriker."

She offered me hers. "Yes, I know. That was your supervisor on the phone."

"Mark Gunn?"

She gave me a puzzled look. "No. Martin Mullarcant."

"Oh," I said, and waited for her to give some explanation as to why he had called, but she offered none. I glanced around the office. A couple of cheap prints of mountain scenes hung on the wall behind her well-used wooden desk. The chair I was sitting on and the one beside me were regulation chrome and orange Naugahyde. A dusty silk plant of some variety stood in the far corner. Marjorie's desk was conspicuously bare, except for a sign about the size of a magazine cover that read "THANK YOU FOR NOT SMOKING."

I indicated it. "I can see your point. It's pretty thick out there."

She gave me a patronizing smile, then folded her hands and laid them purposefully on the desk, the way school principals do when they're about to give a kid a good firm talking-to.

"Emily, I think I need to explain something to you about New Beginnings." She paused. "Our clients come first. And having a place where they can come and enjoy a cigarette is terribly important to them. Therefore, we usually don't make comments about the smoke, because we wouldn't want to offend anyone. This sign," she said, tapping it with a well-manicured finger, "is not for my benefit. It is for the benefit of those clients who choose not to smoke. It was the only equitable way I could handle the situation. Because, Emily, when people come into this office, I have to consider every one's needs and rights."

I don't like you very much, Marjorie Chaperell, and I think you're full of shit, I thought. But I said, "Thanks for telling me all that. I'll keep it in mind."

"You're welcome. Now then, Martin tells me you're replacing Elizabeth and that you will be inviting a few more of our clients to participate in your study."

I wanted to say I wasn't exactly replacing Beth, but I wasn't about to say anything else that would invite another lecture, so I just nodded.

"It was a shame about Elizabeth. We worked together often," Marjorie said.

Beth had never mentioned Marjorie Chaperell. In fact, the only thing she ever said about New Beginnings was that she didn't like recruiting subjects from here, and after meeting Marjorie Chaperell I was beginning to understand why.

"It was such a shock. Such an intelligent young woman, and a very bright future. Were you aware that she was in such distress?"

I shook my head.

"What a pity. Perhaps it would have helped if you had."

I felt my cheeks flush. She struck a nerve, and I got the feeling that's exactly what she wanted to do. I looked at my watch. "Uh, Marjorie, maybe we should—"

She cut me off. "I think it would probably be simpler if you just called me Ms Chaperell." She flashed a practiced smile and a perfect set of capped, white teeth. "There are two of us Marjories here."

I stared at her.

"Well, now, we should be getting on with things, I have a meeting in—"she looked at her watch"—fifteen minutes. Martin assures me you understand the procedure."

I nodded slowly, having decided it was the better part of discretion to keep my mouth shut, lest I say something I might not regret. She looked at me quizzically, no doubt wondering if I had lost my ability to speak.

"Good, then, I have three clients down the hall in the green room, and we really shouldn't keep them waiting any longer." When she came around the desk, I was surprised to see she was shorter than I was. But the tailored suit and coiffed hair gave her an air of height and authority.

I followed her down the hall and into a room that was indeed green. The walls were painted a light hospital green, and a few plaques were hung here and there, stating oil companies' names as beneficiaries to the center. What was left of the linoleum revealed that it too had been a similar shade of green as the walls. Two men and a woman were seated around a battered boardroom table, sipping coffee from Styrofoam cups.

One of the men looked to be in his mid to late fifties. He had a full head of silver hair flowing to his shoulders and a silver beard to match. My immediate thought was that, given the right outfit, he'd make a great Santa. The other fellow was thin and much younger—somewhere in his early twenties. His dark hair hung just below his ears and in his eyes. And, from the look of his nose, he was either an amateur lightweight boxer or a professional street fighter. The woman seated across from them was large-boned with long salt-and-pepper hair. At first glance, I thought she was close to the same age as Santa, but when she looked up and smiled, I subtracted a decade.

"Good day, everyone," Marjorie said effusively. "I'm terribly sorry to keep you waiting."

The younger man spoke up. "That's okay, Ms Chaperell, we don't got nothin' to do anyway."

"Well, thank you. But, no, it's not all right. Because my keeping you waiting sends the message that your time isn't as important as mine, and that's simply not true."

Santa shot the salt-and-pepper-haired woman a look. She averted her eyes and stared deep into her coffee cup in an unsuccessful attempt to suppress a smile. Marjorie pursed her lips and appeared about to say something, but changed her mind and turned abruptly to me. "I'd like you all to meet Emily, er, I'm sorry, what was your last name?"

"Goodstriker."

"Right, Goodstriker." She motioned toward me like a game-show hostess. "Emily is from the university." The way she said it, I was half expecting a slow, sarcastic applause from the audience. She moved around the table, making introductions like a proud mother at Thanksgiving dinner. Marjorie stopped behind the woman and placed her hands on the other woman's tensed shoulders. "This is Irene. Irene helps out with the lunch program. Don't you, Irene?" She said it as though she were talking to someone who had just hit the final stage of Alzheimer's disease.

"Sure I do. Hi, Emily."

"Nice to meet you, Irene."

"Likewise."

"And this is Ken," Marjorie said, moving in behind Santa. "Ken is our resident intellect."

"More like resident drunk," he said. Irene snickered and the other younger man let out a loud, snorting laugh.

Marjorie said in a tight voice, "Now, come on, Ken, you know the rule about using negatives to describe ourselves."

"Okay, Marj, whatever you say. How ya' doin', Emily?"

A lot better now that you called her Marj, I thought. "Just fine, thanks."

"And last, but by no means least," Marjorie said, descending on her final charge, "this is Mike."

"Mick," he corrected her. "Like Mick Jagger."

"Of course, Mick. I'm so sorry. Mick is our handyman."

"Yup, if it's broke, I'll fix it. And if it ain't broke, I'll fix it anyway," he said and slammed his hands down hard on the table, letting out a raucous laugh. He looked over at Ken, who gave him a gentle smile.

"Hi, Mick. It's nice to meet you," I said.

"It's nice to meet you too, Emily. Hope I'll be able to help you with your stuff. Like Ms Chaperell said, I'm real handy. Handyman Mick, they call me." He spoke rapidly and punctuated each sentence with machine-gun laugher. Both of his hands were tattooed. A beautiful yellow and blue butterfly with an arrow through its center graced the back of his right hand. On his left, letters crudely drawn on each finger above the knuckle spelled out M-I-C-K. As he spoke, he ran nervous fingers back and forth over the smooth plastic surface of a very new, very expensive-looking portable disk player.

Marjorie moved toward the door and announced she was leaving. "I'll be right down the hall if you need me," she said. No one responded.

When the door closed, Ken pushed a chair out for me with his foot. "Take a load off, Emily."

I pulled out my files with shaky hands and set about organizing the consent forms.

"Slow down there, Emily, we got all the time in the world," Ken said.

I felt my face flush, and decided the best course of action was to be open and honest. "This is my first time doing this," I blurted out. "I've just taken over for—"

"Beth," Mick said, finishing my sentence.

"Right, for Beth. Did you all know her?"

Irene and Mick said they had seen her around, and knew her to say hi. I looked over at Ken.

"Yeah, I knew her." I waited for him to continue but he

didn't. He put his elbows on the table and steepled his fingers under his chin. The cuffs of his coat were worn and threadbare, and the fur around the hood was ripped and dangling. The rest of the coat was so badly stained it was impossible to tell what the original color had been. "So, Emily, what exactly can we do for you?" he asked in a business-like tone.

"Did Beth ever explain the project to any of you? Because I don't want to bore you by repeating what you already know."

Mick piped in. "Nope, but Jerry Booth told us all about it. He's the one talked us into it. Right, Ken?" Ken nodded. "Jerry said we'd make twenty bucks just by gettin' gassed. Right, Ken?" Mick said, and slammed his palms on the table again and laughed.

"Well, it's something like that," I said. When I caught Ken's eye, I changed it to, "No, you're right, it's exactly like that. We pay you twenty dollars to breath in carbon dioxide and experience anxiety and possibly a panic attack. Then we ask you a few questions about how you felt and what you were thinking during the session."

"So why us?" Ken asked. I spent the next forty-five minutes explaining the procedure and why we were soliciting them for the study. But I was apparently skirting the issue about why exactly we wanted them.

"I still don't get why you want a bunch of drunks like us," Irene said.

"Hey! I ain't no drunk," Mick said defensively.

Irene waved him off, "Whatever."

"Well, I ain't."

"We know that, kid," Ken said gently. "Go on, Emily, tells us why you want us in your study."

I took a deep breath and plowed along. "Part of the project is comparing different populations." I paused to collect my thoughts. "Specifically, we're looking at how alcohol- and drug-dependent people react to a stressor like oxygen deprivation." There, I said it.

Irene raised an eyebrow. "So basically, if I'm following you here, what you're saying is you want to know if pisstanks like us will freak out any different than normal guys when we can't breathe. Is that it?"

"Okay, sure. That's one way of putting it."

"But I ain't no drunk," Mick said.

"No, honey, you fit into the other category," Irene said and patted his butterfly.

"Oh."

"But you have to agree to be sober and drug-free for at least forty-eight hours before coming to the lab," I said.

"Otherwise we might puke all over your nice clean study," Ken said.

"More importantly, it might be dangerous to you."

"Yeah, and we wouldn't want to do anything that's unhealthy now, would we, Irene?" Ken said.

"That's right," Irene said with a smile. "We're pretty health-conscious around here." She turned to me and, in a more serious tone, said, "Don't worry, Emily. I'll make sure we're good 'n clean. We won't wreck your study."

I thanked her and asked them all if they had any other questions. When they said they didn't, I told them that someone from the university would be in touch in a day or so to set up an appointment to take their histories and do an assessment. They signed the consent forms and I thanked them again for their cooperation. And then I left.

When I got to my car, I felt drained and depressed. I had successfully recruited my first three subjects, but I felt icky for doing it. I tried to reassure myself that I had done the right thing. After all, I did believe in the study, since there was always the possibility the results could help somebody else down the road. I wasn't sure exactly how it would help, but that's what I had been told.

While this little ethics war waged in my head, I slipped the key into the ignition and checked over my shoulder before backing out. A man's face appeared in the passenger-side window, and scared the living daylights out of me. He walked around the front of the car and came to the driver's side. I knew who he was, but just the same I slipped my elbow over the lock button and leaned on it until there was an audible click. When he was beside me, I rolled the window down halfway.

"You really startled me," I said.

"Yeah, I noticed that when you locked your door." He poked his head in through the open window and peered into the back seat as though looking for something or someone.

"What can I do for you, Ken?"

"Forgot to mention something."

"Oh?"

"Just thought I should let you know that Beth didn't like her work, either."

"Pardon?"

He raised his voice and enunciated each word. The smell of stale booze and cigarette smoke wafted at me, and I jerked back involuntarily. "I said, Beth didn't like her work. And it looks like this ain't exactly your forte, either. So maybe you better give that some thought, 'cus you know what they say, work-related stress can do terrible things to a person." He winked and clicked his tongue. "Just thought I should mention that." He tapped the side of my car and strolled away across the parking lot, whistling.

Chapter 7

STRANGE GUY, I THOUGHT as I turned out onto Center Street and headed back to the university. I had no intention of letting a person in Ken's condition get the better of me, but all the way back to school his words played over and over in my mind like an annoying song. Beth didn't like her work. What was that supposed to mean? How would he know? He's just pulling your chain, Emily, I told myself. Beth was the most dedicated person I knew. No one could pretend to be that enthusiastic about her work. It didn't make sense. Of course, there were parts of it we all didn't care for, and recruiting subjects from New Beginnings was one of them. No mystery there. Maybe that's what he was getting at. *You know what they say, work-related stress can do terrible things to a person.* I shook my head and flipped on the radio, the sounds of Van Morrison singing to his brown-eyed girl filled the car.

At the school, I found a note on my desk saying Mullarcant wanted to see me immediately. I debated whether I'd do a few things first, like take my coat off, or just go. Just going won out. I knocked on his door and waited for him to summon me in. He was writing furiously at his desk and glanced up only momentarily.

"Good, you're back. Sit down," he said. "I'll be with you in a moment." He continued writing for another fifteen minutes while I sat there steaming, literally, in my winter coat, and figuratively about how much work I could be doing instead of wasting my time watching him get all his done.

For lack of anything better to do, I glanced at the spines in his bookcase. The massive collection covered one entire wall from floor to ceiling. I scanned the shelves closest to me and stopped when something caught my eye. One whole shelf was taken up with titles like *Hitler, A Study in Tyranny*; *Inside the Third Reich*; *The Final Solution*; *Nuremberg Diary*; and *The Limits of Hitler's Power*. Must be where he picks up his supervisory techniques, I thought. I was leaning over, trying to read the spine on a thin report shoved in between *The Final Solution* and *The Hitler State*, when Mullarcant interrupted, "I trust you were successful today."

"Seems like it."

"Either you were or you weren't. Now, which is it?"

I studied him for a moment. This flip-flopping personality of his was wearing me down. In fact, since the Christmas party I had been toying with the idea that Martin Mullarcant was suffering from the same multiple personality disorder the infamous Eve had been diagnosed with in the 1950s. I often felt I was living that movie, only mine was called *The Three Faces of Mullarcant*. Face One was the brilliant, socially challenged, overachieving researcher who was incapable of engaging in any form of socially appropriate interaction. Then there was Face Two, the lunatic mad scientist who exhibited unpredictable mood swings and outbursts of unprovoked anger and rage. Face Three, which he had exhibited at the Christmas Party and when he told me he wanted me to take over Beth's roles, was the awkward academic—the introvert who had no friends in school and who still doesn't, but who tries really hard to join in. And it was this last one that made me the most uncomfortable.

At that moment, I decided, he was exhibiting Face One, the brilliant, socially challenged, over-achieving researcher

Mullarcant face, which was far better than having Face Three rear its smarmy mug and wink at me again.

"Emily, I'm very busy."

I took a deep breath. "Right, sorry. They all signed the consent forms, and if they show up, then I guess—"

"That sounds like a success to me. Let me see the forms," he said.

I handed him the consent forms and waited while he scanned the first two. He nodded his approval. "Good, good. A nice age spread with the woman and this younger fellow." He held up the third form. "This last one doesn't indicate a last name." I leaned closer and, sure enough, Ken had printed only his first name. "Irene and Ken filled out their own," I said. "I helped Mick do his." I apologized and said I'd phone the center.

"It really doesn't matter," Mullarcant said. "As long as we have the correct age or near enough. Many of them give bogus names, anyway."

I asked if he wanted me to do the assessments and take their histories. He said, no, he'd do it himself. "I have something else I want to discuss with you, Emily." He handed over a stack of articles copied from various academic journals. The title on the top one read, "The Role of Situation and Personality Traits on Obedience Behavior in the Milgram Experiment." You've got to love academic articles; nowhere else will you find titles with a dozen or more words.

"Oh, the Milgram project," I said. "Beth was working on this with you. It's the video one, right?" Zac and I had seen a number of subjects come and go when they took part in this phase of the study, but we had not been involved in it.

"Yes, and I want you to familiarize yourself with it as soon as possible. We haven't done a thing with it since Christmas and we need to get back to it. It's a very simple, straightforward procedure. You have the subjects watch the video in the viewing room, then administer the questionnaire. Each subject will be paid an additional twenty dollars to complete it."

"Wow, we must have the best-paid subjects in the country."

He didn't respond. "So, you want me to run the three new subjects through this second phase, then?"

"Yes, and anyone else who participated in the panic phase and hasn't completed phase two."

I felt that familiar pang of sadness and guilt as I took on one more thing of Beth's—like the widower's new wife who is stepping into yet another pair of the first wife's shoes.

"I'll have a list made up for you," Mullarcant continued. "I feel confident you are capable of taking on this part of the research. If you read that first paper, you will see the hypothesis I have made and the connection this second phase has to the first panic phase." He put his head back down and resumed writing like a madman, a sign that our meeting was over.

"Oh, just one thing, Doctor Mullarcant," I said, stopping at the door. "Do you know when Mark Gunn will be back, and does he know I will be working on this next phase?" Mark had been away in Vancouver for the past week.

"That's two."

"Sorry?"

He smiled, a gesture I found strangely unsettling. Oh no, Face Three—it's back! "You said one, but you actually asked two things."

"Oh." I wasn't sure whether I should laugh, so I didn't.

"To your first question, as far as I know he will be back tomorrow for the memorial service." I cocked my head. "For Elizabeth, a memo was circulated this afternoon. It's probably in your mail. And to your second question, yes, I have apprised him of the work you are now doing."

"Thanks," I said and left. I went straight down to the main office to check my mailbox. I found a standard departmental memo that said a memorial service would be held for Elizabeth May Wong in the south block lecture theatre on Friday, January 23rd, at four-thirty p.m. I was pleased the university was doing something to honor Beth.

Back at my desk, I read through the material Mullarcant had given me. As I did so, I couldn't help but be excited at the prospect of doing something other than inducing panic attacks in people. After reading the background paper, I came to the conclusion that whatever else I thought about Martin Mullarcant, the hypothesis and connection he was making between the panic research and this second phase were nothing short of brilliant. By six-thirty that night, I was still reading through the articles Mullarcant had given me and I hadn't made so much as a dent in the pile, but I had to give in and give up when my rumbling stomach told me it was time to head home.

I was happy to see the living room lights were on when I pulled into the drive. Since the term had begun, Rusty and I hadn't had much time to catch up on things. She started back into her art and yoga classes, as well as all the committees and boards she sat on, and I was at school so much, the only time we saw each other was in passing on the driveway. I found her sitting at the breakfast bar in the sprawling room she called the kitchen.

"Ah, Emily, you're just in time," she said, trying to fit a bottle of wine under what looked like some medieval instrument of torture.

"Hi, Rusty. My God, what is that?"

"A relic from the wine cellar."

"Are you sure it's for opening wine and not for some other diabolical purpose?"

"I found it today when I was rooting around down there. Don't you think it will look smashing in the corner over there by the ovens?"

"Yeah, smashing." I said and glanced over to two professional, stainless steel gas ovens. "Oh, and speaking of rooting around in the wine cellar. You know that wine we were drinking at Christmas, the one with the faded label?" She nodded. "I was talking to this guy at the wine store, and he said it was probably a bottle of Rothchilds and worth about eight hundred dollars."

"Really? That's strange," she said, taking a normal wine opener from the drawer and screwing it into the cork. "I didn't think it was all that good. In fact, I like that Australian stuff you bring home a whole lot better."

I never knew if Rusty did this for my benefit so I wouldn't feel bad about the little bit of rent I paid, or if she was still hoping to rock Jerald—a little of both, I suspected. While she poured the wine, I set about making dinner with the things I had picked up on my way home.

"Now then, on with your day," Rusty said, sipping her wine. While I chopped and sautéed onions and celery, I told her about my experience at New Beginnings and what Ken had said.

"Hmmm. I think I'd take that with a grain of salt, dear. What do you know about him?"

"Not much, other than his first name and that he's obviously an alcoholic."

"Didn't you get any personal information on him?"

"No, we usually do the histories and the assessments later. I offered to do them, though, but the Great Man said he'd take care of that part himself. And to be honest, I'm just as happy not to have to do it, anyway. I don't feel good about using people like Ken."

"He's in a bad way, then?"

I nodded. "He looks like a street Santa."

"A what?"

"Saint Nick on the skids. He's got this long silver hair and beard. Looks like Santa Claus after a really good New Year's Eve party."

"Well, dear, it sounds as though the poor soul is in pretty bad shape. I wouldn't put too much stock in what he has to say."

"I don't know, Rusty, I get the impression he's pretty sharp. In fact, the center's director, Marjorie Chaperell, introduced him as the resident intellect."

"Ah, so you met Marjorie, did you?"

"You know her?" I added a cup of cream and a shake of Madras curry powder to the pan.

"I've known Marjorie for years. She was a social worker and a good one, at that. That is, until she was bit by the power bug."

"The power bug. How do you mean?"

"That's a good question. And how do I say it without sounding mean-spirited?"

"Oh, don't hold back on my account, Rust."

"I met Marjorie, let's see now, it must have been twenty years ago. It was at a fundraiser for something or other. Marjorie must have been in her early twenties then. She was with Social Services, but it was pretty clear she had much loftier ambitions."

"How did you know?"

"For starters, she hung on to Jerald all night and insisted she sit next to him at dinner. She talked nonstop about herself and the improvements she could make to this and that agency. It was embarrassing, to say the least."

"What did Jerald think about her?"

"He must have been impressed because shortly after she was made head of Housing For All. Which I thought was interesting, since Jerald was its main benefactor and board chair."

Naturally the first thing that popped into my mind was that ol' Jerald had been stepping out with the very young Marj.

"Personally, I thought she was obnoxious," Rusty said.

"I can see how you might come away with that impression."

"But to be fair, I do believe she was quite competent and genuinely dedicated to the cause. She'd have to have been, otherwise Jerald would never have stood for her, and neither would I, once he was gone." She looked at me thoughtfully for a moment. Then, as if reading my mind, added, "And no, I don't think he was having an affair with her. Frankly, I don't think Jerald would have known how."

"Caught," I said with a sheepish smile. "So you took over after he died, then?"

"Not as chair, but as main benefactor, yes. Hannah Schneider took over as chair."

"Right, of course," I said, remembering that Rusty had mentioned her friend's involvement.

"So how come Marjorie left?"

Rusty took a slow sip of wine and considered the question. "In the end, I was the one who had her removed."

"Removed. I like that. It sounds like you were getting rid of a bad stain."

She laughed. "I take it you had the same impression of her as I did."

"Only I'm not as polite about it as you are." I stirred the rich sauce and then diced a pear, a peach, and a few green grapes before adding them all to the sauce. "So what happened?"

"I took issue with the way she was spending the project's money. There was nothing underhanded or illegal, nothing like that. But after Jerald died, she convinced the board to give her what I considered was an unreasonably large raise. I let it go at first, because I believe hard-working people deserve to be rewarded. At the same time, though, I thought we were setting a dangerous precedent by giving in to her demands. And I was right, because the next year she came back demanding, and I do mean demanding, a further raise. And believe me, Emily, most CEO's in this town weren't making what she was. To make matters worse, she was also spending a significant amount of the project's money on fundraising events that, in my opinion, amounted to nothing more than lavish dinners to satisfy her tastes. Even this would have been fine, if those dinners had accomplished what they were intended to. However, after a while the functions became so extravagant they weren't even paying for themselves."

"Good scam. So why did you let her get away with it?"

"Marjorie's rationale was that she wanted to make the evenings so appealing that over time people would be lining up just to smell the food, but in the interim we would have to put out the initial cash in order to get to that point."

"I don't know much about fundraising, Rusty, but the whole thing sounds a tad self-serving. Not to mention hypocritical. I mean, here are all these rich people getting together over champagne and goose liver pâté to raise money for homeless people." I stopped and looked around the kitchen. "Gee, now aren't I the self-righteous one."

"Exactly," Rusty said, following my gaze. "I felt the same way. That's why I let the parties go on for some time. Who was I to say that she couldn't do what Jerald and I had enjoyed all our lives."

"But you were spending your own money, that's a little different."

"Indeed it is. And once the press finally got hold of what was going on, that was the end of it."

"You canned her?"

"Not exactly, she and the board came to a mutual agreement. She would leave on her own initiative and we would back that up. It was a difficult decision because the woman had, in the early years, done some very good work. It was only in the latter part of her career that she—"

"Became greedy and stupid."

"I suppose you could put it that way."

I stirred the sauce slowly and added a pinch more curry. "Interesting story. So was that when she took over New Beginnings?"

"No, that was when she started New Beginnings. It's Marjorie's project from start to finish. Needless to say, I don't support it financially."

"So who does, the government?"

"I doubt that. I can't imagine Marjorie would ever stand for the bureaucratic red tape. I would think it's mostly corporate donations. Remember, she made a lot of friends through Housing For All."

I nodded, thinking about the plaques with the oil companies' names I had seen in New Beginnings' green boardroom.

"You know, Rust, I was only there for a little while, but I got the impression they are doing some good things. Just in case you're interested, they need some stuff for babies. I'm going to start collecting clothes and other things."

"Good, thanks for telling me. I'm always happy to donate things like that. Now enough about Marjorie, I want to hear how things are going at school."

As we ate I told Rusty about my new project.

"Tell me again, dear, why you are gassing people in the first place and how it ties in with this new project, or does it?"

"Oh it does. As you already know, in the panic project we've been focusing on the idea of control. Mullarcant originally started out with the traditional panic stuff, looking at people who suffer from panic disorder and inducing a panic attack in the lab using carbon dioxide. But then he got interested in the idea of control, and wanted to know if people who felt more in control of themselves and their environment would be less likely to feel panic or anxiety."

"Makes good sense to me," Rusty said. "When I feel I'm in control, I tend not to panic. But why are you using people from New Beginnings?"

"Mullarcant wanted to take it a step further and use people who are more likely to feel a lack of control in their lives."

"Like alcoholics and drug abusers."

"Exactly. So we bring in people like Ken, Irene, and Mick, and let them breath in carbon dioxide, and then we compare their reactions to so-called normal people like your average undergraduate student."

"And the point is?"

"Mullarcant hypothesized that the people who lacked control in their lives would be more likely to keep the mask on longer, because they'd feel they'd have to. He also predicted they would report experiencing more anxiety than other people who took the mask off sooner."

"And have you found this?"

"Of course. Is the Great Man ever wrong? The subjects we categorized as having a lack of control in their lives were more likely to wait for us to stop the gas, and they were also the ones who reported experiencing more anxiety and panic."

"Yet, you're telling me that these same people are the ones who keep the mask on longer? It doesn't make sense."

"I know. In almost all cases we either had to stop the gas or take the mask off."

"You'd think their reflexes would just take over and they'd rip it off."

"But they don't."

"What happens if the person never takes the mask off?"

"We have a maximum time limit of thirty seconds. That way we don't kill anyone."

"That's good of you."

"Hey, we're a thoughtful group."

"Indeed."

"Mind you, Mullarcant keeps upping the time limit, but I won't get started on that. Anyway, another interesting thing we found is that some of the students have been reacting the same way."

"That doesn't surprise me. I'm certain a lot of students feel a lack of control."

"You've got that right. And lots of students have alcohol and drug problems. The only difference between some of us and the folks from New Beginnings is that we dress better." I looked down at my baggy pants and sweatshirt. "Okay, well, maybe not all of us."

"When you're as thin as you are, dear, everything looks good on you. Now tell me, what do these people say when you ask them why they didn't take the mask off?"

"They usually say they didn't feel they had a choice."

"But you tell them they do."

"They say they didn't want to wreck our study."

"It must not be very pleasant for them or you."

"You can say that again. Every time we put that mask on someone, I keep trying to figure out how I got myself into this. And I really hated going down to New Beginnings today."

She nodded her head thoughtfully. "But I don't suppose you have much choice in the matter."

"Not if I want to graduate any time soon. There's hope, though. Being involved in this second phase gives me a nice break and some hope for the future."

"You mean for your PhD?"

"Maybe."

The grandfather clock in the hall let out a resounding gong, announcing that it was half-past the hour. I looked at my watch, it was nine-thirty.

"Rusty, I'm all talked out and full of curried seafood and Chardonnay."

We agreed it was time to call it quits for the night. I insisted on cleaning up the dinner dishes and the horrific mess I'd made in the kitchen. When I finally made it up to my room it was just after ten-thirty.

I was doing up the last button on my PJ's when the phone rang and gave me a terrible start. At that time of night, my first thought was that something was wrong with Dad. When I picked up the receiver, I didn't even get the chance to say hello before a male voice said, "Emily Goodstriker, please."

My heart was pounding against my rib cage. "Speaking."

"I apologize for calling at such a late hour, but it couldn't wait. A file has been misplaced that contains a number of important documents. Have you seen it?"

"Doctor Mullarcant?"

"Yes, yes, of course it is." Of course, how foolish of me.

"Uh, well, I'm not sure if I have it or not. Can you give me a few more details?"

"A file, a regular file. The entire thing is missing. It's labeled Aspen 45 inside the front cover. It's the Milgram phase." It was unlike Mullarcant to lose anything. The man was so meticulous, I was sure he made it his business to find out exactly where his belly-button lint ended up each day.

"Sorry, Doctor Mullarcant, can't say that I've seen it. I know it wasn't in with that stack of articles you gave me. But I'll check around my office tomorrow."

"Don't bother. I've already done so."

"Really?"

"Emily, these documents are extremely important. At the moment I can't concern myself with students' sensibilities. I simply must find that file."

The thought of him rooting around my desk made my jaw tighten. "I'm sorry, Doctor Mullarcant, I apparently don't have it."

"Would you search through your belongings at home then?" He hesitated and then added, "Please."

Why don't you just come over and do it yourself? I thought angrily. "Sure, I'll go through everything in the morning."

"No. Now. Could you do it now? This is urgent."

"All right," I said and sighed.

"I will wait to hear from you. If you find anything, call me immediately. Emily, you will look now, won't you? I can't impress upon you enough how important this is."

"Yes, I'll look. And if I don't call you back in the next half hour or so, you'll know I didn't find it."

"No. Call me back in any case. I'll be waiting." He hung up.

I looked around my room for a moment. This was stupid because I would know if I had a file that didn't belong to me. But just so I wouldn't have to lie, I looked through my desk and file cabinet. I also went back downstairs and looked around the dining room where I sometimes worked, and then called it quits. I phoned Mullarcant and reported back. He wasn't impressed.

"Yes, Doctor Mullarcant, I've looked everywhere. Have you tried Zac?"

"Of course I have."

"Then, all I can say at this point is that I'll sure keep my eyes open for it."

"You do that, Emily, and—thank you for your assistance tonight."

"You're welcome. Good night, Doctor Mullarcant."

When I climbed into bed I was completely awake and pissed off. I knew I wouldn't be able to sleep so I decided to read another article from my never-ending stack. "That ought to put me out," I said as I grabbed my knapsack and pulled out a few readings on the Milgram project. I unzipped the back pocket to look for a marking pen, and that's when I saw it—the blue file folder. I rarely used that pocket, so I had completely forgotten about the folder until that moment, but I knew immediately where it came from. It was the file Beth had given me that last day in the lab. I pulled out the file and opened it. On the inside cover "Aspen 45" was written in black ink across the top.

I reached for the phone and dialed the lab; the line was busy. The file contained a brown letter-sized envelope, which wasn't completely sealed. There was nothing else. I turned the envelope over in my hands. To open or not to open? I slipped a finger under the flap, it came away easily, and I pulled out half a dozen sheets of paper.

The top sheet was an application form to Memorial University, and my heart skipped a beat when I saw "Elizabeth May Wong" typed neatly on the first line. My initial thought was that it must have been an old form, but last year's date was clearly printed at the top of the page. I skimmed each page and everything seemed to be in order. Everything, that is, except for the fact that it made absolutely no sense for Beth to be applying to another school. It had to be a mistake, or a really stupid joke.

I flipped to the back pages and found two letters of recommendation: one was from Mark Gunn, and the other was from my old interim supervisor, Sandra Penny. A quick scan of the letters told me they too seemed legit. Then it occurred to me that she was probably making plans to do some post-doctorate work. But when I looked over the application again, I saw she had indicated, or someone had indicated for her, that she was applying to the PhD program. I looked at the back page where the applicant signs and dates it, and found Beth's signature next to the date of December 16—two days before she died. Stuck under her signature was one of those annoying little yellow sticky notes with the message, "Mail by December 17th," written in Beth's tiny, neat handwriting. Beth was forever writing cryptic notes to herself on those things and then sticking them all over the place. I knew then for certain that Beth had filled out and signed that application form herself. I picked up the phone and dialed the lab. "Doctor Mullarcant, it's Emily—"

"You found the file."

"Yes—but there isn't anything in it." In that split second of hesitation, I decided that what was in that envelope was Beth's business. Since there was no letter from Mullarcant, it was my best guess that he hadn't known about her plans. Better to leave well enough alone, I thought.

"What do you mean?"

"Just what I said, the file's empty."

"Where did you get it?"

"Beth must have given it to me by accident. It was under some forms."

"And there was nothing in the file. Nothing at all?" He knows! I've never been a good liar. But there was no turning back. My mother's words rang in my head: Emily, one lie always leads to another.

"No, nothing."

"Would you mind bringing the file in with you tomorrow?"

"No, I don't mind at all. Good night, Doctor Mullarcant." I put the phone down and set about thinking up a plan to undo my lie. I know, I'll just say the envelope was under the file and I missed it, I told myself. Or maybe I'll just keep quiet about it. Or maybe I'll just go to sleep.

But sleep was, of course, impossible. I spent most of the night tossing and turning and thinking up possible explanations I could give Mullarcant. Some time after three a.m., it occurred to me that the application form was exactly what he was looking for. And it could be for the same reasons I was hanging on to it— he didn't want anyone to know about it, and he was trying to protect Beth—or himself, which was probably more to the point. But how could he have known it was in that file? And what else was missing from it that had Mullarcant in such a panic? He did say "documents." My mind raced from one question to the next. But what was really robbing me of sleep was why Beth was considering switching schools in the first place. She had six months at most to go before graduating. It just didn't make sense. One thing was certain, though. Mark Gunn and Sandra Penny knew what Beth was doing and they were obviously supporting it.

Chapter 8

BY THE NEXT AFTERNOON, I knew exactly what I was going to do with Beth's application to Memorial. I packed up my things, along with the file and envelope, and headed out the door to school. It was a clear day, and the deep blue winter sky stretched unbroken above me to the mountains. I stood on the front steps for a moment and thought about how only a few weeks ago I had wanted to escape to those very mountains. Now I was genuinely excited about finishing the program and being involved in the Milgram project. And in an odd way, I was looking forward to Beth's memorial service. I needed closure, and I believed the service was going to give me that.

On my way across the circular driveway, I pulled the envelope from my bag and tossed it in the trash bins at the side of Rusty's four-car garage. Whatever Beth's reasons were for filling out that application were exactly that—her reasons. Maybe she couldn't handle working under Mullarcant any more. Who could blame her for that? And maybe Mullarcant knew she was trying to leave, and the Great Man would never want anyone to know that. Now no one ever would.

I went in the side door of the garage and slipped into Ol'
Blue—my 1987, metallic, midnight blue, eight-cylinder Buick
Skylark, parked snugly between Rusty's Land Rover and Jerald's
Silver Shadow Rolls Royce. I felt no envy or longing for those
luxury cars. Ol' Blue may not have been much to look at, but
when I saw other fancy cars getting a boost in Alberta's minus
forty weather, I felt smug as all get-out when my old darling
turned over without so much as a moan. I gunned Ol' Blue and
blew a plume of dark smoke as I pulled out of the garage and
headed to school, full of optimism and a renewed sense of calm.

My newfound feelings were short-lived, though, once I
walked into the lecture theatre. It was one of those big, oval audi-
toriums with tiered seats like a football stadium. The place holds
three to four hundred people. During a lecture, it's noisy and
from the back row it's almost impossible to see or hear the
instructor, which makes a perfect resting place for students trying to catch up on their sleep.

Beth and I had taken Cameron Deagle's abnormal psych class in
that very theatre when I was in my first year of the master's program. Beth took it because Mullarcant felt it would be useful review
for the panic project, and I took it because Sandra Penny said I
should. It was during that class that Beth and I became friends.

Although the course was interesting, Beth and I got little out
of it because most of our time was spent laughing and giggling
together over what Cameron was getting up to. It wasn't that we
were inherently cruel, or completely infantile; rather, it was
because Cameron was dramatic, and each of his lectures pro-
vided enough fodder for a good *Saturday Night Live* skit.

His favorite part of the course was substance abuse, about
which he professed to have had a great deal of first-hand knowledge. His introductory lecture on the subject was unforgettable.
Actually, "lecture" is the wrong word; "testimonial-cum-revival"
would be more accurate. Our first clue that this lecture was
going to be a little different was when Cameron came in with
nothing in his hands, no lecture notes, no overheads, nothing
but Cam himself.

Not that Cam needed any props. His appearance alone was nothing short of eye-catching. He had a penchant for wearing hats and pastel colors. That day, which was in November, he was wearing robin-egg blue cotton trousers with a lemon-cream-colored muslin shirt, white shoes, and a sporty kind of white gangster hat.

"He looks like a big Easter egg," Beth whispered.

"More like an Easter stick," I said. Cameron tended toward the leaner side of things. He perched himself on the desk, and for the next ten minutes stared out at the three hundred and fifty or so of us students while we all stared back in nervous silence.

He finally broke the silence with a small chuckle and the non sequitur: "So you think you can handle it, do you?" Shoulders shrugged around the room like a human wave at a sporting event as everyone looked to each other for explanation.

"Go on, then, take a snort, just one little snort," Cam said in a voice loud enough to rouse the back row. He paced the room like a southern preacher on a mission from God, waving his arms and yelling out other incomprehensible messages like, "Come on, I dare ya! Think you're bigger than it?"

A student sitting behind us tapped me on the shoulder and whispered in my ear. "Was there some reading we were supposed to have done for this class?" And another one in front of us turned and said, "What the hell is he talking about?"

"Go on, I dare ya. Just one little line," Cameron raved on. "I'll just do it this once, you say. Just once can't hurt, can it? Well, guess again, friends. Once is all it takes. And remember, it's never just one line. Want to know how I know this?" Obviously a rhetorical question, but one overzealous student put his hand up anyway. Cam pretended not to see him. "Because I've been there, man," Cam said in a throaty voice. At the same time he rolled up his sleeve and offered up the inside of his arm for all to see. Thankfully, only the students in the first row could. "That convince you just one hit won't hurt?"

From there, Cameron took us back to the seventies when he was apparently kicked out of Berkeley for making amphetamines in the basement. Then it was off to Canada to the streets of Vancouver, where Cam claimed he lived for some four or five years, until this "archangel" saved him.

When the substance abuse section was over, we all felt we had lived through detox with Cam, and we were looking forward to moving on. The next section, however, was on psychosexual disorders, which after four, and counting, failed marriages was apparently another of Cam's areas of expertise.

One incident in particular stood out. It was after a long, and I do mean long, lecture on male sexual dysfunction, during which Cameron had displayed a great deal of emotion. Beth and I approached him after class to ask a question about an assignment. He had his back to us and was packing up his lecture notes when Beth said, "Excuse me, Doctor Deagle, we're having a problem, and I was wondering if you could clear something up for us."

Before she got the chance to say what the problem was exactly, Cameron whirled around and in a venomous voice spewed forth, "I'll tell you what the problem is. We men," he said, pounding his chest with his forefinger, "are sick and tired of being told when to get it up, when to stick it in, and when to get it out."

My mind couldn't catch up to my ears, and I was about to say "pardon?" but Beth grabbed my arm and pulled me up the steps. She said something like, "Okay, well, thanks, that helps," and dragged me out the door. When we were out in the hall my legs gave way under the weight of our laughter. It was one of those wonderful moments between friends that only we would understand and share for months, perhaps even years, to come.

That's what I remembered about that room, and that's what I wanted to remember. I wanted to remember it as a place where I came to laugh and learn with Beth, not as a place where I came alone to say good-bye to my friend.

My eyes went to the front of the room, where the podium stood bare as it always did. The only difference that day was the two small flower arrangements placed at its base. I stood at the door, taking in the fifty or so people who were already seated.

Mark Gunn was in the first row, along with Sandra Penny, John Summers, and Daren Oaks. Behind them sat Mullarcant and Cameron Deagle. Next to him was Zac, who waved me over. When I moved across the room, Mark Gunn got up and offered me his seat. I wanted to sit with Zac, but thought it would be rude not to accept the gesture. Zac gave a little shrug and a nod to indicate he understood. Mark took the seat next to me.

I leaned forward and looked down the row to Sandra Penny, who was stone-faced, staring straight ahead. Sandra was a non-descript woman with a generic white-bread face. A nightmare, I was sure, for any eyewitness to have to identify. Her straight, white-blond hair was cropped short, not in any particular style, just short. She worn no make-up and her face was smooth and devoid of lines. When she spoke, she neither smiled nor frowned, the words just came out, which I found distracting because having a conversation with Sandra Penny was much like listening to someone read a speech.

Sandra's area of expertise was Behavioral Psychology, with a specialization in behavioral modification, or B-Mod for those in the know. During my first year, while Sandra was my interim supervisor, I also worked as her research assistant. She was a prolific publisher and had built up an international reputation for her work. Next to Mullarcant, Sandra Penny received more research money than anyone else in the department.

As it happened, it was because of her that I eventually ended up in Mullarcant's lab. Part of my job was assisting Sandra with her aversion therapy sessions. After watching alcoholics puke their guts out once Sandra gave them a few drinks and an injection of Emetinic Hydrochloride, I figured gassing people would be a whole lot easier, if not tidier.

Sandra belonged to the camp of theorists who believed alcoholism could be controlled through classical conditioning, which meant pairing a noxious stimulus with the problem behavior. The first time I was involved in one of those sessions, I couldn't look at alcohol for over a month. Unfortunately, the experience wasn't quite as effective for the poor guy who had actually gone through it—he was back to drinking his daily fifth of rye in about a week.

When I couldn't stand watching people get sick any longer, I went to Sandra and told her I was more interested in her other studies, such as the one where she videotaped people while they were drunk out of their minds. This technique was supposed to work the same way as the injection, with the idea being that subjects would have to watch themselves on video the next day when they were sober, which would, in turn, put them off drinking forever. When I told Sandra I wanted to switch projects, her response was, "So you find the Emic injections distasteful?"

"Yeah, actually I do."

"You know, this isn't new, Emily. In fact, the Romans were the first to practice it." She went on to tell me that in order to stop people from overindulging, medieval Romans put a live eel in a glass of mead or something and made the gluttonous person drink it. I wasn't sure what her point was for telling me this, but I remember thinking at the time that, frankly, I'd opt for the eel over the injection any day. I've heard from my sushi-loving friends that smoked eel goes quite nicely with a glass of Chardonnay.

The upshot was that she had no problem with my switching to the video project, so for a couple of months I spent two days a week serving people copious amounts of alcohol and then videotaping them while they slobbered and blubbered over each other. Sandra eventually gave those studies up and said it was because her new work with Mullarcant was taking up too much of her time. But I think the real reason she abandoned the project was because our subjects were participating with just a little too much gusto and not nearly enough remorse. Toward the end, I got the impression that some of our subjects had come to think of those sessions as their weekly get-togethers. Viewing the tapes became such a source of amusement for everyone involved that I believed they were hamming it up just to outdo each other.

With the video project gone, my only option as Sandra's student and assistant was to go back to the injection room. So when

Mullarcant invited me to work under Mark Gunn in his lab, I jumped at the chance, and Sandra applauded my decision.

Seated next to Sandra was Daren Oakes, our department head, who was reading over what I assumed was Beth's eulogy. Mullarcant was leaning over the seat, reading over Oakes' shoulder and talking into his ear. Every so often Mullarcant would gesture toward the paper, whereupon Daren would dutifully make the appropriate changes.

It was common knowledge that most of the faculty, and Mullarcant in particular, rode roughshod over Daren Oakes. He was, in a word, a gentle figurehead—like the Queen. Aside from showing up at graduations, parties, and memorial services, Daren Oakes didn't do much. When I first met him, the word that popped into my head was "Frangelico"—that hazelnut-flavored liquor that comes in a brown bottle shaped like a monk—because Daren Oakes had this Friar Tuck thing going. His red hair appeared to have been cut with the aid of a mixing bowl and a hunting knife, and his wardrobe consisted of a brown cardigan sweater, a tan sports shirt, brown polyester pants, and brown leather sandals he wore with socks all year round.

Despite my snotty assessment of his fashion practices, I thought Daren Oakes was a very nice man who always had an open-door policy with the students. Not that he actually did anything for us, but he was always willing to lend an ear. I believed he was a man simply caught in the wrong profession. Instead of running USA's department of psychology, he should have been downtown, programming computers. Problem was, when he went through school, there weren't any computers around. By the time he realized what he really wanted to be when he grew up, it was too late and Daren was left with a doctorate in psychology and a really cushy job. He coped with the problem rather well, though, by spending as much time as he possibly could get away with in the computing science department. And to his credit, our psychology department was the best technologically equipped department, aside from computing science itself, in the entire school and possibly the entire country.

The downside was that he wasn't around our department much and seemed perfectly happy to let Mullarcant, or anyone else, for that matter, run the place.

Daren Oakes looked at his watch and then walked up to the podium. Except for the sound of his rattling papers, the room was silent. He looked up at the group of mourners. "Thank you all for coming," he said in a solemn voice. "We have come here today to pay our respects to a fine student, Elizabeth May Wong."

Mark Gunn leaned over and put his hand on my arm. "Are you okay?" he whispered.

I felt my throat tighten and tears fill my eyes. "Yeah. Thanks." For the rest of the service, Mark kept his hand on my arm, giving it a comforting squeeze or pat every so often. Initially, I was a little uncomfortable with it, but since none of the faculty who spoke said anything particularly moving during the service, it was nice to have someone next to me who seemed as genuinely upset about Beth as I was. When Daren Oakes took the podium again to announce that we had come to the end of the service, I couldn't believe it was over already.

I leaned over to Mark. "Isn't he going to have any of the students say something?"

"Sorry, I couldn't hear you."

I leaned in closer. "Why weren't any of the students asked to say something?" I peered over my shoulder and scanned the room. "And where's her family? Didn't they invite her family?"

Mark shrugged. "I just got tenure, remember. My opinion doesn't count yet."

People were getting up and milling around the room. I looked for Zac and spotted him in the corner, talking with Mullarcant.

"Why don't we get out of here and go for a drink somewhere?" Mark said.

"Sounds good. Do you mind if I ask Zac to come with us? He could probably use a drink too."

"No. I mean, no, I don't mind at all."

"Well, that was uplifting," Zac said, coming up beside us.

I shook my head and rolled my eyes in disgust. "Mark and I are going for a drink. Why don't you come with us, and we can talk about it then."

"Good thinking. Where are we going?"

We both turned to Mark, and I thought, how interesting, no matter how comfortable you get with a prof, there's always something that separates us from them.

"Why don't we go off campus somewhere? How about downtown, the Market maybe," Mark suggested.

I knew Mark didn't drive and Zac's car was always in the shop. "Sure. We can all go in my car."

"That's okay. I'll meet up with you later," Zac said. "Mullarcant just asked me to run some stats for him."

"No rest for the wicked," Mark said apologetically.

"Zac, why don't you tell him you'll do it tomorrow or something?" I asked.

He thought about it for a second and then said, "Nah, it'll be easier to just get it done. It should only take me half an hour or so, then I won't have to think about it."

"Okay, we'll wait and you can get a ride with us." I turned to Mark and was about to ask if he'd mind waiting, but Zac cut me off.

"No, just go," Zac said. "I've got my car."

"Oh my God, then we better wait so I can follow you over there."

"Very funny. Look, in the time we've stood here arguing about this, I could be half finished, so just tell me where you're going to be." Mark suggested Cajun Charlie's, and Zac said he'd see us there and then hurried off.

On our way out, I spotted a small, dark-haired woman in a black silk, Chinese print shirt and pants leaving the room.

"Mark, I'll be right back," I said and made a dash for the door. When I was close enough, I tapped the woman on the shoulder. She turned and my heart split open as Beth's grandmother stared up at me through tear-soaked eyes. She held a wad of Kleenex in her hand and made quick, harsh dabs at her cheeks.

The last time I had seen her was at Beth's funeral in December. In that milieu, with all her family and friends around her, she looked strong and in control. In fact, I remembered distinctly that she wasn't even crying. But at that moment, in that big impersonal building, she looked tiny and fragile and very alone.

"Grandma Wong, I'm so sorry," I said as tears filled my eyes. "Are you with anyone?" I said. "Can I give you a ride?"

She looked past me to the front of the auditorium where the bare podium stood. "That no way to honor my granddaughter."

"You're right. She deserved more, much more. I'm so sorry." I suddenly felt ashamed to be a student at the University of Southwestern Alberta.

She looked at me hard and then walked toward the front entrance of the building. I followed silently behind and held the heavy glass doors open for her. But as she passed under my arm, I had the feeling that the power of her grief was so strong she could have walked right through the glass. Outside, a number of cars were parked along the curb, waiting for passengers.

"Do you have a ride?" I asked again.

She studied my face, and a shiver went up my spine. "My granddaughter is no disgrace."

"No, of course she isn't. Beth was a wonderful person, a truly wonderful—"

She cut me off. "You help my Beth. You good friend, you find out who did this to her."

"Grandma Wong, I don't think anyone meant to be disrespectful. I think it was just poor planning."

"They, they did this to her," she said, jabbing a finger back toward the building. Then she gabbed my wrist and held on with such force it hurt. "If you follow them, they do the same to you. Don't forget my Beth."

"I won't forget her," I said softly. She nodded and let go of my wrist, as if satisfied she now had what she had come for. She shuffled toward a dark blue Ford Taurus. Beth's father got out of the driver's side and came around to let his mother into the back

85

seat. Just before she ducked into the car, Grandma Wong looked up and gave a quick, expressionless nod in my direction, as if confirming a pact between us.

Beth's mother was in the front seat, head bowed, shoulders heaving with each sob. I felt like a thief who had stolen something very precious from them. I wanted desperately to give it back, but I couldn't because I just didn't have it any more.

Chapter 9

I WATCHED THE CAR PULL AWAY and felt someone standing next to me. Mark Gunn took my hand.

"Beth's family?"

I nodded.

"You okay?"

Tears were streaming down my face. "No. I'm not okay at all."

"Let's get out of here." He put his arm around my shoulder and led me toward the parking lot.

"I need my bag," I said, remembering I had left it on a chair in the auditorium. He held it up and smiled.

I had stopped crying and pulled myself together by the time we parked at a meter near the Market. We walked in the entrance next to Cajun Charlie's, and I could see that it was busy, as was the rest of Eau Claire Market.

Before the market opened in 1993, downtown Calgary, like many big cities, was a virtual ghost town after six p.m. Then some insightful developers came up with the idea to build an indoor market between Prince's Island Park and the downtown core. The area was suddenly and miraculously transformed into a place where suburbanites actually make a point of coming to on weekends and evenings.

Eau Claire is a Festival Market, which means that it is a combination urban entertainment mall and farmer's market. In Eau Claire's case, it's heavy on entertainment and light on farmers. There are food kiosks that provide fresh offerings, such as fish, breads, specialty meats, and produce. There is a wine market, numerous restaurants, theaters, and lots of buskers.

On our way into the restaurant, we passed Jack E Joker, who was standing on his head, wearing what looked like pink silk pajamas with a matching hood affair, and scuba flippers on his feet. While Jack E waved his flippered feet in the air, he played an energetic rendition of "Happy Birthday" on the kazoo to an appreciative little girl and her father. People seem to love Jack E. So much so, in fact, that he has become somewhat of a city icon whose mug appears regularly in the media and on numerous tourist publications. Jack E Joker is a Calgary drawing card.

Mark and I placed a couple of loonies into Jack E's hat, then went in the restaurant. It was noisy and crowded—the perfect place to drink some wine, eat some gumbo, and get lost for a while. We found a table at the back near the windows and ordered Filé and Smoking Gumbos along with glasses of red wine, but changed our minds to a bottle after the waiter convinced us it would be cheaper in the long run. I guess we looked as if we were in for the long haul. We sipped our first glass and avoided talking about Beth. By the second, and halfway into my Smoking Gumbo, my tongue was getting hot and loose and I couldn't hold out any longer.

"I was surprised Beth's parents weren't at the service," I said.

"So was I. Odd that only her grandmother came in."

I hadn't stopped thinking about Grandma Wong and what she said since we left the university. Was she just a heartbroken old woman who couldn't accept the fact that her granddaughter had committed suicide, or was she right that someone or something had driven her to do it? Then there was Ken, and the application to Memorial, and what Heidi said about Beth's plans after the New Year. And the mystery man. What about him? Maybe there was no mystery guy. But where had Beth been spending those last couple of weeks, and why would she lie to me about it? My mind was spinning out too many questions, and the wine wasn't helping me come up with any answers. Grandma Wong's words played in my mind. *They, they did this to her . . .*

"Penny for your thoughts," Mark said.

"Oh, sorry, I was just thinking about something Beth's grandmother said."

"Which was?"

I looked at him and wondered whether I should I keep it to myself. The wine won out again. "Mark, if I tell you, will you promise to keep it to yourself?"

He traced a sign of the cross on his chest. "Cross my heart and all that. Of course I promise."

I felt foolish once I repeated Grandma Wong's words. "I guess it sounds pretty melodramatic, doesn't it?"

"I don't know. If my granddaughter committed suicide, I think I'd want some answers too. And maybe she's right, maybe the system is to blame. God knows Beth isn't the first student to do it. Maybe it had something to do with her culture too."

"You mean like saving face?"

"Something like that."

"But what would Beth have to save face over? She was a great student."

"I know, but a lot of Chinese students are under tremendous pressure. Remember Lan?"

"Sure, nice guy. Shame he quit, though."

"I felt so bad for him," Mark said. "I saw him after he called his parents, and do you know what they said to him? They said he was a disgrace to his family, and that he was being ungrateful to his country. He was planning to come back. He just needed some time to figure things out."

"It still doesn't make sense in Beth's case, though, because I know for a fact her mother and father were trying to get her to slow down." Then something occurred to me. "That explains it," I blurted out.

"What's that?"

"Mark, last night I found Beth's application to Memorial."

My words gave him a physical jolt. He sat up and took a long drink and stared straight ahead. "Where did you find it?" he said in a hollow voice.

"She gave it to me by mistake, in the lab. It was in a file stuck behind some forms. I was going to return it to her but ..."

"Yeah, but," he said, and finished the last third of his wine in one gulp. "Was there anything else with it?"

"Like yours and Sandra's letters of recommendation, say? I'm sorry Mark, I can see this has obviously upset you. It's just that it doesn't make sense to me. Or I should say, didn't."

"Why didn't?"

"When we mentioned Beth's parents, it occurred to me that maybe they were the ones pushing her to transfer schools. I know they were worried about her, and apparently with good reason. That's the only logical explanation. Otherwise it just doesn't add up."

Mark motioned for the waiter and ordered another bottle of wine. After the waiter left he said, "It's too bad you found that application form, Emily."

"Aside from the obvious, why is that?"

"Have you told anyone else about it?"

"No. I wasn't even sure I was going to tell you."

"Good, because I'm going to tell you what happened and why she wanted to leave. But you have to give me your word that you'll never mention this to anyone. Beth was a good student and a great researcher, and I think it would be a shame for anyone to think otherwise."

"I couldn't agree more. Of course you have my word."

He took a couple of deep breaths as if readying himself for a high dive. "Okay, it's no secret that Mullarcant is a hard guy to work for. He's a brilliant man, but, well ... let's just say his social skills are a little weak." I couldn't help but laugh. It was a bitter laugh, though. "So you get my drift. Anyway, Beth started having problems and her work was suffering because of it."

"Personal or work problems?"

"Personal. She was seeing someone and it wasn't going well."

"Ah ha. So there was a mystery man. Zac and I thought so. But I can't figure out why we never saw him and why she never mentioned his name. So who was he, and why all the secrecy?"

"I'm not going to get into that because it was Beth's business. The only reason she confided in me was because Mullarcant was riding her so much, and apparently that was causing the relationship to go downhill. So when she came to me with that application form and asked for a letter of recommendation, I tried to talk her out of it. I thought she was being irrational."

"Which I can't imagine Beth ever being. She was the most level-headed person I've ever known. But then again, working under Mullarcant for three or four years could make anyone slip off the rails."

"He's tough, I'll grant you." The waiter came with the wine and refilled our glasses. "Oh, and before I forget, Emily, you're doing very well. Martin told me he's happy with you and your work."

"Really. Let's hope it stays that way until April."

"I'm sure it will. And aside from his interpersonal skills, working under him is an excellent opportunity for you."

"So I've been told. Beth always said so too."

"I know she did. And that's why I thought she really wasn't thinking clearly when she showed up with that application form."

"Did Mullarcant know about it?"

"Unfortunately, he did." Just then, the pieces fell into place as the image of Beth's face flashed through my mind. "What is it?" asked Mark.

"He found out that day, didn't he? She was the one he was yelling at in his office. Zac said he was having one hell of a conference with someone."

Mark nodded slowly, and I could see the deep, clear sadness in his eyes. "She told him. I asked her not to, because I was hoping she would change her mind. But Beth wasn't the kind of person

91

who could be dishonest. Frankly, I don't think she could tell a lie if her life depended on it."

"So let me get this straight, she told him the truth, and he went berserk on her. Gee, that's the kind of support a student really needs."

"You're right. He made a mess of it."

"That's the understatement of the year."

"I pleaded with her to think about it over Christmas, but she wouldn't."

"He called me last night, you know," I said.

"I know. He called me looking for it too."

"The file or the application form?"

"Both."

"How did he know it was in that particular file?"

"That's a good question. I have no idea."

"What else was in that file?"

Mark shrugged. "You got me. So where is the application form now? Do you still have it?"

"No, I threw it away. I decided it was Beth's property."

"Good decision. Let's both forget it ever existed."

"Aren't you going to tell Mullarcant I found it?"

Mark thought for a moment. "I'll tell him I found it and that I threw it out. He doesn't need to know you were the one."

I thanked him. "But I can't help but wonder what else was in that file. And what happened to it?"

Mark shrugged.

"Well, at least this explains a few other things. I was beginning to think there was something else going on."

"No, Emily, there's nothing going on except we failed to see that a very bright student was in serious trouble."

"Pretty ironic for a psych department, don't you think?"

"Yup, pretty damned ironic. And you know, I've seen it before. I remember one student who sliced his right arm up two hours before a final exam. The tragic thing was that he was such a bright guy, even if he'd completely blown the final, he still would've passed the course. We never worry about the bright ones, and they're the ones who are probably under the most pressure."

"Beth was certainly bright."

"Extremely. You said it explained other things. What did you mean by that?"

"Oh, nothing. It seems silly to even bring it up now. Forget it. I think I'll just have a little more wine."

Mark topped up my glass. A group of ten or twelve people took up the table next to ours and the noise level rose a couple more decibels.

"You have to tell me now. You've got me all curious," Mark said, leaning in a little closer so he wouldn't have to raise his voice.

"Oh, I was just letting my imagination take over again. My mother always said I tended toward the dramatic. Maybe she was right, I do seem to have this ability to put two and two together and come up with something fantastic."

"Like thinking there's something sinister going in Mullarcant's little lab of horrors."

My mouth fell open. "That's what you call it too?"

"Of course, everyone does." He moved his chair a little closer. "So you have a good imagination, do you?"

"Actually, my mother used to refer to it as wild."

"So how wild is it?"

I could feel my cheeks flush, and I'd be a liar if I said I wasn't enjoying his attention. "One time," I said with a nervous laugh, "I was sharing an apartment in Banff with a friend. For three days in a row I came home from work and found dirty dishes in the sink. My roommate was out of town, so I figured someone was breaking in during the day and playing some kind of psychotic joke on me. When it happened a fourth time, I was almost hysterical and imagined some diabolical person was trying to make me crazy before he—I knew it had to be a he because he never rinsed his dishes—broke in at night and did some dreadful thing to me. So I reported it to the RCMP, who, I might add, found the whole thing hilarious and started calling my intruder Jack The Eater."

Mark laughed.

"Actually, the officer was a friend of mine, and he told me to change the locks on the doors, so I did. That night my room-mate, who had been away for six months, called and wanted to know what was going on because her boyfriend couldn't get into the apartment. I had completely forgotten he was going to be in town working on a construction crew, and might be popping in and out."

Mark's head went back and he let out a laugh, "That's a great story, Emily."

"In my defense," I said, "it had been four months since she mentioned it. It could have happened to anyone. Especially any-one with a good imagination."

"So do you think maybe your imagination has been getting the better of you again as far as Beth goes?" Mark said.

"Oh, maybe. I'm awfully glad I talked to you about this, Mark. I'll always have trouble accepting the way Beth died, but at least now I have some answers. I feel a bit stupid for being so dramatic, though."

"Don't. It's just human nature. When a bad thing happens to a good person, we have an absolute need to make sense of it, and often that means finding someone to blame."

We both sat in silence for a few moments. "Thanks, Mark."

"Any time." He looked at his watch. "Holy cow, it's seven-thirty."

"I wonder where that Zac is."

"Do you want to give him a call?" Mark said. By then the restaurant was filled to capacity with patrons standing three-deep at the bar.

"Maybe on our way out," I said. "He probably just decided to go home."

"Had enough wine?"

"I think so."

Mark was holding the menu up for me. "Then how about a little Gator Gumbo for the road?"

"I've always wanted to sink my chops into alligator, but I'm pretty full just now." He laughed and then beckoned for the waiter to bring us our bill.

"Before we go, Mark, there's one other thing that's been bothering me, and I know I'm not imagining this. Mullarcant doesn't seem to be feeling too badly about this whole thing."

"Oh, Emily, don't be too sure about that. I think he feels dreadful, he just has no way of showing it."

"You give him a lot more credit than I do."

He lifted his glass to me. "Perhaps I do."

As we were paying the bill, the bartender came over with the phone and asked if my name was Emily. Zac was on the line. He was still tied up at the lab and he was heading home in an hour. I told him to give me a call the next day. I was sorry he couldn't come, but not that sorry because I was enjoying Mark's company.

Since becoming my thesis supervisor six months earlier, Mark and I had gone for coffee a number of times and usually talked about work-related things. But since Beth's death, things were changing between us. I'm not usually very perceptive about these things—in fact, according to my mother, I was always completely oblivious to "boys' " affections and assumed they just wanted to be friends. But this time I was getting it—Mark Gunn seemed genuinely interested in me. And I wasn't disappointed.

We decided the better part of discretion was to share a cab instead of driving. When we pulled up in front of his house, I was expecting a polite goodnight, but he surprised me and invited me in for a drink. I turned him down on the drink but said I'd be happy to have a cup of tea. He lived in the fashionable Rosedale district in a modest, elegant Tudor-style home, furnished with antiques and lots of modern art.

"I wouldn't have thought all this new stuff would go so well with all the—"

"Old stuff," he said, carrying in a tray with a pot of tea, cups, and sandwiches. "It's kind of a hobby. I like to shop."

And I like you, Doctor Gunn.

I stayed for the rest of the night, drinking tea and talking, but this time the conversation wasn't about Beth or school, it was about us. We compared our tastes in music, and argued about different books we'd read while we nibbled at cream-cheese bagels and fruit. By the time dawn was approaching, we were dripping honey on toast and talking about his wife, who was living in Vancouver with their only child.

"It just didn't work out here. She's a true West Coaster," Mark said. "Her family's out there too." He shrugged. "But we're still friends and that's good, I guess."

"Better than being enemies," I said, which was lame, I know, but I was uncomfortable talking about her. In fact, at that moment, I didn't want Mark Gunn to have any past or future that didn't include me.

"True. And what about you, Beth?" He looked shocked when he said it. "I'm sorry, I mean, Emily."

"Hey, don't worry about it. She's always on my mind too. I wouldn't be surprised if I called you Beth. What about me?"

"Do you have any husbands hidden away anywhere?"

"No, I'm kind of flying solo these days," I said nervously. It was the first time I felt uncomfortable with Mark all evening. Probably because it was the first truly overt thing he said that would indicate he was interested in me.

"Sorry, I didn't mean to pry."

"That's okay, but I should probably get going," I said and was immediately sorry I had.

He called me a cab and when I was leaving, he kissed me gently on the forehead. "Thanks for making a difficult night into a great night," he said.

"And thank you too. I had a really nice time," I said. My heart was pounding and I felt like a schoolgirl with a crush on her teacher. Which technically was the case, but at my age I guess it would be more accurate to say, school woman. I was searching through my bag for my car keys and house keys. I found the car keys.

"Can't find something?" Mark said, watching me rummage through my coat pockets.

"Just my house keys. I probably left them at home. *Again.* But it's okay."

"Won't you need them to get in if no one's there?"

"No. As long as my garage door opener is still in my car, I can get in that way. We always keep the inside door open, since I forget to take my keys every other day." I knew I was babbling.

He smiled and shifted from one foot to the other. "Emily, I don't know how you feel about this, and if you're uncomfortable because of school, just say so. But I was wondering if I could call you over the weekend. But only if you feel—"

I cut him off. "I'd like that. Do you have my number?" I slapped my forehead with the palm of my hand. "What am I saying, of course you do. You know everything about me."

"I'll call you," he said.

Chapter 10

I PICKED UP MY CAR and was heading across the Center Street bridge with that "just falling in love feeling" that lies somewhere between drunkenness and insanity, when my mood shifted abruptly to feelings of guilt. At the foot of the bridge I spotted Wong's Herb shop. Beth's grandmother's grief-sticken face and her words filled my mind. *Don't forget my Beth. You good friend.*

"No, I'm not, Grandma Wong," I said out loud. "I'm not a good friend at all. Instead of honoring Beth by going home or going to pray at a church or something, I was out whooping it up all night with Mark. Some friend."

I found Rusty in the kitchen at the breakfast bar, reading the morning paper and drinking coffee.

"Good morning," she said. "Up with the birds, I see."

"Up before the birds. I just got in."

"I know. I was just being a smart aleck."

"I deserve it."

"Wearing your new hair shirt, are you? What's the matter, did you allow yourself a little pleasure last night?" She was grinning from ear to ear.

"Before I tell you anything, I want to make it perfectly clear that nothing, and I stress nothing, happened. Just so you'll still respect me in the morning."

"Well, if that's the case, I'm not sure I'll be able to respect you at all. I was hoping you had something really juicy to tell me."

"Sorry, we just talked all night."

"And the 'we' part"—she put down the paper and pondered the question with mock consternation—"wouldn't happen to be the fine young Doctor Mark Gunn, would it?"

"How did you know?"

"Let's just say I'm a bit psychic."

"Okay, Jo Jo, what's your secret?"

"Every time you mention his name your face lights up."

"Oh no, is it that obvious?"

"Yes, but probably only to me."

"Let's hope so."

"Sooo, you talked all night, and let me guess, the two of you are madly in love and you're going to start a dogsledding business in Banff after you graduate, and then live happily ever after."

"Rusty, how do you do it?"

"It's a gift. Now tell me, tell me, tell me. Are you really interested in him?"

"I think so."

"Then why the long face?"

"Because I'm a lousy friend, Rusty. Beth's memorial service was yesterday."

"I know, and I'm so sorry I couldn't make it. The Housing For All meeting went late again. I just couldn't leave."

"You didn't miss anything. Wasn't much of a service. And I was pretty busy drinking wine at Cajun Charlie's and then talking all night at Mark's."

"And that's all you did?"

"Yes."

"Then why are you wasting all that good Catholic guilt on something so dull?"

"Stop it, you're making me feel better. We should have gone to church or something, instead of a bar."

"Or to your room alone," she said. "Stop beating yourself up, Emily. Believe me, you did the right thing. It's far better to be with friends than to be alone. Especially when that friend may turn out to be a little more than just a friend." She rubbed her hands together.

I took a piece of bread from the bread drawer and popped it in the toaster, which in Rusty's kitchen is an industrial-sized eight-slicer that gives off enough heat to warm the entire room. She eyed it for a moment.

"Remind me to buy a smaller toaster, will you, dear? Oh, and while you're at it, remind me to get someone in to look at the furnace, it's been humming away down there all night and this morning."

"Sure." I stopped to listen. "I don't hear anything now, though."

"Of course you don't. It only does it when I'm trying to sleep. And it most certainly won't do it when the repairman is here."

I smiled and watched the toast spring up. "But you know," I said slathering butter on it, "I do like this toaster because it makes toast in about thirty seconds." I looked around the kitchen at all the huge pots and pans and the walk-in appliances. "You must have given some parties in your day, Rusty."

"Oh my, yes, sometimes we'd have over a dozen people staying with us."

"Did you enjoy it, Rusty, all the entertaining and everything?"

"I suppose so. But it's nice not to have to dress for breakfast any more. Now stop stalling and tell me what he's like."

"He's very nice, and he's married. But the wife is gone."

"Gone as in . . .?"

"As in gone west. She's in Vancouver with their son."

"So it looks like it's clear sailing for you. Was it just the two of you all night?"

"Zac was supposed to come, but the Great Man made him work."

"And the university didn't do a nice job of the memorial service for Beth?"

I said no, that they certainly had not. We moved into the living room with our coffee and I described the service and seeing Grandma Wong, and then finally all the things Mark and I had discussed.

"I told Mark I wouldn't tell anyone about this, Rusty, but of course that didn't mean you."

"Don't worry. You have my solemn oath. I won't breathe a word."

"I know that, Rusty."

"You know, dear, I'm pleased you had an opportunity to talk things through with someone who knows what was really going on. And he's right, when bad things happen to good people it's very hard to accept. But perhaps now you can get on with what you need to do."

"You're right. I can't bring Beth back and I can't change what happened. I have to accept that. But I'll tell you one thing I can't accept: no matter what Mark says about Mullarcant, I still think he was a tyrant. And even if he wasn't the entire problem, he certainly added to it. And I'd sure like to know what else was in that file. And where it is."

"Yes, I'd like to know too. But as far as Mullarcant goes, the best thing you can do is make darn sure the same thing doesn't happen to you."

"To me? Why would you say that?"

"It does sound as though you are following in some of Beth's footsteps."

"To a point, but don't forget I'm not planning to stick around his lab. Besides, Mark is my official supervisor, Mullarcant was Beth's."

"But now that you and Mark are getting, well, closer, shall we say, you might have to rearrange things, mightn't you?"

"Rusty, I only have four months left. But I'm glad you brought it up. Once again, I just kind of jumped into something without giving it a whole lot of thought."

"Well, it's a little difficult when it comes to matters of the heart."

"Matters of the heart? Rusty, you kill me. I think you mean matters of lust."

"Semantics, my dear, mere semantics. But getting back to what I was saying, please just be cautious. It's very easy to get caught up and overworked when you are involved with someone like Martin Mullarcant. Just keep your eyes open, and remember that you are the important one here, not him and not his work. Don't let yourself get lost in what he wants."

"Sounds like you're speaking from experience."

She sighed. "I suppose I am. Jerald was a driven man. And I spent the better part of my life just trying to catch up and hang on. Until one day, I learned there really wasn't anything to hang on to. The person in front of me was simply trying to catch up and hang on to someone or something else in front of him."

"I see what you're saying, but I can't imagine Mullarcant is running in anyone else's race but his own."

"Oh, I think you might be surprised to learn what makes a man like him move."

"Anyway, one good thing is that I'll be working on the second phase of the project. And with any luck, I'll be able to stop gassing people."

"That really would be a plus, wouldn't it?" she said and laughed.

"Indeed, but the real exciting thing is that I'll probably get a publication out of this once we're finished."

"Excellent. If you do continue on to your PhD, having a publication will be invaluable. Now tell me about this new project of yours."

"Sure. But we better get another cup of coffee because this might take a while." Once we had our refills, we returned to our serious talking positions: Rusty on the couch and me on the big armchair across from her. "Okay, here's the deal," I began. "Did you ever hear about the Milgram experiments that were conducted in the early sixties?"

"Didn't he have something to do with shocking people?"

"He shocked them all right, and in more ways than one. Stanley Milgram was a social psychologist in the States who was looking at conformity and obedience."

"I can see why he would be. The war had only been over for some fifteen years at that point, and the idea of conformity was still certainly on everyone's mind."

"Exactly. A lot of this type of research came about because of the Nazis and the Nuremberg trials."

"'I was just following orders.' Wasn't that what they all said?"

I nodded. "And Milgram wanted to know how people could commit such atrocities. So he set up these experiments where he had subjects come to his lab and supposedly administer electrical shocks to another person."

"Good heavens, what a dreadful thing to ask someone to do!"

"But the subjects didn't really deliver any shocks; they just thought they were."

"Now you're losing me."

"Sorry, I'll go through it from the beginning."

"Good thinking."

"Two people were brought into the lab and greeted by a guy in a white lab coat—the experimenter—who would tell them they were part of an investigation to test the effects of punishment on learning and memory. One of these people would be a real subject, and the other was an actor named Mr. Wallace, who was working for Milgram. Of course, the real subject didn't know Mr. Wallace was an actor. The experimenter would have the real subject and Mr. Wallace draw straws to see who would be the learner and who would be the teacher. It was rigged so that the real subject always ended up being the teacher and the actor, Mr. Wallace, was always the learner. Are you with me so far?"

"Absolutely, keep going."

"The teacher was given a sample electric shock of forty-five volts so he or she would see how it felt when Mr. Wallace, the learner, would receive it. Mr. Wallace was then strapped into what looked like an electric chair and the teacher/subject person watched all this. The teacher was then taken into another room and put in front of a panel of switches that were labeled "Slight Shock," which was supposedly about fifteen volts, all the way up to "Danger, Severe Shock," which was supposedly about four hundred and fifty volts.

"Mr. Wallace, the learner, was told to repeat a list of words and every time he made an error the teacher was instructed by the experimenter—the guy in the white lab coat—to administer a shock, starting with the lowest level and gradually working up to the highest shock level."

"Now let me get this straight, the teacher who is the real subject thinks he is zapping poor Mr. Wallace each time Mr. Wallace makes a mistake?"

"Right. The teacher couldn't see Mr. Wallace, but he or she could sure hear him. See, Mr. Wallace was given a script to follow for each voltage level. As the shock level rose, Mr. Wallace would begin to yell. The stronger the shock, the louder the yelps. At seventy-five volts, for example, he would moan, at one hundred and fifty he would demand to be released from the chair. At two hundred he would yell that he couldn't stand the pain, and at three hundred he would call out that he had a heart condition and begin to scream."

"My God, that sounds dreadful."

"It was. But remember, Mr. Wallace was an actor and he never received any real shocks; he just pretended to."

"I know, but the subjects didn't know that. But surely no one got to that point anyway. I would expect the vast majority stopped just as soon as Mr. Wallace started to protest."

"Actually, that was the horrifying but interesting part of the whole experiment. Over sixty percent of the subjects went all the way up to four hundred and fifty volts."

"Dear God."

"I know, it's terrible, and it was particularly awful for some of the subjects. Some of those people found the whole thing devastating. While they were delivering the shocks, they'd cry and say things like, 'I can't stand this! I'm going to kill that man.' But a number also said, 'What if something happens to that nice man in there? Who will take responsibility if anything does happen to him?'"

"And what would the experimenter say to that?"

"That was the whole point of the experiment. The guy in the white lab coat would always say, 'You must go on. I will take responsibility for Mr. Wallace.' Things like that. And apparently most of them said okeedokey and went right on delivering the shocks."

"Thank goodness forty percent didn't give in."

"Actually, that's not quite true, either. Almost all of them went as high as three hundred volts. And those who refused to continue simply walked out of the room. Not one of them tried to see how Mr. Wallace was doing."

"Human nature never fails to surprise and disappoint me."

"Take heart. There has been a great deal of criticism leveled against the experiment. And I also like to keep in mind that it was just that, an experiment, and not the real world."

"Yes, and Hitler's was the ultimate experiment. It seems unthinkable what we humans are capable of doing to one another."

"True. But think about all the heroic things people do every day. And Milgram's and a lot of other experiments have shown that it's not that we have some hidden desire to hurt people, it's more that we have this deep desire to be obedient, especially in public places."

"And the Nazis certainly capitalized on that."

"That's an interesting point. Because that's exactly what subjects essentially said when they were asked why they continued shocking Mr. Wallace when they obviously didn't want to. They said things like, 'Because you told me to,' and 'I was just doing my job.' Stuff like that."

"We're a strange lot, aren't we?"

"You should see the film, it's awful. A lot of the subjects were shaking and crying as they pressed that lever all the way up to the top, and yet they did it."

"At least they didn't like doing it. That's something, I suppose. But the really terrifying thing is thinking about how you or I would react in such a situation."

"I'd put money on it that you'd never even give the first shock."

She looked at me thoughtfully. "Yes, you're right, I probably wouldn't do it now. But when I was younger, I'm sure I would have obeyed the experimenter. In fact, I'm sure I would have been one of the ones shaking and crying all the way to the top."

I shook my head. "I find that pretty hard to believe, but I'm not going to argue with you."

"Good, now tell me what this whole Milgram thing has to do with gassing people."

"As I was saying yesterday, in the panic study certain people are more likely to keep the mask on even when they're obviously in distress. Mullarcant made the connection with the Milgram studies, where people were willing to do something just to please the experimenter. So he designed a second phase of the experiment, using the Milgram stuff to find out if his theory is correct."

"Now I'm a bit confused. The people in your study are allowing themselves to be hurt, but in the Milgram study they were hurting someone else, or thought they were hurting someone else."

"Right, but there were other versions of the Milgram study where people punished themselves, and they found the same thing, people were willing to hurt themselves instead of defying the experimenter. It's the whole idea of obedience and conformity that he's interested in. So in this next phase we'll have the same subjects who kept the mask on watch a reenactment of the Milligram experiment on video."

"And what will this tell you?"

"After our subjects watch it, we ask a series of questions, the most important of which is: Who do you think is responsible for what happened to Mr. Wallace, the subject or the experimenter in the white lab coat?"

"Let me get this straight. The people who wait for one of you to take off the mask in the first phase are then going to watch the Milgram experiment."

"Right. Because we suspect these people are exhibiting a particular trait. We want to put them in another non-threatening situation and see if they exhibit the same trait."

"Which trait is this?"

"Feeling powerless and blindly following authority."

"I'd say it's a pretty good guess that the people who are willing to keep the mask on until they expire will say the experimenter in the video is to blame for what happened to Mr. Wallace."

"Exactly. It's a very neat and tidy study."

"Are you just beginning this now?"

"No. Beth and Mark were working on it with Mullarcant."

"So they already have some results?"

"Oh yes. The initial data is just being analyzed and it looks like that's exactly what's been happening. The people who keep the mask on the longest in the panic phase are more likely to say the experimenter in the Milgram study is to blame."

"What do you think, Emily?"

"About what?"

"About the Milgram experiment, do you think the subjects who thought they were shocking Mr. Wallace were to blame for their actions, or do you think it was the experimenter who was to blame?"

"I don't really blame anyone. The situation simply brought out some bad things in some average, decent people. I guess sometimes good people do bad things under weird circumstances."

"But then what about the Nazis and the other German people who stood by and let six million Jews die?"

"You're right, Rusty, everyone has to take responsibility for his or her own actions. But most of our subjects believe they're doing something for science that may help someone else some day, and so did the people in Milgram's lab."

"But who is to blame, the system or the individual?"

"And the whole thing gets really complicated when you consider that the system is made up of individuals."

"The whole is greater than the sum of its parts," Rusty said.

"Gestalt. Hey, I'm supposed to be the psychologist here. You know, Rusty, you really have brought up an interesting point. And it's a terrifying one at that. Because when you think about it, the Milgram study really is about all of us, isn't it?"

"It is indeed."

Chapter 11

FOR THE NEXT FEW WEEKS, much of my time was spent running the undergraduate subjects through the second phase of the study. Mullarcant was off campus a great deal, a huge bonus for me. Rusty was involved in a new art class, and Zac was working like a madman on his thesis. When I wasn't at school, I was with Mark. Overall, I had little to complain about, and because my work had been going so smoothly, it looked as though I'd be finished by the end of April, or mid-May at the latest. Mark told Mullarcant he found Beth's application to Memorial and that he threw it out. Mullarcant, in turn, told me that some documents were still missing, and should I come across anything labeled Aspen 45, I was to bring it to him immediately. After that, the matter was dropped, and my life and academic career seemed to be ticking along beautifully.

But toward the last week of February, my smooth progress was interrupted. It started on a Monday morning after I jumped in the shower and was dressed and out the door in under half an hour, an extraordinary record. I was feeling pumped and nergized, like a runner coming in strong on the last leg. When I stepped out the front door, the warm Chinook air added to my already high spirits. I looked to the west and saw the Chinook arch of soft, gauzy clouds stretch over the horizon like a giant stadium roof opening up to let in the blue sky.

At school, I found a note on my desk from Mullarcant, saying he had scheduled a fourth-year undergraduate for the second phase of the study, and to please see him in his office. I hurried to his office.

"Are you able to run the subject through the procedure today?" he said, tapping his pencil rhythmically on the desk.

"I think so, what time?"

"Nine."

I looked at my watch. It was quarter to nine, and I had my entire morning planned, but like the obedient student that I was, I said, "Sure, I can do it."

"Good, I have a great deal of work to complete and I don't want to be disturbed. I am completing a paper that I think will be of great interest to you."

"Oh, on which study?"

He looked at me as though I had taken leave of my senses. "The second phase, of course."

"Right, of course."

"I will explain more later. At the moment, I must keep my focus." He swiveled in his chair to face the computer. Hunched over the keyboard in his white lab coat with his usually tidy hair sticking up all over the place, he looked like the quintessential mad scientist toiling away in his tower. My Three Faces theory was being borne out.

He waved an arm out to the side. "Thank you, you can go now." He reached around behind him to the desk and wildly tapped at a folder. "Take this. It has the subject's demographics and past results from the panic study."

I reached over and gingerly picked up the folder, lest I disturb the mad genius. I tucked it under my arm, turned to leave, and said quietly, "I'll let you know how it goes."

"Just write the summary results and deposit them under my

door by noon." As I was shutting the door, he summoned me back. "Emily, one other thing," he said with his back still to me. "You can move into Beth's office this afternoon, after you drop off the results. And please close my door tightly when you leave."

I stood outside his office for a few moments, letting what he said sink in. The clock in the hall said ten minutes to nine. I'd have to think later. On my way to the lab, I read over the subject's file. His name was Derrick Grierson, twenty-two years old, male, Caucasian. Results from the panic study indicated he had kept the mask on for the full thirty seconds. It also said he experienced severe anxiety that was close to a full-blown panic attack.

When I came around the corner to the lab, he was already waiting outside the main doors, which made sense in light of his results. Wouldn't want to be late and piss anyone off now, would we, Derrick? I extended my hand.

"Hi, you must be Derrick. I'm Emily." Something about him looked familiar.

"Yeah, that's me," he said, and gave me one of those limp-dick handshakes guys give women when they don't feel comfortable shaking our hands. They just kind of slip their fingers into the palm of your hand, give it a little nudge, and call it good.

Derrick's sandy blond hair, cut in one of those trendy mushroom dos, along with his fashionable wire-framed glasses, made him the perfect poster boy for an eye-wear ad. His features were light, and when he smiled he flashed a perfect set of gleaming white teeth. That's when I remembered where I had seen him before. He was the guy playing with his dog in the commons area. The same guy Beth had been watching from the window in the lab.

"So where's your dog?"

"Petey?"

"I saw you out in the commons area just before Christmas."

"He's at home. Can't bring him in the buildings."

"I don't know why not. He looks pretty smart. You could pass him off for a student."

Derrick laughed. "He is smart. And I think he really wants to be a student here. I just live a couple of blocks away, and one day my roommate let him out and forgot to close the gate. When I came out of my stats lab, he was waiting for me with his frisbee."

"Aw. He's dedicated to you."

"Yeah. Well, anyway, I'm here for the second part of the study."

"Right," I said and fished the key out of the assignments mailbox.

"Hey, good security," Derrick said.

I replaced the key. "You didn't see that," I said, and then led him into the main part of the lab. "I'm surprised you're back, after what they did to you the last time." I was looking over his chart. Beth and Mullarcant had run him through the first phase.

"But we're not doing that again, right? I was told by Doctor Mullarcant that I was just going to watch a movie. But, I mean, I will do the other stuff, it's just—"

"Relax, Derrick, I was only making conversation. You're right, all you'll do is watch a video and then answer a few questions." I took him into the viewing room and settled him in front of the TV screen. He watched closely as I inserted the video and switched on the power, as though he would be quizzed later about every move I made.

"Okay, Derrick, you watch this on your own, and I'll be back in about fifteen minutes." He looked around the room and then up at the ceiling a few times.

"Is there something wrong?" I asked, following his gaze to the sprinkler head.

"I'm looking for a hidden camera, or a mike or something."

"Hmm," I looked around the room a second time. "Can't see any. Don't worry, Derrick, we're not going to leave you alone in here and then watch to see if you do some unnatural act or anything."

"Yeah, well, in Doctor Penny's class she told us about this one study where they hid cameras in men's cans to see if it took guys longer to start pissing when someone else was in the room."

"I remember that one too. And if I'm not mistaken, it did take them longer. Now there's some invaluable information for humankind," I said. "Gee, if only they'd let us do cutting-edge stuff like that around here."

"That gassing stuff you guys do is pretty wild, if you ask me. To tell you the truth, I think I'd rather have someone watch me take a piss than have to do that again."

"Zat's very interesting, young man," I said in my best Sigmund Freud accent.

"Hey, I'm not some kind of weirdo, I just meant—"

"I know, I know. I was kidding. I agree, I think I'd rather have someone watch me go to the bathroom too." I knew I was being completely unprofessional, talking with a subject that way, but sometimes I got tired of playing scientist.

"Can we talk about something else?" he said.

"Sure. It says here in your file that you're in your fourth year. So you're almost done, then."

"Yeah, but I'm going on. What about you? Are you nearly finished?"

"Yup, and hallelujah! I'll be outta here by spring, if everything goes according to plan, that is." I gave the wooden table top a couple of quick raps.

"So you'll be Doctor Emily."

"No, I'm just a lowly master's student."

"But Doctor Mullarcant called you his doctorate student."

"You're probably thinking of his other student, she was . . . ," I trailed off.

"The one who committed suicide. I met her the last time I was here."

"Right. Beth. She was his PhD student. That's probably who you're thinking of."

"No, he said you were. I just talked to him yesterday. I want to get into the master's program next year, so I figured it would be a good idea to do a little schmoozing. And he told me you were his PhD student. I'd take it as a compliment. He obviously has plans for you."

I was a bit rattled and remembered our earlier conversation about moving into Beth's office. Derrick was staring at me.

"Well, that's interesting," I said a little too tartly, "because he hasn't mentioned them to me."

"I'd say count yourself lucky. I'd do anything to work under him. I mean, I've heard that if you get in with Mullarcant, you're set for life: scholarships, good jobs, the whole bit."

"I guess I've never really thought about it. But I suppose you're right, his past students have all done really well, or so I'm told."

"The guy's brilliant. So can you give me any hot tips on how to get in good with him?"

"To be honest, it really wasn't a conscious effort on my part. It just sort of happened. But one thing I know for sure, he likes people who work hard. That's probably the best tip I can offer. Speaking of work, we really should get going on this." I hit the play button, and on the screen appeared a black and white image of two men being greeted by another man in a white lab coat.

"Hey, I've seen this. Isn't this the Milgram experiment?"

"That's right," I said. I pressed the pause button. "All you have to do is watch it, and then after I'll give you a questionnaire to fill out. It's not a test or anything so don't feel you have to take notes, just watch it."

"Oh sure, and you'll probably be watching me to see if I pick my nose or something, right?"

"Wrong, Derrick. Just watch the video," I said and pressed the play button.

As I was leaving, he winked at me and said, "Sure. Gotcha."

I rolled my eyes and came out to find Zac pounding away at one of the computer terminals.

"Hey, Em."

"Hi, Zac, what happened to you Saturday night? Not like you to miss a dinner at Rusty's."

Zac, Rusty, and I had planned to have dinner the previous Saturday, but Zac phoned and left a message on my answering machine, saying he wouldn't be able to make it. I had also invited Mark, but he had to go to Vancouver at the last minute. I still hadn't told Zac that I was seeing Mark. And although we weren't exactly sneaking around, Mark and I were making a concerted effort to keep our relationship to ourselves until after I graduated. There really wasn't much to hide, anyway. Mark and I were spending a lot of time together, but our level of intimacy would make pretty boring fodder for the tabloid crowd.

"What happened to me Saturday night, she asks," Zac said, still typing. "I'll tell you what happened. I was here until after twelve-thirty running stats for the Great Man."

"Get out."

"I'd love to, believe me. And I've been here ever since."

"What? All weekend?"

"Yeah, all weekend."

"Did you get my message on Sunday?" I asked.

"I did and I'm sorry I didn't call you back but"—he put his head in his hands—"I've just been too fucking busy here. Sorry about dinner."

"That's okay, Mark couldn't make it, either."

"You invited Mark?"

"Sure, why not? Anyway, why didn't you call me? I would have come in and helped you."

"Believe me, I suggested that to Himself, but he said you were working on something more important. Looks like you just got a promotion."

"Zac, that's ridiculous. There was no reason I couldn't have helped you. You should have called."

"I was going to but he told me not to bother you. And I hear you just inherited a swanky new office."

"And when did you hear that?"

"Over the weekend."

"That's interesting, because I just heard about it this morning. I was just told by one of our subjects that I was also Mullarcant's PhD student."

Zac stopped typing and looked up at me. "I'd take it as a compliment if I were you."

"Funny, that's what everyone else keeps telling me."

"Believe me, I'd rather be his star student than his slave."

"Zac, I don't want to be his star student. In fact, I'm not even

115

his student. And it really bugs me that he wouldn't let you call me. Who does he think he is? After I'm done here I'm going to have a little chat with him."

"Em, before you do, I just want to say one thing. Don't worry about me because I really don't care. I'm glad things are going well for you. Come April, I'll be outta here. I've already got things set up with Colleen Dresser. She's going to take me as her PhD student in the fall. So I'm laughing. I mean it, Em. And it was Mullarcant who got me set up with Colleen. So I wouldn't want to offend the guy or anything, if you get what I mean."

"Zac that's great. Why didn't you tell me?"

"I just found out on Saturday. I kind of owe him now."

"Well, he's sure collecting."

"And the other great thing is I'll be able to start doing some stuff with Colleen now. So don't think you're abandoning me or anything, okay?"

"Okay, but let me help you. And I don't give a rip what he says. I wouldn't want anything to come between us."

"Like a new, fully equipped office, say?"

"Yeah, like a new fully equipped office I don't even want."

"You want my advice?"

"Always."

"I'd just take all this in stride and start packing. It's a great office. God, Em, you've got your own phone, a brand-new computer, and your very own laser—and did I mention color laser?—printer. Give me one sane reason why you wouldn't want all that. It's every grad student's dream come true. And let's not forget you're only a master's student with a PhD-style office."

"Aside from the fact that the decision was made for me, the other problem is that it's Beth's office. I'd feel like I was . . ."

"What, trespassing?"

"Yeah, or like I just couldn't wait until she was gone to get right in there."

"But that's not the way it is. You know that, and I know that. And who cares what anyone else thinks or doesn't think? It's like when someone dies and people won't give the person's clothes away. It's dumb if the stuff just sits there and never gets used." Zac's jaw was tight as he spoke, and there was tension in his voice. I assumed it was because he was tired.

"When my mother died," I said, "she had this pair of patent leather shoes she had only worn once. My father gave them to our neighbor and I remember how much I resented that woman when she came over to get them. I don't think Dad even knew what he was doing at the time, he was so broken up. And I think Mrs. Wagner felt really sheepish about taking them, but my dad kept insisting."

"Okay, I see what you're getting at. If you really don't feel comfortable about taking the office then don't take it. Who cares?" His cheeks were flushed. This wasn't like Zac, and I suddenly felt foolish for whining about something every grad student would give her or his right arm for.

"Zac, I'm sorry. I know you've been working hard."

He closed his eyes and pressed the balls of his hands against his eyelids. He blew out a long breath. "I'm sorry, Em. It's been a long weekend. I shouldn't have snapped at you."

"Yes, you should. Here I am complaining about being given a nice office. And you've been slaving away all weekend."

"No, no. It is a big thing. But let me just say one last thing. You deserve it, Em. You work super-hard, and I think Beth would be happy to see you have it, because I know I would if I were in her place."

"I'm sure glad you're not," I said and gave him a hug. He returned it with a weary smile.

Derrick came down the hall and stuck his head into the main part of the lab. "Finished," he said.

"Derrick, this is Zac. Zac's also a student on the project."

"Hi, Derrick. How's it going?"

"Better this time."

"No doubt," Zac said.

I took Derrick into the conference room and went through the questionnaire with him.

"Derrick, in the video, the subjects thought they were actually administering real shocks to Mr. Wallace. Who was ultimately responsible for this, the subjects or the experimenter?"

He looked at me suspiciously. "Is this a trick question or something? I mean, it's too obvious."

"No, no tricks, Derrick. Who was responsible?"

"The guy in the white lab coat, who else?"

"Why was he responsible for what the subject actually did?"

He pulled a face and sighed as if I was insulting his intelligence. "Okay, take that big guy who went all the way up to the top. He didn't have a choice, the researcher guy's standing right behind him, telling him what to do. He's got a job to do, so he does it. If the guy didn't follow the orders, he'd be shirking his responsibilities."

"What do you think about the people who went all the way up to four hundred and fifty volts? They obviously didn't want to, and yet they still kept going."

"Yeah, that one guy was really bawling when he had to give old Mr. Wallace one last zap. But he did it, and that's the important thing. He did his job, and he did okay. You know something else, I read all about this study in psych one hundred, and they made out like there was something wrong with all those subjects because they zapped Mr. Wallace. But come on, that's what they were told to do."

"One last question, Derrick. If you had been in that same experiment, what do you think you would have done?"

"I would have done it, but I think I'd have asked the guy in the lab coat to check on Mr. Wallace to make sure he was okay. At the end there it kind of looked like Mr. Wallace bit it."

I finished up with Derrick and handed him a twenty-dollar bill. "Thanks for coming, Derrick," I said and walked him to the door. On our way we passed Zac, who was still hard at it. "And good luck getting into the program."

Zac looked up. "This program?"

Derrick nodded.

"Yeah, well, good luck and be prepared to work your ass off," Zac said. "That is unless you happen to get lucky and become his star student like Emily here." He said it with a smile, but it still stung.

"Thanks, and I don't have a problem with working hard."

"We'll be sure to pass that along," Zac said.

Derrick didn't seem to notice the sarcasm in Zac's voice, but it wasn't lost on me. "I think I have a pretty good chance," Derrick said. "I'm meeting with Doctor Mullarcant again tomorrow to do some other stuff."

"Oh, what kind of stuff?" I asked.

"I'm not sure. He said something about doing another phase of the study. You know anything about it?"

"No, nothing." I looked back at Zac, who shrugged.

After I said good-bye to Derrick, I went down to Mullarcant's office to have a little chat. But when I got there, he had his new 'Conference In Progress' sign up. I leaned against the wall and considered knocking, and then I considered what exactly I was going to say to him. Maybe something like, Now you look here, you have no right to give me a really nice office and then just summarily go around assuming I'll take it. And another thing, how dare you tell people I'm your PhD student when I'm only a master's student.

Yes sir, he'd have a hard time wriggling his way out of that one. What was I doing? The man had offered me—well, okay, it wasn't exactly an offer, more like ordered me to move into— Beth's office. So what exactly was my problem? "Nothing," I said out loud. Except that he wouldn't let Zac call me. I started back down the hall toward the lab.

A voice came from behind me. "Talking to ourselves, are we?"

I felt my face brighten when I turned to see Mark. "Yes, we are," I said. "Only it's more like an argument, and I'm not sure which one of us is winning."

"Well, you know what they say about people who talk to themselves."

"You know, my mother always used to say that and never once did she tell me what exactly it is that they say. So maybe you could finally enlighten me, Doctor Gunn."

He looked over his shoulder to make sure no one was around, and then slipped his arm around my waist before he led me down the hall to his office. "Why don't we just step in here? And I'll be happy to enlighten you." He closed the door behind him and took both my hands in his. "I'm so sorry I couldn't make dinner on Saturday. I was really looking forward to it."

"That's okay. Zac couldn't make it, either. And I think your son is a little more important than a dinner date. I assume he must be better, since you're back."

"Oh, he's just fine. By Saturday night he was asking to go home, and yesterday morning he was doing so well they released him."

"Do they know what it was?"

"To be honest, I think it was just a really bad flu and his mother overreacted a bit."

"Vancouver's a pretty long way to go for a false alarm."

"I don't really mind. If something had been seriously wrong, I'd have wanted to be there. And the poor little guy was feeling so rotten, I was glad to be with him."

"You're a nice dad."

"Thanks. I'll tell you, though, being nine hundred miles away makes it hard." He pulled out a chair. "Enough about me. Come sit and tell me what's going on with you. You sounded a bit upset when you were chatting with yourself back there."

"Oh, it's nothing." I could feel my palms getting sticky. He was leaning against the desk with his arms crossed. Then, for some inexplicable reason, I saw myself sprawled across him on his living room couch, both of us as naked as Mexican Hairless Chihuahuas. It was as though I were viewing it from above, doing a kind of cinematography thing where I moved around the room, zooming in and out on us like a National Film Board documentary.

And I had indeed been on that couch with him in just that same way over the past few weeks, only we were always fully clothed. It was odd, because our little trysts started and inevitably ended the same way. First we'd chat about nothing, listen to music, and have a glass of wine. Then he'd slip his arm over my shoulders and kiss me gently on the cheek and then on my lips. It was a series of gentle caresses and little kisses, nothing too heated or passionate, just soft kisses, and I loved it.

But the last time we were together, things changed slightly and I sensed more urgency in him. Yet, he was still very careful, and guarded, as if he were afraid to wrinkle my clothes or mess my hair—as if that was possible. And just when I thought he was going to ask me to make love to him, he stopped abruptly and announced it was getting late. Just like he always did. I was puzzled, but couldn't say I was too disappointed. Even though I was very attracted to him, for some reason the thought of taking my clothes off in front of this man made my stomach cramp and the blood rush to my face.

"Emily, you look flushed. What is it?" At that moment all I could think of was my old family doctor, Doctor Bruce. Mark was looking at me with the same kindly expression Doctor Bruce had when I was seventeen and trying to ask him for birth control pills.

Outside school I felt more at ease and in control with Mark. But at school I seemed off-balance and constantly fumbled and blushed. I swallowed hard and tried to banish couch scenes and family doctors from my mind.

"Emily, did I do something? Or did something happen with Martin?"

I swallowed and cleared my throat. "He asked me, well, more like told me, to move into Beth's office."

"And you don't feel right about doing it. Jesus, that man can be insensitive."

I let out a sigh of relief. "No. I don't feel right about it at all."

"Of course you don't. You know that it's your choice, don't you?"

"To be honest, I wasn't sure. He didn't leave much room for discussion."

"That doesn't matter, and I don't want this upsetting you." He brushed a hand across my cheek. "So what would you like me to do?"

"I'm not sure I know what you mean."

"Would you like me to go to Martin and tell him you don't want to move into the office? Because I'm quite prepared to do that. And while I'm at it, I'll tell him that he should bring these things to me first before going to you."

"Mark, that's really kind of you, but I think I can handle it myself."

There was a loud, quick rap on the door, immediately followed by Mullarcant poking his head in. "Oh, I didn't know you were with someone," he said, looking at me and then back at Mark.

"I don't see how you could have," Mark said. "The door was closed." Mullarcant didn't seem to notice, or care to notice, the sharp tone in Mark's voice and carried on without skipping a beat.

"It is fortuitous that you are here anyway, Emily. I have a few items I wish to discuss with you." He went around to the other side of the desk, took a seat, and placed a pad of paper down carefully so that it was exactly centered in front of him. He pawed at his hair, went through the cuff-pulling thing, but skipped the pants this time.

I glanced over at Mark, who looked either really pissed off or embarrassed. I decided it was both.

"Martin, we were having a meeting."

It was as though Mark hadn't spoken. After Mullarcant finished his routine, he looked up at me and said, "Firstly, how did the session go?"

I said everything went fine and that I would slip the data under his door just as soon as I was finished with Mark.

"Good, good." He referred to the neatly written list he had in front of him and put a tick mark next to the first item. "Secondly, when you move into the office, please make certain everything of Beth's is placed in cartons. There are empty ones in the library behind the door. And thirdly, I have arranged for one of the New Beginnings participants to be put through phase one and two this morning."

I knew where number three was going. "What time?"

He flipped up the white cuff of his left sleeve to expose a heavy silver watch. "Eleven o'clock, which is in approximately five minutes. It's one of your participants, Emily. The young fellow."

"Mick?"

He scanned his list again. "Let's see," he ran an index finger down the page. "Yes, Mick Rowley. Zacarie will assist you. I won't be there, but I'm sure the two of you are well versed enough to do it on your own. I trust you will be able to accommodate this into your schedule today." It was a command, not a question.

"I guess I don't have much choice."

He studied me for a moment, and I held my breath waiting for Face Two to rear its ugly head and blow its top. But he surprised me again. "Emily, we all have a choice," he said in a low, even voice. "It just depends upon whether we choose to exercise it." He did the swoop thing with his hair and stood up. "How do you wish to exercise your choice today, Emily?"

My cheeks were flaming and I looked over at my supervisor, who was staring at the little man standing behind his desk. There was a fierce anger I had never before seen in the usually easygoing Mark Gunn's eyes. I was looking to him, I suppose, waiting for him to say something, but he didn't, or perhaps he couldn't.

"I'll be there," I said in a hoarse voice.

"Excellent," Mullarcant said. On his way out he brushed past Mark and said, "Come see me in half an hour." He closed the door behind him. The metallic sound of the door clicking into place filled the silent office.

"Asshole," Mark said.

I shook my head and collected my things. "I better get going. Are you going to be there for this one?" I knew I needn't have asked. Mark rarely, if ever, made himself present during the lab sessions.

He busied himself with papers at his desk. We were both embarrassed, because we both knew all his talk about telling Mullarcant to come to him first was garbage. No one told Mullarcant anything, we all just listened.

Chapter 12

"I HAVE THINGS I NEED to get caught up on, so you just go ahead with the session," Mark said. "And, Emily, I'm sorry about all that, I think everyone's a little on edge," he added in a business-like tone.

"Sure, I think you're right," I said and left. On my way back to the lab, I ran into Mick wandering down the hall, holding a piece of paper in his hand and comparing it to signs on the doors.

"Hi, Mick, looking for me?"

"Hi, Emily. I'm here to do your experiment," he said with childlike enthusiasm.

"Well, then you've come to the right place." I led him to the lab, and found Zac where I had left him earlier, still banging away at the computer. "Zac, this is Mick. He's going to do both phases of the study."

Zac looked up, surprised. "Oh, I didn't know we were doing anyone else today." He got up to shake Mick's hand. "It's good to meet you, Mick. Nice jacket."

Mick beamed. "Thanks. It's real leather, not that cheap plastic shit."

"I can tell. The black looks great on you."

"You should feel honored, Mick," I said. "Zac here doesn't give out those kinds of compliments to just anyone."

"It was a gift," Mick said, running both hands down his front over the smooth leather, "for my birthday. Me and Ken had this deal. Said he'd buy me this jacket if I kept straight for two whole months."

"Looks like you must have made it," I said.

"Congratulations," Zac said and gave him a pat on the back. At the touch of Zac's hand, Mick tensed and a wild anger came into his eyes. He spun around to face Zac. I could see Mick's hands clenched in tight fists at his sides, as if readying himself for a fight.

Zac drew back. "Sorry . . . I . . . didn't mean to scare you," he said, holding up his hands, palms forward in surrender.

Like a boxer trying to calm himself, Mick drew a series of short, shallow breaths through his flared nostrils. "It's okay. I just get a bit jumpy sometimes," he said through clenched teeth. "It's a reflex or somethin'."

Zac shot me a concerned look. "Em, why don't we let Mick relax in the viewing room while we get things set up out here?"

"Good idea," I said slowly. "Mick would you like to come with me and I'll get you something to read."

"I'd rather watch TV if you got one," he said. He was now becalmed to the point where I was questioning my perception of what had just taken place. I settled him in front of a television game show he seemed quite familiar with. When I came back out, Zac motioned for me to join him by the main doors.

"Em, I don't feel very good about this. He seems a little over the top. I've seen guys like him before."

"At the clinic?"

"No, sleeping on our front doorstep in Montreal. They're unpredictable, Em."

I nodded. "All you did was touch him, and did you see his eyes? He seems fine now, but if we make him panic, who knows what he'll do?" I opened his file and scanned the personal history and comments section.

"There's lots here, drug dependency, border-line schizophrenia maybe."

"Oh good. Does it say if it's the paranoid type?"

"No, just borderline."

"Why is he here? Didn't you take his history?" Zac asked.

"No, Mullarcant did, it's his handwriting." I showed Zac the file. "I guess he must think it's okay. But I don't think we know enough about him, and to tell you the truth, I don't think it's fair to him."

"Or to us," Zac said. "I don't want to be responsible if anything happens to him."

"I'll go tell Mullarcant what's going on and see what he thinks."

"Or at least make sure he's willing to be here. I really think someone in authority should be here for this. I mean, who's going to take responsibility for him?"

"I will," a voice said from the hall.

Zac and I looked at each other. I poked my head outside and peered around the corner to see Ken's smiling face.

"Ken!"

"Hello, Emily. Nice to see you again," he said, sauntering in.

"Zac, this is Ken. He's one of the other subjects from New Beginnings."

"Subject." Ken said with a rub of his long gray beard. "Well, now, I've been called a lot of things, but I don't think I've ever been called a subject. I kinda like it." He thrust a hand toward Zac. "Pleased to know you. Now what do I get to call you?"

"How about Zac?" Zac said.

"No, no. I mean, if I'm the subject, what does that make you two?" He rubbed his beard again. "I guess you'd be the experimenters, or maybe you'd prefer scientists. Personally, I think I'd go with scientist, more folks know what that is. But wait a minute. You can't really call someone in psychology a scientist, can you? Hmm," he said with mock consternation. "Now that's a philosophical problem, isn't it?"

Zac bristled. "Emily and Zac will be fine."

"No, I think we should keep things on a professional level

here, so how's about I just call you Number One and Number Two Experimenter. And to be politically correct and all, I think I'll call Emily here Number One, since she's the girl."

"Woman, she's a woman," Zac said in a tight voice.

"Thank you, Number Two Experimenter. Woman. I'll try to remember that."

"I'll go get Mullarcant," Zac said.

"Now hold on, Zac," Ken said with a smile. "Don't get your shit all in a knot. I was just havin' a bit of fun with you."

There was a mischievous sparkle in Ken's eyes, and although he was getting under my skin, there was something about him I liked. The white beard and silver hair no doubt had something to do with it. Freud would have loved this, I thought. The analysis would have gone something along the lines that my affections toward a man who looked like Santa were caused by my unfortunate childhood, coupled with my inability to grow up. Which, in turn, caused me to have an unrealistic desire to have the perfect family, and thus fueled my Electra complex and concomitant jealousy of my father's affections toward my mother and subsequent neglect of me. The result, of course, is that I secretly (so secretly, in fact, I am not even privy to it) view my father as Santa and my mother as the meddling Mrs. Claus who always got everything....

"I just came to make sure the kid was okay," Ken was saying. "So don't worry about him. He'll be fine. And if he's not, I'll take care of him, okay?"

I looked at Zac, who didn't appear to be as taken with Santa as I was. Which was odd when I thought about it, because his childhood was way worse than mine.

"I think I'll just let Mullarcant know we have some concerns," Zac said.

"I agree with Zac. In a situation where there's any doubt about a subject's health, it's our responsibility to inform—"

"The Head Cheese Experimenter," Ken said with a raucous laugh. "Oh, that's a good one, get it? Head cheese, because he's probably real brainy."

"You're a laugh a minute, Ken," Zac said, and then left for Mullarcant's office.

"As I was saying, you guys won't have any trouble with Mick," Ken said to me. "He's a good kid, a little skittish maybe, but harmless."

Mick popped his head out the viewing room door. "Ken! I didn't know you were going to do the experiment today too."

"I'm not, kid. Just thought I'd come down and watch 'em gas you, seein' how I ain't got nothin' better to entertain myself with today."

"Yeah, well, you make sure they don't give me too much."

Zac was back in moments. "Doctor Mullarcant said he's apprised of the situation and for us to go ahead."

"There now, that make you feel better?" Ken said with a smirk.

We put Mick through the panic phase without incident. In fact, he reached a perfect four, and he didn't pull the mask off until we did it for him.

When I asked him why he didn't stop the procedure when he was obviously in such distress, his response was, "I wanted to do good for you guys." His responses to the Milgram video questions were also right on the money, except for a couple of comments he made toward the end.

"See, the guy giving the shocks didn't have any choice because the scientist guy in the white coat told him he had to do it," Mick said.

"If you had been in that same experiment, what do you think you would have done, Mick?"

"You mean if I was the guy giving the shocks or taking them?"

"The one giving the shocks."

"If it'd been me shocking that old guy, I would have let him shock me back."

"But that wasn't the way the experiment was set up, Mick."

"Yeah, I know, but to be fair I'd give that guy a chance to take a shot at me."

"Why would you do that?"

"Because it's fair and then I wouldn't feel so bad after." Even though this part of the conversation went well beyond the scope of the study, I was curious so I continued plying him with questions.

"But, Mick, you do understand that by the end of the experiment the subject thought it was possible Mr. Wallace may have died?"

"Yeah, I understand that. So I'd just let someone else shock me, then."

"Even if it meant you could die yourself?"

He shook his head and let out a sigh as though he was trying to explain something very simple to a child too young to grasp the concept. He leaned across the desk. "See, that doesn't matter. The dying part, I mean. What matters is putting things right."

"And allowing someone else to shock you to death would put things right?"

"It would if I had done it to someone else. Listen, Emily, here's the thing, you either even the score now, or you wait until your next life and get it right then. So the way I figure it is, why not just get it over with now. With that experiment, see, I wouldn't have shocked that guy in the first place if I wasn't willing to get shocked myself. And I would have told that scientist guy that right at the beginning. That's where that other guy went wrong, 'cus I got the impression he didn't want to be doing what he was doing. And I'll bet money on it there was no way he'd let anyone shock him." He folded his arms and leaned back in his chair, obviously satisfied with himself. "I won't do nothin' to nobody, unless I know I'll let them do the same thing to me."

"Do unto others as you would have them do unto you."

"I guess so, but you just said it more complicated."

"Getting back to the original question, then, who was to blame for what happened in the experiment?"

"The scientist guy, I already told you that. He made that guy do something he didn't want to, 'cus the guy giving the shocks probably wouldn't let no one else shock him. And besides, you told me that Mr. Wallace never even got shocked. But if he had, then I would have let him do it to me, okay?"

Mick's logic was beginning to make my head hurt. Science allows for neat and tidy yes/no answers, not bits of Biblical references and reincarnation theories. "Thanks, Mick, you did really well. Here's your money," I said, and handed him two twenty-dollar bills.

"Easiest money I ever made." He stuffed the bills into his jacket pocket.

"I don't know if I'd call it easy. Not being able to breathe is a pretty terrifying thing."

"That was nothin' compared to when my stepdad used to hold his hand over my face when I was a little kid. Now that was scary. 'Cus I never knew if it was going to end, or if it was going to be the end of me," he giggled at his little joke. "I figured you guys would make sure I'd be okay. Just like in that video, they made sure everyone was okay. No one really got hurt."

It made me slightly uncomfortable, knowing how much trust people actually put in us. I wondered if I had the same trust in myself. I placed the questionnaire next to his assessment and history forms.

"Hey, where'd you get all that stuff about me?" Mick asked, craning his neck to read his history.

"From you. Don't you remember when Doctor Mullarcant asked you all these questions?"

"Nobody asked me nothin' except you."

I looked over the forms again to make sure it was Mullarcant's writing. "Gee, Mick, I don't know, it's all here in Doctor Mullarcant's handwriting. Are you sure you don't remember talking to him?"

"Sure I'm sure. But anyway, I gotta get going. I'm gonna buy Ken a big fat bottle of his favorite booze, and then I'm gonna go eat about six burgers. Can I go now?"

"Sure." When I brought Mick out to the front, we found Ken sitting in the reception area, reading an *Omni* magazine.

"How'd ya' do, kid?" Mick held out the money and flashed a broad grin like a kid who had just come from the dentist's office with a prize. Ken's mouth curled at the edges and with cat-like quickness he snatched the money from Mick's hand, and then stuffed it into his own pocket.

"Hey, no fair," Mick whined, then slumped down on the couch.

"Let's go, kid. This old man needs a drink."

I felt the anger well up through my body and stop in my throat. "Excuse me, but that money belongs to Mick."

Ken stood up and took a couple of steps toward me. Fear tightened my chest, but I didn't move. He put his face close to mine. "Listen, Ms Scientist, why don't you mind your own fucking business."

I looked around for Zac, but he was nowhere in sight. Mick stayed sitting on the couch, kicking the floor with the heel of his boot. I stared hard at Ken as he metamorphosed before my eyes from a benevolent Santa clone to an evil troll.

"Why don't you just give him back his money?" I said in a trembling voice.

Mick got up and stood beside Ken. He was at least half a foot taller than the older man. "Come on, Ken, let's go. You can keep the money, I don't care."

"Well, I do, Mick. It's your money," I said.

"That's right, and he just gave it to me," Ken said to me. "So why don't you butt out, and go do whatever it is you do." My anger was so intense I felt sick.

"See you later, Emily," Mick said, as though nothing had happened. I followed them out into the hall and yelled after them.

"He was going to buy you something with that money, you know." Neither of them looked back, and I felt like an idiot for saying it.

Just as I was about to go back into the lab, I noticed Sandra Penny stick her head out of her office to see what was going on. As Ken and Mick neared her, Ken lifted his hand in a gesture of greeting. He paused in front of her and looked as if he was intending to stop and chat. But he didn't get the chance; Sandra returned his greeting with a crisp "hello," and then ducked back into her office and closed the door in his face.

Chapter 13

"WHAT WOULD YOU EXPECT from such people, Emily?"

"I don't know. I just thought we should do something, like call the police."

"Sit down, Emily." I took a seat across from Mullarcant's immaculate desk. File folders were placed with mechanical precision in an upright file holder. A pad of paper lay in front of him with a pen resting directly in the center.

Mullarcant also kept precise records of everything, and lab reports were detailed to the point of distraction. Even a subject's slightest nuance was recorded. Only Mullarcant's hair, it seemed, was allowed the luxury of getting away on him, particularly when he was working hard on something. Freud believed we all have a certain amount of anxiety we must rid ourselves of. Building on this theory, my hypothesis was that Mullarcant's occasionally disheveled hair functioned as a kind of release for his pent-up stress that was caused by his usual hyper-vigilance. It was obvious he had been hard at it all day, and I tried to keep my gaze from settling on the sprouts of dark hair that clumped and swirled at the top of his head.

Mullarcant set his fingers under his chin. A look of concern crossed his face. "Emily, I think you need to think more carefully about what we are doing here and its importance. Research is not always a pleasant thing. No matter what they may tell you in those sanitized little descriptions they provide in textbooks, animal studies cause pain; human studies cause pain. But in both cases there is also gain." He looked pleased with himself and his little rhyme. "And what you must learn is that here we are dealing with personalities, characteristics, and behaviors. Scientists"—he paused—"good scientists, do not concern themselves with the other aspects of their subjects." He leaned back in his chair and placed his hands behind his head. "And this, Emily, is how we become good researchers." He paused for another moment, letting me absorb his brilliant words.

"Emily, does the word 'objectivity' mean anything to you?" he finally said.

"Of course it does, it's just—"

"This is a hard lesson, but all good researchers must learn it. Do you understand what I'm getting at?" He cocked an eyebrow.

"You're saying that what happened between Mick and Ken was none of my business." I knew it was a mistake to come to talk to him. But I was hoping he could do something for Mick.

"Not quite, but you are on the right track. What transpired between the two subjects was your business, but only from a scientific point of view."

"I'm sorry, but I don't follow you," I said wearily.

"You told me that this Mick fellow didn't even put up a struggle when his friend—what is his name?"

"Ken."

"When this Ken—this is the same Ken you interviewed, is it?"

"Yes."

"Oh, too bad I didn't know he was coming in today. I would have liked to meet him. I'm having trouble getting his history. He's a hard man to pin down."

My conversation with Mick came to mind. "Speaking of that,

Doctor Mullarcant. How do you get the subjects' histories? Mick mentioned that he didn't meet with you, and he was wondering where we came up with all his personal information."

"My point exactly. You expect too much from these people, Emily. This Mick fellow was either playing games with you, or he simply forgot. Now, back to the matter at hand. When this Ken took the money from the subject, the subject did not put up a fight, correct?"

I nodded.

"And did this same subject put up a struggle when you placed the mask on his face? Did he take it off even when he was air-hungry?"

"No. He was a perfect four."

"Ha!" he said and clapped his hands. "Don't you see, Emily?" This is just one more piece of evidence to support my theory. We are talking about personality traits, unbending, unwavering personality traits. Emily, the importance of this finding is monu-mental. We will be able to determine how people will react in all circumstances, not just in the lab. And as you well know, this has always been the main criticism I have had to endure from my not-so-learned colleagues. 'Your findings are not generalizable outside of the lab, Mullarcant,' they all say. But they are wrong. Now then, do you understand the importance of this lesson, Emily?"

"Sure."

"In that case, tell me what it is."

I took a deep breath and fought back my overwhelming desire to tell him to go to hell. But like a good student I said, "I should remain objective at all times so that I am open to discovery."

"Exactly. And you see what happened. You missed a very important observation by allowing your emotions to cloud your objectivity. But don't be discouraged. As a student it is your job to make the odd mistake." I felt the corners of my mouth turn up. The odd mistake. My God, the generosity of this man obvi-ously knows no bounds.

"Something has amused you, Emily?"

"No, I was just agreeing with you. What you said about being open to discovery really struck a chord with me."

"And so it should." He pulled at his cuffs and considered me for a moment. "I am pleased you have said so because I have a little surprise for you. I was going to wait until it was published, but I think you could use a boost today."

I shifted my gaze to the floor and suddenly felt as uncomfortable as I had when he winked at me at the Christmas party. He opened the side drawer of his desk and produced a large, brown envelope. He smiled proudly and handed it over like a father presenting a gift to his child. I took the envelope and placed it on my lap. For some reason Beth's application to Memorial ran though my mind, and I felt beads of perspiration forming under my arms.

"What are you waiting for, Emily? Go on, open it."

I opened the top flap and took out a research paper. In the middle of the front page the title, "The Influence of Perceived Control on Subject Behavior: Another Look at the Milgram Experiment," was typed in bold letters. But the title wasn't what held my attention, it was the line underneath it that read: "Emily Goodstriker and Martin Mullarcant."

"There you are, Emily, your first publication. Congratulations."

I looked up slowly. "But I didn't write this, Doctor Mullarcant."

"Consider it a gift."

"I'm sorry?"

"A gift. I'm giving you a gift."

"I just started working on this project. I haven't even read this."

"But you are working on the project now and that's enough. Emily, I am a little surprised at your attitude. Most students are extremely grateful, to say the very least."

"Don't get me wrong, it's not that I don't appreciate it. It's just that I can't—"

"Can't what, Emily?" he raised his voice. "What is the problem?"

135

"Isn't this wrong? I mean, isn't it wrong to put someone's name on a paper they didn't write?" What am I saying? I thought. Of course it's wrong, and he knows damn well it is.

His face was red, and he leaned over the desk farther. If he gets any closer, I thought, his head will be in my lap. "Emily, I am very surprised and disappointed by your attitude. I have gone out of my way to ensure that your future as a graduate student is secure here. You know perfectly well that your chances of gaining acceptance into the doctoral program are considerably diminished without publications of this nature. And you have the audacity to sit in my office, after I have just handed you a gift that most students would give their lives for, and tell me that what I have done is wrong. You know, I had very high aspirations for you as a researcher. Up until now you have shown a great deal of initiative, but I'm beginning to wonder if I was wrong, and perhaps a little too hasty in giving you authorship on this very important study. And another thing," he said, wagging a finger at me, "I failed to mention that this paper is about to be published in the most respected academic journal in North America."

"Dr. Mullarcant, I didn't say I wasn't grateful for what you're trying to do for me."

"Then I suggest you show it." He whirled around in his chair and resumed banging at his computer.

Our meeting was over. On my way out of Mullarcant's office, I passed Sandra Penny, who was on her way in.

"YOU JUST STAY PUT, dear, and I'll be back with some brandy and tea," Rusty said before she breezed out of the living room.

I wrapped the blanket around my shoulders and stared out the window to the back grounds where half a dozen stone statues, looking terribly cold and underdressed in their scanty attire, stood knee-deep in snow. The one closest to me held a Venetian vase on her shoulder, under which her right breast was exposed to the elements. I felt like throwing a parka over her shoulders and popping a toque on her head.

A blue jay swooped from a birch bough into a feeder of bird goodies. Her (I decided it was a her) cerulean blue, payne's gray, and black feathers made a striking contrast against the backdrop of glistening snow. She strutted around the feeder, snapping her saucy little face and "Jerry Lee Lewis feather do" to and fro, defying anyone to invade her space. She nabbed a peanut in her beak, spread her wings, and then glided over the ground before she sailed up to the highest bough of a pine that rose sixty feet in the air. The peanut still firmly in her mouth, she perused the world below. I wished I had her confidence.

The grandfather clock chimed six o'clock. It had been just after two when I left Mullarcant's office. I knew I wouldn't have been able to get any work done, so I had stopped by the lab and told Zac I was going home. He could tell something was wrong and asked me to stay and talk, but I said I wasn't feeling well. Which technically wasn't a real lie because I was feeling pretty rotten.

Rusty came back into the living room with a big pot of tea and an even bigger bottle of Louis XIII Cognac. "Let's see if we can't make a dent in this hooch," she said, holding up the dusty bottle.

"Rusty, I swear you do these things just to get a rise out of that poor man."

"Whatever do you mean, Emily?" she said with a wicked smile, and then poured two good shots into oversized snifters. She passed one to me and raised her glass to the ceiling. "To Jerald," she said before taking an unladylike like swallow. I followed her lead. "To Jerald, thanks for the brandy. Rusty, we're terrible."

"Maybe, but at least we know how to have fun. Now, let's get down to business." She took a seat in the chair across from me.

"Wait," I said, "I can't talk from here."

She looked around the chair and then back to me on the couch. "Oh, you're right, we'll switch." I pulled the blanket with me over to my chair. Rusty took up her usual place on the couch. "Much better," she said. "Now then, you were saying that the paper is about to be published. So that means there still may be time to get your name off it."

"How will I do that? I can't very well just call up the journal and say, listen, my supervisor put my name on a paper I had nothing to do with. Besides, he didn't even mention which one it's going to."

"Yes. But he did say it was one of the most respected journals in North America. Surely that narrows it down for you."

"It's one of three, I'm positive of that. But if I call them and tell them he did this deliberately, what would that do to his reputation?"

"Never mind his reputation, Emily, let's concentrate on you."

"The way I see it, I have two choices. One, I phone the journal and quit the program. Or two, I say nothing and stay in the program. Or, okay, looks like we have three, I don't say anything and quit the program. Either way, I'm screwed. Rusty, this is like being given a really nice present you know is stolen."

She looked at me thoughtfully. "You're absolutely right. This is exactly like a father who has given his child a lovely piece of stolen jewelry. And regardless of his intentions, he has put that child in a very awkward, not to mention dangerous, position. It's wrong, and it is not a gift—it's a conspiracy. We have been talking on here as though what Martin Mullarcant has done is in your best interests. Well, it's not. And I don't give a damn what he says his intentions are. He says he's doing it for you. But is he really? The only thing he has done for you is put you in a terrible situation. And it should be up to him to fix it, not you."

"Sure, but he won't listen to me, Rusty."

"Then perhaps he might listen to the head of the department."

"Daren Oakes?"

"Yes. He is still head, isn't he?"

"Well, he still occupies that office. So you think I should talk to him about this?"

"I really can't see any other solution. You can't very well handle this on your own. This is a departmental issue. And don't forget, Emily, the department's reputation is at stake here too."

"You're right. I have an obligation to tell someone about it. Rusty, I just had a terrible thought."

"And I'll bet it's the same one I just had. You're wondering if he's done this before."

"I think he said something about other students being grateful. But if that's the case, wouldn't someone have noticed by now?"

"Oh, my dear, I think you'd be surprised to learn what people can get away with. Someday I'll tell you a few stories. But right now I think we better figure out exactly what you're going to say to Daren Oakes tomorrow."

Chapter 14

Daren Oakes' office was as messy as Mullarcant's was tidy. File folders in every imaginable color were stacked on his desk, forming a precarious fort. I suspected the colors had been some earlier attempt at organization but had broken down early in the process. When I took a seat across from his desk, I could just see the top of his red head over the folders. He tried to rearrange some of them so that he could see me, but eventually gave up and came around to my side.

"Why don't we sit over here," he said, motioning to a small table, also piled high with books and loose papers. A black leather couch at the far end of the room was buried under stacks of journals, newspapers, and magazines. While I took in the chaos, I saw that there actually was some order to this landfill. Files on the desk, library books and correspondence on the table, and print media on the couch. We settled down at the table and I kept my knapsack and coat on my lap, afraid that if I let go of them they'd be lost forever.

"Here, Emily, let me take your coat and bag."

"No, that's okay," I said a little too quickly.

"Don't worry, I'll put them where you can keep an eye on them," he said, taking my things and placing them at the summit of a newspaper mountain. "There, they won't get buried if they're way up here," he said with a smile. He took a seat across from me, folded his arms, and said earnestly, "Now then, I'm sorry I wasn't able to see you earlier, but I've been terribly busy these last few days. But never mind that, what can we do for you today?"

I took a deep breath. "Uh, well, this is a little difficult for me to explain, but it's about Doctor Mullarcant."

"And speaking of Mullarcant, I think you should know he has been giving you glowing reports." He leaned forward. "Just between you and me," he said in a conspiratorial tone, "things are looking good for you, as far as the doctoral program goes."

Great, now I'm going to sound like the biggest rat in the world. "Actually, Doctor Oakes, that's part of what I need to talk to you about."

"I'm all ears." There was a knock on the door, and he sprang to his feet as if happy for the interruption. It was Mrs. Kenny, his secretary, announcing a delivery had arrived.

Mrs. Kenny had been the department head's secretary for so long she should by rights, have taken over the position herself when the last one left. When anyone wanted or needed anything, we went straight to Mrs. Kenny. She was a career secretary, one of the old-fashioned ones who was smarter than most, if not all, of the people she had worked under. She was loaded with common sense and had a deep-seated distrust of anyone who relies on jargon and verbalizes nouns. Mrs. Kenny was not into "conferencing," "memoing," or "networking." Nor was she proactive, pronurturing, prowomen or promen. Mrs. Kenny was simply prowork.

"Sorry to interrupt, Doctor Oakes," Mrs. Kenny said. "But you said you wanted to sign for this yourself."

"Yes, wonderful," Oakes said, taking a clipboard from her. "Right in here, gentlemen."

When the two burly men negotiated their load through the

door, the first one couldn't help himself and let out a long whistle when he got an eyeful of the office. The other shook his head in amazement. Daren Oakes, however, didn't seem to notice, he merely grabbed a pen from his shirt pocket and scrawled his name across the delivery slip.

"Thank you, gentlemen, and you have a lovely day," he said, closing the door behind them. "Emily, do you know what this is?"

"Uh, more computer equipment?"

"Yes." He looked disappointed that I had guessed so quickly. But he bounced back quickly enough, and slid his hand across a box as someone might across the hood of a new Jaguar. "This isn't just computer equipment. This is a system that will allow us to process data faster and more efficiently than anyone else in this entire university. Now we can bypass computing services because we have it all right here on our own workstation. No more overnight waits, Emily. No more fighting with those officious operators. We can do it all ourselves."

"That's great."

"Yes, it is great, it is very great. No other psychology department I know of has this capability. You should be proud to be here, Emily."

I smiled and nodded, something I did a lot of whenever I talked to Doctor Oakes. His unbridled enthusiasm for things I didn't much care about, like computer equipment, say, tended to make me and others find alternative routes past his office. He managed to tear himself away from his prize and sat back down across from me.

"No more interruptions. Back to business. Now, what were you saying?"

"This is a little difficult for me. It's about some work I have been doing. I'm sure you're aware of Doctor Mullarcant's research." While I stammered along, Daren Oakes kept glancing back over his shoulder to the boxes. "I've been working on the panic project, and the Milgram one."

"That's good, Emily, but I must tell you, I'm really not involved in Martin's work."

"Right, of course you're not. But I just wanted to give you a bit of background." He glanced at the boxes again and then down at his watch. Okay, time to pick it up. "Doctor Oakes, I'll get right to the point. What I'm trying to tell you is that Doctor Mullarcant wrote a paper and put my name on it, and it's going to be published in a very esteemed journal."

"Well, congratulations, Emily. And now I suppose you'd like to talk about the PhD program, would you?" he said, his eyes bright and expectant.

"No, Doctor Oakes, I don't. I didn't write the paper, and I didn't even work on that particular study. Well, not until very recently." Now that got his attention. "I'm sorry to have to bring this to you. But I felt it was the best thing to do under the circumstances."

"Yes, yes, of course it is. This must be very difficult for you. But maybe Martin just made a mistake. Perhaps you should discuss this with him."

"He gave me the paper yesterday and got pretty angry when I said I thought what he was doing was wrong."

Daren Oakes got up and paced the room. "Now, you say you had nothing to do with this study?" he said, stopping in front of me.

"Well, next to nothing. I started working on it only a few weeks ago. So the paper he wrote is obviously about results I had nothing to do with."

"But you're working on the project now?"

"Yes, but—"

"Then I think we're splitting hairs here."

"I didn't even read the paper. I couldn't tell you what the results are or what method he used, or how many pages it is."

"I think we should concentrate on the positive side of this, Emily."

"Which is?" He walked over to the boxes and started tearing off the packing tape. "Doctor Oakes, I know this is a difficult situation, and I wouldn't want anything to jeopardize the reputation of this department or Doctor Mullarcant's. That's why I'm telling you this."

"I appreciate that, Emily, and I'm glad you brought this to my attention." Yeah, you look ecstatic. Daren Oakes was a Teflon kind of guy; anything that had to do with running the department seemed to slip away from him like greased egg. I tried to keep my composure as he leaned into one of the larger boxes and extracted handfuls of green, pink, and white Styrofoam chips, and carefully laid them on the couch. There was a garbage can near my feet.

"Would you like a garbage can?" I pushed it toward him.

"No, thank you, I'll need these if we ever move the department."

Oh my God, he's going to leave those on his couch for the next forty years.

"Doctor Oakes, what should I do about this paper? I'm pretty upset about it."

"I don't think you need to get too troubled about this. It'll all work out in the end. I'm sorry I have to cut this meeting short, but as you can see I really have a lot to do here. Now, I don't want you to worry, though, because I will look into the matter." His head was down inside the box, and my stomach was tying itself into knots.

"Doctor Oakes, this paper is about to be published."

He came up holding a keyboard. "Emily, I will do something about it. In fact, I'm meeting with Martin later today. So please, just put it out of your mind, and get back to your migraine studies."

"That's Milgram."

"Good. I wonder if I could ask you to keep this little misunderstanding confidential? I'm sure it's just an oversight on Martin's part. He is an extremely busy man, you know." Now it's a little misunderstanding. I wonder on who's part, Doctor Oakes? There was no point staying any longer, so I collected my things and headed for the door.

"Thanks for your time, Doctor Oakes. I'll check back with you later this afternoon, if that's okay. Around four, say?"

"Absolutely, and thanks for stopping by."

When I left his office, I knew perfectly well that Daren Oakes was going to forget all about this conversation, and that he wouldn't be in his office at four, nor would he ever mention our conversation to Mullarcant.

But I was wrong.

Within half an hour, he sent Mrs. Kenny to find me, and I was back sitting at the same table across from Daren Oakes and Martin Mullarcant.

"Emily, I am extremely disappointed you have taken the attitude you have about this paper." He smoothed his hair, aligned his cuffs, and waited for my response.

"Well, now, hold on there, Martin," Oakes said. "To be fair, I think the problem is that Emily here just hasn't had much experience with publications, and she doesn't understand how things sometimes work around here."

Well, now hold on there . . . ? Emily here . . . ? Within the past thirty minutes the good Monk Oakes had somehow turned himself into a good ol' cowboy. And I was turning into a very angry ol' gal.

"I do know that it's wrong to put your name on someone else's work. I believe it's called plagiarism."

Mullarcant threw his hands in the air. "Emily, this is not a case of plagiarism. You are working on the project. You are causing a problem where there is none. And just what exactly did you think you would accomplish by bringing this matter to the head of the department?"

"I hoped he would talk to you and—"

"And what? What, Emily? Perhaps you would like me to call the *North American Journal of Psychology* and tell them I made a mistake by putting your name on the paper. What do you think would happen then?"

"They'd take my name off?" I chanced. He slammed his hands on the table, sending papers flying. Daren Oakes and I both jumped.

"You don't understand, Emily," he said, leaning across the table and poking the requisite index finger at my face. "So I will explain it to you. If you or anyone else informs the journal editors about this so-called error, you will start a formal investigation of this department by the journal first, and the Psychological Association second, and then finally by the president of this university. In other words, Emily, you, a second-year master's student, will throw this department into disgrace. And let me ask you this, have you even considered what this will do to your reputation?"

"My reputation?"

He sat back in his chair and smiled. Again, an unsettling experience. "Yes, Emily, your reputation. If you call this journal and tell them your name is on a paper you didn't write, well then, I guess you would be admitting to plagiarism, wouldn't you?"

"But I didn't put my name on it."

He looked at me with a triumphant little smirk. I was beginning to get the message.

"And I don't suppose you'd tell them you put it on there for me?"

"Emily, do you really think I would jeopardize this entire department just to appease your misguided sense of ethics?"

"To be honest, Doctor Mullarcant, I don't know what to think. And for the life of me, I can't understand why you're doing this."

"Why am I doing this? I should think it obvious. I am trying to help you, and this department. Without publications you are nothing, this department is nothing, the university is nothing."

I looked over at Daren Oakes, who was picking lint balls off his polyester pants. "Doctor Oakes, I'm really confused."

He looked up sheepishly and said in a soft voice, "I know you are, Emily, but Martin is right. Our department runs on funding. And as you know, the more we publish, the more funding we receive for our research. No papers, no funds, no research." And no computers, I thought. "It's as simple as that. Your supervisor thought he was doing you a favor. It's very important that our students demonstrate they are capable of producing publishable work. Isn't that right, Martin?"

"Yes, yes. Of course. Emily, my only concern is this depart-ment and the students. It is imperative that we let the world know that our department and its students produce work that is every bit as brilliant, and hopefully more so, than the big-name universities. Emily, we must strive to be number one and dismiss those who delight in mediocrity.

"Oh, I know what you're thinking," he continued, "that I am being overly dramatic. But I'm not, Emily. If you make a fuss about this paper, it will have far-reaching implications for the entire department, not to mention for your own fellow students. Don't forget, Emily, with research money comes research scholarships."

They had me, but I thought I'd make one last stab. "Okay, I get the message. I won't say anything. But I'd like to ask you one thing, Doctor Mullarcant. Would you consider calling the jour-nal and telling them there was a mistake? Maybe say the person who typed the paper made an error. I'll bet that kind of thing happens all the time," I said hopefully.

"But, Emily, that would be a lie," Mullarcant said with a sly smile.

Oh, good one, but I can do better. "And I wouldn't want you to have to lie, Doctor Mullarcant, so I'll just call them myself and say I typed it and that I made—"

Daren Oakes piped in. "But I think that would have the same effect, worse, in fact. You would sound as though you had tried to slip your own name on—"

Mullarcant waved him off. "I suspect she just came to that realization herself." He stared at me for a moment and then said something that surprised the hell out of me.

"I'm sorry," he said.

I looked over at Daren Oakes, who appeared to be praying with his hands folded neatly under his chin and his eyes half closed.

"I didn't enjoy putting you through this," Mullarcant went on. "I just wanted to make a point. I'll call the journal today and tell them there was a typing error, if that's what you want. And your name will not appear on the paper." His tone was soft, and coming from anyone else it would have been soothing. But in Mullarcant's case, it was simply unnerving.

"Thank you," I said through clenched teeth. I stared at the strange little man before me, and a feeling of absolute disdain began to consume me.

I left Oakes' office, made a dash for the ladies' room, and ducked into a stall before the tears began to flow. I stayed there for close to half an hour, waiting for my eyes to clear, because I couldn't risk bumping into those two clowns and giving them the satisfaction of knowing they had gotten to me. But the fact was they had, and they knew it. The worst part was that I had given in, and I felt as though I had just discovered something despicable in myself. If Mullarcant hadn't agreed to say it was a typing error, I couldn't have done anything, or wouldn't, which was more to the point.

Chapter 15

I LEANED OVER THE SINK and stared at myself in the mirror, and for a split second Beth's face stared back at me. No wonder you wanted out, Beth, if this is the kind of crap they pulled on you. Then the proverbial light came on in my mind. Did Mullarcant do the same "favour" for you, Beth? And was this what Grandma Wong meant when she said they did this to you? Oakes and Mullarcant made me feel there was no way out. They knew there was nothing I could do but go along with them. Is that what they did to you, Beth? Maybe there was one way I could find out.

A final check of my eyes told me I was passable, and I left the confines of the ladies' room. I headed over to the library with Daren Oakes' words at Beth's memorial service playing over again in my mind. *Elizabeth Wong was a dedicated student and a prolific researcher. She has numerous publications to her credit, and because of that she was an invaluable asset to the department. . . .* Well, let's just see how invaluable you were, Beth.

A few people hurried by me as the university emptied out for the supper hour. The freeway that paralleled the commons area was busy with rush-hour traffic. In summer, the cars roared up and down the street with deafening persistence. But in February the snow-covered streets and early dusk created an enveloping hush. The sun was setting in a canvas of violet, amber, and rose, casting a tranquil haze that seemed to calm the traffic to a purr, as the city headed home in a quiet procession.

I was rounding the corner past Danmoth Hall when a pink frisbee sailed over my head, immediately followed by a black and white streak of dog who caught the toy in mid-air. He gave me a polite wag of his tail and then zipped off back around the corner to where I knew Derrick would be waiting. I wasn't in the mood to make small talk about the best way to gain brownie points with Mullarcant, so I took a circuitous route that led me behind the buildings and came out at the library's west doors. I stole a glance in the direction the dog had gone and spotted Derrick standing next to the oil-pump jack wearing the same blue duffel coat. There was nothing unusual about the scene except for the fact that he wasn't alone. This in itself wouldn't have been out of the ordinary, either. It was *who* he was with that made the tableau so compelling. Mullarcant, clad only in a suit and white lab coat, was laughing and playing, with the exuberance of a twelve-year-old, with Derrick's dog, Petey.

The dog spread his favor equally between his two playmates. After Derrick tossed the toy, Petey retrieved it and then returned it to Mullarcant, who allowed the hound to lick his face and press his paws against his chest. Mullarcant would throw the frisbee over Derrick's crouched back, and watch as the dog flew over the human obstacle and cleared it by at least half a foot. Derrick would then do the same to Mullarcant, who appeared to have streaks of brown mud smeared up and down the back of his usually pristine white lab coat. It was a bizarre sight that made me question my own sanity.

Was this the same man who just humiliated and browbeat me? How could someone who seemed so genuine with that animal be so despicable to humans? Then again, I thought, even Hitler apparently liked dogs.

Yes. This was the same man. And if someone didn't do something to stop him, Derrick and many others after him would end up feeling exactly the same way I had not thirty minutes earlier.

It was just after five when I took a seat at one of the computer terminals. The library, like the rest of the university, was quiet. Only a few keeners were scattered about the tables, absorbed in their textbooks. I glanced over my shoulder, afraid that Mullarcant would see me and know what I was up to. Which was a ridiculous, since doing that type of research was customary for all graduate students, although it was more customary for me to be doing it in his lab.

I logged on to the Internet, and went to the psychology literature site, where I selected "Author" and typed in "Wong" at the prompt. I hit enter, and watched as about six hundred Wongs came up. I narrowed my search to "E Wong," one hundred and fifty this time. I tried again with "Elizabeth M Wong" and got fifteen listings. I brought up each one and scanned the title and abstract.

By the time I was through, I found ten publications that were Beth's, and four which she couldn't possibly have written or been involved in. I knew this for certain because Beth had told me so herself.

It was on a Friday, shortly after we met in Cameron Deagle's class. We were having coffee at a place called Brewed Awakenings on Edmonton Trail in the northeast. It was close to Beth's parents' house, in Bridgeland, and had become our favorite haunt because Robert, Brewed's owner, made the best lattes in town, and customers could still smoke. Beth was a smoker, but not a particularly good one. She was one of those people who looked awkward when she smoked, and she had a habit of holding her cigarette between her thumb and forefinger about two feet in front of her, as if she were hanging on to it for someone else. On that particular day, we were sipping extra-large lattes, chatting about school, and I happened asked her if she ever got bored with her work.

"I'm always so busy I usually don't have time to think about it.

But once in a while I think it would be nice to get into another area."

"Like what?"

"Oh, I don't know, maybe something more on the social side of things."

"What about animal research? Sandra Penny told me Mullarcant has done some pretty amazing stuff."

"Never," Beth said vehemently.

I was pleased we shared the same view on that subject. "I know what you mean. I couldn't stand it, either. Did you ever see any of those experiments?" I asked.

"No way, I refused. He did ask me to get involved in one pain study with lab mice during my first year, but I wouldn't do it."

"I'm surprised he was okay with that. I'm getting the impression your supervisor isn't the kind of guy who takes no for an answer."

I remember her sitting back and smiling. She looked stunning that day. She was wearing black tights, a short black skirt, and a silk top that went to the hem of her skirt. Her long, black hair flowed down the front of her shirt, and it was nearly impossible to tell where the hair ended and the silk began.

"You catch on fast," she said. "You're right. He doesn't take no very well. But I told him right from the start that animal research was out. And if that wasn't okay with him, then I'd transfer to another area."

"And what did he say to that?" I asked, wide-eyed.

"Nothing. He never brought it up again. It was forgotten."

Well, Beth, maybe you forgot about it, but it looks like someone else didn't, I thought. The first title on the printout was "The Effect of Pain Tolerance on Panic in Laboratory Mice." Directly under the title, the names "Martin Mullarcant, Mark Gunn, and Elizabeth M. Wong" appeared in bold type. There were three more, similar citations, all with Beth's name on them.

Publish or perish, huh, Beth? Well, it looks as if you managed to do both. The image of Beth sprawled in the snow flashed through my mind, and I felt the sting of tears and the familiar pang of anger in my gut. That bastard! She probably never even knew about these until that day. Yet I knew that couldn't possibly have been the case, because three of the four papers had been published over two years earlier. Beth would have to have known.

And so would Mark.

And so would anyone else who cared to check her publication record. Was this such a common practice in Mullarcant's lab that no one even questioned it? What had Mullarcant said? *Most students are extremely grateful . . .*

The hair on the back of my neck prickled, and I had the distinct feeling someone was watching me. I scanned the room, but the only other person I saw was a big guy behind the information desk who was completely absorbed in a book. I shoved the listing into my bag and left.

Outside, the campus was still and dark. I glanced at my watch. It was after six. The temperature was falling, and the sun wouldn't begin to warm our part of the planet for at least another fourteen hours. A few stars winked dimly in the blue-black sky. The air was cold on my face, but it felt good, and I breathed it in deeply as I walked across the grounds to the parking lot.

I looked back at the science building and wondered if Zac was still around. I headed for the entrance, but as I pulled open the front door, I changed my mind. I didn't want to run the risk of bumping into Daren Oakes or Mullarcant, or Mark, for that matter. I had to regroup and needed to get away from school to do it. Rusty would be waiting to hear what happened with Daren Oaks, and I was looking forward to a nice, quiet evening at home with her. Maybe I'd go for a run before dinner to clear my head.

I walked past the parking lot pay-booth and turned up the ramp toward Ol' Blue. I came within fifteen feet of him, and stopped short when I saw a man perched on the hood. He waved and gave me a bright smile. I looked back at the guy in the pay-booth and considered asking him to call the police. What for? To arrest a guy for sitting on my car? I hadn't even asked him to get off yet. Another glance back over my shoulder and a wave to the guy in the booth told me he could see me when he waved back.

I took my keys out of my pocket and held them like a weapon, between my right index and middle finger. Actually, it's not like a weapon at all, it's a key held in an awkward position. When women do this, it's for purely psychological reasons. Everyone knows it'd be next to impossible to inflict even so much as a bruise with an ignition key. I walked with what I hoped was an air of authority to the driver's side door.

I was about to put the key in the lock when the intruder jumped down and said, "Here, Number One Experimenter, let me get that for you," before he swung open my door.

"Hey, I locked that door this morning."

He gave me a wink. "Thought I'd save you a bit of time."

"Very clever, Ken. You know, I could call the police."

"And what, have them charge me for opening a door for you? I didn't know you could get arrested for being politically incorrect."

"Save it, Ken. I'll have you arrested for breaking into my car."

"But I didn't break into your car."

"Look, just go away. I'm in no mood. I locked the doors this morning. I know I did because I couldn't remember if I had. I made a special trip back to check. So knock it off, I've had a really bad day."

"What's the problem, Emily, not enjoying your job?"

"Ken, I'm leaving now, and I would appreciate it if you'd stop showing up at my car."

"I was thinking maybe we could have a cup of coffee together."

"Yeah, well, think again," I said and turned the key in the ignition. I tried to pull the door closed but he held it open. "Excuse me," I said, yanking on the door.

"So tell me, find anything interesting in the library?"

I stopped pulling. "Yeah, Ken, I found all sorts of interesting things in the library, that's kind of what they're about. You might want to try it sometime, maybe check out the personality disorder stuff. I think you'd find it fascinating."

He put his finger to his lips. "Hmm, not a bad suggestion. But I was thinking animal research might interest me more. I think some pain and panic studies might just keep me turning the pages all night."

I turned the engine off, and let out a sigh of resignation. "So where did you want to have that cup of coffee?" I leaned across to open the passenger door, but he had it open before I got the chance. Ken got in, and then crouched down in the seat as if hiding.

"What are you doing?"

"I don't think it's a good idea if anyone sees us together."

I narrowed my eyes at him. It had been a really stupid day, and it looked like my evening wasn't going to shape up to be much better. "Where to, Ken?" He suggested his favorite haunt—Dickey's Donuts on Fourteenth.

"Now this is where a guy can get a good, straight cup of coffee," Ken said as we walked into the smoke-filled restaurant. "None of this Gucci-woochi-cappuccino shit here. Just good ol' black-as-tar-make-your-Mama-proud coffee."

A few of the patrons recognized Ken and waved. I guess I hadn't been paying attention to what he was saying about the coffee because when we went to order, I asked what flavors they had. A tall woman behind the counter who bore a striking resemblance to Flo from *Mel's Diner*, but who wore a name tag that read "Lexy," smirked and said, "Coffee flavor."

Undaunted, I plowed ahead. "Okay, I'll have decaf then." Flo held up a pot. "We got one kinda' coffee. You want some or not?"

Ken stepped in to save the day. "We'll take two, Lex, and we're gonna stay."

"Okeedokee, Kenny. Two coffee-flavored coffees coming up." No tip for you, Flo.

We took a table near the back, where all the smoke from the entire restaurant was drawn to, as if by a huge fan. I'm not an anti-smoker fanatic, and I'll even accept a cigarette from time to time when the mood strikes me, but I really don't enjoy places so thick my eyes water. When I sat down across from Ken and looked toward the front of the restaurant, I had a hard time seeing the counter. With all those donuts stacked neatly in their baskets, with nothing covering them, I had to wonder what they would taste like.

"The other thing I like about this place," Ken was saying, "is I can enjoy a smoke without having some yuppie brat bunch his nose up at me like I'm yesterday's garbage." The nose-bunching response probably had more to do with the emission of Ken's bodily odors, I thought. I watched him take out an unfiltered roll-your-own and fumble with the match. I was going to say lighting it in there would be redundant, but then thought better of it.

"Okay, Ken, we're here. You've got your coffee. Now, what is it you have to say?"

He took a long drag, and looked thoughtfully at me as he blew a stream of white smoke over my head. "You know, Emily, I'm getting the impression you don't really want to be here."

"No kidding. Look, Ken, let's cut the games, okay? I know you don't like me, and that's fine. I just want to know—"

"I don't dislike you, kid. Hell, I don't even know you."

"Gee, you know, that's exactly what I was thinking. You don't know me, and yet you've gone out of your way to be rude, not to mention spooky."

"Spooky," he let out a loud, hoarse laugh. "I've been called a lot of things in my day, but never spooky. But I like it. So now I'm a spooky subject. How so?"

"Oh, you know perfectly well. Waiting around my car and saying little weird things about Beth. Just get to the point, Ken. I'm tired." I took a sip of coffee and then dumped half a dozen creamers and three packs of sugar into it.

"What are you trying to make, a milkshake?"

"It's a bit strong."

He extracted a silver flask from somewhere deep inside his coat and poured a shot into my cup. "Here, this'll thin it out for ya."

"That's okay," I said but it was too late.

He picked up his coffee cup and took two good swallows, and then emptied the flask into it. "Fuckin' thing doesn't even hold a cup. But I use it anyway, 'cus I'd insult the kid if I didn't. He likes to buy me stuff. Got no sense of money."

Oh, and you do, I thought dryly.

He lifted his cup in a toast. "To a new friendship."

I reluctantly lifted mine, and then took a sip of the liquid that stole my breath and made me choke so badly I thought I'd fall off my chair. "My God, what is that?" I gasped.

"My Newfie Cocktail." He held up his cup to the light as if he were inspecting an expensive Beaujolais. "It's a fine blend of Newfoundland Screech and Everclear, comes out to about one hundred and sixty proof. Ha! That'll put hair where ya want it. A friend of mine gets me the Everclear and I mix 'em." Some friend, I thought. "I wouldn't suggest lightin' a match right about now," he said with a giggle.

He toasted me again and drained his cup. His cheeks were flaming and his nose was aglow. The children were sleeping all snug in their beds. *Not a creature was stirring, except Santa who was behind the bar stirring Martinis and pissed out of his mind.* I shook my head.

"As I was saying, Emily, I don't dislike you. In fact, I'm even going to help you."

This from a man who just tried to kill me with over-proof alcohol.

"I know what you're thinking."

I doubt it.

"How's this old drunk going to help me?"

I told him the thought had crossed my mind, and that I also had a couple of questions for him. The first of which was why he would want to help me, since up until then he had been nothing but rude. And the second was why would he think I needed help in the first place.

"To answer your first question," he said, fishing around in his coat for what I assumed was another cigarette, "I was rude to you because I don't like what you do. But I noticed you weren't

157

exactly enjoying it yourself, so I figured maybe you're worth saving."

"Thanks."

From the depths of his overcoat, he produced a juice jar filled with dark, evil-looking liquid. He reached over to pour some into my cup, but this time I was ready.

"No thanks, I'm fine," I said, placing a protective hand over my cup.

"Suit yourself. Anyway, where was I?"

"You were saving me."

"Right. See, I could tell when you came down to the center you didn't feel too good about what you were doing. And in your lab, I could see you weren't exactly enjoying the show. So I started kind of watching you. And when I saw you in the library tonight, I figured I knew what you were looking for."

"I knew someone was watching me. And it was you. So tell me, Ken, what was I looking for?"

"A few papers that our friend Beth didn't exactly write herself, but somehow got her name all over them."

"How do you know about them?"

"What you're really asking is how does this drunken ass, who probably can't even read, know anything about academic papers?"

"That's not what I was thinking, but since you're the one who said it ..."

"Let's just say I've had a little experience with the university."

"Mind telling me in what way?"

He waved me off. "That's not important. The important thing is we know we're talking about the same thing, and we both know what it means."

"You're wrong there, because I'm not sure about anything right now. And I can't believe Beth would have gone along with something like that."

"And you haven't? I would have thought your friend Mullarcant would have done a paper or two for you by now. That's how he gets them, you know."

"How do you know that, Ken?"

"Me and Mullarcant are old friends, Emily."

"Oh, did you participate in other studies with him?"

"No."

"Well then, how do you know each other?"

"Never mind that right now. Let's just leave it at that I know. And I know him well."

Let's just leave it at that you're full of it, I thought. I had no intention of telling this indigent Santa anything. As far as I knew, no one but Daren Oakes, Mark, and Mullarcant knew about the paper, and I intended to keep it that way.

"He has done it, hasn't he? I can see it in your eyes." I returned his penetrating gaze and stared into Ken's deep green eyes. I had never seen irises that color. They were the emerald and teal green of ammolite, and they made a disquieting impression. It was as though those eyes were capable of boring right through me to the truth.

"No . . . well, almost, I guess." So much for keeping it to myself.

"What do you mean, almost?"

"It's a long story."

"I got time."

"First, tell me what you know about Beth. What did you mean when you said she didn't like her work?"

"Just that. She didn't like what she was doing. See, we kinda became friends. A couple of weeks before she took a dive, she came to the center to bring us some things. Beth was always donating stuff." I shifted in my seat. "She was looking pretty down, so I followed her out to her car."

"This is a habit for you, isn't it?"

He shrugged. "Anyway, she was sobbing away and I got her to come have a coffee with me."

"Another habit, I'm seeing a pattern here. And that's when she told you about the papers?"

"No. That came later. On that day, she told me some other stuff I won't get into."

"Personal stuff?"

"Yeah, personal."

"Boyfriend personal?"

"Maybe. Anyway, it wasn't until the day she took a dive that she told me about the papers."

"She phoned me that day, and said she was at the center."

"I know," he said. "I was standing next to her." I felt a lump in my throat.

"Why would she tell you then?" I said. "Those papers were published two years ago."

He shrugged again. "That's what I wanted to know. Maybe conscience. Maybe something else. At the time, I figured it was like saying confession. Or maybe she was trying to tell me something, I don't know. She was pretty ripped up about Carmen. That much I do know."

"It was terrible, and I know she took it hard. Maybe it was all just too much, the boyfriend, the papers, and then Carmen."

"And let's not forget Carmen was one of your participants, or I guess I should say subjects."

"Right, and so is Mick and about a hundred and twenty-five other people. What are you getting at?"

"I don't know, it just seems strange, that's all. Don't you think it's strange?"

"No. Are you trying to be dramatic?" He gave me a disgusted look and waved me off. "Anyway, how did you know what I was looking for tonight?"

"Like I said, I've been kind of watching you. And when you left the library you didn't clear your screen."

"You're right, I didn't."

"Don't worry, I did it for you."

"Thanks," I said cautiously. "This doesn't make sense. Why would Beth tell you about the papers?"

"Kid, I got no answers for you. Maybe she needed to get it off her chest and figured a dirty old guy like me would be a safe bet. She didn't know anything about me." He stared off for a moment, lost in thought. "She was a good kid, you know. So don't think she was a cheat or nothin'. She just got caught up, that's all. You know what I'm saying?"

"I think I do."

"Ha! I was right. That bastard did the same thing to you, didn't he?"

"Looks like it. But I think I caught it in time."

"Oh?"

I told him the whole story, and by the time I came to the part where Mullarcant said he would notify the journal, Ken was laughing and shaking his head. "And you believed him?"

"What else can I do? If I contact the journal, I'll call attention to myself and put—"

He finished my sentence. "The whole department at risk. I've heard it before, kid. And it's a crock of shit. And I'll tell you another thing." He leaned across the table jabbing his index finger at me—which, I might add, I was getting pretty tired of people doing. "When that paper comes out, you can bet your bottom dollar your name's going to be on it. So my suggestion to you, Number One Experimenter, is you better do something about it yourself before you end up with your face planted in the snow."

"What's that supposed to mean? You think the papers are what drove Beth to kill herself?"

"Let's just say I think that was part of it. And who said anything about killin' herself?"

"Oh, come on, Ken, now you're saying someone killed her. I was there. Believe me, I know what happened."

"Did you actually see her jump?"

"Well, no. But I sure as heck didn't see anyone else in there. And I didn't hear a thing other than ..."

"Than what?"

"Than someone screaming ... and ... ," I trailed off.

"And what?"

"The water and the hand dryer." It was the first time I'd thought about it. "Come to think of it, why would someone who's about to jump out the window take the time to wash and dry her hands?"

Ken clapped his hands. "Now you're thinking, Number One Experimenter." He wagged a finger at me. "But don't think too much. I've heard of people doing weirder stuff than that just before they off themselves."

"Like what?"

"Like people who take a walk out into the middle of the Atlantic in November. They strip down naked and fold everything up real neat and tidy and them kill themselves. Or like putting' plastic over all the furniture so's not to get the upholstery messy. Weird shit like that."

"How do you know about all this, Ken?"

"Like the song says, I get around, sweetheart. But I'm glad you told me about the dryer and the water, 'cus I figure the papers are just part of the whole dirty business."

"You're confusing me, Ken. One minute you're saying she didn't kill herself and the next you're convincing me she did. And what's the rest of this so-called dirty business?"

"I don't know yet, but I have my suspicions."

"Care to share them with me?"

"Not yet."

I was irritated, and I was also starting to question my own sanity. Why was I sitting there talking conspiracy theories with a guy who looks like Santa and smells like a sewer? "I should be getting home," I said.

"Suit yourself," he said, extending his hand. "And congratulations on your first publication."

I was getting really tired of this guy. The smoke was stinging my eyes, and the Newfie cocktail was burning a hole in my stomach. "He said he would contact the journal, and there isn't a damn thing I can do about it if he doesn't, so I'm going home now because I've had a really bad day."

"Sit down," he snapped, "and quit feeling sorry for yourself. If you want to do something about this, you can. That's if you can lower yourself enough to take some advice from an old bum."

I looked at him for a minute and then slumped back down in my chair. I rested my chin in my hands and, in a resigned voice, said, "Ken, why are you doing this? Why would you possibly have any interest in what goes on in my life, or my lab, or my university, for that matter?"

"You know what your problem is?"

"No, but I have this sinking feeling you're going to tell me."

"Your problem is you think everyone will leave you alone if you just keep going along with them. But guess what, kid? The more you do that, the more they come after you."

Okay, this guy's delusional, and I'm about to join him. "So it's better to be a maverick like yourself?" I said, and then immediately wished I hadn't.

"Fuck you. You don't know shit," he said, breathing sour breath in my face.

"I'm sorry, I didn't mean it."

"Yes, you did. Why can't you just say what you mean and stick with it?" My stomach was really burning up now. He pulled another small bottle from inside his coat and started to pour the liquid into his cup, but then thought better of it and poured it directly into his mouth. That's right, cut out the middle man. He took a long drink and wiped his mouth in a way reminiscent of Clint Eastwood in every western he's ever made. "If you want to stop this thing, you can."

"Okay. How?"

"Send a fax to the journal's editor."

"Good plan, Ken. I already told you that if I do that Mullarcant will tell them I was the one who put my name on the thing in the first place."

"Emily, you're not thinking. You send the fax from him. You don't even have to sign it. Just type it out on department letterhead, stating that there has been an error. Just say that, Emily, whatever your last name is—"

"Goodstriker."

"Okay, Emily Goodstriker is working on a related study and the typist was in error. Add a sorry for the confusion, and then type his name."

"But if they call to verify it, he'll say—"

"What? He can't say a thing. If he does, then he'll be screwed, and we know he sure as hell can't afford to do that."

"No, he can't, because that would raise suspicions in his direction. But wait, he'll know it was me who did it."

"That's right," Ken said. He raised the jar to offer me some. I eyed him thoughtfully. He was right, it was just that simple.

"Sure, give me a shot. You know, Ken, this just might work." He shrugged as if to say, what did you expect? "So now will you tell me how you know so much about this kind of stuff?"

"Like I said, I had a little experience with the University of Southwestern Alberta in one of my past lives."

"Do you mind telling me in what way?"

"Yeah, as a matter of fact, I do. But I'll tell you anyway, just so you'll stop asking me. I used to be a professor there, full tenured professor, that is." I suspected he liked telling people this and enjoyed seeing the shock on their faces. "Listen, kid, we weren't all born on the streets. Some of us had to work real had to get here. And I'll tell ya', getting from the university to the street takes real tenacity. I had to show up drunk every day for about a year and a half before they even noticed. And when I wasn't fallin' down in the halls, I was perched on a bar stool in the faculty lounge. Ha! and the beauty of drinking there was, they'd never cut you off."

"When did they finally make you leave?"

He tilted his chair back and laughed. "Make me leave? I just stopped showing up. I'd still be sucking a paycheck out of them today if I'd been able to stomach it. Actually, that's wrong, I still do."

"Your pension?"

"Pension, my ass, just another form of welfare."

"I don't know about that, you earned it. So what department were you in?"

He smiled. "Psychology. Social psychology. And guess what my last research paper was about?" I shrugged. "The social behavior of gamblers and night club patrons. I'll bet you think I'm pulling your leg, don't ya?"

"No. I believe you. And I'm sure it was very interesting."

"Then I'd say you're in worse shape than I am."

I didn't say anything and looked out the window.

"Don't you fuckin' feel sorry for me," he snapped. "'Cus I'm the one who's pitying you." He jabbed his finger at my face, again. "You got that?"

"I got it." The alcohol was clearly starting to do its intended work. Time for me to go. "I should get going, Ken. Do you need a ride somewhere?" Please God, let him say no.

He was leaning his chair against the wall, staring up at the ceiling. "Nope, I got more work to do tonight. But you could buy me another cup of coffee and one of them jelly things on your way out."

I asked Flo to send over another cup of coffee with a sandwich, a bowl of soup, and a jelly donut, and then ordered a sandwich to go, for myself. After I paid her, and left a tip, I walked out into the cold night air. My clothes smelled heavily of smoke and I felt nauseated from the coffee and booze. I did a quick calculation of time and liquor consumption, and felt I was okay to drive. I ate the sandwich and hurried off to my car.

When I turned onto Fourteenth Street, I spotted Ken coming out of the restaurant with a steaming cup of coffee in one hand and the donut in the other. I pulled over to the curb to watch him stroll down the sidewalk. He stopped at the far end of the building, where a grocery cart filled with green and orange garbage bags sat between a garbage can and a bike rack, as if it had been parked. Ken set his coffee in the cart and chomped down on the donut while he pushed the cart with his free hand. He made his way down the street, stopping periodically to riffle through garbage bins. I pulled out and drove past the restaurant. Through the window, I could see the soup and sandwich left untouched on the table.

Chapter 16

FOR A MOMENT, I THOUGHT I was in the wrong house. The entire foyer was draped with white painter's tarps, and some sort of wire contraption was planted squarely in the middle. A stepladder was set up next to it, with a pan full of thick, pasty stuff placed at its base.

"Ah, Emily, you're home. Wonderful, I've been waiting to hear from you," Rusty said, rounding the corner with an armload of unbleached cotton strips.

"Hi Rusty. Looks like you've been busy."

She moved up the ladder with the gait of a twenty-year-old, and then proceeded to dip the strips of cotton into an ice-cream bucket full of goop before gently pasting them on the wire. "Can you tell what it's going to be?" I moved around the soon-to-be sculpture. It was at least ten feet tall, cylindrical, with a slightly thicker part at the top. I was trying to come up with something profound, but all I saw was a giant lipstick tube. "If you say a space shuttle, I won't be offended because the most important parts aren't attached yet."

"Actually, I was going to say an upside-down lipstick tube."

She tilted her head back. "Yes, or a dildo."

"Rusty, I'm shocked! You've been in Jerald's wine cellar again, haven't you?"

She gave me a wry look. "No dear, I've been into *my* wine cellar again. And if you go into the living room you'll see I've left you some of today's spoils."

"You know, Rusty, you'll never get rid of me at this rate."

"Good, then my plan is working. Why don't you run and get yourself a nice glass of whatever it is I've got in there, and then come tell me what happened today."

I moved a piece of tarp out of the way and hung my coat in the hall closet, which was more like an opera-house coat check than a closet. "Thanks, but I think I'll skip the wine. I just finished cocktail hour." I picked up a few strips of cotton and a pan of paste. "Want a hand?"

"Start dipping. Oh, and before I forget, Mark Gunn called." She said his name in a singsong voice. When she didn't get a reaction from me, her expression changed to concern. "I don't mean to pry, dear, but for someone who's supposed to be in lust, you don't look very excited."

I took a piece of cotton and dipped it in the gooey substance and then draped it over the wire. "Am I doing this right?"

"I have no idea, but as long as the wire is eventually covered I think we'll be in business." She said it cautiously. "I'm getting the impression your meeting with Daren Oakes wasn't altogether positive."

"Oh, you could say that."

She wiped her hands on a rag. "Should we go into our office to discuss this?"

"Actually, Rust, I wouldn't mind using the other side of my brain for a change. Do you mind if we do this for a while and I'll fill you in?"

"Absolutely. I'm happy for the help."

While we dipped and pasted, and dipped and pasted, I recapped the day, starting with Mullarcant and Daren Oakes and ending with my chat with Ken, and his advice about faxing a letter to the journal.

167

Rusty rested her elbows on the top rung and looked down at me thoughtfully. "Emily, this is very, very serious and I am extremely concerned about you. Obviously Martin Mullarcant, and apparently Daren Oakes as well, feel that plagiarism is an acceptable practice. This is a dreadful spot for you to be in. Would you like me to approach someone at the university? Because I don't mean to sound high-handed, but I'm just curious as to why you're considering advice from this Ken fellow."

"Right, I forgot to mention that it's Doctor Ken."

"Oh my. A medical doctor?"

"No. Ex-USA prof. Psychology prof."

"Is that a fact? When was he there?"

"I'm not sure. But I get the impression he's been on the streets a while."

"I don't know, dear. Do you really think he's telling you the truth?"

I thought for a moment. "Yes. I think so. Or he reads an awful lot."

"The reason I ask, Emily, is that since working with Housing For All, I've met my fair share of characters who have told me some pretty wild stories. Like this one fellow, Morris. What a hoot he was. He claimed to have been an astronaut, that is, until his back went out on him."

"Be pretty tough to sit in a spaceship for days on end with a bad back, Rust."

"Indeed it would, but Morris had never been outside Alberta. I wasn't aware of a space program here. And there was another fellow, now what was his name? Doesn't matter. He claimed to have been a dentist until he became addicted to laughing gas."

"I believe the dentist. Have you ever tried that stuff?"

"Yes. But he was never a dentist. In fact, he hadn't even made it to the end of grade eight, poor soul."

"But it does happen, Rusty. I knew of one man who was a friend of my father's. He owned his own oil field supply company. Ended up dying on the streets. And when Ken was in the lab yesterday, he stopped to speak to Sandra Penny. And come to think of it, Sandra was on her way in to see Mullarcant when I was on my way out, just after she saw Ken."

"Which could have been a coincidence," Rusty said. She climbed down off the ladder and wiped her hands on a rag. "Well, Emily, there is one simple way to find out if Ken is telling the truth."

"Phone the university and see if he was on their faculty list."

"Exactly. But in the meantime, what are you going to do about all this paper business?"

"To tell you the truth, I don't have a clue. But there is one thing I do know, I can't fight the whole department on this. I mean, who am I? Just some second-year master's student. Even if I, or you for that matter, went to the ombudsman or the president, Mullarcant and Oakes would twist things so badly I'd wind up looking like a lunatic. And then I'd never finish at this or any other university in the country."

"I hate to say it, but I think you're right. And from what you've told me, they seem pretty well versed in twisting things to suit them. What about Mark Gunn? Do you think he knows anything about this?"

My stomach did a flip flop. "His name was right before Beth's on most of the papers."

"Oh dear. Emily, there has to be something we can do about this. We need to come up with a plan for you. What they are doing is wrong and it can't go on. It simply can't."

"You're right. But right now I'm tired, and all I want to do is dip these things in this stuff and paste them on your sculpture."

"Okay, dear, let's change the subject for a while and maybe we'll come up with something later."

For the next couple of hours we chatted about happier things and dipped piece after piece of cloth, gradually covering the wire. One of the things I enjoyed most about Rusty was that no matter how serious things got, we could always cut the tension by finding something to laugh about. By the time we were finished that night, Rusty and I had the top and the bottom two feet almost entirely encased. We stood together across the foyer on the bottom stair, admiring our handiwork.

"There now, we have a vibrator with a grip," Rusty said triumphantly.

"Rusty, I don't think I'm going to let you hang out with that wild artsy crowd any more."

"It always amuses me when you young people think you're the ones who invented sex."

"Just sex without clothes."

Rusty let out a hoot. "How did you know Jerald always wore socks?"

"Lucky guess. But let's not talk about it any more, I'm getting this unnatural vision of Mr. Monaghan wearing nothing but a pair of black brogues and executive hose with sock suspenders."

"Okay, dear," she said with a laugh, and then looked at her watch. "Oh my, it's after ten. I think I'll grab a sandwich and head off to bed—alone," she said with a wink. "But Emily, before I do, I just want to say one thing. Think carefully about what you are going to do. I have a very uneasy feeling about all of this."

"Me too. And the first thing I'm going to do tomorrow is call the university and find out if Ken is who he says he is."

Rusty snapped her fingers. "I think we can do better than that. If Ken was associated with the university, we need to know the whole story. And I'm pretty sure I know just the person who can tell us it."

"Oh, who's that?"

"Hannah Schneider."

"Why Hannah?"

"She was on the university's disciplinary board for over twenty years."

DOCTOR HANNAH SCHNEIDER was standing at the living room window with a cup of tea in her hand, scrutinizing the Monaghan grounds. The morning sun poured in through the beveled glass patio doors, bathing the handsome woman in an ethereal glow. Rusty had called her after breakfast and she came over immediately.

Hannah and her husband Steven had been friends and loyal bridge partners of the Monaghans' since shortly after the Second World War. Both Schneiders were doctors, and when I was a child they fascinated and terrified me. Physically, they were large-boned, imposing figures, but it was their personalities that took up the better part of a room.

My mother told me they were German Jews who had escaped from Germany during the war. Which, to my seven-year-old mind, meant they must still be on the run.

"Hi, Hannah."

"Oh Emily," she said, giving me the requisite bearhug. "Look at you. You are all grown up. You know, the last time I saw you, you were this quiet little pixie. And now you are a lovely young woman. Come," she said, taking my hand and leading me to the couch. "Rachel has told me you may have met an old friend of mine."

The idea of the straight-backed Hannah and the foul-mouthed Ken ever being friends was stretching my imagination.

"Now, let us see," she said, busying herself with a stack of old faculty yearbooks. "The man I am thinking of still would have been at the university until the late seventies or early eighties. He didn't tell you his last name, Emily?" I shook my head. "Well, from what Rachel tells me, I'm guessing it's Ken Cox. With any luck there will be at least one picture of him. But of course he will have changed."

You can bet on that, I thought.

Rusty produced a tray of little sandwiches with the crusts cut off, and for a moment I was transported back to my seventh year when I sat in that very same spot, nibbling those same little sandwiches, listening with rapt attention to Doctor Hannah recount one of her many adventures. Hannah was a great talker and an even greater storyteller, and I loved to listen to her recount their experiences, especially the one about Cairo.

"We were picnicking near some ruins, when along came this nasty scorpion and stung me right here," she would tell us, indicating the back of her right hand. "I ran around and around the table with Steven chasing after me, waving a bottle of brandy. When he finally caught me, he threw me down on the ground and was about to pour that liquor all over my hand. But I grabbed it just in time and said, 'Good God, man, don't waste that good alcohol,' and I poured it down my throat instead." Then she would turn to her husband and say with deep affection, "And you call yourself a doctor." Whereupon, no matter if it was the first or the fifteenth time we'd heard it, we'd all laugh uproariously.

"This was a most difficult case, Emily," Hannah was saying. "It brings back very sad memories. Yes. Here we are." She passed me a 1978 USA yearbook. Down the left-hand side of the page were four black and white photos of people with bad haircuts, two of whom were smiling: a woman and a man. The other two, both men, looked as though they were in a police lineup. The picture at the bottom of the page fell into this latter category. It was of a man who appeared to be in his early forties. He had light, shaggy hair, a clean-shaven face, and wore no glasses. I didn't need to study the picture long to know it was Ken. Even in black and white, the eyes had that same piercing quality.

"Is it him, Emily?" Under the picture, a biography detailed his academic background and research. It was brief, and said only that he was a graduate of Harvard, and that his current area of interest was social psychology, with an emphasis on group dynamics and reaction to stressors. I took a closer look at the eyes.

"Yes. I'm sure it's him."

"And how is he?"

"Not too good."

"Yes. I suspected as much. What a waste of a brilliant mind."

"Was he a good researcher?"

"Oh my, yes," she said loudly, her German accent becoming more pronounced. "And he was a wonderful teacher. Completely unconventional, you must understand, but brilliant nonetheless. As I say, it was one of the most difficult cases. Now, how are you connected with him? I had a faint hope you were going to tell me he was making a comeback."

"Afraid not, Hannah." I explained our study and how I met Ken. Rusty and I had agreed we wouldn't mention the paper incident. Not yet, anyway.

"And what can I tell you about him? There's so much, I really wouldn't know where to begin."

"What happened, Hannah?" Rusty said as she filled our cups with more tea. "How does someone so bright just up and throw it all away?"

Hannah sat back and collected her thoughts. "When I first heard about Doctor Ken Cox, it was in 1980. By that time he was drinking all the time, and his behavior had become a nuisance at the very least, and an acute embarrassment at worst. When he did show up for meetings, he was drunk. And the odd classes he didn't pass off on to his teaching assistants were more like vaudeville acts than academic lectures."

Hannah explained that when the case was brought before the disciplinary committee, her initial reaction was simply to have Ken fired.

"Not that it is a particularly easy task when someone has tenure. But the evidence against him was so grave, and he certainly didn't try to make things any better for himself. In fact, he seemed bent on helping us along."

"You mean he was trying to get fired?" Rusty asked.

"It certainly appeared that way, and I for one would have been more than happy to oblige him."

"Until?" I said.

"Yes, until I happened to meet a young woman named Leslie Donaldson, who was a former student of Ken's. Part of our committee's task was to look back at Ken's academic record and his success with graduate students. Leslie Donaldson's case caught my eye. She had been a very average undergraduate student who was just barely making it through the psychology program, and her chances of getting into graduate school were nonexistent. Then she met Ken and joined his—"she paused, "let's call them study groups, I'll explain those in a moment. She stayed with Ken and his study groups for the next two years, and doesn't she graduate with honors. The next year she is in the master's program with Ken as her supervisor."

"And she went on to Harvard and is now a brilliant psychologist practicing in Manhattan?" I asked.

"Not quite, Emily," Hannah said. "She is now a brilliant ophthalmologist in Vancouver."

Rusty and I exchanged a look.

"When I contacted her, she claimed that it was because of Ken that she ended up doing what she was meant to do and loves. She also convinced me that he had done the same thing for many others."

"And that's when you became more interested?"

"Absolutely. I looked back over his graduates and contacted at least thirty of them, and many of them had similar glowing reports."

"Did any of them stay in psychology or did they all go on to become brain surgeons?" I asked.

"About a third stayed, and the majority are doing very well as clinicians, researchers, and academics. Extremely well, in fact."

"And the rest?"

"Again. Almost all the others went on to pursue something interesting. I spoke to people who were enjoying careers in everything from architecture to medicine. One fellow I spoke with was in Hollywood, creating animated characters for Disney. All these people had one thing in common."

"Ken."

"Yes. And they said it was because of him they ended up where they were. Ironically, one of the main criticisms Ken's colleagues and his department leveled against him was that he didn't teach, and that he had a poor record for getting his graduate students through. It was a unanimous sentiment: Ken Cox didn't teach because he was a lazy drunk."

"So his drinking wasn't something that just suddenly came about at the end?"

"Oh, heavens no. He had been drinking for years, and he prided himself on drinking with his students. But he functioned well enough. It was only toward the end that things got completely out of hand."

"But, Hannah, if his students all did so well, how could they say he didn't teach?"

"He didn't teach. Not in the conventional sense, anyway. Ken, as I mentioned, had these study groups."

I smiled. "That met in a bar?"

"Precisely. I learned through his students that Ken Cox's teaching philosophy was if you're interested, show up; if not, stay home! You see, Ken wasn't interested in preaching, as he put it, to a crowd of three or four hundred bored students."

"I'm sure no one is," Rusty said. "But everyone has to do it, otherwise no one would teach those classes."

"Yes, but Ken had a rather ingenious way of getting around it without violating department code. On the first day of class, Ken would inform the students that all exam questions would come directly from the textbook. He'd say he intended to give a lecture each day, but that no exam questions would come from his lectures."

"Gee, and I'll bet the next class was a little sparse," I said.

"Certainly. The following day he would come back and collect those students who had enough interest to show up, and then he'd whisk them off to the bar. Once there, he would make damn sure they learned something far more valuable than what they would get from his recycled notes in an overcrowded lecture theatre. So those few students who were keen enough to show up when they didn't have to, learned exactly what was going to be on the exams. In return, they took on special projects they didn't get credit for."

"Wow, I think I would have enjoyed one of his so-called classes."

"I believe you would have. His students loved him. They fed

off his brilliance, and I suppose he, in turn, must have fed off their passion for learning. And according to Leslie, her case was apparently typical. It was Ken, she said, who during her master's program persuaded her to do a study under one of the other professors in the department who specialized in vision and perception research."

"And the rest, as they say, was history," I added.

"What a shame," Rusty added. "He must have been a very unhappy man, though. Otherwise he wouldn't have been drinking so much."

"You are absolutely right, Rachel."

I thought about the man I had been sitting with the night before. The man who digs through garbage cans and who guzzles overproof liquor. "So what happened in the end, Hannah? Did his drinking just get away on him?"

"Yes. But it was my impression that something happened to trigger his decline."

"And you have no idea what precipitated it?" Rusty asked.

"No, but I do know that by the end of '79 the president, Norman Dessier, had taken all Ken's graduate students away from him and forbade him to take on any new ones."

"Because of his drinking?"

"That was the official reason. The documents we received stated the president felt that until Doctor Cox completed treatment for his addiction, he was not equipped to supervise students. Seven months later, when our committee was trying to figure out what to do with Ken, his behavior had been getting steadily worse. But what puzzled me was that some of Ken's students I spoke with had graduated as recently as the end of 1978, and not one of them said Ken's drinking had affected them."

"Maybe they were just being loyal."

"I considered that possibility too. But their academic records spoke for themselves. After I completed my investigative work, I went to our president and asked exactly what had happened that made him take such drastic action against Ken. I was met with a curt and dismissive response. Norm said he was so fed up with the whole Ken issue, that what transpired the year before wasn't worth repeating and that he considered the matter closed. In fact, by that time, no one wanted to talk about Ken Cox. No one except his students."

"So did you fire him?"

"Not really. In the end, the committee finally agreed on a forced retirement. The university doesn't often fire people, Emily. It was a formality, really, because by then, Ken Cox had disappeared."

AFTER HANNAH LEFT, I spent the remainder of the morning mulling over what she told us, and the better part of the afternoon trying to decide whether to take Ken's advice and send a fax to the journal. When I couldn't stand it any longer, I went for a run to clear my mind. I ran through the neighborhood past the sweeping snow-covered lawns, across Seventeenth Avenue, and down Twelfth. Another chinook had blown in and the temperature was climbing steadily. By the time I reached Good Earth Cafe, where half a dozen brew hounds were sitting outside, warming their faces in the sun, I had already shed two layers of clothing.

Calgary is said to have the third-best climate of Canadian major cities, behind Vancouver and Victoria. Calgary also has the most bizarre climate, where the weather can change from a bright sunny day to a major storm in literally minutes, and where the temperature can rise or fall twenty degrees in less than twenty-four hours. It has been known to snow in August, and hit plus nineteen Celsius in December. The coffee culture in front of Good Earth Cafe that day was enjoying a balmy plus eleven.

The smell of java and fresh baking beckoned me in, but I "stayed the course," and headed down to the bike paths that snake through the city and follow the rivers. The ice was breaking on the Bow River, sending mini bergs down its icy, aquamarine waters. I crossed the Tenth Street bridge, determined to put everything out of my mind and just enjoy my run. I stopped on the north bank of Memorial Drive to watch a man, silhouetted by the downtown office towers, cast his fishing line into the frigid water. Calgary is one of the few major cities in North America with two rivers running through its heart that are still clean enough to fish and swim in. In a few months, people in canoes, rafts, and boats would be sailing down that river, as well as swimming and floating on air mattresses down the smaller Elbow River.

As I headed toward the northeast, I watched the cityscape zip by on my right. With the clear rushing water of the river, and the snow-covered park that borders the downtown core, I thought that we Calgarians have it all.

I headed toward Bridgeland, my destination being the hill where Beth's parents lived. My run was turning into a half marathon, but it felt so good I just wanted to keep going, even though I knew I'd pay through the joints for it the next day.

Just before I turned up the path and came out on Edmonton Trail, I passed a group of five or six people huddled together under the Langevin bridge, sharing a bottle. One of the men looked a little like Ken. He stared up at me through empty eyes. I lifted my hand and said hello. He turned away as I drew closer. The one woman in the bunch also looked up, but she gave me a warm, gap-toothed smile. My exuberance left me, and I suddenly felt very tired. Apparently only some of us Calgarians have it all, I thought as I turned around and headed home, wondering how my legs were going to carry me.

Chapter 17

BY THE NEXT MORNING, I finally made the decision to go with Ken's advice (since I certainly didn't have any of my own to go with) and send the fax. Moving into Beth's office was still under review, though. I was leaning toward not doing it, because the thought of being physically closer to Mullarcant was more than I could bear.

The door to our office was locked, which meant Zac hadn't been in yet. I turned on my computer and took a couple of deep breaths before I slipped down the hall to the lab to swipe a few sheets of department letterhead and the most recent copy of the *North American Journal of Psychology.* Thankfully, Mullarcant nor Oakes was around. Back at my desk, I flipped to the front of the *Journal* and found the mailing address and fax number. After that the rest was easy. When I was satisfied with the letter, I printed it off, gave it another read, and went to the main office.

Darla Sheeny, our department secretary, was at her desk, and in her usual helpful way told me to do it myself when I told her I needed to fax a letter, which was exactly what I was counting on. Even though Darla could be downright rude, I made a point of getting along with her, simply because when I worked in offices during the summers of my undergrad years, I learned first-hand what it meant to be support staff. I also learned that although support staff may appear to have little overt power, they do, however, possess a tremendous amount of covert power. And nowhere is this more evident than in the university system. The secretaries are the gatekeepers; they decide who sees whom and when, whose forms are ready on time and whose aren't, and who gets to use the photocopier and fax machine and who doesn't. But more importantly, they are the purveyors and disseminators of essential communiqués and departmental gossip.

"So how's it going, Darla?" I asked offhandedly, as I waited for the fax machine to perform its magical communication function. Darla had a head of big, dark hair, and hands ending in long red nails that clicked on the keys when she typed. Whenever Darla was in possession of a tasty morsel of gossip, she had a habit of flicking the underside of each fingernail with her thumbnail. And this was precisely what she was doing at that moment.

I waited patiently for a response, knowing full well she'd have to flick the pinkie before sharing. It was all part of Darla's charm and, no doubt, her way of heightening the suspense.

"Flick." She hit the pinkie and on cue, said, "So did you hear?"

I moved over to her desk. "What's that, Darla?"

"Well, actually," she said, looking over her shoulder, "I'm really not supposed to know about this, so maybe I shouldn't say anything."

"Oh, come on, Darla, you've started it, you have to finish it." I leaned against her desk. "You know I won't say anything."

She looked around the office again. Satisfied no one was in earshot, she said, "Looks like we lost another one."

"Another what?"

She lowered her voice. "Student." I assumed she meant another graduate student had dropped out of the program, but I couldn't think of who it might be.

"Who?"

"Derrick someone, I couldn't catch his last name."

I narrowed my eyes. "We don't have a Derrick in the graduate program, do we?" I was beginning to question Darla as a credible source.

"What program?" she snapped. "He's an undergraduate, one of your gas chamber kids." Darla had a lot of creative names for our experiments and our subjects.

"Oh yeah, him. What about him?"

She looked at me as though I were deficient. "We lost him," she said and made a diving motion over the edge of her desk with one long, red fingernail. "Out the window, just like Beth."

Her words knocked the wind out of me. "Oh my God. Why? What . . . what happened? Who told you this?"

"Look, I just overheard them this morning, so don't say I said anything, okay? And for God's sake don't tell Rita Kenny. She'll kill me. So, did you know him?" Darla asked. I felt like someone had just slammed me in the stomach. "So! Did you know him?"

"Uh, no, I mean yes," I said. "I met him in the lab the other day. I just saw him in the commons with his dog. Oh no, what's Petey going to do?"

"Who's Petey?" Darla said.

"His dog. Jeez, Darla. He seemed like a nice guy. Really eager to get into the master's program. What happened? Are you sure about this?"

"I'm sure."

"Who told you?"

"No one exactly, I just happened to overhear Mullarcant and Oakes this morning. But, hey, you didn't hear it from me. Okay?"

The fax machine announced with a beep that my message had been successfully sent. I turned toward the machine and watched it expel my letter.

"Okay?" Darla repeated.

"Sure, Darla, sure. I won't say a thing. What else do you know? What did Mullarcant and Oakes say?" She started flicking her nails again, but this time I found it irritating.

"Just that it doesn't look very good for the department."

I grabbed the letter and took off back to my office.

Once there, I started emptying out a cardboard box of old files that I kept under my desk. Since Beth's death, my gut had been telling me something was going on, but I kept rationalizing it away and making excuses. Grandma Wong tried to tell me and so did Ken. Things didn't add up, and I couldn't keep ignoring the signs—Beth's application form, the publications, Daren Oakes' reaction, and now Derrick.

For a second, I thought maybe it was just coincidence. But then Derrick's words ran through my mind. *I'm meeting with Doctor Mullarcant again to do some other stuff. He said something about doing another phase of the study. . . .* What other phase? Zac obviously didn't know anything about it, and Beth never mentioned it. And I had never come across anything other than the panic studies and the latest Milgram one. It was time I did some digging. I left a note for Zac, telling him where I'd be, and then lugged the box down the hall to the lab. I steeled myself for the moment I'd see Mullarcant, and decided the best course of action would be to pretend nothing was wrong, and that our meeting and the paper were forgotten. With any luck, the journal wouldn't contact him once they received the fax, and Mullarcant wouldn't know what happened until after the thing was published. I crossed my fingers as I made my way down the hall. Along the way, I ran into Mark.

"Well, hiya, stranger."

"Mark!"

"Gee, you look like you didn't recognize me. You okay?"

"Sorry, you startled me."

"Did you get my message the other day?" he said, taking the box from me.

"I did, and I'm sorry I didn't get back to you. It was late when I got home that night. And I haven't been feeling too well the past couple days." I was nervous and I was talking too quickly. During my brief hiatus at home, I had effectively put Mark Gunn out of my mind. Not because I didn't want to see him any more. No. That definitely wasn't it. I just had too many other things to deal with. But there he was, standing beside me, looking more handsome than ever. And there I was with no clue what to do or say.

A look of deep concern crossed his face. "Are you feeling better now?"

"Oh yeah, fine. Just a cold or something."

"I would have called you back again, but I had to take off to Vancouver."

"Your son?"

"No, it was his mother this time. She got what he had and needed me to look after him. But then she was okay by last night. So I'm back."

"At least you were able to spend a little time with him."

"Actually, that part was great, but I always get bummed out when I have to leave him. So where are we headed with this?" he said hefting the box.

"Beth's office."

"You're moving in? I mean, I think that's a wise decision. But are you okay with it?"

I was having trouble looking at him. "I'm not actually moving in, not yet, anyway. Just thought I'd do a little housecleaning. I need some journal articles."

I hadn't set foot in Beth's office since before Christmas. Since before she died. But it was evident someone else certainly had. Beth had been as neat and meticulous as Mullarcant. Her desk was always conspicuously clean. Her in-basket was typically empty, and all file folders were either out of sight or arranged alphabetically in a file organizer.

The mess that was on and around Beth's desk now looked as though the place had been burgled and vandalized.

My first thought was that Mullarcant must still be searching for the missing Aspen 45 file documents. But messiness was not Mullarcant's trademark. If he searched her belongings he wouldn't have been able to stop himself from cleaning it all back up again.

The expression on Mark's face gave away his surprise. "What

the hell? Wow, Martin must still be looking for those missing file documents."

I doubted it was Mullarcant, but I didn't say anything.

"Emily, don't feel you have to clean this up. I'll have a word with Martin when he gets back." Mark went to the door and closed it.

"Where is he?" I asked.

"Off campus, at a research meeting, I think." I felt the tension in my shoulders ease. Mark moved closer and I took in the scent of his expensive cologne. "I couldn't stop thinking about you the whole time I was away," he said. He kissed me lightly on the lips, and then he drew back. "I'm sorry, shouldn't I have done that?"

I was completely unnerved and wanted to tell him about the papers, about Derrick, and the fax, and about Ken. But something said, don't. "I guess I'll just have to get used to you again," I said.

"I was only gone a day."

"I know, but it seemed a lot longer."

"Aw," he said and put his arms around me. "I was beginning to think you were losing interest. How about dinner tonight at my place?" He kissed me on the forehead and then on the cheek, and all my anger and confusion were wiped away with each kiss.

"That would be nice," I said, my voice raspy. "What time?"

"Seven okay?"

"Perfect." Right, perfect. I'm a perfect idiot, I thought. "I guess I should get started here."

"Are you sure there's nothing wrong?" Mark asked.

I sat down at the desk and rested my cheek on my hand. In front of me was Beth's billboard with yellow, green, and blue sticky notes arranged neatly according to color. Seeing her handwriting gave me a stab.

Mark followed my gaze to the billboard and then looked back to me. "Maybe it's too soon for you to be in here. Why don't I look for whatever it is you need?" He knelt down in front of me and took my hands in his. "Emily, is there something else bothering you? If it's about us, or school, or anything else, please, I want you to tell me."

His kindness and the sincerity in his eyes made me want to weep.

"There is something, Mark. But I've been sworn to secrecy. Of course, if I know, then I'm sure you must already know too."

"Derrick?"

I nodded. "Mark, what's going on here? First Beth and now Derrick?"

"I know, it's terrible. But I'm not surprised."

"You're not?"

"No. We try to keep these things quiet, but word gets around. I'm just hoping no one else does it." He sighed. "The stats aren't in our favour, though."

"Stats? I'm not following you."

"The contagion factor. You know, where there's one suicide, there's usually more to come."

"You think that's what happened to Derrick? He was following Beth?" "Seems like it. I don't know if you know this, but he had pretty high aspirations about getting into this program next year."

"I did know that. He mentioned it when he was in the lab. Mark, that was on Monday. And he seemed pretty up to me. But, come to think of it, he did mention Beth."

"I talked to him myself a couple of times. Last week he came to me asking for a recommendation. He was really pumped about getting accepted. I told him to take it easy. I don't know, maybe everything just got to him. And he kept mentioning Beth's name to me too."

"Really, what did he say?" I asked.

"Please keep all this confidential."

"Of course."

"He said he couldn't believe she would throw it all away when she had everything going for her, things like that."

"You think he was following Beth's lead? But why?"

"When ordinary people, young people in particular, see someone like a rock star or movie star commit suicide, they think,

Look, that person has everything, and yet he checked out. And here's me with nothing. So my life must really be worthless."

"I see what you're getting at, but Beth wasn't exactly a star."

"At that moment she seemed like one to him, because she had everything he wanted. I really shouldn't be telling you this, but to be honest, Derrick wasn't master's material. At least, Martin didn't think so."

"And I suppose he felt compelled to communicate this to Derrick in his ever-so-subtle way."

Mark stared at the floor. "I'm afraid so." He looked up and our eyes met.

"But I saw him late Tuesday afternoon, Mark. He was out in the commons area playing with his dog, and Mullarcant was out there with him. Derrick didn't look devastated then. In fact, the whole thing was a bit bizarre. Mullarcant and Derrick looked like best buds."

Mark's brow furrowed. "Are you sure?"

"I'm positive."

"Well, then, I guess Martin must have told him right after that. Because I talked to him yesterday morning."

"To Mullarcant?"

"No, Derrick."

"But weren't you in Vancouver?"

"One of the undergraduate secretaries called me. Said Derrick was really upset."

"So you called him."

"Yes."

"Because you knew Mullarcant had just devastated him?"

"I had my suspicions."

"My God, Mark. You should have seen him playing with that dog. Poor Derrick, he must have thought he was in for sure. What kind of a man can do that to someone?"

"I don't know, Emily. And to be perfectly honest, I don't think I can take much more of this. Derrick was devastated when I talked to him. Beth was having problems and . . ." Mark rubbed his eyes with the palms of his hands.

I was relieved he was finally admitting his feelings about Mullarcant. "Maybe we can talk about this some more tonight," I said.

Mark looked up into my eyes, and I found myself staring back into the face of a man who suddenly looked very worn-out.

"I was hoping I could steer Derrick toward something else," Mark said. "But it looks like his heart was set on this. And with Beth's suicide still fresh in his mind . . . ," he trailed off. "Well, Emily, I just pray we can keep this one quieter than Beth's."

"Derrick said something about meeting with Mullarcant to work on another phase of the study. Do you have any idea what he was talking about?"

"I have absolutely no idea," Mark said. "Derrick was a little overzealous."

"But why would he say there was another phase?"

"Who knows. I'm getting tired, Emily, I'll tell you that . . . ," he trailed off again. "God, Emily, I just hope we don't start an epidemic on campus."

"Isn't there something that can be done?"

"It's a 'catch twenty-two' situation," he said as he stood and smoothed the wrinkles from his slacks. "If we talk about it, we bring more attention to it. So the short answer is no. The best thing for all of us to do is to keep quiet about it. All we can do is cross our fingers and keep an eye out for anyone we think might be at risk."

He leaned over and gave me a kiss on the forehead. "I've got a meeting to get to. I'm sorry, I'd like to stay with you, but I'm going to be tied up for the rest of the day. I will see you tonight, though, won't I?"

"I'll be there."

"Good, I'm looking forward to it. And, Emily, don't spend too much time in here."

After he was gone, I wrestled with my feelings. There was no question I liked him, and I wanted to trust him. But there were the papers. He knew as well as I did that Beth's name was on them right alongside his. And if I knew she had nothing to do with the studies, then he sure as hell knew too.

But maybe Mullarcant had done the same thing to Mark. Maybe he just got in too far, like Beth had. That was it, I reasoned. Mark knew about the papers, of course, and therefore he must have suspected they were the reason, or one of the reasons, Beth killed herself.

I went over our night at Cajun Charlie's when he convinced me that Beth's death had nothing to do with the department. Personal problems, he said, a boyfriend. Ah, the mysterious boyfriend. It occurred to me then that maybe Derrick was the boyfriend. Was this a Romeo and Juliet thing? I thought back to the last day in the lab, how Beth had stood at the window, watching Derrick. How I had been taken aback with her tone of voice when she said, "You know, he goes out there and plays with that dog every day." But when Derrick came to the lab, he gave no indication he knew her personally. And unless he was a really good actor, my feeling was that he was off the list of suspects.

Perhaps it was time I found out more about this troublesome fellow, whoever he was. I glanced back up to Beth's mosaic of notes and spied the name of someone I was pretty sure could help me out.

Chapter 18

BOTANICAL SMELLS OF ROOTS, herbs, and tea filled my nose as I descended the stairs to the narrow, overly stocked store. Grandma Wong was behind the counter, filling an order for a customer. I watched from the stairs as she opened wooden drawers and extracted roots, plants, and animal parts, weighing each carefully on a brass scale before grinding it to a fine powder.

As I watched her work, I remembered the first time I stepped into Grandma Wong's world. I was fighting a terrible cold at the time, and Beth suggested we make a visit to Chinatown. I was skeptical about Grandma Wong's curative powers. If someone had a cure for the common cold, surely one of the giant pharmaceutical companies would have it packaged as yet another lemon-flavored drink. But I did want to meet her, so we had lunch at the Silver Dragon and then went off to Wong's Herb Shop.

When Grandma Wong saw Beth, her face lit up, and she took her granddaughter's hands in hers and kissed them.

"Hi, Grandma. This is Emily, she's a friend of mine from school."

"Ah, you must be good person, if you friend of my Beth," she said, patting Beth's hands.

"It's nice to meet you, Mrs. Wong."

"You call me Grandma, everyone call me Grandma." She studied me for a moment. "But you got bad head."

"Yeah, Grandma, Emily's got a really bad cold. I told her you could fix her up."

"Oh sure, we got lots for cold. Come, come," she said, still holding on to her granddaughter as she led us to the counter.

We followed her down aisles past all kinds of wonderfully exotic-looking things lining the shelves and counters. I gazed at one wall that held dozens of quart sealer jars filled with everything from giant seed pods to dried beetles. Down the length of the glass counter, behind which Grandma Wong was busy at work, ginseng roots, neatly arranged like root-soldiers, filled Pyrex trays.

"So what's the difference between this one," I said, pointing to the tray closest me, "and that stuff at the end?"

"About fifteen hundred bucks," Grandma Wong said over her shoulder.

"Holy cow. They all look the same."

"But they're quite different," Beth said. "The stuff at the end is wild Asian Ginseng and it's the most potent of the ginsengs, whereas this cheaper, wimpier stuff is American."

"It not wimpy," Grandma said as she measured out a scoop of brown powder onto the scale. "Just different."

Under the ginseng, on the bottom shelf, were little leathery things that looked like tiny, black, change purses. "Hey, what are these?" I asked.

Beth knelt down to get a better look. "Seal penises. Want to know what they're used for?"

"No. But you can tell me about those," I said, indicating a jar on a shelf behind Grandma, which was filled with long, dried buggy things tethered to popsicle sticks.

Grandma Wong looked up from the scale. "Oh yeah, dried centipedes. Good for skin rash."

"So what do you do, rub it on?"

Grandma and Beth both laughed. "No, no, make tea." Grandma made a fist with one hand and placed it in the palm of her other to make a grinding motion. "Make a powder and drink it. Very good," she said with a huge smile and sparkling eyes.

"It tastes good?" I said suspiciously.

"Oh no, tastes terrible, but good for skin."

"Have you ever had centipede tea, Beth?"

"Are you kidding?" She gave an exaggerated shiver. "Never."

Behind the counter, Grandma Wong was grinding a ginseng root to a yellow powder. "Oh, she try it. She just don't know. I tell her it something else."

"I never did, Grandma," Beth said, taking the lid off a tiny jar to smell the contents. Grandma gave me a wink and went back to her grinding. "Hey, Grandma, is this ginseng creme any good?" Beth held up the jar.

The little woman squinted her eyes at it. "No, got no ginseng. I make you a better one."

"You know, Grandma, I think I need more vitamin C," I said. "What can you give me for that?"

"An orange." She shook a disapproving finger at me. "Chinese medicine for whole person. It not like taking a pill for this or that. You eat right foods, drink lots of water, and sleep at night, and then take a walk in the morning. You young people want only one thing to fix everything, quick, quick. Each day that matter, little by little. Chinese medicine is about balance. You keep everything in balance. Beth, she work too hard, out of balance."

"Oh, Grandma, you worry about me too much. I sleep, I go for walks, and I eat oranges."

"Oh, yeah, and how about your love life anyway?"

Beth looked startled, and then changed the subject abruptly. At the time, I really didn't think anything of it. I probably wouldn't want to discuss my love life, or lack thereof, with my grandmother, either.

"So what did you whip up for Emily?" Beth said inspected the mess of herbs, roots, and powder her grandmother had piled on a piece of brown butcher's paper. Mani Wong studied her grand-daughter for a moment. She seemed about to say something, but changed her mind and then bundled up the mixture.

"Here you go, Emily, you make tea three times a day for three days, and you feel better. You add lemon and honey too. Taste lots better that way, okay?" I thanked her and dug out my wallet, but she wouldn't accept any money. "You don't pay me. You just take care of my Beth. You good friend." She placed the packet in my hands and gave them a good squeeze.

Now, after Grandma Wong's customer paid for her herbs and left, I approached the counter. When she saw me her face lit up, but the brightness I remembered in her eyes was gone.

"Hi, Grandma Wong."

"Ah, Emily, I been waiting for you." She came around from behind the counter and slipped her arm through mine. I was sur-prised at how tiny and frail she seemed then. Her grief over the loss of her granddaughter was literally eating away at her small frame. When I met her that first time, she appeared aged and small in stature, but she carried herself with a sense of strength and good health. She exuded a sense of balance. Now she seemed off-kilter.

"Come, come we have tea." The word "tea," from Grandma Wong, made my stomach lurch at the memory of those three days I drank the potion she had prepared for my cold. My stomach rebelled each time I took a sip of the stuff, but by the end of day three, I had to admit I was feeling great. She sensed my hesitancy.

"Don't worry. We just have green tea. Unless you got cold again."

"No, no, I'm fine," I said it a little too quickly, and I noticed the corners of her mouth curl up. She led me behind a red cloth curtain to a small room at the back of the store. The room served as office, lunchroom, and storage area. It was tiny and cramped, but oddly comfortable. There was an old, battered desk with a solid oak chair on castors, two smaller chairs, and a table that held a black porcelain teapot with a gold dragon painted on it. Half a dozen matching teacups were placed neatly on a wicker tray around the pot, as if on display.

Beth's grandmother motioned for me to take a seat in the big chair, while she opened the curtain to ensure a view of the front of the store, and then busied herself making the tea.

"Grandma Wong, I'm sorry I haven't come to see you before now."

"That okay. You here now," she said, sprinkling a few green leaves into the pot.

"A number of things have happened and . . . ," and I didn't know where to begin. She sat down on one of the small folding chairs and waited patiently for the kettle to boil and for me to collect my thoughts. "Maybe I won't go over everything right now," I said. "Would it be all right if I just asked you a few questions?"

"Sure, sure, you ask."

I was feeling awkward, because the last thing I wanted to do was cause this woman any more grief. I weighed my words carefully. "Grandma Wong, I've thought about what you said at Beth's memorial service, and I don't have anything specific to tell you but—"

She pointed a finger toward the heavens. "But you know my Beth didn't do this. You know they do this to her, right?"

"Actually, no. I don't know that for certain, but there are a few things that don't make sense, and I was hoping you could give me some answers."

"Okay good, I tell you anything." She poured two cups of tea and handed one to me.

"Thanks, Grandma."

"You know my Beth was here that day."

"The day she . . . died?"

"Yes, that day. I close up for lunch, and when I come back I know Beth has been here."

"You didn't see her? How did you know?"

"I don't know, I just know. I can feel her. She was here."

193

"If she did come to see you, then I'm awfully sorry you missed her."

"Oh, she not come to see me. If she come to see me, she wouldn't come at lunch. She come for something else."

"Had she ever done that before? Come here when you were out?"

"No. No reason. That day she had reason."

My suspicion was that if Beth had come to the store that day, it was because she needed desperately to talk to her grandmother. If Beth Wong was contemplating suicide, then I was almost certain she would have wanted to see her grandmother one last time. With that sad thought, I changed the subject.

"Grandma, do you remember that first time I was here and you mentioned something about Beth's love life?" She nodded. "What did you mean by that? Was she seeing someone?"

"Oh yeah, she seeing someone all right."

"Were they having problems?"

"Yeah, they got big problems. He have a wife and a kid. But that only part of their problems. He not Chinese, and Beth's father want Chinese husband for Beth. My son is very traditional, he doesn't understand that things are different here for young people. Beth not want to disgrace him. So she has to lie about this guy all the time. Say she not seeing anyone."

"But she told you."

"Sure. She can't lie to me. I see it in her eyes."

"That must have been awful for her. Beth wasn't the kind of person who could lie easily."

"Yeah, and her father always bring home nice Chinese boys for Beth."

"And what about you, Grandma Wong? What did you think?"

She shrugged. "Oh, sure, better if he Chinese, but I live a long time now. I see old ways changing. I don't know, I just know my granddaughter very, very unhappy. That's what I know."

"Did you ever meet him?"

"Sure, I see him. Once Beth bring him here to meet me."

"What did you think of him?"

"He okay, but too old for her."

"I'd like to talk to him. Can you tell me his name and where I can get hold of him?"

"Sure I know his name, and so do you."

"Oh?"

"I think he a good friend of yours too," she said and gave me a sly smile.

I felt the color drain from my face.

Chapter 19

I SAT IN OL' BLUE FOR CLOSE to half an hour, letting my emotions transmogrify from shock to seething anger. I thought about our evening at Cajun Charlie's and how convincing he had been. That son of a bitch, how could he sit there so smugly and tell me Beth had personal problems? "Yeah, well, Doctor Gunn, looks like you just happened to be the biggest one!" I said out loud.

I pounded the dash with my fist. "How could I have been so stupid? He knew about those papers, and he probably knows about the one with my name on it too. He's nothing but a little messenger boy. That's why he stayed so close to me when I went to talk to Grandma Wong. And then all that crap about how bad things happen to good people and—God, he's good!" I hit the dash again, this time too hard. I rubbed my bruised hand and glanced at the clock on the dash—it was nearly noon, and I really needed to talk to someone.

I pulled out into Chinatown traffic and headed for New Beginnings. Why I picked there is still a mystery to me. Maybe it was for the same reason Beth had—because it seemed safe.

The foyer was just as thick with smoke as it had been the last time I'd been there. All the tables were occupied with card players and coffee drinkers. I noticed Mick and Irene playing checkers at the far end of the room. Irene spotted me and waved me over. Mick jumped up and pumped my hand effusively.

"Hey there, Emily, how you doin'?"

"Hi, Mick." I pulled my hand away as gently as I could without seeming rude. I turned to Irene. "Hi, Irene, how are you?"

"Just peachy," she said between drags of her cigarette. "Have a seat, honey, you can play me just as soon as I whip this kid's ass and take all his money."

"I'll be the one takin' your money. Unless of course you cheat again," Mick said, taking his seat.

"Crybaby," Irene said. She moved a red marker over two of the black ones. Mick shook his head in disbelief.

"Thanks, but I think I'll pass. Looks like you're a bit of a shark there, Irene," I said.

"Well then, sit down and have coffee with us."

Mick jumped up again. "I'll get you one, Emily."

I really didn't want coffee because my nerves were already on edge, but I didn't want to refuse him. As soon as Mick was out of sight, Irene plucked two more black checkers off the board and shifted two red ones in their place. When she was satisfied with the new configuration, she leaned across the table. "I win the kid's money from him and then buy him stuff he needs," she said in hushed tones. "Otherwise he just pisses it away or gives it to some low-life."

I thought about Ken taking Mick's money. "Does Ken do the same thing?"

She looked over her shoulder and around the room. "Yeah, but you didn't hear it from me."

"That's nice of you to do that for him."

"Not really, but it's necessary. That kid would give his ass away if it weren't attached. You watch, he'll run down the street and find the most expensive cup of coffee in the city. So anyway, what brings you down to my private club?" Before I could answer, she added, "Oh yeah, and when am I gonna get my turn in that study of yours? I could use a few extra bucks right about now."

"Actually, that's one of the reasons I'm here," I lied. I dug my wallet out of my knapsack and handed her a twenty-dollar bill. "I'm not going to be doing much of that any more, but policy is you get paid anyway." In fact, I thought, if Mullarcant finds out about that fax any time soon, I may not be doing anything at USA for the rest of my life.

"You're full of shit, you know that?" Irene said. She snatched the money from my hand and stuffed it into her shirt pocket. "Listen, Emily, I'm gonna let you in on a little secret," she said, sounding an awful lot like Ken. "Just because we're a little down on our luck doesn't mean we're all stupid." She lit a cigarette and blew a long stream of smoke out of her facial cavities and into my face.

I felt my cheeks flush. "Sorry, I didn't mean ... I just wanted ..."

"Yeah, yeah, forget it. And when Mick gets back, don't try and pay him for the coffee, just say thanks, and maybe get him next time or something." I felt as though she had crawled inside me and unearthed a dark secret. But then her voice softened and she said, "Listen, honey, don't mind me, I get a bit cranky now and then. Do-gooder types kind of get under my skin."

"I didn't know I was one."

"You are when you're giving out twenty-dollar bills."

"I just wanted to do something." I rested my chin in my hands and let out a long sigh. "I've been having kind of a bad day."

"Let's hear about it, and I'll tell you if it's bad or not." I didn't want to tell her for a hundred reasons, not the least of which was that I knew anything I'd have to say would sound insignificant next to her troubles. But if I didn't tell her, I'd run the risk of pissing her off again. Sometimes I think too much, I told myself.

"I just found out this guy I've been seeing had been seeing a friend of mine."

"That friend wouldn't happen to be dead now, would she?" I studied Irene's lined faced while I let her words sink in. She put her fingers to her temples. "Wait, I'm getting something. I'm a bit psychic, you know. Was her name Beth?"

"How did you know?"

"Me and Kenny figured it out the other night. We knew Beth was seeing someone and she was all bent out of shape over it. And when Ken told me about your little problem with the paper and that you were seeing that Mark Gunn guy, I just put two and two together."

"Ken told you about the paper?"

"We go back a long time, honey. But don't worry, it stays with me."

"Irene, what happened with Ken?"

She took a drag of her cigarette and blew a chain of fluffy smoke rings into the air above my head. "You mean why did he blow off the professor thing?" I nodded. "Ken never belonged at that university. It sucked the life out of him. Only thing he got any joy out of was the students and some of his research. But that bastard sucked that away from him too."

"Who?"

"Your boss."

"Mullarcant?"

"Yup. Him."

"But they were in completely different areas." An image flashed in my mind of Sandra Penny ducking into her office when Ken greeted her..

"That's not for me to get into. Kenny can tell you if he wants to."

"Did you know him back then?"

"You ask a lot of questions, don't you?"

"Sorry."

"I guess it really doesn't matter. Yeah, we knew each other back then. Met at a bar. I was bartendin' and trying to keep myself from gettin' killed by my sick freak husband, and Kenny was bein' my white knight. He was also being a cheatin' asshole on his wife and his kids. And I told him that." She took another drag off her cigarette and then stubbed it out. "But shit happens,

I guess. Anyway, Ken was real bright. Do you know that he went to Harvard?"

"Yes. I did know that."

"Yeah, well, his parents thought they were doin' him a huge favor. So they gave the family farm to Ken's brother and sent Kenny off to a fancy school. Worse punishment they could have ever dished out."

"Why, because he wanted to stay on the farm?"

"Yes ma'am. And I'll just bet you find that pretty hard to believe, don't you, Emily? I'll bet you're thinking what everyone else figured back then, that all those brains of his would be wasted growing Idaho spuds. Boy, they sure were right, weren't they? Now he's got all this," she said and spread her arms to take in the splendor of the room. "Life is stupid, Emily, and the sooner you and everyone else figures that out, the easier it'll get." She lit another cigarette, the last one in the pack.

"Anyway, let's get back to your problem. I don't want to talk about Kenny's shit any more. So we were right. Both you and Beth have been bedded by this Gunn fellow."

"Not quite both of us."

"What's wrong? Haven't let him get to third base yet?"

I decided to ignore the last comment. "Does Mick know about any of this?"

She gave a derisive snort, and apparently decided not to push it. "No, and we don't want him to either, okay?"

"Don't worry. I'd rather no one knew."

Mick came bounding back with two large cups of coffee and a paper bag under his arm. "Chocolate Amaretto," he said proudly and placed one of the coffee cups in front of me. "I got about twenty creams too and lots of sugar. Ken was telling us how you like flavored coffee with all kinds of stuff in it." I'll bet he was, I thought. "I like the flavored ones too," Mick chatted on. "But Ken and Irene only like the normal stuff. Right, Irene?"

"That's right, Micky. We leave that flavored stuff to the kids."

"Thanks, Mick. I love Amaretto."

"I figured so," he said happily stirring his coffee with his finger.

"What ya' got in the bag, Mouse?" Irene asked.

Mick rolled his eyes and turned to me. "I told her a million times to cut it out, but she never listens." Irene sat back and sipped her coffee, pretending not to hear him.

"Why Mouse?" I asked.

"Micky Mouse," Mick said with a disgusted look. "But Ken calls me Rat, which I prefer. Right, Irene?"

"Right. What's in the bag?"

"Oh yeah, I got you a present." He dug into the bag and pulled out a carton of cigarettes. He went to hand them to Irene, but stopped just short of her reach. "I'm only going to give 'em to you if you promise not to call me Micky or Mouse any more, okay?"

"Yeah, yeah, whatever," she said, grabbing the cigarettes. "What'd you do, go and spend all the money I'm going to win off you?"

"Nope, I got other money too."

Irene looked at the cigarettes and then back at Mick. "Is that so, Micky. And where might you have come into this money?"

"It's a secret."

"Well, it better not of come from where I think," she said in a stern voice.

"I told you I don't do that no more. Jeez, and stop calling me Micky, you promised." He looked at the checkerboard. "Hey, you moved these, Irene." He turned to me. "Emily, did you see her move these?"

"Yeah, as a matter of fact I did." Irene shot me a look. "What am I going to do, lie to him? You just gave me hell five minutes ago for lying to you. Besides, he just bought me a coffee. A really good coffee." One side of Irene's mouth curled into a grin.

"I knew it. I'm going to have to watch you a whole lot closer from now on," Mick said. "Who's move is it?"

"Mine," Irene said, and then proceeded to clear off three more of Mick's black markers.

Ken appeared beside me, holding a cotton ball to the inside of his arm. He looked paler than usual and his hands were trembling. "Ah, Number One Experimenter," he said in a halting voice. "To what do we owe this pleasure?"

"I was in Chinatown—"

"And thought you'd drop by to join us for a mocha cappuccino."

"Actually," I held up the cup, "it's chocolate Amaretto."

"Hi ya, Ken," Mick said without looking up. "I got something for you, since you had to get a needle today. But don't open it in here." Ken sat down next to me with the bag. He peeked inside it and let out a long whistle as he extracted a bottle of Glenfiddich scotch.

"Put that away or we'll all get kicked out," Irene snapped. Ken took a quick look around and then slipped the bottle back into the bag. "Thanks, Rat."

"Okay, Irene, I'm not playing with you any more," Mick said. He collected the board and markers. "I'm gonna go play with Rod and them guys. See you later, Emily."

"Thanks again for the coffee, Mick. I'll get you next time." He nodded and moved to another table where two men were playing checkers and a third was watching.

"Where do you suppose he's getting the money for this stuff?" Irene said. She held up the carton of cigarettes to Ken.

"I have no idea, and at the moment I really don't give a damn because I need some lunch before I fall down here. Anyone want to come?" I said I would, and Irene said she'd catch up with us in a few minutes. As soon as we were out on the street, Ken twisted the paper around the neck of the bottle, screwed off the cap and lifted the bottle to his lips. "Ha! that'll separate the men from the boys," Ken said and then drew a sleeve across his mouth.

"And burn a hole in your empty stomach," I said.

"Don't pick me, kid. I'm in no mood." He took another couple of swallows, each one returning more color to his face. "Damn, that's good stuff. I used to drink shit like this all the time at the faculty club. And the best part was it was cheap there too. Well, compared to normal bars, anyway." He rubbed his cheek. "I feel all aglow."

"You do have a little more color."

"I call it my Irish tan." He held up the bottle like a trophy. "When you got this, who needs the sun? So what brings you around today, Ms Scientist?"

I was about to ask myself that same question, I thought wearily. "Some things have happened," I said as we turned the corner to the Royal York Hotel.

Every city in North America has a Royal York Hotel that appears in various incarnations. The exterior is usually painted a salmon pink or weird green color perennially splashed with bodily fluids. On weekends, these establishments fuel the legal system with myriad assault charges, drunken behavior infractions, along with various and sundry drug offenses. These are the places you drive by and peer at every day, and you never dream of stopping in.

"I thought we were going for lunch," I said as I followed him into the dingy, smoke-filled bar.

"We are. I'm going to have a dozen or so barley and tomato sandwiches and you can have whatever you like." We made our way down the length of the room past pool tables, video machines, and old men sipping glasses of draft beer and smoking roll-your-owns. "And, uh, listen," Ken said over his shoulder, "don't go asking for anything fancy, okay? Just order something normal like a beer."

I shot a look to the back of his head. Yeah, I wouldn't want to embarrass you in a place like this, I thought. We took a seat at the back of the bar. Ken ordered four draft beer and two tomato juice. I wanted something with a little more sustenance, but the only items on the menu were chips, and those horrible pickled eggs suspended in cloudy liquid that reminded me of biology class pig fetuses swimming in formaldehyde. I settled on the chips and a bottle of beer—"No glass, thanks."

When the beer and juice came, Ken downed his first two "barley and tomato sandwiches" in about thirty seconds. He wiped his mouth with the back of his hand, and with a satisfied belch leaned back in his chair.

"Okay, so what's going on?"

"Another student committed suicide yesterday."

He let out a soft whistle. "Friend of yours?"

"No, I only met him once in the lab. His name was Derrick, a participant in the study. Undergraduate in his last year. He was trying to get into the program next year."

"He tell you that?"

I nodded. "He'd been in before Christmas. Beth and Mullarcant ran him through the first phase, the gassing stuff. And then on Monday I put him through the Milgram phase."

Ken put his hand in the air and made a circular motion with his finger to indicate he wanted another round. I was going to tell him not to get another beer for me, but figured I probably needn't worry about it going to waste.

"That the one Mick did, the video thing?"

"Right."

"So what do you think all this means, Number One Experimenter?"

"I don't know, but Derrick said something that got me thinking. He said he was going to be working for Mullarcant on another phase of the study. I have no idea what he was talking about and neither does Zac."

"So now maybe you don't think I'm so full of it any more. I knew damn well there was more to this whole stinking business," he said. He looked around impatiently for the waiter.

I heard a muffled voice behind me. I turned to see a little man in a dark suit shuffling toward the table next to ours. "Sorry, pal, that's taken," Ken said. The old guy didn't even bother to look up, he merely continued to mumble softly, and then shuffled back to where he had just come from.

I turned back to Ken. "That wasn't very nice. What'd you think, that he's one of Mullarcant's spies?"

"I like my privacy."

"Apparently."

The more Ken drank, the more together he seemed to get. His hands no longer shook, and his speech was controlled and articulate. The street-talk slang fell away, and for a moment I could see the academic.

"I'm beginning to think maybe you're right that there is more going on. And the other thing I found out today—" I paused. "Well, I guess you and Irene already figured it out." I lowered my eyes and felt my throat tighten. Ken pushed my beer toward me.

"Here, take a swallow." I did as he said. "Irene and I just kind of put it all together. Look, kid, the guy's an asshole, Okay? So bonus for you. You found out before you did a swan dive out the bathroom window."

"What's that supposed to mean?" Before I got an answer, the waiter appeared with a tray of beer and placed it down on the table over the bills and loose change from our first round.

"Christ, I thought we were going to die of thirst here," Ken said. The waiter looked around impassively as though he hadn't heard Ken's remark. He was a big man, in his early fifties, I guessed, with the face and expression of a man who had been working in places like this since he was old enough to drink.

He picked up his tray and said, "That's seven-fifty."

"Nice try, asshole," Ken said, and peeled two bills off the bottom of the waiter's very wet tray. The waiter said nothing; he merely collected the money he was owed and left.

"Hey, that's a dirty trick," I said.

"You don't get out much, do you, kid? Anyway, as I was saying, I knew there was more going on in that psycho psychology lab of yours." He took another haul on his beer. "So what are you going to do now?"

"I have no idea, and I'm not even sure why I'm telling you all this."

"Well, you better figure it out, and quick, because you need a plan—an action list."

"An action list?" Just then it occurred to me that maybe I was being duped by a guy who had an axe to grind with the university, and apparently with Mullarcant in particular. "Okay, Ken, how about the first thing I put on that list is you. Why don't you tell me why you're so interested in this whole thing?"

He studied me for what seemed like a long time, and I felt the tingle of icy fingers go up my spine. He narrowed his eyes at me. "I'll tell you why I'm so goddamned interested. It's because people like you come down here and wave a few bucks in our faces, and then you hook us up to some machine that sucks the fucking air out of our lungs. And believe me, you and your friends aren't the only ones doing it to us. Know what they were doing over in the medical arts building last year? Been over there lately?"

I shook my head.

"Oh that was a good one. They injected us with some shit that made us feel like we'd gone to hell and back, just another creative way to induce panic. Using people like us ain't a novel concept, kid. I'm sure in your psychology 101 class you learned all about the—" he made the sign of quotation marks in the air, "studies that they got the guys in jail to participate in, and those poor souls in mental hospitals. Oh, and let's not forget the poor bastards in the army. Now, there's where they got real creative. Ever been pumped full of LSD and left alone in a room for a couple of days?" His face was flaming, and there was spittle in the corners of his mouth.

"You're right, those studies were horrible. But they happened years ago. They don't do them any more."

"And just what the fuck do you think you're doing when you put that mask on someone like Mick?"

I knew it was pointless argue the benefits of such studies. And the truth was, I wasn't even sure I could. Ken drained another beer and slammed the empty glass on the table.

"That's why I'm so goddamn interested. And maybe that's why you should be too. Two kids are dead, Emily. Two kids who were both associated with that lab of yours. Beth had her name on papers she didn't write, she was seeing that asshole Gunn, and so are you. Gee, I don't know, Emily, but I'm beginning to see a pattern here."

"Okay, Ken. Nice speech on the ethics of human experimentation, but you left out the part about you and Mullarcant. I know something happened, so why don't you start being straight with me and tell me about that."

Ken's nostrils flared as he stared a hole right through the center of my forehead. "And why don't you start by getting off your high fucking horse, Ms Scientist, and start figuring it out that I'll tell you whatever the fuck I feel like telling you."

I felt a presence behind me and turned to see Irene leaning against a video game. She gave me a wink. "Don't let him get to you too much, honey. Bark's worse than the bite." She moved over to the table and took a seat next to Ken. Ken motioned for another round and I pushed my second, untouched, beer toward Irene.

I weighed my options. I could just tell this drunken ass to take a flying leap, but I needed him. He knew something. In fact, my sense was that he knew a lot. I swallowed my desire to tell him to go to hell.

"Okay, I agree there's a pattern."

"Well, hallelujah."

"Ken, I'm not an idiot. I did come to talk to you about this. And I did send the fax to the journal like you suggested."

"Good. Because there was another one, you know."

"Another what? Paper?"

He shook his head slowly, not taking those penetrating eyes off me. "Another student. Suicide."

"No, when? Who?"

"Twenty years ago. Girl by the name of Christine Stevens. Another one of Mullarcant's."

"Really," I said, letting the news sink in. "But twenty years is a long time."

"Not if you're Christine Stevens. She would have been in her early forties now, probably just at the height of her career."

"You're right. It was a stupid thing to say. I just meant it was so long ago, I can't see there being a connection. It's probably just be a coincidence."

"Probably," Ken said. Not believing it for a second.

"So what are you going to do, honey?" Irene asked.

"Two things. First, I'm going to have a talk with Jerry Booth. I was thinking about him while Ken here was yelling at me before. The last time he was in the lab was the day before Beth died, and there was something strange going on between him and Mullarcant. I didn't think anything of it at the time, but now I'm beginning to wonder. And didn't you tell me Jerry was the one who suggested you three do the study?"

Irene lit a cigarette. "Sort of. He talked Micky into doing it. So me and Ken went along."

"But we knew about it through Beth," Ken added, "and a couple of Jerry's buddies, Norm Sager and Jack Landers. Ever meet them?"

"No. But I may have seen them in the lab or seen their names on the lab reports." I took out a pen and notepad and flipped it open to a clean page. "I think I'll have a chat with Jerry. And who did you say the other two guys were?"

"Jack and Norm, but they're not around any more," Ken said.

"Not for two or three months at least," Irene added. "In our neighborhood people tend to move in and out a lot."

"That just leaves Jerry, then. Do you think Jerry will be at the center today?"

"Normally I'd say yes, but he hasn't been around this week, as far as I know."

"And good riddance too," Irene said. "That little weasel was a thief and a liar. And so were those other two half-wits."

"Do you know if any of them are still in the city?"

"Haven't got a clue. Jerry said some shit about going some place hot for the winter," Ken said.

"Yeah, well, it was getting pretty hot for him at the center," Irene said. "He probably only made it as far as Vancouver, and I'd bet my last dollar, which he stole from me, I might add, he hooked up with those other two."

"Were they friends?"

Ken snickered. "Like they say in the movies, guys like that don't have friends, they only have associates."

"Oh," I said and arched my brow.

"No one could prove it for sure, but everyone knew they were stealing from everyone else," Irene explained. "Wallets would go missing regularly, and then turn up a few days later, but without the cash, of course. It was getting to be kind of a joke. When they left, it stopped. But then started again just recently. Since Jerry hasn't been around this week, guess what?"

"It's stopped again."

"You don't have to be a genius to figure who's been doin' it. 'Course people still steal stuff, but it's more normal again."

"That's right," Ken said with a laugh. "If some asshole steals your wallet now, you know it's not coming back."

I had no idea what significance, if any, this had, but I had a feeling there was a connection. "Would Marjorie know where these guys are?"

Irene exchanged a look with Ken. "Doubt it, she's been pretty tied up lately, planning her daughter's wedding. Probably hasn't had too much spare time to keep track of her clients, as she likes to call us."

"I may as well give her a try."

"So what's the second thing?" Irene asked.

"Sorry?"

"You said there were two things you were going to do."

"Oh yeah, the second is I'm going to tell Mark to go to hell." Just as soon as I said it, I knew I really didn't mean it. In fact, at that moment, I didn't know what to think or what I meant.

Irene put her head back and let out a throaty laugh. "Good for you, Emily. Let the bastard have it."

"Wait a second," Ken said. "Not that I wouldn't love to see you do it, but why don't you just hold off for a day or two?"

"Why? You were the one who just said he was an asshole," Irene snapped.

"And speaking of that, why do you keep calling him an asshole, Ken? You don't even know him."

Ken belched. "Lucky guess," he said. He turned back to Irene. "I think she might be able to get some info out of him if she doesn't let on she knows anything yet."

"Which shouldn't be too hard, since I really don't know anything."

"And if she does tell Gunn that she knows about him and Beth, and the papers, he might go straight to Mullarcant. Unless, of course, Mullarcant didn't know about the relationship."

"Hey, maybe that's it, you guys," I said seeing a bright spot.

"What's that?"

"Maybe that's why he didn't tell me. Maybe he didn't want anyone to know. Maybe we're not thinking this through clearly. We're pointing the finger at Mark and maybe he's not to blame at all. We don't know what the circumstances were between him and Beth. There wasn't anything wrong with it. Maybe they were just going through the usual stuff."

"So why didn't he tell you about it, then?" Irene asked.

"I don't know, to protect her. I know her parents wouldn't have been too thrilled about the arrangement."

Ken was shaking his head. "And what about the papers? He sure as hell knew about those. That his way of protecting her too?"

"I don't know about that, either. But I think you're right, Ken. We need to find out more before we point the finger at him."

"Oh, don't get me wrong, kid, I am pointing the finger at him. I just figured we could use him. Don't go twisting my words to suit your hormones."

"I know you don't want to hear this, but he is a very nice person."

"Holy shit, here we go," Ken said.

"What happened to telling him to go to hell?" Irene asked.

"I think I need to find out a little more before I completely write the poor guy off."

"Now he's the poor guy. What happened to the asshole?"

"Your word, not mine." I wasn't in the mood to argue the point any further. "I'm going to have a talk with Marjorie and see if she knows anything about Jerry and the other guys. I'll get back to you guys later," I said.

"Give Mark a kiss for me," Ken said.

I marched off toward the front door, but stopped just as I was about to push the handle. I turned around and then marched right back to the table.

"Forget something?" Ken asked.

"Yeah, I did. At a the risk of getting my head chewed off again, I'd like to ask you three things."

"You always carry lists around with you, don't you, Emily?"

I didn't bother to answer, and launched into my first question. "Did Beth know who you were?"

"Yes," he said it without hesitation.

"But you told me at the donut shop that she didn't know who you were."

"I lied."

"Okay. Second question. Are you ever going to tell me what happened between you and Mullarcant?"

"Some other time, you're in a hurry now. And your nickel's running out. So tell me, what's your third wish?"

"How did you know I was seeing Mark?"

He shrugged. "Something you said."

I knew he was lying.

Chapter 20

THE BRIGHT SUN SHOCKED MY EYES when I stepped out onto the street. There's always something disconcerting about being in a windowless bar in the middle of the afternoon, where time seems to meld into one interminable midnight hour. They probably build those places with that very intention in mind.

As I walked back to New Beginnings, I felt the rush of excitement I get when I'm about to do research. Not the kind of research I was doing in Mullarcant's lab, but the kind where I have to search the library and archives to find just the right thing. Hey, maybe if this psychology thing doesn't work out, I'll look into becoming a private investigator or a librarian, I thought. I wonder which one pays more?

Mick was still at the center playing checkers when I crossed the foyer to the reception desk. Heidi, the receptionist, recognized me and sent me straight back to Marjorie's office. Her door was open and I could see she was poring over a magazine with a white wedding cake on the front cover. I knocked softly, and looked forward to watching her scramble to put the magazine away. But she disappointed me when she summoned me in without even looking up. She eventually put the magazine down, but not before she marked the page with a sticky note.

"Yes, Eleanore, what can I do for you?"

I knew what she was doing. It's a passive aggressive thing stupid people do to piss off other people when they can't think of anything more creative.

"Hi, Marion." Okay, so I'm stupid too. "Sorry to bother you, but we're doing follow-ups on some of the study participants and I wanted to okay it with you first."

"It's Marjorie," she said through a tight smile. "Martin didn't mention anything about this to me."

"Oh, it's just routine so he sent me to do it." I thought being self-effacing might please her. I was right.

"Yes, well, we are busy people."

"I'll just need to talk to— Let's see," I flipped to the page in my notebook where I jotted down the three names, "Jerry Booth, Jack Landers, and Norm Sager."

"Well, that's a problem, Eleanore, because as far as I know Jack and Norm haven't been in here for quite some time, and Jerry seems to have disappeared too," she said, pleased with herself.

"Do you know where I might be able to contact them? And it's Emily."

"Right, Emily. Sorry. I don't think you understand something, so let me try to explain it to you. Our clients share with us only what they wish. We provide a warm, comfortable place for them to come for a nice cup of coffee, to see some friendly faces, and to receive medical and dental attention, all with a no-strings-attached policy. We don't care where they come from or why they are here. They just are."

"Right. I just thought you might know where I could reach them."

"My only suggestion would be to try the Mission Street Shelter. I know Jerry sleeps there, and I think the other two may have as well."

I thanked her and left her to her magazine. On my way out, I looked for Mick in the foyer but couldn't see him. Just outside the main front doors, three or four teenagers were huddled together, talking and smoking cigarettes. When I tried to pass, a young woman who looked no more than fifteen stepped in my way.

"Excuse me, ma'am." Ma'am! "Could you spare some change?" she said, flashing a winning smile. "I need it for busfare home." She held her cigarette down at her side as if trying to hide it. I dug through my coat pockets and came up with a gum wrapper, an old dry-cleaning receipt, and a lot of lint. I then fished out my wallet. While she waited, she combed her hand through her hair every five seconds or so, and tried to make small talk. "Did you just start working here or something?" she asked.

"No. I was meeting with Marjorie," I said and handed her two loonies.

"Hey, thanks. I've seen you around before. I figured maybe you were a social worker or something."

"Nope, just a student. I'm working on a project with some of the people here."

The door opened behind us and Tom, the social worker, came out and spoke to the group. "Okay, you guys, you know the rules."

The girl's friends moved off down the street, and the girl gave me a quick wave and said another thanks before running off to catch up to her buddies.

I was about to say hi to him, but he spoke to me as if he didn't recognize me. "Excuse me, but we don't allow panhandling out here. So please don't give them any money. It's against center rules," he added sharply. "If you wish to make a donation, then please do so, but don't give it to them directly."

I opened my mouth to say I was sorry, but apparently he wasn't interested in my apologies and was back inside before I got a word out. I made my way down to the shelter, feeling lousy. It was the second time I'd been yelled at for giving money away.

By the time I entered the shelter's back door, I was really feeling sorry for myself. My self-indulgence passed quickly enough, though, when I got a load of the gymnasium-like room that served as bedroom, living room, and dining room to some three hundred homeless people each night.

The clock on the wall, which looked exactly like the white clocks I remembered from my high school gym class days, said it was five minutes to three, and the place was deserted. I walked between rows of neatly made cots, feeling a mixture of pity and fascination. I had never seen anything like it. Even the sun wasn't welcome here. Wooden framed windows that started about ten feet above my head looked as though they hadn't seen a drop of water or a squeegee in decades. The brightness of the sunlight was filtered out through the grime, leaving only a hazy glow across the cots and floor. The smell of old socks, damp wool, and stale booze hung in the dead air. I listened to the sound of my feet echo on the badly scuffed floors until a male voice stopped me.

"Excuse me, no one's allowed in the hall until after six."

I spun around to face a bearded and mustachioed man who would look right at home riding a Harley Hog. He wore a gray T-shirt, black jeans, and work boots. The long salt and cayenne pepper hair and shaggy beard made it hard to pin an age on him—somewhere between forty and sixty, for sure.

"Sorry, I guess I came in the wrong door." I extended my hand. "I'm Emily Goodstriker. Marjorie from New Beginnings said someone here might be able to help me."

"Okay," he said, and gave me the limp shake, which, in light of the size of the man's hands, was a blessing this time. "I'm Murray. I run the check-in. What can I do for you?"

"I'm working on a project at the university and we're trying to locate three of our study participants. Marjorie said they sleep here quite regularly."

"What's their names? I got a pretty good head for names."

"Jerry Booth, Norm Sager, and Jack Landers.

"Nope, if they're the Jack and Norm I'm thinking of, they haven't been around for a dog's age. But Jerry, he's a regular. Only I don't recall seeing him for the last day or two, either. Let's go back out front and I'll check my records."

I followed him out to the front to a high counter stacked with blankets, pillows, and sheets. "I'll just need to see some ID, so I can make a note of who you are and all that." I gave him my

driver's licence before he slipped into a back room. Within a couple of minutes he was back with a computer print-out. He handed
me back my licence. "Monday was the last night he was here."

"This past Monday?"

"Yeah, the twenty-second, says so right here," he said, pointing a kolbassa-sized finger at a line of type.

"Do you have any idea where he might be staying now?"

"Not a clue. But I expect he'll be back. Been sleeping here for
about two years."

"I don't suppose any of them left a forwarding address?"

He pulled a face.

"Just thought I'd ask."

"Half the time we don't even know a person's last name.
Especially if that person don't want to have a last name, if you get
my meaning. But wait," he snapped his fingers, "Jerry did say
something about getting a job a while back. Said he was going to
make some good cash working for the government or something.
I just figured he was full of shit, but hey, who knows."

"Did he mention anything more specific?"

"Not that I remember, but if you come back tonight there's a
guy here who hangs out with Jerry, name's Zip."

I wrote down "Zip" in my notebook. "Does he have a last name?"

"Imagine he does. Listen, I got to get some things ready for
tonight," Murray hefted an industrial-sized laundry bag over his
shoulder.

"Sure. I'll get out of your way, then. Thanks for your help.
What time should I come by tonight?"

"Any time after six," he said over his shoulder. "Zip's always
here by six-thirty or seven."

"If I don't come tonight, I'll be by tomorrow, if that's all right?"

"Whatever," he called out from the back room.

"Thanks again," I yelled, but there was no reply. I was interested in this government job of Jerry's. Maybe this Zip guy
would know something about it. I decided it would be helpful to
be prepared for my meeting with Zip, so I headed back to school
to take a look at Jerry's file. When I got to the lab, Mullarcant

was standing by the window in Beth's office, going through a file.

"Ah, Emily, your timing is impeccable. I just came down to speak with you. I see you are getting settled in. I do apologize for the mess."

"Are you still looking for the Aspen 45 file documents?"

He hesitated before he answered. "Uh, yes," he said.

I wasn't convinced as I took in the mess around me. If Mullarcant had done this, he was developing a new, fourth face. Because none of the Martin Mullarcant personalities I knew would never conduct a random, messy search. He would have gone through each file with the methodical precision of a tax auditor.

"I do intend to clean up this mess today," he said. "In the meantime, let me know if there is anything you need. And Emily, I hope we can put that whole unfortunate matter about the paper behind us and carry on with our work."

I felt the moisture forming in my armpits. Guilty consciences make perspirers of us all. "Thanks. Uh, sure, yeah, I'm sure we can," I stuttered.

He looked at me kindly, and then he winked. I turned away and gave an involuntary shudder. Thankfully, I still had on my coat. He placed the file he was holding on the desk and pulled the chair out for me. I took a seat and immediately saw the name "Irene Benner" typed across a standard lab-assessment form. "I want you to contact this subject this afternoon. We have a paucity of data on women and I believe this is remiss on our part. Wouldn't you agree?"

I thought about poor Carmen. "Uh, I suppose so."

"I'm in a hurry for this, so please set up an appropriate time to run her through both phases, the sooner the better. Do you have any questions?"

"Will we be running Ken as well?" There was a pregnant pause. I kept my head down.

"Possibly." He said it slowly. "Did you know he was once a member of this faculty?"

I was staring at the forms in front of me. All the information was there: Irene's birthdate, height, weight, social insurance number, previous employers, number of times in rehab, previous arrests—there had been two, both for drunk and disorderly behavior. Further down the page where it said "number of dependents," there was a "2" typed beside it.

"Emily, I asked you a question?"

"Sorry, I was just going over this. Yes, I just learned that the other day." I looked up at him. His face was wearing an expression of someone pleased with himself.

"Do you have any questions or concerns, or can I expect you will have this completed before the weekend?"

"I'll do my best to get her in here by tomorrow."

"Good. I'll expect you to report back this afternoon, then." He turned to leave and then hesitated. "It's a shame you didn't mention you were dropping by New Beginnings today. It would have saved you making two trips." He glanced at his watch and then left.

He knows! And he's toying with me. Marjorie told him I had been there. But did she say I was asking about Jerry and the other two guys? Of course she did. Then why didn't he ask me about it? Oh God, am I letting my imagination run away on me again? Have I blown everything out of proportion? I held my head in my hands and leaned on the desk. Maybe I'm just being overly dramatic, and I'm letting people like Ken and Grandma Wong get the better of me. Mullarcant must think I'm some kind of nut. Then I thought about the papers with Beth's name on them. Whatever else he may or may not be doing, those alone were wrong. I slipped Irene's file into my bag and went to the file room to grab Jerry Booth's file.

I PARKED ACROSS from the Royal York in one of those outdoor lots where you have to put about a dozen quarters in a machine before it spits out a ticket. On my way into the hotel, I spotted Mick coming out of the restaurant at the side of the building. He held a burger in one hand and a milkshake in the other.

"Hi, Emily," he said through a mouthful of burger.

"Oh hi, Mick, I was just going in to see Ken and Irene."

"You won't find them in there," he said, motioning to the bar-room door.

"Oh? Do you know if they went back to the center?"

"Nope. You want me to show you where they are?"

"Sure." We walked down Eighth Avenue Mall, past stores, buskers, and panhandlers. Every so often Mick dropped a quarter or loonie into an outstretched hand or hat. We stopped to listen to a guy, a regular along the outdoor mall, belt out opera tunes. Mick and I both dropped toonies into his hat before we turned off at First Street and entered a part of Calgary I believed existed only in other, larger North American cities.

The back alley was strewn with garbage, scrap lumber, and industrial waste bins in various states of dilapidation. We passed worn, dirty mattresses, littered with syringes and used condoms, that were pushed up against soot-covered walls with a disquieting sense of permanence.

We stopped at the back of a low brick building and looked up a wrought-iron fire escape about six feet above our heads that curled at the top of the building. To our right, someone had strategically parked a shopping cart full of bottles and cans, and green and black garbage bags.

"Looks like they're home," Mick said, glancing at the cart. He handed me his milkshake, and then hiked himself up the ladder and disappeared over the top. I looked around nervously as I waited at the bottom for him. I wasn't sure what I was looking for, and I felt foolish standing there. Mick popped his head over the edge and yelled down.

"Yup, they're here. Coming up, Emily?"

"Okay," I said hesitantly. "But I'm not sure I can get up this ladder."

"I'll come down and give you a hand." He skipped down each rung with the agility of a little kid descending his tree fort. He gave me a leg up, and I grabbed hold of the rails and eased myself up while Mick pushed my feet. I've never been a fan of heights, and as I negotiated each rung I felt my legs turn to rubber and that old familiar feeling of panic surge through my gut. I reminded myself not to look down and banished thoughts about how I would make it back down again.

I wriggled over the eaves onto the roof of Grey's Men's Wear, and I realized then that I was holding my breath. I stepped away from the ledge and took a couple of deep breaths. The roof was just what one would expect: snow-covered and windy. It wasn't a particularly cold day for late-February, but the chill winter wind went right through my jacket and sweater. Beside me, Mick hugged himself against the cold.

"Hey, honey, the kids are home," a voice said from somewhere to my left. A gust of wind came up and blew little tornadoes of snow around us. Mick grabbed my arm and led me to a far corner of the roof where Ken and Irene huddled together under a pile of dirty blankets. Irene's hand poked out from under the pile and passed Ken a bottle.

When I crouched down next to them, I noticed a flow of warm air coming from a duct just above Irene's head. Mick sat down at the foot of the makeshift bed and picked at the blankets absentmindedly. Ken offered him the bottle, but Mick declined with a shake of his head.

"Thanks for the gift, kid," Ken said, waving the near-empty bottle at him. Mick nodded and continued to pick lint balls off the blankets. "I'd offer you a chair but our set-tee is out getting reupholstered," Ken said with a giggle.

He was clearly drunk, drunker than I had ever seen him. And for the first time I thought I understood exactly what he was. In a bizarre way it was like visiting a slaughterhouse for the first time. It's okay to eat the stuff as long as you don't know where it comes from. And that's what it was like with Ken. I knew he was a drunk, but as long as I didn't actually have to see it to that extent, I thought I could live with it—even romanticize it. The brilliant professor who gives up on society to live among the street people. The intellectual angel, champion of the down-and-outers. But what I saw that afternoon on top of Grey's Men's Wear was a pathetic drunk who had given up on himself and everything else.

"Gimme that fucker, you hog," Irene grabbed for the bottle.

"Fuck you," Ken said, leaning away and falling over.

"Cocksucker," Irene said. She turned awkwardly to root in a shopping bag propped at her side. "Ha!" she said triumphantly, as she extracted an unopened bottle of Five Star rye.

"So wha's goin' on, Number One Experimenter?" Ken slurred.

"Maybe I'll talk with you about it later. Now's probably not a good time."

"Look, Irene, we've made her *uncomfortable*. I told you not to drink in front of the kids," he said and shook a disapproving finger at her. She laughed and put her head against his shoulder.

"Okay, I'll hide it," she said and slipped under the covers. "Fuck that. I can't see anything," she said, fighting with the blanket. I pulled it gently off her face, but she ripped it violently from my hand. "Don't you ever fucking do that again, you snotty little bitch," she hissed. I fell back on my heels and then scrambled to my feet.

"Oh, now look what you've gone and done, Irene. You've hurt her feelings."

I grabbed my backpack and started toward the fire escape. "Go to hell," I said under my breath.

"We heard that," Ken yelled after me, and then let out a roar of drunken laughter.

Mick jumped up and came after me. "Don't let them pick you, Emily, it's the booze talking. They get like this and then—"

"Turn into assholes," I finished his sentence. Mick looked hurt, and I wished I hadn't said it. "I'm sorry, I didn't mean it, Mick. I was just caught off-guard, that's all."

He nodded. "Are you going to be okay getting down on your own?"

"Sure, fine," I lied. "But do you want a ride anywhere, Mick?"

"No thanks, I'm going to stay here tonight. I don't like to leave them when it's cold like this."

"You guys aren't going to sleep here, are you?"

"We are if we don't get caught," Mick said.

"I know this is none of my business, but it's going to get a lot colder tonight. I heard it on the radio coming over here."

"Don't worry, we've done it a million times. That duct spews out hot air all night. Well, it usually does, anyway."

"Don't you think you should take them to the shelter?"

"Can't stay if you're drunk."

"But, Mick, you're not drunk."

"I know. I don't like to leave 'em when they're like this, in case they do something stupid."

Like sit on the top of a building in the middle of winter and drink themselves to death, I thought. "Well then, can I get you anything, like some extra blankets or something hot to drink?"

"Or a bedpan," Ken yelled out.

Mick tried to hide the smile on his face with his hand. I got the message. So I took a deep breath and then inched down the ladder. It was close to four o'clock when my feet hit the ground and rush-hour traffic was starting to pick up. I found a phone and left a message on Mullarcant's voicemail, explaining that Irene was unavailable. I was about to hang up and then thought, what am I doing? "Actually, she's really drunk," I said into the receiver. I hung up and felt better for saying it.

I had exactly three hours before I had to be at Mark's—one dinner date I wasn't looking forward to. But with any luck, I'd get some information out of him and the evening wouldn't be a total bust. Was that the only reason I was going? On my way back to the car, I tried to sort out my feelings. My biggest problem was that I liked him. I really liked him. Another problem was that I had been out of commission for some time. The last serious relationship I had had was with a guy in Banff three years earlier, when I took a year off from school. It had been pretty uncomplicated, as resort-town relationships tend to be. In fact, the whole thing was a lot like meeting someone on a holiday and falling madly in love for ten days. Only up there, the vacation can last for years. His name was Rob, a ski instructor. I know, how cliché. But in a place like Banff, it's pretty hard to meet anyone who isn't a ski instructor, especially if you happen to work in a ski shop. Rob and I met in the shop when he came in, looking for a new jacket. I picked out the most expensive one and gave him a fifty percent discount. Naturally, he was hooked.

About three months later, we moved in together and began performing social gymnastics in an attempt to hide the fact from my father that we were living in sin. When I moved back to Edmonton to finish my undergraduate degree, Rob stayed on in Banff. We tried to keep things going, but over the course of a year the phone calls became fewer, as did the drives back and forth. We finally decided to end it officially, and not surprisingly, there were no broken hearts. We're still good friends and provide free accommodation for each other whenever Rob comes to Calgary or when I go to the mountains. But those visits are becoming fewer and fewer.

At twenty-five and a half years old, I was beginning to take stock of my single existence, and Mark was looking like a pretty good addition. Consequently, it wasn't hard to talk myself into believing that Mullarcant was the evil one who had done to Mark exactly what he had done to Beth and tried to do to me. By the time I was driving down Sixth Avenue, I was convinced that Mark and Beth were just nice people who had had bad things done to them. And was it so bad that two nice people got together? No, of course not. Where else was he going to meet people, but at school? And then I clinched it by thinking back to that day in Mark's office, how he had been so cowed by Mullarcant. The same thing was true of Daren Oakes: he was completely run over by Mullarcant.

When I swung Ol' Blue into the driveway, I had decided not only to make the most of the evening, but I'd also decided to confront Mark about the papers and his involvement with Beth. My plan was to convince him that if we all started standing up to Mullarcant, he wouldn't be able to bully any of us any more. "That's just what I'll do," I told myself as I turned the key in the front door lock. If those papers were part of the reason Beth killed herself, then she won't be the last. And Derrick, was his suicide just a coincidence? It was time I was honest with Mark and he with me. But first I needed to get out of the jeans I was wearing and slip into something a little less comfortable.

In the foyer, I gazed up in awe at the looming figure, which had miraculously sprouted wings the size of a small aircraft. The head still looked somewhat phallic, but the wings did a nice job of averting your attention. That is, if you didn't concentrate on the big hunks of cotton strips that had fallen away and now dangled haphazardly from the wire frame, giving the thing the appearance of something unearthed from one of those teen horror movies.

"Emily, I'm in a terrible mess here," Rusty said, hurrying into the foyer with a bucket of goop. "Look at this." She held up one of the dislodged strips. "It's all coming apart. And my art instructor is coming over tonight to look at it."

"Well, maybe we can fix it up." I said and picked up a paint brush. "Okay to use this?"

She was up the ladder, smoothing out a patch of wing. "Use anything you like as long as this thing starts looking like one of God's messengers instead of the Creature from the Dark."

I stood back a couple of paces. "I don't know, Rust, I think you might be onto something here. It'd make a great security system."

She pulled a face. "A little cumbersome, don't you think?"

"You could custom make them. Apartment-size Creatures from the Dark all the way up to corporate-size."

"Very funny. Start dipping."

I dipped the brush into the bucket and gently brushed it over the fallen-away strips.

"Don't be delicate, Emily. We're in crisis mode. Just slop it on. And speaking of crisis, anything new?"

"There is indeed. But I'll have to give you the Reader's Digest version because I'm meeting Mark in about an hour."

"Well, don't let me and my apparition keep you, dear."

"That's okay, I'll help you for a while and fill you in." I told her about Derrick and then about Mark and Beth.

She put down her brush and studied me from on high. "Emily, this is very disturbing. Two students are dead, and both were involved in Mullarcant's laboratory. I know I can't tell you what to do, dear, but I do wish you would consult someone else about this. The ombudsman would be the most likely place to start, and failing that, I suggest the president himself. I also think it's time you got some legal advice, don't you?"

I knew she was talking about my father, and I had no intention of calling him. Not yet, anyway. "Rusty, I know what you're saying. But if I go to someone too soon, Mullarcant will be able to cover things up and I'll be the one who looks like an idiot."

She came down the ladder and stood in front of me. "But you already have the papers. That's proof enough."

"Is it? Think about it. It's my word against theirs. Beth isn't here to back me up, and even if she was, who's to say she would? And Mark, well, I have no idea what he'll do, but I guess I'll find out tonight."

"Oh Emily, I just hope you know what you're doing. Whatever happens, you know I'm always here."

"You're the best," I said and gave her a hug.

"Careful, dear, don't get this stuff all over you," she said, holding out her goop-covered hands. "And you better run along and get changed. Oh, but before I forget, I used that black patent purse last night and found a lipstick and a key you must have left in it. I put them in the kitchen in the little dish."

The image of Beth putting that lipstick on her lips sent a pang of sadness through me, which turned immediately to jealousy at the thought of those lips joining Mark's.

Rusty was staring at me. "What is it, dear?"

"Oh nothing, just exploring the darker side of myself again." I went off to the kitchen and retrieved the lipstick and the key from the raku dish we kept odds and ends in, like paper clips, elastic bands, and keys. I turned the heavy brass key over in my hand. It had a big, square top with the words "Swallow Mountain Lodge" and the number 12 engraved on the back. I took it back out to the foyer. "Rusty, this must be yours from a long time ago. It's a Swallow Mountain Lodge key."

"A what?"

"Swallow Mountain. It's an old ski hill on the way to Banff."

"Never heard of it. I know there's a Swallow Mountain, but I had no idea there was anything there."

"Maybe Mr. Monaghan stayed there or something, because that place hasn't been open in years."

"I don't think so, dear, Jerald didn't ski. And besides, how would he have gotten it into my purse? I bought that bag just before Christmas. Oh dear." She raised an eyebrow. "Perhaps Jerald is getting a little hot about the wine cellar and he's trying to tell me something."

"Stop it, you're scaring me."

She laughed. "And you didn't notice it in there before you went to your party?"

"No, but I didn't go through it, either. Where was it?"

"Loose in the bottom. And I know for a fact that bag was empty when I gave it to you that night. The reason I'm so certain is because I had misplaced one of my diamond earrings the night I went to dinner with Heather Baxter. That was before I lent it to you, and I went through every inch of that bag looking for it."

"I must have picked it up somewhere, then. But I sure don't remember."

"It was a difficult night, dear," Rusty said gently.

"That it was. But you know, I do remember leaving the purse with Beth in the washroom, and then someone handing it back to me later, but I can't remember who it was." It was strange how the details of Beth's last words and the sight of snowflakes floating in through an open window were burned indelibly into my mind, but the face of someone handing me back my purse was gone.

"Someone must have put that key in there, and I'm wondering if it was Beth. In the washroom that night she used my lipstick and put it back in my bag."

"But why would she have a key to a place that's been closed for years?"

"I don't know. Or then again, maybe it was the person who handed it back to me."

"And you don't know who that was?"

"I can't remember, maybe Zac or Mark."

"Ah, the good Doctor Gunn."

"Rusty, I do think he's good, and so was Beth. I just think they got caught up in Mullarcant's bullying. The same way I almost did."

"Be careful, Emily. Don't just see what you want to see."

"I know, I know, but. . . ." I looked at my watch. It was after six. "I better get going." I held out the key to her. "Would you mind hanging on to this for me?"

"Absolutely, just slip it into my smock pocket and I'll make sure it's safe. In fact, why don't we just leave it in the little dish? That way we'll both know where it is." She looked at me as though she had just remembered something. "Emily, where exactly did you say Swallow Mountain Lodge was?"

"I've never been there myself, but as far as I know it's just a few miles off the highway right after Deadman's Flats. I don't even know if there's anything left. Rob was the one who told me about it. His grandfather worked on the original building or something."

"You know, the university purchased some land around that area. Oh, let's see, it must have been ten or fifteen years ago."

"Way out there, what for?"

"There was talk of a forestry research park, and then there was talk about a conference center. But like everything else, it was shelved due to funding. Why don't I check with Hannah and a couple of my old board friends and see what I can come up with?"

Chapter 21

HALF AN HOUR LATER I WAS SITTING on Mark Gunn's brown suede couch, sipping a glass of Merlot and listening to Renata Tebaldi belt out Puccini's "Vogliatemi bene" from *Madame Butterfly*.

"Are you an opera fan?" Mark said sifting through his CD collection.

"Once in a while I go with Rusty when her opera buddy can't make it. But I really don't know one from the next. Except *Tosca*, it's Rusty's favorite."

He looked at me quizzically, "Rusty?"

"I've told you about her. I live in her house. Her name is actually Rachel, but she changed it to Rusty." I was nervous and I knew I was talking too quickly. I took a deep breath.

"Rusty, of course. I'm sorry, my mind's someplace else tonight."

Mine too. I wanted to blurt out that I knew all about him and Beth. And I wanted him to tell me that, yes, he had been seeing her, but he liked me much, much more. Oh, for God's sake, Emily, try to keep it together. Maybe he's the kind of guy who changes students to correspond with the academic calendar. Get hold of yourself.

"Does she have red hair?"

"Who?"

He gave me a puzzled look. "Rusty."

"Oh, Rusty, right. No, it's silver. Why do you ask?"

"I knew this woman and everyone called her Rusty because her hair was red." Hrrumph, must have been the one before Beth, I thought sulkily. He sat down next to me on the couch with a few CDs in his hand. My heart lurched. I've always been a sucker for magazine-guy good looks, and Professor Mark Gunn had 'em. And to make matters worse, he smelled as gorgeous as the scratch-and-sniff cologne cards that go along with them.

"You like living with Rusty?"

"It's great," I said, feeling my cheeks heat up. "She's got this incredible house up in Mount Royal. But you know that."

"Yes, of course. I'm looking forward to seeing it. Judging from the address, it must be quite a place."

"Oh it is. And Rusty's quite a person. I've known her for years. My father used to do work for her husband. She's a wonderful friend." Slow down, Emily, slow down.

"Sounds like a student's dream come true." No. I'll tell you what a student's dream come true is, I thought, gulping in his scent. I let the wine and his handsome face push any doubts I had straight to the back of my head, where they would have to stay until I was forced to deal with them in the bleached morning light.

"Cheers." I raised my glass to his.

"Cheers. To a wonderful evening." He put his glass down on the coffee table and took mine, just like they do on soap operas, and then put his arms around my waist. He brought his lips to mine and we sank back on the couch and held on to each other. He pulled me on top of him, and I felt his hands move up and down my sides. He touched my face with feather-like kisses, and I breathed him in deeply. He pulled me up gently and handed me back my wine, and I did battle in my head over whether I'd

229

say yes when he made his big move toward the bedroom. In the end, it was a moot point because his big move was to pass me a pile of CDs.

"Here, why don't you look through these and pick out a couple while I go check on dinner."

I couldn't decide whether I was relieved or disappointed. A little of both. I read the title on the first CD—*The Opera Lover's Collection*. Under it was *Turandot*, and I was pleased with myself for recognizing the name, although I didn't have a clue about the music. When I came to the third one, I couldn't read the title because there was a piece of paper stuck over it. On it someone had written, "You're being watched. Don't look up. Don't talk. Come to the kitchen." My first reaction, of course, was to look up, but as soon as I did, the part of my brain that wasn't numbed by the wine told me to keep looking through the CDs. I slipped the one with the note under the pile and looked at the fourth. It occurred to me this might be some romantic little trick on Mark's part. But with everything that had been going on, I knew it was just wishful or lustful thinking.

Mark stuck his head out the kitchen door. "Find anything worth listening to?"

I tried to stand and found that my legs had turned to jelly. "Well, I'll tell you," I said, trying to sound casual, "I recognize the titles and a couple of the names. How about we make this a committee decision?"

"Good thinking," he said, and held the door for me. In the kitchen, I didn't know what to do. I felt pale and shaky, and by the look on Mark's face it was obvious this wasn't a joke. He took the CDs from me and shuffled through them until he came to the one with the note. He held it up and put his finger to his lips. I nodded.

"Okay, let's see here now," he said loudly. "How about *Tosca*? Since you know it. I just got that new system and Prevedi and Sutherland sound fantastic. I'll go throw it on. Back in a sec." He went out to the living room, and in a few seconds the sound of Bruno Prevedi's booming voice filled the house.

When he came back, he took my hand and led me down a set of stairs that went from the kitchen past the back door and down to the basement. I flicked on the light as we descended the stairs. I still hadn't said a word. He took me over to the far end where there was a washer and dryer. The basement was unfinished and I hugged myself against the chill from the bare concrete floor. Although the upstairs of the house looked as though it had been built in the past year, the basement was testimony to the house's eighty-year history. The low ceiling and the musty root-cellar smells created a claustrophobic atmosphere, which stretched my already taut nerves.

"Mark, what's going on?" I said in a whisper.

He took a deep breath and ran his hand through his hair. "It's okay. We can talk down here. It won't be able to pick up anything."

It! My imagination was off and running. "What do you mean, it? You're really scaring me."

"I'm sorry," he said. He put his hands on my shoulders. "Look, Emily, I can't say too much."

"Oh, I think you can. I'm standing in your basement because you're telling me there's something upstairs watching me. I think you can say a whole lot. What's going on, Mark?" It occurred to me that perhaps Mark Gunn was a lunatic. I mean, how much did I really know about him? I took a quick look around to determine exactly how I would make my getaway, if the need arose.

Mark picked up on what I was thinking. "Don't worry, I'm not going to do anything. I'm trying to help you."

"Really," I moved his hands off my shoulders. "The same way you helped Beth?" I said.

He shook his head slowly. "I knew you'd find out about that. That's what I kept trying to tell him."

"Him who? Wait, let me guess, Mullarcant?"

"Who else?" he said, a look of exhaustion and resignation in his face. For a moment, I felt sorry for him. Then it finally hit me, and I covered my mouth with my hand. "Oh my God, is that who's watching upstairs?"

"No. I mean yes. Well, not exactly. It's a video camera."

"Why would you want a video of me?" Suddenly, the image of Beth and Mark together naked on the couch became as clear in my mind as if I were filming it myself. I drew back and slapped him hard across the face. He stood rock-still, accepting the blow as if he were expecting it and perhaps even grateful for it. A red welt was forming on the side of his face, and I waited for him to say something, but he bent his head and stared down at the floor like an abused mule. At that moment, all his good looks appeared as fake and stupid as the cardboard Ken dolls I used to play with as a kid.

"You did this to Beth, didn't you?" I didn't wait for his response. I already knew the answer. "What did he do, tell her he'd send a copy to her family?" He nodded and kept his gaze fixed on the floor. The sight of him disgusted me, and his cologne now offended me to the point of nausea. "Why, Mark? Were a few publications that important to you?"

"You don't understand. It's not that simple. You have to listen to me, Emily, and stay out of this. It's not just about papers, okay?" When he lifted his head, he had tears in his eyes. Which, under other circumstances, would have moved me, but at that moment it filled me only with contempt.

Then the image of me rolling around with him on the couch came to mind. "What were you going to do tonight, Mark? Seduce me and capture the moment on film? And then what? Give it to your friend as a gift?"

"Emily, he's not my friend." He stared at me with pleading eyes.

"Why, Mark? So I wouldn't talk about the paper? This doesn't make sense. Why is he doing this? Why are you doing this?"

"The *Journal* contacted him today about the fax you sent."

"Oh."

"Right, oh. Emily, why didn't you come to me?" I had no intention of dignifying his question with a response.

"Let me see if I understand this. He put you up to having dinner with me tonight and told you to make the video?

Mark nodded.

"For a little insurance? What was he going to do with it, Mark? Try to blackmail me by threatening to send it to my father?"

"Yes."

"Is this what he did to Beth?"

"Yes. He told her he'd send it to her family."

"He showed it to her the day she died, didn't he?"

Mark lowered his head.

"And you went along with all of this? My God, Mark, how could you have done this to her?"

"That's why I'm telling you now. I want it to stop. I can't do it any more," his voice cracked. "Beth is dead. Derrick is dead. My name is on papers I didn't write. Emily, I don't blame you for hating me, but you just don't understand. I'm trying to help you. I don't want to see you get hurt, like ..."

"Like Beth. Say it, Mark," I yelled.

"Yes, like Beth," he whispered.

"Well, gee, call me crazy, but based on the way you *helped* Beth, I think I'll pass on the offer, thanks."

"I really do like you."

"Shut up, Mark." I turned and started toward the stairs.

"Where are you going?"

The glorious and dramatic sounds of Puccini's *Tosca* drifted down from the living room and filled the basement, adding to the already melodramatic scene I was playing out.

"Upstairs to find that handy camcorder of yours. Then I'm going to sit down with you and you're going to tell me absolutely everything that's going on." He ran to me and grabbed my arm.

"Wait, you can't. He'll know if we turn it off. And then he'll know—"

I pulled away from him, and, in a deep, throaty voice that surprised even me, I said, "Mark, let me go and get upstairs before I smack you again."

"Emily, please, you don't understand, he's crazy. You have no idea what he's capable of."

"Oh, I think I'm getting a pretty good idea. But I'm not going to be bullied by him or you or anyone else ever again. Got it? It's time someone stood up to that little maniac."

He still had his hand on my arm, and I could see the terror in his eyes.

"Mark, for God's sake, we're talking about papers here. A few studies, that's all. And look what's happened. It's time it ended." He sat down on the bottom step of the stairs, and put his head in his hands.

"No. No. It's not just about a few studies. It's about money and power, and award ceremonies and bigger offices and respect."

"Maybe for you, Mark, but for Beth it was just about getting through."

He looked up at me with tear-soaked eyes. "Is that right? And is that all it's about for you, Emily, just getting through? Just getting the degree? Where are you headed? You aren't just getting through, you're on your way somewhere. Don't ever lose sight of that."

"Oh, save it, Mark. Where's the camera?"

"In the stereo cabinet," he said in a resigned voice.

"Good one, Mark. You were able to flip it on just as soon as I showed up. Isn't that right?" I pushed past him up the stairs.

"Wait, please just hear me out. I'm scared for you, please." Something about the desperation in his voice made me stop. I came back down and stood in front of him.

"Thank you," he said hoarsely. "I can't take this any more. All of it. I want out. Beth wanted out. We were going to go away together."

"You were both planning to go to Memorial?"

"Yes. That's why I wrote that referral letter for her, and then I talked Sandra into writing the other one."

"But you must have known how Mullarcant was going to react."

"I didn't care. I just wanted out. Beth was miserable. We both were. You have no idea what it's like having to work under him. I wanted to do my own research, legitimate research that would have my name on it."

"What about the tape, Mark? If you were so dedicated to Beth, how could you betray her like that?"

"I made a mistake. And look what it cost me."

"You? Look what it cost Beth. She had no one to turn to except—"

Mark hit the banister with the palm of his hand. "Except Ken? Don't talk to me about Ken, Emily. Yeah, he was a big fucking help. If he would have kept his big, fat mouth shut.... That ... that drunken ass." Mark's face was contorted with anger. He shook a finger at me. "And I know he's been working on you too. But you've got to stay away from him, Emily. He's dangerous."

"More dangerous than someone who was about to make a home porn movie of me?"

He stared at me with a hard, determined look. "Yes, Emily, much, much more dangerous." He said it with the conviction of a man trying to save my life.

"How would you know that, Mark?"

"Doctor Kenneth Cox was my supervisor." That took the wind out of me. "I guess he didn't bother to mention that."

"No, he didn't."

Mark was enjoying the shock he was seeing in my face, and I was sure he was planning to use it to his advantage. "I'll bet he didn't. Some time I'll tell you all about it, Emily. But right now we need to work out a plan, and you need to stay the hell away from Ken Cox."

He stood up and put his hands on my shoulders again and looked me in the eye. "Okay, here's what we'll do. We'll go back upstairs and go through the evening just like we planned. We'll have dinner, and then after, I'll say I want to make love to you." I felt like retching when he said the words. "But you say, no, that you're not ready, or make up some reason."

"Have you stepped off the edge and slipped into the deep end? Why on earth would I do that?"

"Because it's the only way he won't get suspicious. We can work together."

I shook my head. "You're delusional. I really think you need help. And I don't care what you have to say about Ken. He didn't make a disgusting video of Beth. You did."

"Emily, I'm warning you. Go ahead and hate me, but believe me, if you keep trusting Ken Cox, he will destroy you just like he destroyed Beth."

His words were getting to me. But I hung on to my instincts. "It's over, Mark." I pushed past him up the stairs.

Joan Sutherland was praying to the gods when I opened the cabinet and found the camera, which was easy to spot if you were looking for it, but would go virtually undetected if you weren't. I flicked off the power button and set it on the table, and then went back to the basement stairs to get Mark.

"Mark, I'm waiting." I called down the stairs.

Silence.

I felt a cool breeze on my feet and saw that the back door was ajar. I grabbed my coat and bag and was about to head out after him, but stopped and went back for the camera. I also collected the half a dozen or so tapes that were neatly stacked behind some old LPs. By then it was too late to go after Mark, and in a way I really didn't care. I had the feeling I probably wouldn't be seeing Doctor Mark Gunn for quite some time.

Chapter 22

WHEN I PULLED OL' BLUE OUT onto Mark's quiet, residential street, I knew exactly where I was headed. I drove down Center Street, took a right on Fourth, turned in on Seventh, and stopped in front of the Anderson Apartments on Eighteenth Avenue. I looked up to the top floor to see if Zac's lights were on. They were.

The first time I saw this building, I fell in love with it. In Alberta typically we don't let a building stand for more than a decade, but somehow this 1912 brick beauty survived the decimation of the sixties and seventies. And Zac loved to tell people how he lived in the oldest apartment building in Calgary, and how he, against all odds, was able to find one tiny corner of Calgary that reminded him of his beloved eastern birthplace.

I pressed the buzzer next to the sticker that read, "Z. Farnham." Zac answered immediately and buzzed me up.

"Hey, Em. Good timing. I just made a pot of Red Zinger, and I was thinking how much I'd enjoy a chat with someone."

"That's good because I've got a whole lot to say."

He looked puzzled, but didn't ask any questions. Instead, he made small talk while he fixed a tray. In someone else, this total lack of acknowledgment of my obvious upset would annoy the hell out of me. But with Zac it had a surprisingly calming effect. In fact, whenever I came to Zac's place, I always felt comfortable and calm. A lot of that had to do with his ability to put people at ease. But it also had something to do with his flair for decorating. When he moved in, the first thing he did was paint over those "goose-shit green walls," as he liked to call them, with a deep forest green in the living room, a sunny yellow in the kitchen, and a deep maroon in the bedroom and bathroom. He went about collecting old tables and chairs from thrift stores, sanded them down to their original wood, then finished them with a clear coat of lacquer. He had a couple of futons in the living room, and a circa 1965 vinyl director's chair he splashed with the same green, yellow, and maroon paint. Over the windows he draped lengths of various complementary fabrics. And for a grand total of nine hundred dollars, the place looked like something out of one of those chic decorating magazines. I seem to gravitate to people who have good decorating taste, probably because I myself am devoid of it.

In his flamboyant way, Zac poured the tea by holding the cup about a foot below the pot. Once he passed me my cup and was seated on one of the futons, he was ready.

"Okay, now we can begin."

"Finally. Are you sure you don't want to make some cookies or anything?"

"Look, when someone's got news, I like to be settled and have everything in place. Kind of like going to a movie."

"Zac, sometimes you drive me out of my mind."

"Drink your Red Zinger and start talking."

I looked into my cup at the bright red liquid. "Have you ever noticed you drink a lot of red stuff?"

He looked at me thoughtfully. "I've never really thought about it, but I suppose you're right. As a kid I only drank cream soda. God, that was a beautiful shade. Do they make that stuff any more?"

"Yes, but I think it's clear now."

"No wonder I stopped drinking it."

"Anyway, if you're finally ready, I'll tell you what I came to tell you."

"I'm all ears."

I started at the beginning with Beth and went slowly through almost everything. By the time I got to the paper Mullarcant put my name on, Zac stood up abruptly. "Wait a second, I'm going to write this down." This was another of his habits—making notes, lists, and little graphs, and then presenting them back for clarification. No doubt this practice would prove useful as a therapist, but as a friend it was just plain irritating. He jotted down a couple of points.

"Okay. Continue," he said.

I shook my head and pressed my thumb and forefinger against my eyes.

"What?"

"Nothing, but let's skip the graphs today, okay?" I carried on and told him what Ken had said about Beth. I neglected to tell him what Mark had said about Ken, because I wanted to leave that alone until I talked to Ken myself. I went on to tell Zac about the papers I discovered with Beth and Mark's name on them.

"Beth didn't do animal research," Zac said. "At least that's what she told me."

"Me too. But there's more, lots more." I told him about my meeting with Grandma Wong, and I ended by lifting the video camera out of my bag.

"He was taping you while you were there tonight?" Zac said incredulously.

"I switched it off myself."

"And you have no idea where he went?"

"No. But my guess is Vancouver. And frankly, I really don't care."

"Aren't you worried he'll go to Mullarcant?"

"No, he's terrified of him. Mark will concentrate on saving himself. That much I'm sure of."

"I didn't know you were seeing him. Okay, I had my suspicions but ..."

"Yeah, yeah, I imagine the whole department did. I didn't want anyone to know because, well, I guess I was a little embarrassed."

"No doubt."

"Thanks."

"Sorry, it's just that I don't know about these professor/student relationships, but if it gets a girl her own office ..."

"Zac, what are you getting at?"

"Nothing, sorry, I was kidding."

"Well, it hurt. I don't understand you sometimes."

"Sorry, Em. It's just that I don't think students should date their profs."

"Maybe we can argue the finer points of that one later. Right now I need your help." His words were still stinging.

"My help? Em, you need more than that. You said yourself Mark's terrified, and with good reason, I might add. And I think you should be too."

"You know what I think. I think Mullarcant is just this little bully who's been allowed to terrorize that department for too damn long."

"And what, you're going to be the one to stop him? Get real, Em. This is serious business."

"I couldn't agree more."

"Good," he reached for the phone. "Then tell the police exactly what you just told me. I'm in shock, Em. And to be honest, I'm having a hard time believing it. But I do believe you."

"Put the phone down for a minute, Zac. That's exactly what I'm thinking. Who's going to believe me?"

"But it's true. Isn't it?"

"Yes. But we need something more concrete. If I go running to the police now, I can just see it. They'll come in and be all apologetic with Mullarcant about having to bother him with this and blah, blah, blah. And then he'll be in a perfect position to cover everything up. And get rid of that porno tape of Beth. If he still has it."

"I see your point. But what about the papers? And what about the one he tried to pull on you?"

"It's not even published yet, and remember, I sent a fax."

"But what else can you do?"

"That's where you come in."

"No, that's where I pick up the phone again."

"Just hear me out. I have a plan. Well, an idea anyway."

Zac took a deep breath. "Why do I get the impression I shouldn't be listening to this?"

"But you are, so here's the deal. Mullarcant wants me to run Irene."

"Who?"

"Irene, she's one of the people from New Beginnings. Mullarcant wants to run her through both phases of the study."

"So?"

"So, if there's anything else going on, this might lead us to it."

"Em, I think your imagination's getting the better of you. We should put this into perspective. The only thing I can see that's going on is Mullarcant's writing papers for other people."

"Oh really? How about blackmail? I'd say getting Beth on film with Mark is a little more than just plagiarism. And another thing, you might want to ask yourself this, why is he writing papers for other people in the first place? What's his gain?"

Zac rubbed his eyes. "It's just that it's hard to . . . God, poor Beth. What an asshole."

"Assholes. Mark wasn't doing it for his own entertainment. I'll tell you, Zac, based on what Mark said, and the fact that he took off, I know there's more going on."

"I was just thinking about how upset Beth was that last day in the lab. I wonder if that was what they were fighting about when I went past Mullarcant's office. God, she must have felt so betrayed."

"Not to mention trapped. But I don't think Mullarcant showed her the tape that day. Mark said on that day Beth went to see Mullarcant about her application to Memorial."

"As if we can believe him. So when did he show her the tape?"

"The day she died. Which, I might add, was just after Beth found out Carmen had died."

"So?"

"So, I'm just wondering if there's a connection."

"She was a drunk, Emily. She torched herself. It's not a new phenomena. Shit like that happens all the time in Montreal. I think you're making too much of this. Don't get me wrong, what Mark and Mullarcant are doing is bad, but I don't think it's anywhere near as bad as you're suggesting."

"Maybe. But speaking of New Beginnings participants, do you remember Jerry Booth?"

"Sure, the skinny, nervous guy."

"Right. Do you remember when Mullarcant came in and talked to him?"

Zac nodded. "Poor old Jer was a wreck. But I wouldn't read too much into that. Mullarcant tends to have that affect on most people."

"I know, but I got the feeling he and Mullarcant knew each other."

"Jerry had been in the lab before. But now that you mention it, it was a little strange. Usually Mullarcant pretends to be human when he deals with the subjects, but that day he was his usual charming self."

"That's what I thought too. So I went down to New Beginnings and the Mission Street Shelter to talk to Jerry, and no one's seen him for a couple of days."

"People come and go in places like that all the time. Something you Mount Royal girls wouldn't know anything about."

My nerves were already ragged and Zac's last comment sent me over the top. "Zac, is there something bothering you? Did I do something, because these snotty little comments are really getting to me."

He looked down at his hands and picked at his cuticles. "I'm sorry, Emily. No. You didn't do anything. I've just got some of my own stuff going on. It's nothing compared to what's happening to you, though."

"Zac, tell me. What is this? Why does everyone feel like they can't tell me anything?" Zac cocked his head. "Beth was one of my closest friends, at least I thought she was, and she didn't tell me anything. Maybe if she had told us, we could have helped her. So if there's something going on with you, could you please let me help. Or better, let's help each other."

"I'm running out of money again. And Daddy Dearest"—Zac's pet name for his stepfather—"won't give me a cent."

I suddenly felt guilty as hell. "Jeez, Zac, I had no idea. I can help you out. I'm really sorry I came here and dumped all this on you."

"Don't be. I'm glad you came. I'll figure it out. Always do. But thanks." He smiled, but it was a weary smile. "I just need to make a few decisions."

"Please let me know if I can help. I want to."

"I know that, Em, and thanks. Anyway, we have more important things to discuss here. As I was saying, guys like Jerry Booth don't tend to stay in one place more than a month or two."

"Maybe that's true for most of them, but Jerry's been sleeping at the shelter every night for the past two years. And that's not all, the manager of the place said Jerry had been talking it up about some job he had with the government."

"Oh, Em, guys like Jerry bullshit all the time. Believe me, I met my fair share of them back home."

"I've got a feeling there's a connection somehow. Oh yeah, and there's another thing, Ken and Irene said Jerry was a thief."

"Oh now, there's a stretch."

"Zac, just because someone's a little down on his luck doesn't automatically make him a criminal."

"No, but I think it's a pretty good guess in Jerry's case."

"Is that your professional assessment?"

"No, personal."

"Anyway, it looks like you're right because Irene said wallets went missing when Jerry was around. But it stopped when he was gone. And the weird thing was that the wallets would turn up again later."

"So how does this tie in with the lab?"

"Have you ever wondered where all the subjects' personal data comes from? Have you ever filled out one of those forms yourself?"

"Of course, dozens. And so have you."

"Not for the New Beginnings subjects. Just for the students."

"That's true. I assumed Mullarcant was interviewing them, or Beth."

"So did I, but that's not the case."

"Why do you say that?"

"Because Mick said I was the only one he talked to. And I didn't take his history."

"Really? What about Marjorie, or whatever her name is? It probably comes from her."

"No way. She told me herself that half the time she doesn't even know their last names. And I'm sure that suites Marj just fine."

"So what, Em? You think Jerry was working for Mullarcant stealing wallets?"

"I'm beginning to think that. Unless Marjorie is lying. Or—hey, maybe she steals the wallets. Oh God, I hope so. But truthfully, I don't think she'd involve herself in anything other than collecting a paycheck. She probably just identifies the people she knows are alcoholics and drug abusers. And, hell, I could do that just by visiting the place."

"Okay, Em, I'm going to make another pot of tea," Zac said, picking up the tray. I followed him into the kitchen and sat up at the breakfast bar on one of the brightly painted stools that reminded me of big Smarties.

"Zac, do you remember when Derrick mentioned something about working on another project with Mullarcant? Do you have any idea at all what he might have been talking about?"

"Only the animal studies. But as far as I know, they stopped doing those before we started."

"That's all I could come up with too."

He plucked the box of teabags from the top shelf. "Now what

are you thinking, that there's some diabolical research going on that no one knows about? I'm sorry, Em, but my imagination stops there."

"Well, mine doesn't. And if you'd seen Mark tonight, I don't think yours would, either."

"Why don't we just give Derrick a call and ask him about it?"

I stared at him.

"What? I don't think it's such a bad idea. Even if he doesn't tell us exactly what—"

"Zac, he's dead."

Zac froze with the teabag in one hand and the kettle in the other. "He's what?"

"Sorry, there's been so much happening, I just assumed you heard."

"Jesus, no! I haven't heard a thing. I've been working here for the past couple of days, trying to stay out of Mullarcant's way. My God, what happened?"

"I don't know anything other than that he killed himself just like Beth."

"You mean he jumped ?"

"So Darla says."

"Oh God, Darla, the communication nerve center."

"Never mind. She's the most reliable source I've got."

"Poor Derrick," Zac said. He pulled up a blue Smartie next to my yellow one. "So you think his death is connected to Beth's?"

"It's looking pretty suspicious, wouldn't you say?"

"What about letting someone else like the police or the university president look into this? If you're right, this is big, I mean really, really big."

"At this point all the police, or God forbid the president, will do is send some committee in there that will take about a year or two to get going, and in the end"—I threw my hands up in the air—"they'll say, 'Well, guess what? We didn't find any wrongdoing. But we did find that the student who brought this to our attention is clearly a troublemaker and she is no longer attending this or any other academic institution.'"

"But if there is something big going on, the university should know about it. And aside from anything else, the papers and the tapes are big enough."

"Zac, I don't ever want to go to the president. I know how they operate. I want hard evidence that I can take to the police. And I don't have enough, yet."

"So what are you going to do?"

"You mean, what are *we* going to do. First, I'll go see Irene and see if she's willing to do the study. And if she is, we'll see where that takes us."

"What about Mark?"

"Let's call Darla tomorrow and see if she's heard anything. My guess is that Mark will have called in to say he's had a family emergency that's going to keep him away for quite some time. How about you try to set up an appointment with him?"

"Doesn't he usually make his own?"

"Tell Darla you've been trying to get hold of him and he's not answering his voicemail."

Zac put his hand on my shoulder. "Hey, Em, I'm sorry things worked out this way for you."

"Thanks. I'm just glad I didn't, you know, with him. Because believe me, I was considering it. At least he did redeem himself a bit and tell me about the camera. He didn't have to."

"Yeah, well, don't give him too much credit. He sure as hell didn't give Beth the same courtesy."

I glanced at the geometric clock on the wall over the sink. The hour hand was a triangle and the second hand an elongated blue rectangle. There were no numbers or marks to indicate the hours, and as near as I could tell it was somewhere around nine o'clock. I got to my feet and collected my things.

"Where are you going? To see Irene?"

"No. I expect Irene won't be taking any callers until sometime tomorrow. I'm going down to the drop-in shelter to see a man about —"

"A dog?"

"No. To see a man named Zip about a Jerry."

"Zip? Can I come?"

"Sure. I'll explain in the car, but we need to go before they shut the doors for the night."

IT WAS NINE-THIRTY when we walked into the Mission Street shelter, and the place was completely transformed. The check-in desk and foyer were a buzz of activity, with clients lined up a dozen deep at the counter. Zac and I took our place at the end of the line behind a burly fellow who was muttering a stream of obscenities to no one in particular. I felt someone slip in behind us, and turned to face an elderly woman who, except for the dilapidated condition of her clothes, looked as if she belonged in a children's nursery book as Grandma Good. She smiled graciously and brushed a few strands of silver hair out of her eyes.

"It's a breezy one out there tonight, isn't it?" she said in a thin voice.

"It is," I agreed, and immediately thought of Beth's friend, Carmen.

"Would you mind asking Murray to save me a place next to you, dear, when you get up there?"

I swallowed hard. "No, I wouldn't mind at all, but I'm sorry I'm not staying here tonight."

A look of disappointment crossed her face. "Oh, that's too bad. I like it better when I'm beside another woman. Maybe Anne Marie will be here," she said more to herself than to me. Zac looked back at the woman and then at me.

"My name's Emily, and this is my friend Zac," I said, extending a hand.

"I'm Alice. Nice to meet you, Emily, and you too, Zac," she said with a warm smile and a surprisingly firm grip.

"Alice, I know this is none of my business, but is it safe for you to sleep here?" She looked at me as if I had descended from another planet. "What I mean is, isn't there some other place you can go?" I felt Zac's elbow in my ribs. I ignored it. A look of panic crossed Alice's face. She went up on her toes and craned her neck to see to the front of the line.

"Why, did they run out of spaces again?"

"No, no, it's just...." It's just that I wanted to say, 'I'll take you home, Alice.'

"Nothing," I said apologetically, and turned back to stare at the big guy's back. We waited another few minutes, and I was surprised at how quickly Murray had everyone signed in.

"Next," Murray yelled from behind the desk. It was our turn. I tugged at Zac's arm to stand aside.

"Oh, thank you, dear," Alice said, stepping up to the counter.

"Hiya, Alice. Looking for a room?" Murray said. "I think I've got a nice corner suite for you tonight. Anne Marie's here." Alice thanked him and hurried off into the noisy dorm.

I reminded Murray who I was, and he told me that Zip was in bed number twenty-four. "About a third of the way down and along the back wall." As we walked through the rows of the now-occupied beds, I tried to keep my eyes on the ceiling. The room was rank with the fresh smells of damp clothes, old shoes, and stale booze. By the time we found number twenty-four I was breathing through my mouth, but the smell was so strong I could taste it.

To look at where his head lay on the pillow, you would have thought it a normal posture, but as soon as you got to the feet, you knew something was askew. Zip's knees were bent at the end of the bed and his feet were planted firmly on the ground. A quick bit of math, and I guessed him to be about seven feet tall, and, as my mother used to say, he weighed about as much as a drink of water. Zip was wearing a green denim shirt and pants like the ones janitors or gas jockeys wear. His eyes were closed, and I looked at Zac for a suggestion on what to do next, but he just shrugged. I finally took the bull by the horns and nudged Zip's shoulder.

"Excuse me," I said over the din of the place.

"Yeees," came the fully alert voice.

Zac and I both jumped slightly, which I'm sure was Zip's intention.

"Hi, uh, I'm Emily, and this is Zac," I said hesitantly. Zip's eyes remained closed. I studied his face. He was somewhere in his mid to late thirties. His skin was as pale as paper, and contrasted alarmingly with his jet-black hair. He sat up slowly, like a corpse rising from a coffin, eyes still shut tight. I was amazed at how he bent at the waist with his feet still on the ground. And into my head came the thought, that this is one lean, mean beanpole of a guy. He turned slowly toward us and then finally opened his eyes.

"Hi, I'm Emily," I said extending my hand, "and this is Zac."

"I know," he said, and lifted a long, branch-like arm to shake my hand.

"Sorry to disturb you. Hey, how did you know our names?"

Zac elbowed me. "You just told him."

"Oh." I couldn't remember telling him, but I let it slide.

"You're not disturbing me," he said in a strangely effeminate voice. "I always enjoy company, especially when it's young and pretty."

I decided to let that slide too. "The manager told me you might be able to help us. We're looking for a friend of yours, Jerry Booth."

"Jerry's been gone for a few days. Got a good job with the government."

"Do you have any idea where we might find him? Or maybe you know something about this job?"

He cocked his head and said in a soft voice, which I supposed he thought was sexy, "Now, why would I want to tell you anything about my friend Jerry? How do I know you're a friend of his?"

"We know him through the university. He was involved in a study with us. It's important we find him," Zac said with slight irritation in his voice.

Zip snapped his long, sinewy fingers, "Oh right. It wasn't the government, it was the university. That's it, the university."

Zac and I exchanged a look.

"He said he was going to work for the university?" Zac said.

Zip closed his eyes and laid his head back down on the pillow.

"Maybe, but then again, maybe not. My memory's not too good, if you know what I mean."

I took out my wallet, extracted my last twenty-dollar bill and held it over his face. "Think this might jog your memory?" His eyes snapped open and his hand shot out to the money like a gecko's tongue to a fly. But I snatched it back just in time.

"Don't wave that around here! I'll get rolled the minute you leave," he hissed.

I thought about Alice and looked around the expanse of the room trying to spot her. This was probably where poor Carmen had spent the last days of her life.

I was about to hand Zip the money, but Zac intervened just like one of those TV cops. "Not until you give us what we came for," he said. I felt a smile tugging at the corners of my mouth. I bit my lip.

"Jerry said he was going away to work on an important research project for the university. He was waving fifty-dollar bills around. Said it was his advance. I thought he was full of shit, but now that you guys are here, I guess he wasn't. He packed up his stuff a few days ago. We share a locker over at the bus depot sometimes. So I ask him, 'If you got this great job, how come you're leaving?' And then he says he has to go up to the mountains. So then I really figure he's full of it 'cus the university's right here in town. That's all I know, so give me my money."

I looked over at Detective Zac, who gave the official nod. I handed over the money. On our way out, I scanned the room for Alice and spotted her in the far back corner. A woman was sitting on the cot next to Alice's and I could see they were chatting and occasionally laughing.

"Do you want to go over and talk to her?" Zac said following my gaze.

"No. Maybe when I can actually do something for her I will."

Chapter 23

I WOKE THE NEXT MORNING with a sense of dread and a pounding headache. My spirits lifted a bit, though, when I saw the glass of orange juice and the note Rusty had left on my bedside table. The note said she was off to meet with some ex-board members and Hannah, and that she would be home later that afternoon.

I sipped the juice, mulling over what I had to do. It was just after six-thirty. My first order of business was to find out where Mark had gotten to. Was he telling the truth about Ken? And if so, then why hadn't Ken told me about being Mark's supervisor? I decided to let that alone for a bit. When the timing was right, I'd spring it on Ken and see how he reacted. Then there was Irene. My initial thought was to wait until the afternoon to go see her, but then it occurred to me that a better course of action might be to catch her when she woke up (assuming she went to sleep), before she tied into more booze. At that thought, I leapt out of bed and hit the shower.

The sun wasn't up yet, and the alley was only dimly lit by the few remaining security lights that had somehow escaped the stones, sticks, and bullets of vandals. Morning traffic inched by on Center Street, with each passing car sending beams of light like long, silvery fingers down the alley. As I stood under the fire escape, it occurred to me what a quick step it could be from where all those commuters were in their toasty warm cars to the place I was about to ascend to that morning. I thought about a story my father told me about a colleague of his: a man named Ted Allister. Mr. Allister was one of the most successful attorneys in Edmonton. He had a beautiful house in the fashionable Old Glenora area of town. His wife was a lovely woman who was involved in every charity going. They had three nice kids, all grown and doing fine. Then one day Ted came home and found his lovely wife had strung herself up in the garage. He never got over it. So Ted gave up his practice and bought a Winnebago with the intention of traveling the globe. He made it as far as North Battleford, Saskatchewan, where he sold the Winnebago, and then spent the better part two years drinking himself to death. He started out in a motel room, and then finished the job on the street.

I looked up the ladder and then down the alley. The coast was clear—of what I wasn't sure—but clear, nonetheless. I found some old wooden crates, stacked them under the bottom rung, and clenched between my teeth the Tim Horton bag I had picked up on my way over. I grabbed hold of the rails and hauled myself up to the roof of Grey's Men's Wear. Like most things, the second time was much easier.

The rising sun lit up the east sky in ribbons of pink, mauve, and gold. I thought back to the shelter, where the sun didn't seem welcome. But up there on the roof of Grey's Men's Wear, I felt as if I was part of its glory. Then a chill wind came up and brought me back to the moment and to the task of surviving. It was blowing an unusually damp cold that morning, with each gust screwing my back into little spasms.

Calgary tends to be crispy-dry all year. In the summer, the foothills are brown and wind-blown. And during the winter months, it's as cold and dry as a well-made martini. When a little moisture sneaks in every now and again, we Calgarians have absolutely no coping mechanisms.

Hugging myself against the cold, I moved away from the ledge and stood a few yards back from the makeshift bed, watching it like a Peeping Tom. The two bulges in the pile of rags and blankets were testimony to the bodies under them. It occurred to me they might be dead. Then, thankfully, the bulges moved. I heaved a sigh and went quietly to what I thought was the head of the bed. I knelt down and was about to give what I hoped was Ken's shoulder a nudge, when suddenly he sprang up from the other end of the bed, wielding a baseball bat and yelling like a madman. I screamed and stumbled back, flinging the bag with the donuts and coffee in the process.

"It's me, damn it! It's me!" I hollered.

Ken dropped the bat after enough neurons fired to let his brain know that it was, indeed, just me.

"Jesus Christ, girl! What the hell are you doing?"

"What am I doing? What are you doing?"

"What the fuck's goin' on?" a muffled voice said from under the blankets.

"It's okay, Irene," Ken said as he slumped down on the covers. He rubbed his eyes and set his elbows on his knees. He was wearing oversized, red longjohns over layers of clothing. *Heeere's Santa, with a bat and a baaad attitude.* The image made me smile.

"You know, this ain't funny, kid. I could have bashed your skull in."

I tried to salvage the donuts from the lake of coffee in the bottom of the bag. I picked out the chocolate-covered one, gave it a shake, and held it out to Ken. "Breakfast?"

He shook his head in disbelief, and plucked the soggy pastry from my hand. "Don't ever go sneaking up on people when they're sleeping." He spied the bag. "Hey, you got coffees in there?"

"Had coffees. I had coffees until you tried to bludgeon me to death." I pulled out the one cup that hadn't spilled and handed it to him. His eyes lit up, and he leaned over to give Irene a nudge. "Wake up, honey. Room service is here," he said before taking a greedy gulp of the coffee.

Irene struggled out from under the covers. "What the hell is going on?" She looked around bleary-eyed and then grabbed for the coffee.

"Hi, Irene," I said, producing a raspberry-filled donut for her. She waved it away. "Hiya, kid. Where's Micky?"

"Took off a while ago. Said he had to do some work or something," Ken said.

I was surprised at how coherent they seemed in light of the condition I had left them in the night before. Ken finished the rest of the coffee and handed the empty cup back to me.

"Okay kid, you've done your good deed for the day, so we'll be seein' ya." He reached under the covers and brought out a bottle of wine. His hands were shaking as he brought it to his lips. Not such good shape, after all, I thought.

"Actually," I said hesitantly, "I need to talk to you guys about something. I need your help."

Irene let out a laugh that turned into a rough, hacking cough. When she finally caught her breath, she said, "Yeah, well, check back in three or four days. We're on holidays here."

"That's right, we're gonna be away for a while," Ken said. He passed the bottle to Irene.

I know I sounded like a four-year-old, but I couldn't help myself. "You mean you actually plan to be drunk for four days?"

Irene giggled. "We call it our little getaways."

Ken held up the bottle of wine. Sauterne Cooking Wine was printed on the white and green label. "Yeah, but this year we're in economy class," he said. "How the hell do you think we do it? Nothing just happens, kid. You got to plan in this world." He lifted the bottle over his head to see how much was left.

"Okay, well, do you think you could plan to cut your vacation a little short? I really need your help."

Ken looked at Irene and cocked an eyebrow. "My God, Watson, she's turned my brilliant speech back upon us." Irene giggled and I couldn't help but smile.

"So before you consume that whole bottle, could you just hear me out?"

"No, 'cus we'll need to consume this whole bottle and one more just like it, so we can hear you."

While they drank to the point of functioning, I told them everything that had happened since I had seen them the day before.

"Told you, Irene," Ken said. "That bastard was packing little Beth." I shot him a disgusted look.

"Never mind him, Emily," Irene said, giving Ken a sharp elbow to the ribs. "Show a little more respect for the dead, for Christ sake." Irene was sitting up now, and after consuming the better part of a bottle she was starting to get some color back in her cheeks. "So what do you want us to do?"

"I think you might be able to lead us to what Mullarcant is really up to." I explained how Mullarcant wanted to run Irene through the study and how I hoped this might give us some answers.

"Sounds like a good plan to me," Irene said, "seein' how you already paid me. So when do you want to do it?"

"Today. This afternoon, if possible."

"Oh, I don't know, honey, I might be a little under the weather for that."

"Don't worry about it. Zac and I will only pretend to administer the gas. And we'll just fake the results. But you have to come in so it looks legit."

Ken looked skeptical. "And then what?"

"We hand the results over to Mullarcant and see what he does next. If my suspicions are correct, I don't think we'll have to wait long."

"Wait a minute," Ken said. "Won't Gunn tell Mullarcant what happened last night?"

"I don't think so," I said and crossed my fingers. "Zac's looking into that right now. By the way, Irene, did you ever talk to Mullarcant, or anyone else from the university?"

"Nope, just to you."

"That's what I thought. So what do you say? Think you can postpone the trip for a day or two?"

Ken looked around their little camp, and then at Irene. "Well, what do you think, Watson?"

"What the hell, the weather hasn't been with us this year anyway, Sherlock."

We all laughed.

After I left Irene and Ken, I stopped in at a coffee shop and grabbed a java to-go, then found a pay phone and called Zac. "It's just like you said, Em," Zac said. "Mark called in last night and left a message."

"Lemme guess, family emergency?"

"Bingo. Darla said he was going to be away for at least a week, and probably longer."

"Perfect. Irene's coming in this afternoon around one. Well, I should say her body will be in. I can't make any promises on her mind."

"Huh?"

"Never mind, I'll see you in the lab at one. And in the meantime I'll drop in and tell Mullarcant that everything's a go with Irene, and hope to God he won't want to be there when we run her."

I replaced the receiver and turned with a terrible start. A face was pressed up against the glass. Ken's face. His eyes were closed and for a moment I thought he might be dead. But then I noticed that each time he exhaled, his breath steamed up the glass. I tapped the glass and gave him a start this time. He staggered back and opened the phone booth door for me, eyes blinking as if I had just roused him from a dream.

"Come on, kid," he said. He threw an arm around my shoulder. "Buy me another cup of coffee and I'll tell you a story."

"Okay, but why don't you start it by telling me how you knew where to find me just now?"

He pointed to the heavens. I let my gaze follow his nicotine-stained index finger up to where Irene was standing on the roof of a red brick building. She was waving at us. "That's why we rent the penthouse, kid. Get a nice view of the skyline."

We traipsed down the block and over to the drop in-center

where Ken took an hour-long shower and found a change of clothes. Aside from being a little shaky and a bit on the pasty side, he looked quite dapper in this new cords and sweater vest. In fact, he looked like a university professor who smelled like shampoo and soap instead of the streets.

We drove over to 17th Avenue, where I suggested we stop in at my favorite haunt, Good Earth Cafe, and breakfast on some fresh bagels, scones, and maybe a bowl of homemade soup. But Ken said it was against his better judgment to eat anywhere that had the words "good" or "earth" in its name. "Particularly when they're both in the same name. Don't have to be a rocket scientist, kid, to figure out a place like that ain't gonna' let a man enjoy his morning smoke." We settled on Phil's on 14th, where Ken ordered black coffee, ginger ale, and dry toast. I, on the other hand, ordered Belgian waffles with strawberry sauce, vanilla ice cream, and whipped cream.

By the time the toast and waffles came, Ken had surreptitiously consumed the better part of a mickey of rye we had picked up on our way over. The only discernible difference in his behavior was that his hands stopped shaking and he seemed more aware and awake.

"I expect by now you know that Gunn was my student."

"He mentioned that last night."

Ken snickered. "Took you long enough find out."

"That's right, it did, because you certainly didn't tell me."

"Nope, I didn't. But what with you sleuthing around the library and settin' up bogus experiments, I would have thought you'd have known all about me long ago."

"I know a few things."

"Yeah?" He leaned forward across our booth table. "Like what?"

"Like you taught your classes in bars. And that you caused quite a stir with the disciplinary committee before they canned you."

"That it? Nothing about my working relationship with your boss?"

"Sorry, you'll have to fill me in on that one."

"Hmmm, I'm disappointed in you, Emily."

"Okay, Ken, knock it off. I'm not one of your students."

He raised a bushy gray eyebrow. "Too bad, you would have been good."Mark's words played in my head: *He'll destroy you just like he destroyed Beth.* "Are you going to tell me what happened any time soon, Ken? I have to get to the lab."

Ken gave a snort at my sudden impatience. "So now, what else did Mark Gunn tell you about me? That I'm baaad, and he's good, and if you hang around me, I'll take you down with me?"

"Something like that."

He pulled himself up and, with a serious countenance, said, "Okay, Emily, here's my story and you decide who you believe."

I ordered us more coffee and then sat back to listen.

"See, when I was teaching, the majority of students who showed up for my little weekly meetings were genuine; they had a keen desire to learn. But occasionally one or two would slip in who were just there to be seen and get a good grade. They were easy enough to spot, though. They were the ones who talked too much and listened too little, bought one too many rounds, and quoted psychology textbooks as if the content was simply too close to them not to."

"I'm getting the impression Mark fit into this category."

Ken nodded. Mark had joined Ken's study group when Mark was in the second year of his undergraduate program. He did well under Ken, and went on to graduate school with Ken as his supervisor.

"But why take him on as your grad student if you knew he was a fake?"

"I didn't know, kid. Gunn was good. So good, in fact, he fooled me for three years. See, he was an expert at getting other people to do his work for him. He loved group work. He also had lots of money from his wife's father, so he spoiled his fellow group members with free dinners and beer."

"And in return, his group members did all his work and never mentioned a word," I said.

"Exactly, and it wasn't until his thesis year that I started noticing something was off. What was off was that he wasn't getting the damn thing written. During this same time he was working as my research assistant on a project I was collaborating on with your man Mullarcant."

"Really? But you were in social psych. Hasn't he always been in experimental? And 'never the twain shall meet' was my understanding. Especially back then."

"Right again. Even though it was almost unheard-of to mention qualitative data in the same breath as experimental, Mullarcant couldn't help but be interested in what I was finding. See, I was getting a lot of attention in the research community over the panic stuff I was doing. But so was he. It made sense to get together."

Ken explained that his research was looking at individual responses during real-life mass panic situations like bomb threats, hurricanes, and the like. Mullarcant, on the other hand, was studying individual responses to panic under artificial conditions created in the lab.

"Like he's doing now."

"Yes, similar."

"So where does Mark fit into all this? Or does he?"

"Sure does. He's central to everything. See, Mullarcant and I had a healthy respect and mutual dislike for one another. I always got the feeling Mullarcant was pissed because I came from a big-name university and he didn't." Ken snorted. "Poor fool. Anyway, we were both smart enough to agree to use Mark as the go-between. Christine Stevens was working in Mullarcant's lab at the time. And Mark was also collecting data for me in the field, with the intention being that he could use some of the data for his thesis."

According to Ken, Mark was responsible for interviewing half of the one hundred and twenty-five study participants—people who had been involved in some form of mass panic situation. Then one day, Ken noticed something didn't look right, and it didn't take him long to figure out that Gunn was falsifying the data.

"He was too busy playing campus Casanova to do more than about a dozen legitimate interviews."

"Campus Casanova?"

"Kid, that guy would sleep with his mother."

"Please."

"It's true. He was a busy guy back then, and his prick was even busier. Apparently it still is."

I cleared my throat.

"And I always suspected he was making it with Christine Stevens. Why the hell wouldn't I? He was making it with everyone else. See, kid, that's how I knew Beth was seeing him and then you. It wasn't hard to figure. You're both young and pretty, and you both worked under Gunn. When Beth used the expression 'boyfriend troubles,' I knew it could mean only one thing—Mark Gunn."

I wanted to get off this topic. "So how did he fake the data?"

"Simple, he just made up responses based on what the first twelve said."

"Did Mullarcant know?"

"Not until I told him. This was new research we were working on, so it didn't affect our earlier work together. It certainly slowed down things, though."

"And you told Mullarcant?"

"Sure did."

Once Ken was certain Mark was falsifying the data, he went to Mullarcant and to Daren Oakes, and started making moves to have Mark expelled.

"Then what do you know?" Ken said. "Guess who goes to the university president and intervenes on Gunn's behalf?"

"Mullarcant?"

"Precisely. He marches off to the president and tells him that poor little Mark had his head too far up his ass to know that what he was doing was wrong."

"Norman Dessier. He was the president then."

"Right, and Mullarcant had him in his pocket."

Ken admitted that his reputation for drinking and not teaching made it easy for Mullarcant to convince Dessier that Ken was the one in the wrong. In the end, the president concluded that Mark Gunn made legitimate errors that any inexperienced student could make, especially one who was unlucky enough to be working under an alcoholic supervisor.

"And wasn't it fortunate that Doctor Mullarcant had the presence of mind to intervene and rectify the situation before it ruined a very good student's reputation, not to mention his future," Ken said mockingly. "A few weeks later, the whole dirty business was put to rest," Ken said. "Gunn switched departments and became Mullarcant's student. Finished up his MA and then did his PhD under Mullarcant. And I'll just bet Mark wouldn't know what was on page one or sixty-one of the thing. No matter, though." Ken made no attempt to hide the bitterness in his voice. "Mark Gunn, as you know, has been enjoying a brilliant academic career ever since."

"Wow. That is quite a story," I said. I wondered if it was true. "But I don't get why Mullarcant would go to the wall for Mark. What was in it for him? Did he really believe Mark had made a mistake?"

Ken raised his eyes to the ceiling. "Mullarcant knew there was no mistake. All he knew was that Mark Gunn was exactly the kind of student and future assistant he was looking for. It was also a perfect opportunity for Mullarcant to take credit for my research. See, having Mark as his student meant that Mark would bring along his thesis work. Which was my work."

"And Mullarcant could pretend it was his." I suddenly remembered reading a couple of earlier papers of Mullarcant's that dealt with this very topic. "He won awards for that research. I read those early papers. It was your work?"

"You bet it was. And after Mark went over to Mullarcant's lab, Mullarcant lobbied hard to get me kicked out. And he was doing a pretty good job. Dessier took my grad students away and wouldn't let me take on any new ones. But the real kicker was, he did it just after Christine Stevens kills herself."

"By the way, did it ever come out why she killed herself?"

"Family problems, was the party line. But I figured it had something more to do with her working for Mullarcant. No one seemed to be interested in exploring that theory, though. So ain't it great. That fucker's student kills herself, but it's me who gets his students taken away. I could never figure that one out. But the university's always been famous for making asshole policies. Anyway, I didn't really care one way or the other, because I was only hanging around back then to make Mullarcant sweat. And I sure had some fun during that last year. You ought to try it some time, Emily. Try and get yourself fired. It's not as easy as you might think."

I smiled, but it was forced. I suspected Ken was having anything but fun back then. A thought suddenly came to me. "Ken, did it ever occur to you that Mullarcant may have put Mark up to falsifying the data in the first place?"

He looked far off into space, as if he was mentally transporting himself back to 1979. After a moment he said, "Jeez, kid, damned if I won't admit it. But no, that thought never crossed my mind. Shit. I think you might be on to something. Mark was probably playing both sides right from the beginning."

"But the irony is that Mullarcant was the one doing the playing," I said.

"You bet he was. It's all starting to make sense now. Mullarcant wanted to make sure my side of the research would jibe with his," Ken said.

"And what better way to do it then to custom-make your own results."

"This might explain why Mullarcant was so quick to defend Gunn," Ken said.

"It certainly might."

"You're a smart girl, Emily—I mean, woman."

We both smiled.

Chapter 24

"EMILY, NICE YOU COULD MAKE an appearance," Mullarcant said as I followed him down to his office.

I ignored his sarcasm. "I just came from meeting with Irene. Zac and I will run her this afternoon." I was trying to act natural, but I was having a very hard time being in the same room with him, and I knew my tone was clipped.

My mind raced with questions. Had Mark contacted him and told him what happened last night? My instincts told me no, and that Mark probably did call and leave a message saying everything went as planned—that he had a tape of me. Mark would then probably lie low for a while until he figured out how he was going to save himself.

But the fax.

Mark said Mullarcant knew about the fax, that's why we were supposed to be making home movies together. So what was Mullarcant's next move going to be with me? I knew I had to keep it together long enough to find out what he had planned for Irene, and me.

"So Ms Benner has managed to sober herself up enough,

then, has she? Excellent. I'd like to be there," Mullarcant said. "I'm quite interested in how a female subject with Ms Benner's background will respond."

Damn! I took a seat across from his desk and pulled out my notebook. "Why the interest in this particular subject, Doctor Mullarcant? Are you expecting her responses to be appreciably different?"

His eyes lit up. "I'm glad you asked. You see, my theory is that she will be even more compliant than the men who succumb to addictions. Based on my gender research, it makes sense to hypothesize that this subject won't even dream of resisting, and she will keep the mask on indefinitely. Yet, I have absolutely no doubt she will report experiencing even greater distress during the procedure than the men. A woman's desire to please, especially an alcoholic woman, will far outweigh her desire to save herself. That is my hypothesis, Emily."

Yeah, well, you haven't met Irene, I thought. "And what about in the second phase, what do you expect there?"

"Oh yes, I could almost write the results myself."

That's what I'm counting on, I thought. "But I wonder if we'll be surprised," I said.

"I hardly think so. Just for fun, I'll tell you what I think and then we can compare it with the actual results." Oh joy. "During the second phase this woman will place unequivocal blame on the white-coated researcher. She will put herself in the subject's place, and will see herself as merely an extension of the machine that administers the shocks. She will not see the arm moving the lever up to the danger levels. Rather, she will see and feel only the experimenter's push to go ever higher." His eyes rolled back in his head as he savored each of his words.

I broke the spell. "But in the original Milgram experiment, I didn't think there were any differences between the men and women's responses."

"Ah yes, but you're not thinking like a researcher, Emily. I am using people with dependencies, people with flawed personalities. Weak people who can't control themselves, let alone anyone else." My mind drifted back to Ken's words. *Nothing just happens. You've got to plan in this world.* Mullarcant glanced at his watch, "I must be going. What time—"

I cut him off. "Oh, before I forget, are you free any time this afternoon? I have a lot of things I need to go over with you about my thesis."

He opened his Daytimer and ran a finger down the page. The thought of that same finger pressing the play button on a video machine and those beady eyes watching Beth's naked body commingling with Mark's made me ill with anger. I wanted to upend his desk and slice him in half with it. I closed my eyes, drew a couple of deep breaths, and told myself to hold it together.

"I have one meeting this morning and then I am free until three-thirty, at which time I will be off campus with Daren Oakes. What time is our subject scheduled for?"

I threw my hands up. "Wouldn't you know, three-thirty."

"That's quite all right. I will simply move my meeting with Daren up to twelve-thirty, which should give us plenty of time to be back here by three. However, that will also mean we will have to postpone our meeting."

"That's okay, I've got some prep work and—" And he was out the door before I could finish.

Then, just as suddenly, he popped his head back in and startled me so badly I nearly wet myself. "Oh, and by the way, I'm planning to run Ken Cox through both phases within the next few days."

AT ONE FORTY-FIVE THAT AFTERNOON, Ken staggered into the lab three-sheets-to-the-wind. "Hey, hey, Experimenter Two, how the fuck are ya?" he said, slapping Zac on the shoulder.

Zac stared through him. It was going to be one of those days. Irene came in shortly after. "Kenny figured there was no point in both of us suffering today."

I studied her for a moment. "Are you sober?"

"Close enough."

Ken was over by the bed, fiddling with the tubing from the CO_2 tanks. "I don't think it's such a good idea to have him here," I said to Irene. She went over to Ken and slipped her arm around his shoulder.

"Kenny, you're going to blow it if you don't get the fuck out of here, okay?" He tried to focus on her and then looked over at me before making an unsteady exit.

Zac was setting up the tanks and attaching the mask. He turned to Irene. "Hi, Irene, I'm Zac."

"I'm sorry. I forgot you guys haven't met."

She took Zac's hand and gave him the death grip. Zac winced under the pressure, and I couldn't help but smile. I straightened the paper sheet on the bed, gave it a pat, and said, "Okay Irene, up here. We've got to get this done before Mullarcant gets back." I turned to Zac. "Do you have all the forms?"

He held them up, "Right here."

I leaned over Irene, who was now stretched out on the bed. "Okay, here's the deal. We're going to do everything just as we normally would, except of course we're not going to gas you. As we go through all the procedures, I'll explain how you should be feeling, and what I'm going to report happened to you." Zac was giving me a puzzled look. "I talked with Mullarcant this morning, so I know what he's expecting. I want Irene to be able to discuss it as though she's really gone through it."

Zac nodded.

"Do I get a say in this?" Irene said.

"Sure."

"I say just do the damn thing and then we won't have to worry."

"Irene, it's not a particularly pleasant thing to go through. I'd rather not. And besides—"

"And besides it's my body, and I'll make the decisions. Gimme the gas."

"Irene, there could be serious problems if you have alcohol in your system. I won't take that risk."

"Well, I will. Gimme the gas."

I was about to protest again but Zac said, "Em, it's her choice. We can still write the results the way we need to, but this will make it more authentic. And she's obviously not drunk." I glanced at the clock, it was twelve minutes after two, and I calculated how long it would take to get Irene through both phases. Zac followed my gaze. "Em, don't worry about it. I think the best thing is for us to act normal, and if he does show up, so what?"

"Okay. Irene, I'm going to slip this mask on your face." I fitted it over her nose and mouth. "Zac is going to run the gas. It's carbon dioxide, and once it hits, you will experience oxygen deprivation."

Irene lifted the mask. "You mean I won't be able to fucking breathe."

"Right, you won't be able to fucking breathe." Zac laughed. "I'll just go down the list of instructions, okay?" She nodded, and waved her hand for me to get on with it. "Right. Okay, Irene what we're doing here is inducing a simulated panic attack. We ask that you keep the mask on for as long as you possibly can. But you are free to stop the procedure at any time by taking the mask off or by having me do it for you."

At that point the researcher in me couldn't help but wonder how a person like Irene would react in this situation. "Now, this is the important part. The more authentic our data, the better, so from now on we're not pretending any more. Treat this as the real thing and remember, the longer you can keep the mask on, the better it will be for the study. Ready?"

She nodded, and I could see she was reacting much the same way other subjects had. She clenched her fists and her breathing became shallow. "Try to relax as much as you can and keep your breathing even. Okay, Zac, turn on the gas."

Irene took a number of deep breaths, and it was immediately apparent when the gas hit her face. Her breathing became more rapid, and the whites of her knuckles showed. I kept one eye on the stopwatch. Only fifteen seconds had lapsed when Irene sat up, ripped the mask off, and spat the words, "Fuck that!" as she gulped air into her lungs.

"Are you okay?" I said, patting her back.

She looked at me with a wild expression in her eyes. "What are you guys, a bunch of Nazis?"

"I told you I didn't want to do it."

Zac laughed. "Right, Em, you were just following orders."

"Very funny."

"So how'd I do?" Irene asked, regaining her composure.

"You did great. Except this isn't what we're going to tell Mullarcant."

"So I didn't do so good, then?"

"No, you did. You showed us that you have a mind of your own and that you're not going to do something just to please someone else."

"It also shows that I enjoy breathing. So what did your boss expect I'd do?"

"He thought you'd keep the mask on to please us. And that's what we're going to tell him."

Zac piped in, "If he asks, that's what you should say too."

I went through the follow-up questionnaire with her, making up the responses as we went along. "Question three. Irene, when you were experiencing oxygen deprivation, translation when you couldn't breathe, what were you thinking?"

"That I can't fucking breath."

"Here's your answer. I felt like I was going to die, and I wanted to get away. Number four. Why didn't you take off the mask?"

"Because I didn't want to disappoint anyone," Irene said mockingly.

"Now you've got it." I jotted down her response and went through the rest of the questions, while Zac set up the video in the viewing room.

"Ready to roll," he said, rushing back in. We led Irene back to the viewing room. "This part is a little easier. All you have to do is watch the video and answer some questions." She looked at me suspiciously. "No really, that's it. But we better get moving."

Fifteen minutes later Irene poked her head out the door to say she was done. I grabbed the clipboard. "What did you think?"

"I think you people do really strange things to other people. That poor sucker was really choked up when he thought he was electrocuting that other guy. And then it turns out it's all fake."

"It is kind of mean, that's why we don't do that sort of thing any more. Some people think it's too emotionally damaging."

"But gassing them isn't?"

"Yeah, well, let's not get into that right now. We could argue that one forever."

"Be a pretty weak argument from your camp," Irene said.

"Let's just get this finished up. It's the same thing as before. I'll ask you the questions, Irene, and you answer them. Then I'll tell you what you really said."

"I think you got that backwards, but go on, shoot."

"Whatever. Question one. In the film, who was ultimately responsible for delivering the shocks, the person moving the lever, or the experimenter in the white coat?"

"The guy pushin' the lever. I mean, it wasn't like the white coat had a gun to his head or anything." I smiled and thought, well, Doctor Mullarcant, it looks like your bone-headed gender theories are a little flawed.

Irene was watching me. "What?"

"Nothing, I was just thinking about something Mullarcant said earlier. That's the perfect answer. But I'm going to put down that you said it was the guy in the white coat because he was in charge."

"Whatever. But, jeez, I hope I don't screw any of this up if I do have to talk to the guy."

Zac was standing behind me. "You won't. Just say the opposite of what you really think. Besides, he probably won't ask you anyway."

"Zac's right, Mullarcant will only be interested in the results."

"In fact," Zac added, "the reason he probably won't ask you anything is because Emily and I are out of our minds thinking that he's going to lead us anywhere."

"Zac. I thought you were with us on this?"

"I am. It's just that I think we're being a little dramatic. I really don't think we're going to find anything other than what we've already found."

I heaved a sigh. "Maybe you're right. Maybe I'm nuts."

"Come on, Emily," Irene said. "Gimme the next question." We exchanged a smile.

"Number two. At what point did you think the guy pushing the lever could have walked out of the study?"

"Right from the get go. Just as soon as he found out what they were up to."

"And your answer," I looked to Zac for help.

"Say there was no opportunity because the experimenter needed him to stay. No wait. Say the experimenter never gave him an opportunity because he said he had to continue."

"Perfect," I wrote it down quickly. "Question three." I paused and we all looked toward the main doors as the sound of approaching voices drifted down the hall. "Oh no, it's Mullarcant. Irene, just do the best you can," I whispered.

"Ah, good thing I'm early," Mullarcant breezed in. He walked over to Irene and extended his hand. "I'm Doctor Mullarcant, and you must be Mrs. Benner." He seemed excited to the point of agitation.

She took his hand tentatively. "Yeah, that's me."

"Never mind the preamble, Emily, I'm anxious to get started. Would you like to come up on the bed, Mrs. Benner?"

Irene looked at me for help.

"Uh, actually, Doctor Mullarcant, things got a bit mixed up," I said.

"Oh?"

"I kind of screwed up with the time," Irene said and slapped her forehead. "I thought I was supposed to be here at one-thirty instead of three-thirty. And I sure as hell wasn't going to hang around for a couple of hours once I came all the way down here."

"We thought it was best to run her since she was here," I said.

"Yes, we wouldn't want to inconvenience our subject," Mullarcant said, scrutinizing Irene. "Where are you then?"

"Question three, second phase."

"Then you're nearly done." He became excited again. "And where is the data from the first phase?"

"Here." I passed him the forms.

He snatched them from me. "Bring me the second phase data just as soon as you have it completed. I'll be in my office." Then, thankfully, he left with his head buried in the forms.

I finished up the last few questions, gave the results to Zac, and asked him to run them down to Mullarcant. When he returned, the smile on Zac's face communicated all that was needed.

"I take it he was happy with the results."

"Ecstatic is more like it. The man's a lunatic, he was practically jumping up and down, saying, 'Genius, genius, absolute genius'."

"Looks like you made some brownie points with your boss," Irene said.

"I think he was referring to himself."

Zac gave Irene her forty dollars for participating in the study. She was about to hand back a twenty, but changed her mind and stuffed both bills into her coat pocket without saying a word. I gave her my home phone number and asked her to call me if Mullarcant contacted her or if anything else came up.

"Sure thing," she said, pocketing the little slip of paper. "Well, it's been a slice. I'll be seein' ya'."

I walked her to the door and watched her make her way down the hall, her worn overcoat swishing from side to side across the calves of her blue jeans. She stopped to peer down hallways and into open doors, looking for Ken, I presumed. And for one guilty moment, I hoped she wouldn't find him so that she could go on being the person she had just been with us.

When she passed Mullarcant's office, the Great Man himself stepped out in front of her, giving her and me quite a start. I ducked back into the lab, but not before I saw Irene go into Mullarcant's office.

Chapter 25

RUSTY WAS WAITING WHEN I CAME through the door. "I've got news," she said excitedly.

"Great, but first, did Irene call?"

"No, dear, the phone hasn't rung all afternoon." She waited for an explanation.

"I'll fill you in later. Let's hear your news."

"Yes, good. Hannah is here and says she has some rather unsettling things to tell us." Rusty leaned her head close to mine and whispered, "But don't worry, I haven't told her anything other than that you find Mullarcant to be a bit of a tyrant."

"Rusty, I never worry with you."

"I wish I shared the same sentiment about you," she said.

"Things will be okay. Let's go hear what Hannah has to say."

"SO, NOW," HANNAH SAID, "you are having trouble with the lunatic Mullarcant are you, Emily?"

"Yes, a bit."

"Well, my dear, I will tell you something, I would be more

worried about you if you weren't," she said, taking a sip of her tea. "He's crazy, you know. I'm not kidding, I truly believe the man is, you know." She made a whirling motion around her ear with her index finger. "And at the risk of sounding like an alarmist, I believe he is dangerous. But I can't seem to get anyone else to join me in taking any definitive action against him."

"It's interesting you should say that because my impression is that the man terrorizes the entire department."

"Oh," she said loudly, her German accent becoming more pronounced, "he is terrorizing the entire university, as far as I'm concerned. He bullies his way into meetings and then holds court. And don't even talk to me about seminars and conferences. The man is an embarrassment to the university. And he should be stopped."

"But, Hannah," Rusty broke in, "you and I both know that when someone is bringing in the kind of funding he is, it's almost as though he's earned the right."

"And don't I know that. It's a shame, we are turning our universities into paper mills."

"Publish or perish," I said.

"And it is the universities that will perish in the end. With this race to publish we are forcing people to produce inferior and even fraudulent research." That made me swallow. "Well now, enough speeches about the decline of academic integrity. What are we going to do for you, Emily? How can I help you? Oh, but before I forget, I must tell you I have been doing a little more investigating since we last met, and I found out more about our Doctor Cox."

"Oh?"

"Yes, and I am rather disappointed. After we spoke I became more curious about that matter Norman Dessier refused to speak of. So I gave him another call and squeezed out a little more information."

"Did it have anything to do with Mullarcant and research?"

Hannah looked at me with a blank expression. "No, nothing like that at all. Frankly, I wish I could say it had. It's all quite bizarre. I'm still having trouble believing it. Especially in light of the fact that neither I nor any of the other members of the disciplinary committee were informed of it." I was literally on the edge of my seat, holding my breath. Rusty too was leaning a little further forward in her chair.

"Go on, Hannah. What was it?" Rusty said.

"Well, it has to do with another student who committed suicide, back in 1979."

"Christine Stevens," I said.

"Yes." Hannah looked disappointed. I suspected she was enjoying creating the suspense. "She was one of Mullarcant's students. According to Norman Dessier, there was rumor that she had been having an affair with—"

"Mark Gunn?" I said.

"No. Ken Cox."

My lungs collapsed and expelled the air in them along with any hopes I had of believing in Ken."Aw shit," I said.

"That was my reaction too, Emily." Hannah said. "I remember the case, of course. It was terrible. Bright young woman, I understood. But I don't remember there ever being any talk of an affair. In fact, we were told it had something to do with family pressures and marks."

Rusty piped in. "You did say it was a rumor, though."

"Yes, but Norm Dessier told me there was a note."

"What did it say?"

"Norm didn't go into the details. Believe me, I did well getting what I got out of him."

"I'd say you did exceptionally well."

Hannah's face beamed with pride. "I am a researcher at heart, Emily. I just did the medical degree on a lark." She let fly her booming laugh. "Maybe I should have been a detective."

"Maybe. So answer this for me, Detective Schneider. If there was a note implicating Ken, then why didn't this all come out?"

"Ah, Emily, you obviously don't understand the politics of academia. The university wouldn't want that kind of thing associated with its good name. And besides, it was a suicide, not a murder. An unfortunate number of students end their own lives each year. And who could say anything she wrote in that note was true. No, the university would not let that out."

"This explains why the president stopped letting Ken have students."

Hannah looked at me thoughtfully "Yes, it does, Emily."

"Did Ken know about the note?"

"I don't think so. Norm said he never discussed it with anyone."

"Well, unless he was the one who discovered Christine and her note, then he must have discussed it with whoever did."

"Quite right you are, Emily. And I have no idea who that would have been."

"Wasn't the university taking a terrible chance hiding that note?"

"Not really. Back then, the death certificates in these cases often indicated the death was accidental. You have to understand, suicides were not discussed."

"They're still not," Rusty said. "So why would Norman Dessier tell you all this now?"

"Because he lives in Palm Springs, and perhaps he doesn't care any more. And it was nearly twenty years ago."

"Or perhaps he needed to get it off his chest and clear his conscience."

"Yes, Rachel, you may be absolutely right." Hannah turned to me. "Just out of curiosity, why are you still so interested in Ken Cox?"

"No reason, really." Hannah gave me a skeptical look. "He knew Beth Wong."

"Ah, did he now? Emily, in light of what I have just told you, I would suggest you consider very carefully how much time you spend with Doctor Ken Cox."

"I think you might be right, Hannah. But don't worry, I'm not planning to have an affair with him any time soon, and unless Beth had unusual tastes in men, I doubt she had one with him, either."

Hannah smiled. "Ah well, regardless of his social practices," she said, "I still believe it is a grave pity he turned out the way he has. That man had a brilliant mind. Now, enough about the past. How can I help you today with the lunatic Mullarcant?"

"Why don't you tell her about Swallow Mountain, Hannah?" Rusty suggested.

"Oh yes. Have you been up there, Emily?"

"No." I was still reeling from what she had said about Ken and was having trouble collecting my thoughts. "Uh, wasn't it a ski resort?"

"It was, but it went into bankruptcy some twenty years ago. As Rachel has probably already told you, the university acquired the land for a research site. But with all the unexpected cutbacks, the project was abandoned almost as soon as the university finished paying some expert to tell us what we already knew—which was, of course, that the cost of converting it would be prohibitive. And there it sits. Or, I should say, there it sat, until Martin Mullarcant started pumping some of his abundant research money into it."

"What's he doing with it?"

"As far as anyone knows, he's been renovating the old hotel."

"What for?"

"I have no idea, and much to my chagrin, neither does anyone else, it seems. He is an impossible man to pin down. And to be quite frank, no one is particularly interested in trying."

"Hannah, tell me something. Why is he allowed to run roughshod over everyone? I don't get it. I mean, he's only one man. And a little one, at that."

"That's an excellent question, Emily, and I don't have an answer. Except, of course, the money. In these economic times of slashing and burning, the educational system is suffering."

"So if a professor brings in enough money, he's entitled to a reign of terror?"

"It appears so. But, Emily, I'll tell you this. Beth's suicide, don't think that has escaped the board's attention. At least it hasn't escaped mine."

"That's good to know," I said.

"And now this other young man."

"Derrick."

"Yes. Derrick. Now we have three."

"And they all have one thing in common," Rusty piped in. "Mullarcant."

"That's true," I said. "But Derrick wasn't even in the program yet, and Christine's death was apparently because of Ken."

"Perhaps it is only coincidence, Emily. But"—Hannah took my hands in hers—"Rusty has told me how hard all this has been for you. And I would like to say something to you now, Emily. I have lived a great deal and I know that nothing is worth that. If you need my help in any way to get a transfer or to change supervisors, you know you have my support. I still have a little clout around there."

"I'm sure you do, Hannah. And thanks, I may just take you up on that."

"Good, because I don't want to tell you what to do. But I do think that if you are unhappy working under that man, and I can't imagine who in this world wouldn't be, you really must make some changes."

Then, as if on cue, the phone rang. I excused myself to take it in the other room. Irene was on the line.

"Emily, I'm at the York with Ken. Can you come down here?"

"I'll be there in a few minutes." I hung up and dialed the lab. Zac answered and I told him where to meet us. While I was on the phone, I fished the Swallow Mountain key out of the little dish and slipped it into my pocket. I wasn't even sure why I took it.

I went back to the living room and thanked Hannah for her help. I explained I had to meet with someone.

"It sounds like an unexpected meeting," Hannah said suspiciously. It was hard to get anything past Doctor Hannah.

"Actually, I was hoping the person would call. I'm sorry to run out on you." I hugged her and added that I would take her up on her offer for backing when I decided what I was going to do.

"Just remember, Emily: nothing is insurmountable. And no

matter how impossible a situation may seem, there is always a solution."

"Thanks, I'll keep that in mind."

I headed for the front foyer and stopped momentarily to gaze up at our archangel. Rusty had followed me out. "I think the head is an improvement," I said. She had added a simple, round head with no features. It now looked like a cross between the Virgin Mary and the Angel of Light. "The white paint really solved the problem of keeping those strips in place. "It's beautiful, Rusty." And it was.

"Was that Irene on the phone?" I nodded. "Just please, please be careful, Emily. I don't want to see you get hurt. This is all making me very nervous."

As I was gazing up into the angel's faceless face, it suddenly occurred that I hadn't asked Hannah something.

I went back into the living room and asked, "Hannah, just out curiosity, how did Christine Stevens kill herself?"

"Same way as your friend. Only in Christine's case it was off the top floor of the Administration Building."

I FELT LIKE A YORK HOTEL regular when one of the old guys and the bartender waved to me as I made my way to the back of the bar where Ken, Zac, and Irene were sitting at our usual table.

Ken spread his arms and said, "Hello Dolly."

"Hi everyone." I pulled up a chair.

Ken picked up a glass of beer and poured about a quarter of it into a glass of tomato juice. I was seeing him in a different light now, the light of suspicion. Aside from Rusty and Zac, I wasn't sure who I could trust any more.

Why hadn't Ken mentioned anything about his relationship with Christine Stevens? Was that what he was alluding to when he said, *What else did Mark Gunn say about me? That I'm baaad, and he's good and if you hang around me, I'll take you down with me.*

One part of me wanted to blurt out what Hannah had said about him and Christine, just to see his reaction. But I decided to play my cards close to my chest for the moment. I needed to find out what else, beside plagiarism and blackmail, was going on in Mullarcant's lab. This mysterious third phase of the study Derrick had mentioned was still eating at me, and my hope was that Irene was going to lead us to the answer. If I sprung the Christine Stevens incident on Ken, and Irene didn't know anything about it, it could screw things up.

I turned my attention to Irene, who was lighting a cigarette. "So tell me, what did our man Mullarcant want?" She looked around, checking for eavesdroppers, and then dug into her jeans front pocket.

"Get this. He offered me two hundred bucks, and this here's the first installment," she said, waving two fifty-dollar bills in the air.

"For what?"

"A trip to the mountains."

"Let me guess, Swallow Mountain?"

"Yeah, that's right. He said all I had to do was participate in another study and I'd get the other hundred."

"Swallow Mountain? I've never heard of it," Zac said. I took the key from my jacket pocket and handed it to him.

"It's an old ski resort," Ken piped in. "Used to take the kids there years ago. But it went bust, I heard, about the same time I did." He giggled at his little joke. No one else joined him.

"That's right, now it belongs to the university." I went on to tell them what Hannah had told me.

"So what the hell is he doing up there?" Zac said.

"More to the point, *why* is he doing it up there?" I turned back to Irene. "What else did he tell you?"

She took a deep breath. "Okay, he said all I had to do was meet him tonight at the university at eight in the"—she hesitated—"shit, was it the east or west parking lot?" Come on, Irene, think. "Wait," she said and dug out a crumpled piece of paper from her coat pocket. "I wrote it down." I saw Zac's shoulders relax. "East parking lot."

"And did he tell you what you would have to do? What kind of study it is, anything at all?"

"Yeah, but slow down, Emily. You're making me all jumpy and then I can't think straight."

"Sorry."

She took another deep breath, and a sip of beer. "It's okay. He said it was like the study I just did. And when I said I didn't think I was too interested in gettin' gassed again, he said no, it was like the second part of the Mill . . ."

"Milgram study."

"Yeah, that's it, Milgram. Well, anyway, the video one."

Zac and I looked at each other. "He's replicating the original Milgram experiment," we said in unison.

"Can't be," Ken said. "Wouldn't make sense. Irene's seen the film, she knows it's a set-up. Unless . . . well, unless he's going to use her as the confederate."

"The what?" Irene said.

"The guy in the film who was pretending to be getting shocked in the other room, the Mr. Wallace guy. You could play that part, the learner," Ken said.

"But he could get anyone to do that, he'd hardly need to pay someone two hundred dollars," I argued.

"He would if he wanted them to keep quiet about it," Ken said. "No one does that experiment any more."

I glanced over at Zac for his input, but he was staring at Ken as though he were watching someone speaking in tongues.

"Ken used to teach at the university," I said. Zac looked even more astonished. "I'll explain it all later."

Zac tipped his glass toward Ken. "I'd say it's pretty self-explanatory."

"Fuck you."

"Okay, Kenny," Irene said, patting his arm. "Let it go." She shot Zac a look. "So why wouldn't he want anyone to know he's doing the study?" she asked him quickly.

"Because it'd never get ethics approval."

"But gassing people does?"

Zac looked tired all of a sudden. "They're two different things."

Ken snorted.

"Okay, okay, let's not get into this," I said.

"So how come it's so unethical? I mean, I saw the tape," Irene said.

"But what you didn't see was how upset the real subjects were after. Some of those people thought they discovered something pretty evil about themselves," Ken added.

"Think about it," Zac said, "if you believed you were capable of doing that to another human being, it'd be pretty hard to live with. And remember, many of those people really believed that the old guy in the other room was dead."

"I get your point. So why would he want to do it all over again?"

"Fame," Ken said.

Irene looked exasperated. "But someone else already did it."

We were all silent for a moment, none of us able to come up with a plausible explanation. And then Ken said, "Well, he's got to be doin' it for some reason. So what now?"

"I know what I'm gonna' do," Irene said. "I'm going to collect my other easy hundred bucks, and the rest of you can do whatever you like."

"I don't know, Irene. I'm not so sure it's going to be that easy. We don't know what he wants you to do," I said.

"And let's not forget Carmen." We all stared at Ken.

"Carmen? She died on the streets, Ken."

"Yeah, Kenny, what the fuck are you gettin' at?" Irene said.

He scratched at his beard. "I don't know, I've just been thinking. Kind of added things up, or bodies." We all waited, each making our own mental tally. "Carmen is dead. Jerry Booth is missing, and is supposedly doing some government work in the mountains. Beth is dead. That other kid, Derrick, is dead. Hmmm. Who else? Oh yeah, Norm and Jack haven't been heard from in months." Irene shifted in her seat, and her eyes went to me and back to Ken.

Zac piped in. "This is asinine. What are you saying, Ken, that Mullarcant is doing *your* people in?" He put a little too much emphasis on the "your."

"Better watch it, Number Two Experimenter," Ken returned, his green eyes penetrating Zac, as if reading the younger man's past. "You never know when we'll all become *your* people."

Zac's jaw tightened as he glared back across the table at Ken.

"Okay, everyone," I said. "This whole thing has us all a little on edge."

"Emily's right. Let's just cool it," Irene said. She tried to get Ken's attention, but he was still locked in a stalemate gaze with Zac. "And, Kenny, I don't care what you think is going on up there, I'm going."

Ken averted his gaze from Zac. "Okay, Irene. I'm going too, 'cus I'd really like to find out what that little fucker's up to." He picked up his glass of tomato juice and tipped it up to Zac, and then he drained the rest of it in one gulp.

"Since I'm the one who started all this, I better go too," I said.

"Well, I'm in too, then," said Zac.

I looked around the table at my team. "Okay, now all we need is a plan."

Chapter 26

AT EIGHT-THIRTY THAT SAME NIGHT, Ken, Zac, and I were on Highway One heading west toward Swallow Mountain with absolutely no clue what we were going to do once we got there. Zac was driving and Ken was navigating.

"It's about two miles past the Deadman's Flats turn-off," Ken said. "But slow down, the first turn comes up real quick on your left."

I was in the back, fighting with Mark's video camera. I'm sure a kid in grade two could have figured it out in about fifteen seconds flat, but techno wizardry was not something that came easy to me. Zac had suggested we bring the camera and tapes just in case we needed to collect evidence. Zac had obviously missed his calling as a private dick.

"How's it coming back there, Em?"

"An instruction manual would be handy. I can't get it to do anything."

Ken leaned over the front seat and pushed the play button on the top of the machine. "How about that?"

I looked through the view-finder. "Still nothing."

He took it from me and popped open the side panel, and then handed it back. "Might want to try a tape."

"Good thinking," I said sheepishly. And then I thought, for a guy who keeps himself as well lubricated as Ken does, he seems awfully sharp. I eyed the back of his head suspiciously and wondered if what he had in his flask was real booze. Maybe I'd ask him for a sip and while I was at it, let the words "Christine Stevens and affair," slip out in the same breath. Not just yet, I told myself, and went about busily sorting through the tapes I had swiped from Mark's place.

"Em, have you looked at any of those tapes yet?" Zac asked.

"No, but I'm hoping this one is blank. There's no label on it. I'll check it, though, to make sure we don't wipe anything out."

My head started to spin from keeping it down so long in the moving car. I gazed out the window and watched the lights of the houses whiz by. No matter how many times I make that drive, I'm always inspired and awed by it. The highway cuts through Morley Flats, a wind-swept expanse of land owned by the Stoney Tribal Band. From there, it funnels down into the Bow Valley to the base of the mountains, where the Rockies seem to rise up out of nowhere like giant castles.

Another thing that seems to rise up out of nowhere is the cement plant: a massive concrete structure that sits obtrusively on the shores of Lac Des Arcs. It's hard to miss, especially at night because the place is lit up like a power plant. The glow from the factory lights cast enough light to see the silhouette of the raked mountainside sitting decapitated and denuded behind the factory.

The tape went in with a resounding pop. I pressed the rewind button and then the play button. Pictures of mountain scenes, obviously taken from a moving vehicle, filled the tiny video screen.

"Hey, a travel log."

"Not blank?" Zac said.

"No, but it doesn't look like anything important, just some mountain scenes." A picture of the factory came into focus.

"Hey, it's this drive." I fast-forwarded it and watched as mountain peaks, pine trees, and highway sped by. Then suddenly, an image of Mullarcant flashed across the screen. "Oh, wait a second," I said and pushed the stop button.

"What?" Ken and Zac said in unison.

"There's stuff on here with Mullarcant." I reversed the tape and stopped it at the place where Mullarcant, dressed in a white lab coat, was standing in a rustic-looking room. I rewound the tape again and then let it play through. The sound of Mullarcant's voice filled the car. "Tuesday. February, twenty-three, nineteen hundred and ninety nine, seven p.m. Swallow Mountain Research Centre."

Ken leaned over and picked up the video machine and extracted a pair of those little sponge headphones you have to stick right into your ears. He plugged them into the side of the machine. "Here, you can give us a blow by blow after."

Zac was looking through the rear-view mirror at me. "Why can't we all listen to it?"

"Because you're a lousy driver, and you need to listen to me," Ken snapped.

I fitted the little phones uncomfortably into my ears and watched again as pictures of mountain scenes rolled by and then abruptly changed to the scene with Mullarcant. The scene switched again. This time it was of Derrick seated at a table in front of a control panel. Mullarcant stood behind him. Except for the rough wood walls, everything looked exactly as it had in the original Milgram experiment.

My stomach tightened as I watched Derrick lean forward and push the lever up to the first level. A man called out from somewhere in the distance, "Hey, that hurt!"

Derrick turns and looks back at Mullarcant. Mullarcant's arms are folded over his chest, his face is expressionless. Curiously, though, the look on Derrick's face is one of embarrassment, as if he thinks the whole thing is a ridiculous joke. But Mullarcant is stone-faced.

"Please continue," Mullarcant says in a deadpan voice.

Derrick's expression turns to boredom as he pushes the lever up to the danger level. A scream is heard from another room. Followed by the man yelling, "You said there wouldn't be any shocks!" Derrick smirks and shakes his head before he puts the lever up even higher. A distant howl fills my ears.

"He's good," Derrick says with a chuckle.

Mullarcant responds, "Please, you must continue."

"Okay," Derrick says lightly, taking the lever all the way to the lethal level. An eerie silence follows. Derrick looks back at Mullarcant. "Must have missed his cue." He turns in the direction the screams have been coming from and calls out, "Hey, Jerry, I hit the big one." There is no response.

Mullarcant places a hand on Derrick's shoulder. "How do you feel right now, Derrick?"

"To tell you the truth, a little silly."

"Really, but you have just killed a man, Derrick. Surely you must feel more than just a little silly."

"Well, it's like I said, I'm not too good at this role playing stuff. I flunked drama. Thought it'd be easy credit..."

"Don't you even want to go and check on Mr. Booth, Derrick?"

"Oh sure, right, I get it."

Derrick walks out of the camera's view. Footsteps can be heard, followed by a brief moment of silence, which is abruptly broken by the sound of someone screaming. Derrick comes back in view. He is hysterical.

"I think he's dead," he bellows. "You killed him. You killed him." Derrick grabs Mullarcant and shakes him. "Help him. Jesus Christ, you killed him. You killed him. You gotta help him."

He tries to drag Mullarcant along with him, but the steel-faced Mullarcant says, "Derrick, there is nothing you or I can do. He is dead." Derrick drops to his knees, and pounds the floor, sobbing. "You killed him, you bastard. You killed him."

"No, Derrick, you killed him."

Through tear-soaked eyes he pleads, "But you told me to. You said we were just doing a role-play."

Dying by Degrees

Mullarcant squats down beside the hysterical young man. "I know, Derrick, you were only following orders."

I dropped the camera on the seat and tore the headphones out of my ears. The contents of my stomach were threatening to surge up into my throat, and I couldn't catch my breath. My head was spinning as though I had just received a sharp blow.

Zac was looking at me through the rear-view mirror. "Em, are you okay? What's on the tape?"

Ken turned around. "Hey, kid, speak." I tried to say something, but it was like being in one of those dreams where you open your mouth to scream, but nothing comes out. "What? Are you choking, kid?" He leaned over the back seat and handed me his flask. "Here, take a hit off this. You're lookin' a little pale."

I did what he said and didn't mind as the alcohol burned down my esophagus on route to my stomach. I did, however, mind that I couldn't catch my breath for a second or two after. There was no longer any doubt in my mind that the stuff was real. I finally managed to say, "H-how close are we?"

Ken looked down the highway. "I don't know, five, ten minutes, maybe." He pointed to a side road. "Take that left up there."

"Em," Zac was yelling now, "what's on the goddamn tape?"

"He's killing people up there," I heard my voice say. "And either Irene's next, or she's going to be the next one to do it."

Zac pulled the car off the road and slammed on the brakes, sending us all flying forward and then back again as our seatbelts did their duty. He spun around to face me. "What are you talking about?"

"Zac," I said, pushing his shoulder, "drive. We don't have time."

Ken reached for the video camera and pressed the rewind button. He didn't have the earphones in and the car filled with the sound of Derrick's howling sobs.

Zac pulled the car back on to the road, his face the shade of milk. "We need a phone."

"Fuck that! Irene's up there." Ken grabbed the wheel and yanked it sharply to the left.

"Get your hand off the goddamn wheel," Zac barked, trying to regain control of the car.

"Just drive!" Ken commanded. We spun onto a narrow road that hadn't seen a snowplow all winter. We slewed in and out of the ruts like a toy car in a fair ride. The road went straight up, and Zac was driving as fast as he could to make it to the top.

"Slow down or we'll be driving down to hell," Ken said, pointing out the passenger-side window. Until then, I hadn't noticed that on our right, the road was a sheer drop that plummeted down into the valley.

"Yeah, slow down," I said. "There's nothing between us and God on the right here."

"And turn your lights off," Ken ordered. "We'll see the hotel just as soon as we make it over that rise. No wait, cut your engine here, and we'll walk it."

"And what, just leave the car in the middle of the road?" Zac said.

"If we get any closer, he'll hear us."

"I agree. Let's walk," I said.

Ken handed me the video camera, and I took the tape out and replaced it with one I hoped was blank. I was about to put the tape of Jerry Booth and Derrick under the front seat, but Zac said it would probably be safer to take it. He slipped it into his jacket pocket, and I threw the camera into my backpack and opened my door. We climbed out and immediately sank up to our knees in snow.

"Here," Zac said, extending a hand to me. He helped me and then Ken into the middle of the road where we were able to run in the ruts. Ken stumbled and fell a couple of times, but in light of the fact that he had been drinking all the way up in the car, I was amazed he was able to run at all. Fear is a great motivator.

At the top of the rise, a dark structure appeared in the distance. As we neared it, the shape and detail of the old hotel became clearer. It was a three-storey log building with a large, open front verandah. All the windows were dark except for two rooms on the top floor and one on the main. Thankfully, it was a bright evening.

The sky was clear and the moon illuminated the bright white snow. If it had been overcast, we literally would not have been able to see our hands in front of our faces. As we drew closer to the hotel, my heart picked up its pace and so did my feet. Ken put his hand on my arm and whispered, "Slow down."

"Yeah, Em, you'll wipe out or something," Zac said. "We've got to keep it together here, so let's just go easy."

I took a couple of deep breaths and realized that my rapid-fire breathing wasn't because I was jogging, it was because I was scared out of my mind. The vision of Derrick screaming and crying on the floor played over and over again in my head, and Jerry Booth's moans and howls made my chest tighten. I told myself to think about something else, otherwise I knew I wouldn't have the guts to keep going.

When we were about fifty yards from the hotel, we stopped and ducked in behind a stand of pine trees. Zac pointed to a path that led around to the back of the hotel. We started to move toward it but stopped when another light in a main-floor window suddenly came on. We moved quietly behind the trees as a door creaked open and voices drifted out.

The first voice I recognized immediately as Mullarcant's, but the other was female and although it seemed familiar, I couldn't quite place it. I strained to hear what they were saying, but we were too far away. Their footsteps on the wooden verandah indicated they were moving closer to us, and I heard Mullarcant say, "I assumed she would be more cooperative. This is very unexpected. She thinks we're trying to trick her."

Right on, Sister Irene.

"But he's compliant enough," the woman said. "And I think he'll talk her into it. And remember they want their money."

"True," Mullarcant said. "Well, that should be long enough," he added. "Let's see how eager they are to get paid." Footsteps went back inside. We waited until we heard the door close, then we started down the path. At the back of the hotel, we came to a small parking area. A Ford Explorer I didn't recognize was parked next to Mullarcant's circa 1982 Pacer, a hideous little car that looks like a mobile fishtank. The perfect car, I thought, for a perfectly hideous little man.

To our right, a narrow set of stairs led down to what I assumed was the hotel basement. I moved quickly down the steps to the door and found that the door handle was missing. In its place, someone had stuffed a rag into the hole. The door was slightly ajar, and I stuck my fingers in the hole around the rag and pulled the door easily toward me.

A faint noise that sounded like a yelp came from above as we moved into the dank basement. Except for the narrow streams of light shining through cracks in a boarded-up window, we were in complete darkness. From upstairs, we heard the yelps turn to hollers. I pushed past Zac back toward the door. "I'll prop it open so we can get some more light," I whispered. When I went to open the door, it was closed tight. I felt for the rag, but found only a smooth metal plate with a key lock covering the hole.

Zac came up behind me. Gently he took my hands from the door and said almost apologetically, "Forget it, Em, we're not going anywhere. It locks from the inside."

"How do you know?" The realization of what he said hit me like a slap. My knees went weak and tears filled my eyes. "Oh, no, Zac, not you." A stream of moonlight shone through a crack and fell across his face. His eyes were wide and shiny with tears, and I felt my heart break as I stared into them.

He sank down to the floor and put his face in his hands. "I'm so sorry, Em. I tried to get you to stop. I wanted to, I wanted you to call the police."

"Zac, my God. How could you? Have you known all along?"

He gazed up at me with a pathetic, pleading look. "Em, I had no idea it was this bad. I didn't know, I only—" His sentence was cut short as a chair crashed down on his head. Ken was standing over him with what looked like an old bar stool poised above his head, waiting for any sign of life. I bent down to help Zac.

"Forget it. Just get the tape," Ken said through labored breaths. Gingerly, I picked the tape out of Zac's jacket pocket and was trying to look at his head, when Ken grabbed my hand

and pulled me into the darkness. "Come on. There's a door over here somewhere."

I pulled back. "How do you know?"

"This used to be the bar," he said leading me around, and occasionally into, pillars and tables. "Aw, ouch," I said, bumping into a high bar table. Just then, a scream filtered down through the floorboards and we both froze. Ken led us up a flight of stairs. When we stopped at the top, I ran my hands over the surface in front of me, searching for a door handle. Suddenly, the area was illuminated. Ken had struck a match.

"Why didn't you do that before?"

"I was in a hurry."

We were standing in front of a door. I tried the handle, but of course it was locked. I faced Ken. "How do I know you're not one of them?" I said.

"Come on, kid. There's a dumbwaiter over behind the bar," Ken said.

I held my ground. "Well? How do I know you're not in this with Zac?"

"Oh, fuck it," he said, and retreated down the stairs. "I don't have time for this. Irene's up there."

I was left standing in complete darkness. "Okay, I believe you." I said in a thin voice. His match had gone out and I had no idea where he was. I suddenly felt like I had when I was a little kid and the babysitter locked me in the basement and turned off all the lights. Why? Because she was a very sick thirteen-year-old who thought it was funny.

A flash of light went up in front of my face and I could see Ken's face. A yelp escaped from my lips. He shushed me and told me to follow him.

I held onto his coat as he led the way back down the stairs with another match. We went behind the bar, which was an immense old mahogany beauty. My eyes were adjusting to the dark and I could see the bar mirror was still there, but it was discolored and cracked. At the far end, we stopped in front of a miniature elevator. Ken lifted the door and held a match inside.

In the corner, half a dozen dead cockroaches lay in various states of decomposition.

"Aren't there any other stairs?" I asked.

"Jump in."

Again, I stood my ground.

"Aw shit." he said, and dropped the match as it burned his fingertips.

"Here," I took the matches from him. I lit one and held it over the corpus delicti.

"Oh, for God's sake," Ken said. He leaned into the box and swept the roaches out with his hand. "There, now get in."

I was going to tell him that it wasn't the bugs I was most concerned about. Rather, it was the thought of getting into that small, dark space and being hoisted up to God knows where that had me paralyzed. Another scream tore through the floorboards. I jumped in.

"You'll be okay," Ken said. "We used to put this little guy in here all the time when his wife came looking for him." He lowered the door after I folded myself in. His assurances gave me a small sense of relief, until I remembered the hotel had been closed for twenty years.

"Wait," I said, stopping the door with my hand. "Where am I going?"

"To the kitchen."

"Okay, the kitchen. Hey, how do we know this thing still works?"

"We don't. And we never will if you don't let me try the button."

"Okay, but what if it doesn't and the cable breaks or something?"

"You'll end up in the basement." He said it deadpan, and started to close the door again.

"Wait." I put my hand under it again. "Once I get to the kitchen—if I get to the kitchen—then what am I going to do?"

"Unlock the door for me."

"Right."

"And I'm the one with the problem," he said dryly.

"Look, I'm scared, okay?"

"You're doing fine," he said evenly. "It should stop at the kitchen, but keep opening the door whenever it stops to see where you are. When you get to the kitchen, run around to the right and you'll see the door we just tried."

He brought the door down, and I was in complete darkness. There was a low hum of the motor and the sensation of being jerked and then hoisted up. I hugged my knees closer to my chest and tried to steady my breathing as panic welled inside me. A couple of seconds later the elevator stopped. I lifted the door and pushed my hand out into the darkness and hit solid wall. I closed it again, and up I went. It stopped two more times and I was beginning to worry I had gone too far, but on the fourth try, light seeped in at the top, and I thrust my hand out into open space. At that point it occurred to me that Ken and I hadn't made up any sort of code that would tell him he needed to hoist me up or down. There was about two feet of space to crawl out above my head. I hit the bottom of the elevator box with my foot a couple of times, and to my surprise the waiter jerked up a few inches. I climbed out easily onto a metal dishwashing table, and then jumped down and ran around to the side door where Ken was waiting as promised.

He led the way up the back stairs. The screams grew louder and more piercing with each flight we climbed. I felt tears stinging my eyes and fear seize my gut. Ken had to stop a couple of times to catch his breath, but waved me on. At the top, I burst through the fire door and ran down a hall toward the screams, all the while yelling for Irene to stop. I followed the screams down to a door with a brass number "12" on it. The door handle was locked. I started banging on the door and then remembered the key. I fumbled wildly for it in my pocket and then slipped it into the lock. Still calling out to Irene to stop, I flung open the door.

But it was Mick who looked up at me from the control panel.

Chapter 27

STANDING BEHIND MICK WAS MULLARCANT, in a white lab coat, staring with icy reserve. My first thought was that they were all in on it and that I had been duped. But the innocent smile on Mick's face told me he couldn't possibly know what was actually taking place.

"Hello, Emily, come to observe?" Mullarcant said.

I didn't bother to exchange pleasantries. I ran into the next room. It was empty. I rushed back to where Mullarcant and Mick were still in front of the control panel.

"Mick, where is she?" I said. When he pointed toward an accordion partition that divided the room, he seemed almost amused by me. The partition was open at one end and I slipped through to the other side. There, Irene was strapped to a chair that was an exact replica of the one used in the Milgram experiment. The only difference, of course, was that this one actually delivered high-voltage shocks to its occupant. I tore the extension cord from the wall socket, and ripped the wires from the armrests. I was undoing the straps that held Irene's arms, when Mick came sauntering in, smiling.

"Hey, Emily, chill. It's not real. It's just like the video you showed me. See—" He stopped when he saw Irene's head lolling to one side and her tongue hanging out. He came closer, still grinning. "Aw, come on, Irene, cut it out. You're scaring Emily."

"Mick," I said sharply. "It's real."

His face blanched, and his body crumpled to the floor like a puppet. "NO, NO! Something went wrong. She was just supposed to be pretending."

"Doctor Mullarcant!" he called out. "Something went wrong."

I tore the restraints from Irene's chest and felt for a pulse. There was none. I dragged her to the floor, tilted her head back and pressed my lips to hers, and desperately tried to breathe life back into her.

Ken burst in and knelt down beside me. He buried his face in Irene's chest and wept.

I tugged at his shoulder. "Do you know CPR?" I said, between breaths. I felt for a pulse again—still nothing. Ken pulled himself together and brought himself up over Irene. With determination on his face, he pressed his palms into her breastbone over and over again in a steady rhythm.

He jerked back. "I felt something."

I put my hand to her neck. "It's faint, but it's there."

"Come on, woman," Ken said. "Don't you leave me. Give her another couple of breaths, kid."

I did as he said and brought my lips to hers and filled her with my breath. Ken leaned back into her with another series of compressions.

"She's coming to, goddamn it," he said, wiping his brow. I looked around for Mick and spotted him curled up in the corner of the room.

"Are you okay for another minute or two?" I asked. I pointed to Mick.

"Aw shit," Ken said, holding Irene's hand. She was now drawing shallow breaths on her own. "Hey, kid, it's okay. Look, she's okay, kid."

Mick didn't respond.

"We need an ambulance," I said.

"Yeah, for two. He's gonna' be like that for a while."

I went to go to Mick, but Ken pulled me back. "Leave him, I'm the only one he'll let near him when he gets like this."

Mullarcant's voice drifted in from the adjoining room. "I will deal with this as I see fit," he was saying to someone.

"Ken, we've got to get help," I whispered.

"Closest place is Deadman's Flats, but I got my doubts that fucker will show us to a phone," Ken said.

Mullarcant drew back the partition like the master of cere-monies at a Broadway musical. Daren Oakes and Sandra Penny entered from the wings as though taking a curtain call.

"Well, Emily, it looks like you have ruined a perfectly good experiment," Mullarcant said, taking his place between his two stars.

I stared in disbelief at Sandra Penny, who looked pale and drawn, and was obviously unwilling to make eye-contact with me.

"What are you people?" I said.

"Scientists, Emily, we are scientists," Mullarcant said. "And so were you, but I see you've changed career paths and have now chosen social work." He was picking at his coat cuffs like a bird pecking at a seedball. I was beginning to see, or perhaps it was just hope, that there was a connection between his compulsions and his conscience.

"No, just humanity."

His smile was sardonic and patronizing. "I do like your spunk, Emily."

"We need an ambulance," I said. Irene was gaining conscious-ness, and color was returning to her face. She moaned and Mullarcant knelt beside her.

He looked at Ken. "Well, Doctor Cox, I see you've regained your interest in my research."

Ken had his head down and didn't move until Mullarcant reached over to feel Irene's neck. With prize-fighter swiftness

Ken drew back and delivered one wallop of a punch to Mullarcant's jaw.

"You stay the fuck away from her," Ken spat as Mullarcant reeled from the blow. Before he hit the floor, Sandra Penny and Daren Oakes rushed to his side.

"I'm going to find a phone," I said. A glance around the room told me it had probably been some kind of banquet or conference hall. The vaulted ceiling measured at least sixteen feet and was supported by solid wood beams. The hardwood floors were dusty and scuffed from years of shoes, boots, and pumps dancing and tramping across them. But other than the chair Irene had been strapped into, the room was empty.

"Don't bother," Mullarcant said, getting to his feet with the aid of his confrères. "There aren't any. And I suggest everyone just settle down for a minute and listen to what I have to say." He rubbed at his cheek gingerly and stared at Ken. "I suppose you've been waiting a long time to do that, Doctor Cox." Ken didn't even bother to look up at him.

"Doctor Mullarcant," I said, "I really don't think you're in any position to be suggesting anything to anyone."

"Oh, on the contrary, Emily. I am in a perfect position to do exactly as I please."

"Not any more, you're not. I'm going to tell the police everything." I looked over at Sandra and shook my head. "I can't believe you went along with this."

In a tiny voice that bordered dangerously on a whine, she spoke for the first time. "I didn't have a choice."

Daren Oakes, who had also been silent, parroted her. "None of us did."

"Everyone has a choice, right, Doctor Mullarcant?" I said. And for the first time in my life, I felt my own power as the depth of the stupidity of these people began to sink in. "Ken, you stay with Irene and Mick, I'm going to get help."

As I passed Mullarcant on my way out, a wicked smile crossed his face. "But, Emily, how can you be sure your friends will be here when you get back?"

"Look, if you lay one hand on them—"

"You'll what? Say we three eminent professors from the University of Southwestern Alberta disposed of three useless drunks?"

"Mick's not a drunk," Ken said in a hoarse voice.

Mullarcant ignored him. "Please, Emily, don't disappoint me. I've always thought more of your intellect."

He had me—again. If I left and he did do something to them, I'd never forgive myself. But if I stayed, how would we get out?

"What do you want, Doctor Mullarcant?"

"Please, call me Martin. I'd say it's time, wouldn't you?"

"Okay," it stuck in my throat, "Martin."

"Emily, I assume you know by now that part of my plan was to bring you out here, and it worked beautifully, wouldn't you all say?" He looked from Sandra to Daren and then back at me. "Well?" he demanded. They nodded their heads in agreement My disgust for them was so complete it was almost palpable. "Oh, and by the way, where is our friend Zacarie?"

"He's in the basement, and someone should go and check on him, " I said.

Ken chuckled. "Yeah, he might have a bit of a headache." Mullarcant turned to Daren Oakes and ordered him to go and see to Zac.

"Now then, as I was saying, my plan was to get you to come here, although you were a little early."

"So you were the one. You put the key in my purse, didn't you? You wanted me to come here."

He smiled. "No. That wasn't me, it must have come from Elizabeth. But regardless, my plan worked perfectly. Except for one small detail. Zacarie was supposed to keep you in the basement until such time as all the data had been collected."

"You mean until such time as you murdered Irene."

"Emily, you still disappoint me. We don't kill things in laboratories, at least not in the way you are suggesting. And we don't murder things in laboratories, either. We conduct experiments on subjects and follow procedures, and we record the results.

And then we dispose of those things that have served their purpose. Your objectivity is still very much lacking."

A sound came from the far end of the room where Mick was, a sound more animal than human. Ken moved over to him and cautiously stroked Mick's shoulder, but the boy didn't respond.

"Doctor Mullarcant," I said impatiently.

"Martin."

"Martin," I swallowed it, "could we please hurry this up. We need to get help."

"Patience, Emily. Aren't you at all curious as to why I had you come here?"

I let out a sigh. "Okay, sure why?"

"Because I believe you have potential and I would like to see you develop it."

"And by having me come out here and witness this," I swept my arms out, "that'd do it?"

"That's right, Emily. Now you are a part of it, and you always will be. But I had to consider your feelings too. Because I can see that you share many of the same qualities as Elizabeth. So you see, I had to handle things a little differently with you."

"Answer one thing for me, will you?"

"Certainly."

"Did you kill Beth and Derrick?"

His look was of complete shock. "Of course not. Emily, I'm a scientist, not a monster."

I wasn't about to argue the point. Daren Oakes came back supporting Zac, who was holding a towel to his head. Zac sat down on the floor and leaned his head against the wall. He wouldn't, or perhaps couldn't, look at me. One side of me wanted to go to him and comfort him, and the other side wanted to slap him.

"I'm sorry, Em," Zac said as tears streamed down his face.

"Well, then, help me get these people to a doctor," I said. But he just shook his head and kept repeating he was sorry.

"Since our friend Zacarie is back, I think it will be instructive to have our department head explain the way things are now. So go on, Daren, tell us please."

Eileen Coughlan

The good Monk Oaks took a deep breath and, in a monotone, said, "Emily, you can't ever tell anyone about this. Because if you do, we'll all say that you are lying and delusional." It was as though he were reading from a script. "We'll say that you have psychiatric problems. We'll also say that you tried to put your name on other papers you didn't write."

"Oh, and Emily," Mullarcant interjected, "the fax you sent to the journal using my name. That is fraud, you know."

"Don't listen to him, kid," Ken said. "He can't prove you wrote it or sent it."

Mullarcant smiled at Ken. It was the smile of a chess player about to call checkmate on his opponent. He pulled a computer disk from his lab coat pocket. "I believe I can," he said. "I made a copy from your computer, Emily. And, really, I might make a suggestion that you stop taking advice from a man who is capable only of ruining his own and other people's careers."

"Ha!" Ken let out a hoot of laughter. "That's rich, coming from a guy who has either driven his students to kill themselves, or, more likely, who killed them himself."

"Oh, please," Mullarcant said. "Enough dramatics. We have work to do here."

"What's the matter, Mullarcant? Can't stand to hear the truth? You're the one who ruins your students. Look at Gunn. He was a bright guy once. Lazy, I'll give you that, but bright. Now he wouldn't know how to run a lab rat through a one-way maze. The only thing he's any good at is being your henchman."

"Oh my, yes, you're right. Far better these innocent minds have the opportunity to study under the likes of you, Doctor Cox. The liberal education you can offer them in bars and in your bed is much more valuable than anything I can offer them, such as a brilliant future."

"Fuck you," Ken said. "What the hell are you talking about, *in my bed*? You're obviously confusing me with your loyal assistant, Gunn."

Mullarcant laughed. "Come now, Ken, is your mind so polluted it has washed away the memory of poor Christine Stevens?"

I stared at Ken.

"What the fuck are you talking about?"

"She left a note. It said she couldn't live without you, or some such nonsense. If only the poor girl had known what she was throwing her life away for."

"Why, you son of a bitch." Ken was on his feet, moving slowly toward Mullarcant. "Who told you this crap? Or did you make it up, so you'd have something to tell Dessier?"

Mullarcant smiled another triumphant smile, but took a step back.

Ken moved in closer and said, "I never touched that girl. That was Gunn's department. He was sleeping with her and anyone else who'd let him. If there was a note it had his name one it."

A moment of confusion registered on Mullarcant's face, which wasn't lost on Ken.

"Who found the note, Mullarcant? Gunn?"

Mullarcant straightened his shoulders. "Whatever happened twenty years ago makes little difference now. One undeniable fact remains. You still can't leave them alone, Doctor Cox. You still have to drag them down with you. First Elizabeth, now Emily. You were a loser back when you were a faculty member, and nothing has changed except you are now where you belong—down in the gutter with other losers." Mullarcant appeared to be gaining the upper hand again.

Irene moaned, and Ken retreated to her side. There was some truth in Mullarcant's words, and everyone in the room knew it. But there were other truths he was leaving out.

I cleared my throat. "If Ken was a such a loser, Doctor Mullarcant, then why did you steal his research and his students?"

Mullarcant lifted his eyes to meet mine. Silvery cold fingers slid up my spine and pinched the base of my neck. But I didn't avert my eyes.

"I didn't steal his research, Emily. I saved it. And I did the same for his students, and I am trying to do the same for you." I caught Ken's expression of amusement out of the corner of my eye. "Now please continue, Daren," Mullarcant said.

"Yeah, Daren," Ken said. "Continue telling Emily how you and your boss here are going to save her by telling everyone how crazy she is."

Mullarcant piped in enthusiastically. "And who better to make such an assessment than the most esteemed psychologists in the country. Go on, Daren, tell her the rest. Tell her what will happen to her friends if she does say anything."

"Don't bother. I get the message." I said. It was beginning to dawn on me just how far gone this guy really was.

"And with no proof of your outlandish accusations, well, Emily, who will believe you?" he cocked his head waiting for an answer.

I felt the bulge of the videotape in the inside pocket of my jacket. "Okay, I get your point. But tell me something. Why in God's name are you doing this?"

"Because this is the most brilliant research project since Milgram himself. Don't you see? It's all about compliance, obedience to authority, and most importantly, self-preservation. Milgram was clever, oh yes, but I am brilliant." He paced the room, his excitement growing. "Milgram's experiment was incomplete, you see. Certainly he got people to comply, but it is after the initial compliance where I am most interested. Think of the Nazis, Emily. How does a man get an entire nation to follow him? With compliance certainly, but there has to be something else, and my hypothesis is self-preservation. Do you see now what I am after here, Emily?"

I said no.

"Emily, you disappoint me."

"So you've said."

"I want to see what happens to people once they commit the ultimate sin against another human being. In other words, how far will they go to save themselves after they have annihilated, even inadvertently annihilated, another human being. The results are already clear. Look at your friend Zacarie. He brought you here. He sacrificed you. Just as Mr. Booth sacrificed these—" he hesitated as if searching for an appropriate term to describe Ken, Irene, and Mick"—these subjects."

"Zac, you killed someone?"

He shook his head. "No. No. Of course not. I didn't know about any of this until you played that video tonight."

"Excellent, Emily. Does this mean you have all the videos with you?" Mullercant asked.

"No. Just the one where you murder an innocent man and psychologically destroy another one." I caught the sadistic pleasure on Mullercant's face, but turned my attention back to Zac. "You took us to the basement."

"All I knew was that there was an experiment going on here," Zac said. "I didn't know what it was. I knew that I was supposed to bring you out here. I assumed he was replicating the original Milgram study. That's all I thought. I went to him after we all met in the bar, and I told him I didn't want any part of his projects. He told me we were being melodramatic and to bring you out here, and he would show us all what was really going on. I was as shocked as you were."

"Why didn't you say something?"

"I was scared. "

"Oh now, Zacarie, you're not telling the whole story," Mullarcant said, obviously enjoying the show. "What he was afraid of, Emily, was that he wouldn't be allowed to finish his degree. And did he also mention he has his first publication coming out this month?"

"Zac, you sat there in your apartment pretending to call the police. How could you lie to me like that?" He looked so pathetic, I actually felt sorry for him.

"Em, one part of me really wanted to call the police. But I felt trapped too."

"I came to you for help and told you everything Mark did. And after you saw the tape tonight you knew what was going on, and yet you still brought us here. I'll never understand how you could do that to a friend."

"I'm sorry," he said in a whisper. "I thought it was too late. Too late for all of us. I worked so hard for this, Em. Just before I went back home for the holidays he asked me to run some data for him. The data files were in Beth's desk, and so was the Aspen 45 file with the research proposal."

"That was the file you called me about," I said to Mullarcant. "Why would you call me if you already had what was in it?"

"Zacarie only had part of the documents," Mullarcant said.

"What I found was a pretty sanitized proposal for a project to replicate the original Milgram experiment," Zac said. "It didn't mention any of this other terrible stuff, Em. You've got to believe me. I had no idea until tonight. Beth must have had the results of the actual experiments."

"Not quite, Zacarie," Mullarcant said. "Unfortunately, Elizabeth came across the Aspen 45 file and reacted in a most unexpected manner. The documents she found were results of a replication of the original Milgram experiment. The only difference was that we were using very low-grade electrical shocks. We started with the original version and then modified it."

"I'll say you modified it. You killed people."

He continued as if I hadn't spoken. "A week before her untimely passing, Elizabeth ran around the department trying to solicit letters of recommendation for her application to another university. But of course you already know this, since you found her application."

I looked at Sandra Penny, who was leaning up against the wall, picking at her cuticles. "You and Gunn told him, didn't you, Sandra?" She wouldn't look up.

I turned back to Mullarcant. "That's when you had Gunn make the home movies. You were worried and needed a little insurance just in case she threatened to blow the whistle."

"She was acting irrationally. I assumed she would eventually see that."

"You son-of-a—" I stopped in mid-sentence as everything started to become clearer. "You set her up, didn't you? This was your whole plan. She didn't just come across that file. You made damn sure she found it, didn't you?"

He clapped his hands excitedly. "Emily, you are every bit as bright as I thought you were. Yes, yes, you're exactly right." Then his brow furrowed and a look of disappointment crossed his face. "But her reaction was somewhat unanticipated."

"Yes. I'm sure it was. The night we found out about Carmen, that's when Beth knew you were doing more than shocking people. She knew Carmen didn't die on the streets. She knew you killed her." The magnitude of what I had stumbled upon came to me in one fell swoop. "Dear, God. You killed all those people, didn't you? Jerry Booth, Jack Landers, Norm Sager—my God, how many others?"

"You forgot Christine Stevens," Ken said.

"Please, Doctor Cox," Mullarcant said. "You'll have to take credit for that one."

"You made it so Beth couldn't get out. And that's exactly what you were trying to do with Zac and me. Zac didn't just happen to find that proposal, did he?" Zac looked up. "Oh, don't look so shocked, Zac." I snapped. "Use your head. After Beth died and then Derrick, didn't you stop and think? People were dying, for God's sake."

"I know, I know," his voice broke. "I just wanted out, Em."

I cut him off and turned my attention back to Mullarcant. "And that's when you showed her the tape, after she found out about Carmen. She came to you, didn't she? She was going to the police."

"Yes, yes. So she said." The corners of Mullarcant's mouth were slightly upturned. He's enjoying this, I thought incredulously.

"You told her you were going to send it to her family."

"Go on, Emily, you're doing fine."

I imagined the scene in his office. Beth crushed and defeated with no one to turn to. Too humiliated—trapped. Then something occurred to me that didn't make sense. "What time did this happen, Doctor Mullarcant?"

"In the morning."

"Why would she wait until that night to do it?"

Ken spoke up. "Because she had no intention of killing herself, kid. My guess is that this bastard or his bastard assistant killed her. Just like they killed Christine Stevens."

My eyes shot from Ken, back to Mullarcant, and back to Ken again. "But I was in the washroom, Ken. I would have heard something. We were alone."

"You absolutely sure about that, Emily?"

My mind made a visual sweep of the washroom, down the long row of stalls to the open window. I thought I heard her say something to me. Was it possible someone was hiding in a stall?

"No, I guess I can't be absolutely positive."

"Come, come, Emily. You're letting this drunken fool play with your mind. You must learn to trust me. I am the one who is truly concerned with your future. Tell her, Zacarie."

"I'm not telling her anything," Zac spat the words. "He was blackmailing me. He said if I told anyone he'd ruin my chances of ever getting my PhD. And I needed the money. I'm so sorry. I guess I just didn't want to know."

"You knew enough to call Mullarcant and rat me out. And what about when Irene was in the lab, did you tell him about all that too?"

"No. After you came to my place and told me about Derrick, I was getting suspicious too. I wanted to find out what was going on just as badly as you did. All I told him was that you were coming out here. He said to keep you in the basement until he came for us. That's how I knew the door locked from the inside. Em, I never dreamed any of this was going on." Zac buried his face in his hands and let the sobs rake his body.

I imagined what must have been going through Beth's mind the day she learned the truth. She would have felt so responsible because she was the one recruiting the subjects. And on top of that, she would have felt so betrayed by Mark.

"So Mark has known about all of this from the beginning," I said to Mullarcant. "And I presume you put him up to going out with me." He flashed a triumphant smile. "What about Derrick?"

"Yes, Derrick. Now I'm sure you can imagine my surprise when he reacted the same way as Elizabeth. But this could just be a coincidence. Obviously, it's far too early to speculate."

My God, he sees these deaths as nothing more than pieces of

data, I thought. I needed to keep him talking so I could buy some time to figure out what the hell I was going to do. "So Jerry Booth, was he working for you, then?" Mullarcant nodded. "He stole the wallets and gave you names, right? And what about the other two, Norm Sager and Jack Landers?"

"Yes, yes, they were my first subjects and good ones, at that. It went off like clockwork. First Norm recruited his friend Jack and they came up here. Norm then recruited Jerry and —"

"And Jerry killed Norm, and then you moved on to students and had Derrick kill Jerry."

"You have to admit it's an elegant study."

The only thing I'll admit is that you're certifiably nuts, I thought. "But your experiment is flawed, Doctor Mullarcant," I said. "You tricked your subjects into believing there were no shocks being delivered."

"Not at all, Emily. The study is the exact opposite of the original Milgram experiment, therefore it is perfect. They trusted me, just as they trusted Milgram. Milgram tricked his subjects into believing they were delivering shocks to the subject. I led them to believe they were not. I simply take the study to new heights. Milgram and I are doing exactly the same thing. We lead people to believe."

"Milgram didn't hurt anyone."

"Now that depends on who you speak to. Why do you suppose we can't do that experiment any more?"

"You killed three people and drove two others to their deaths. I'd say that goes a little beyond a philosophical discussion of ethics."

"Emily, let's get something straight. I didn't kill anyone and I didn't drive anyone to their deaths. In all cases, it was the individual's choice. They did what they did because they wanted to."

"Your participants didn't know they were either going to kill someone or be killed themselves. Forgive me if I sound slow, but I still don't see what you think you'll accomplish with this."

"Think, Emily, think. In the original Milgram experiment, many subjects thought it was possible that they had killed that old man. But, of course, they had not, and they later found out as much. I take it a step further and ask the question, what if they had actually killed the person? Then how far will they go, how compliant will they be in order to save themselves? I came up with the notion when I saw how subjects reacted in the panic project—how they would keep that mask on just to please authority. But it was also because of my colleagues. I saw how they reacted toward me when I gave them publication gifts. By simply putting their names on papers I had written, I automatically became the authority figure in the department." He made a sweeping motion toward Daren Oakes, Sandra Penny, and Zac. "And you can see the outcome of this. They will do anything to protect themselves."

"Answer one other thing for me."

"Certainly."

"Why would Jerry Booth and the others be willing to let themselves be strapped into that chair? Jerry knew what happened to Jack Landers and Norm Sager."

"Obedience, Emily. Blind obedience and an unwavering faith in authority."

"In other words, you lied to them. You gave them a script to follow, just like in the original Milgram experiment, and convinced them they wouldn't receive any shocks."

"Exactly, Emily. It's an integral part of the project. The fascinating thing is how easy it is to get them to comply. Because I truly believe they all know, at least subconsciously, what's going to happen. Yet, they just can't resist authority."

This is a game for him. Just a bizarre game that he's been playing with all of us, and only he knows the rules. "But Beth got you, didn't she? You still can't find those original documents that say you were replicating the original Milgram experiment with real shocks, can you?"

"You wouldn't happen to have them, would you, Emily?"

It was my turn to smile. "But the office, Mullarcant. That wasn't like you. You left Beth's office in a terrible mess."

"Oh yes. No, that wasn't me."

"Who was it, then?"

He looked around the room, and I followed his gaze. Zac was still sitting on the floor with his head in his hands. Daren Oakes and Sandra Penny were leaning against a wall, staring down at their feet. Across the room, Ken was kneeling next to Irene, her head on his lap. Her eyes were open and she looked to be fully conscious, although she hadn't said a word. Mick was still in the corner, curled up. Mullarcant's eyes rested back on me.

"I'm tiring of this, Emily," Mullarcant said. "Let's move on. As far as Elizabeth goes, it was unfortunate that she chose to leave this world so prematurely." He fingered the cuffs of his sleeve and drew them down, and then repeated the action at least half a dozen more times. "Thankfully, I had you to fill her shoes."

I felt my jaw clench as the truth struck a nerve. "You tricked me."

"Did I really? Well, it certainly wasn't difficult, was it? Remember, Emily, we see only what we wish to see. Only those of us capable of looking beyond ourselves will seek the truth. Oh, don't look so defiant. Think about Mark Gunn for a moment."

"I'd rather not."

"He shows a glimmer of interest in you and you're ready to fall into bed with him. Why? Because it suited your ego. And what about the paper? I'll grant you did put up a little protest, and you were the only one, by the way. But in the end, just like Elizabeth, Mark, Daren, Sandra, and Zac, you walked out and left it in my hands. Although I did applaud your attempt to inform the journal about the so-called mistake. Fortunately, I was able to rectify the situation. Your name will appear on the published version. Aren't you going to thank me, Emily?

"Go ahead and stare through me, Emily. But you know what I'm saying is the truth. You recruited subjects and then placed a mask on their faces until they panicked. Never once did you ask why. Never once did you question this. Why? You believed it was the right thing to do because I said it was. You didn't like what you were doing, yet you did it anyway. This is precisely what Milgram was getting at. We go along because we think we are supposed to. We do as we are told."

He was pacing the room like the brilliant professor delivering his last great lecture. "Why are you even in school, Emily? And don't tell me it's to obtain a degree. Tell me why you want that degree." He waited for an answer. My stomach squeezed into a tight knot. "Well!" he boomed.

"Because I want to learn."

"Bullshit, it's because your father wants you to get a degree so he can tell all his friends what a bright little girl he has."

"So," was all I could come up with.

He shook his head in disgust. "Well, Emily, now you have to make another choice. You can continue your studies with me and be rewarded with academic accolades, or you can go against me and—well, we've been over that, haven't we?"

"You'll have to excuse me again if I sound naïve, but I really don't see how this research is of any use to you or anyone else, since no one can ever know about it. I fail to see its value. And, therefore, I fail to see any benefit in going along with you."

"Good, Emily! Now you are thinking like a scientist. Excellent point. That is precisely the beauty of this research. It is so grand that at the moment, no, we cannot publish it. But once we have replicated it enough times, we will have something so great, with such far-reaching implications, the ethics will, of course, be overlooked."

Of course. Clearly mad, I thought. The man is clearly mad. I glanced over at Zac, who was bent forward, his head hanging down between his knees. I turned back to Mullarcant, who was studying me with detached amusement. Okay, time to switch gears.

"I see what you're driving at," I said. "You're probably right, once you do release it, everyone will overlook the ethics."

"Of course they will. Now I'm not so foolish to think I will escape criticism altogether, but so goes the life of history-makers. Do you see now how fortunate you are to be involved in such a magnificent project?"

I nodded, and tried to collect my thoughts. "Okay, I understand what you have said, Martin, and I need some time to think about my level of involvement. I have a lot of mixed emotions, and I'm sure you can understand that."

Irene was trying to sit up.

"In the meantime, I think we should get Irene and Mick to a hospital," I said.

"We can't very well have an ambulance showing up here, can we?" Mullarcant said. "Perhaps we should drop them somewhere."

"Like the old east-side stockyards? Where you dropped Carmen, Jack, and Norm?" I said.

Mullarcant put his hands deep inside his pants pockets and rocked back on the heels of his shoes. "Emily, you still seem to believe I am some kind of a monster. I am a scientist and so are you. And as such, you need not concern yourself with such matters. Believe me, there are plenty of people out there, just like your friends here, who, for a few dollars, are more than happy to throw a little gas on a pile of rags and dispose of them for us."

"A pile of rags?" I said. "You mean a pile of people."

He ignored me and turned abruptly to Zac as if something had suddenly occurred to him. "Zacarie, I assume the tape you were referring to earlier is the one with Derrick and Mr. Booth?" Zac put his hand inside his jacket and then looked up at me. I held my breath and shot Ken a look. Mullarcant followed Zac's gaze. "Emily, why don't you let me hang on to that," he said, extending his hand.

"Run, kid!" Ken yelled. "It's the only chance we've got."

I bolted for the door, and ran down the hall to the back stairs, taking them two, three at a time. I tried the second-floor door. Locked. Panic coursed through every cell in my body. I glanced over my shoulder to see if Mullarcant was coming after me, but there was no one.

I ran down the second flight of stairs and tried the door. Locked again. I heard a whimpering sound and looked around half-crazed to find its source, but I realized it was coming from me. I raced down to the main floor. *Please God. Please God.* My prayers were answered when I burst through the door and ran like hell down the hall toward what I thought was the front of the hotel then I heard them coming down the front staircase. I spun around and headed back to where I knew the kitchen was. I slammed through the swinging doors and made for the exit door. It was stuck and wouldn't budge. My legs gave out and I slid to the floor. I heard them coming down the hall, pausing, I imagined, to poke their heads into the empty rooms along the way.

Then I spotted the dumbwaiter. For a split second my claustrophobia made me abandon the idea, but a greater fear lifted me off the floor and hoisted me into the little box. Once inside, I reached out and hit the button. The box jerked up, and the last thing I saw was Mullarcant's face peering up at me, and the words, Dumb Emily, Dumb, Dumb, Dumb, pounding in my head. The button was on his side. As I was lifted skyward my panic rose too. Anxiety squeezed the air out of my chest. Then suddenly, everything stopped and I was left suspended in complete darkness. I thrust my hand out into the darkness and hit solid wall. I imagined the air was getting thick and I started to pound wildly on the sides of my metal cage. It swayed and I became even more panic-stricken at the thought of plummeting to the basement.

My legs were vibrating. I brought them up close to my chest and hugged them to me. Tears welled up in my eyes and then I remembered a relaxation technique I'd learned in a drama class. I breathed in deeply and visualized the air rushing into my lungs and then flowing softly out my nose. For a second or two it worked, until I remembered I was running out of air. My deep breathing turned into quick, desperate breaths, and panic tore through me like an electrical current. That's when I lost it. I started to yell, and I pounded on the bottom and the top of the box with reckless abandon. The box swayed but I didn't care, better to plunge to my death quickly than to suffocate slowly.

The box jerked up, and then, as if changing its mind, reversed. I was going down. I tried madly to find someplace to hide the videotape, but as the light began to seep in at the bottom, I knew it was too late.

Chapter 28

I HELD MYSELF TIGHTER, trying to stop vibrating, and closed my eyes. A throwback to my childhood: If I can't see the monsters, they can't see me.

I heard voices, and a woman calling my name. When I opened my eyes, Rusty was standing there. For a second, I thought maybe I was dying from lack of oxygen.

"Emily, Emily, it's all right, dear. Give me your hand," she said, extending her arm across the dish table. An RCMP officer stood next to her, and near the back exit Ken was talking with another officer. I took Rusty's hand—could this be real?—and climbed out. The officer gave me an arm down. "Are you all right, Ms Goodstriker?" she asked.

"I—I think so," I said haltingly. Rusty put her coat over me. "I can't believe it. Rusty . . . how, how did you—"

"Never mind, dear, I'll tell you all about it later." She placed her hands on my shoulders and scrutinized my face. "Are you really all right?"

"Now that I can breathe, I'm fine, just fine."

Ken was beside me now. "How you doin', kid?"

"Better now. Where's Irene and Mick? They need—"

"On its way," Rusty broke in.

We all looked up to the ceiling as the whirling sound of a helicopter filled the room. Ken shook his head. "Irene's gonna hate this, not too big on heights, you know."

"How is she?"

"She's coming around."

"Mick?"

"Not so good, but he'll get over it."

The other RCMP officer came up to Ken. "Excuse me, Doctor Cox, I'll need to finish taking your statement. And if you're up to it now, Ms Goodstriker, the other officer would like to ask you a few questions as well."

"Sure, but for starters," I said, handing him the tape, "why don't you hang on to this." I turned to Rusty. "How did you know?"

"Beth." When I gave her a puzzled look, she produced a brown manila envelope with "Aspen 45" scrawled across the front in Beth's handwriting.

Chapter 29

RUSTY, KEN, AND I STOOD TOGETHER on the front verandah, watching the air ambulance attendants load Irene onto the side of the helicopter. The RCMP officers had already taken the others away. One of the pilots ran up to us and said they were taking Irene to the Foothills Hospital. Ken said he'd ride in with Mick.

"Okay, a van's on its way," the pilot yelled over the drone of the chopper, before he ducked under the blades.

Ken waved to the helicopter as it floated above the tree line. I noticed a purple bruise forming under his eye. "Where'd you get the shiner?"

He put his hand to his face and chuckled. "Oh yeah, you should've seen it up there after you took off. I was great. Grabbed that asshole Mullarcant around the knees, got him to the ground and just started pounding him in the back of the head. And the monk—"

"—Daren Oakes."

"Yeah, Oakes. You know, when I was in the department, Daren Oakes was this sniveling little guy who locked himself in his office and read computer literature all day."

"Not much has changed," I said.

"How the hell did he manage to stay on as head?"

Rusty laughed. "Just another of life's little mysteries, I suppose."

Ken snorted. "Anyway, he jumps me and starts wailing on me. Then I figure I'm dead when Zac gets into the act, but doesn't he go and drag the monk off me, and then they start fighting. It was like watching slapstick. But then Mullarcant gets away from me and takes off after you, with the rest of us following." He let out a hoot of laughter. "We were something, all right, like the Keystone Cops."

"Zac was trying to help us?"

"Maybe, who knows."

"It certainly sounds like that to me, dear," Rusty said. She looked up at the grand hotel entrance.

Ken followed her gaze. "Used to be quite a place. Wouldn't know it now, though."

"It must have been lovely in its day," Rusty said.

"Oh, it was. That wood's all cedar, you know," Ken pointed to the solid beams. "And the rooms, every one of 'em had its own fireplace, and a big old pine bed, with pretty quilts too. Wife loved those quilts."

"When did you stop coming up here?"

"About the same time I started spending more time in the bar than on the slopes. No point wasting all that money on something I wouldn't remember anyhow. Speaking of which." He reached into his coat pocket and extracted his flask. "To a happy ending," he said before taking a long celebratory swallow.

An orange and white van with flashing lights was winding its way up the road toward us. "Looks like my ride's here," Ken said. He took another long drink. "Now let's see if I can talk the kid into comin' along."

"I hope he's going to be okay," I said. "Where will they take him?"

"To the Lougheed Hospital first, and then, depending how things go, maybe out to the Nut House."

"You mean Alberta Hospital?" I said.

"Yup. That'll be home for a while."

"Well, if it comes to that, I sure hope he won't have to stay there for too long."

Ken stared at me for a moment. "Won't make much difference one way or the other, places like that have been the nearest thing to a home for him since he was about sixteen."

"That's a terrible shame."

"Yeah well, that's what happens when it's your dumb luck to end up with a demented, drunken stepfather who doesn't have the good goddamn sense to get the fuck out."

RUSTY DROVE US BACK to the city in my car, as she had come out in one of the police cruisers. We stopped in at the police station to give more statements, and by the time we pulled into the driveway it was after two in the morning. We sat in the car for a few moments under the security lights. I took the envelope off the dash and pulled out the Aspen 45 report.

"I probably wouldn't have understood its significance, but Hannah certainly did," Rusty said.

"How did Grandma Wong find it?"

"Well, it's all very interesting, and I'm still having a hard time getting my head around it. She's quite a character. To put it bluntly, she said that Beth told her."

"Really. How?"

"In a dream. Grandma Wong said she went to bed and dreamed of Beth. She said something about how she knew Beth had come to the store for something the day she died."

"She told me that too. To hide the file?"

"Apparently so. Because Grandma Wong claims Beth told her where to look for it."

"Did she say she actually saw Beth?"

"No. She said after you came to the store, she dreamed of tea."

"Makes sense, we had tea together."

"But then last night just after she went to bed, she suddenly woke up and all she could think about was a teapot Beth had given her some years ago." The image of the black and gold pot came clearly to my mind. "She said she knew it was a message and that she had to go down to the store. And what do you know? Under a tray she keeps her teapot on was the file."

"Then she called me?" I said.

"Yes. But of course you weren't here. I told her who I was and that I was worried about you. She said she was worried too and told me she found something that looked like it had something to do with the university. So I got on the phone to Hannah and we whipped down there pronto. Hannah knew immediately what was going on and the danger you were in. I also noticed the key was gone, so I knew you must have gone up there."

"And you called the police."

"Yes, and they contacted the RCMP. It would have all been very exciting if I hadn't been out of my mind worrying about you."

"I'm sorry, Rusty."

"Oh, don't be, dear, you've done a wonderful thing."

"Please, Rusty. All I've done is save myself."

"Nonsense. It's time we went in."

I was suddenly too drained to even put Ol' Blue in the garage, so we left him on the drive and went in through the front door. In the foyer, Rusty's angel still loomed large and we both stopped to look up at her.

"It really does take up an awful lot of room, doesn't it?" Rusty said. "I think I'll have it taken down next week."

"No. Leave it, Rust. I've become kind of attached to her."

"Me too. Ah well, it's a big house. Why don't you go and take a hot bath, Emily, and then try and get some sleep."

"I don't think I can. There are a million things spinning around in my head. I think I'll go over to the hospital and check in on Irene and Mick. And Ken needs some place to sleep tonight."

"I've taken care of that. While you were giving your statement at the station, I called the hospital and talked to Ken. He said Irene is going to be just fine—and Mick, well, time will tell.

There's nothing anyone can do. And as for Ken, I told him to take a cab over here, but he would hear none of it. So I suggested he check himself into the Marriott for tonight. Tomorrow we'll figure out a more permanent arrangement. If that's what he and Irene want," she added.

"You're an angel, Rusty."

"I hardly think so, and I'm pretty sure our friend Ken doesn't think so, either. He was a little hostile when I said I'd pay for the hotel."

The untouched sandwich and the bowl of soup came to mind. "He doesn't seem to appreciate unsolicited gifts."

"Well, there really isn't much else we can do, other than offer. But we can get you off to bed."

Even though I was exhausted, sleep was impossible. I tried to turn my mind off, but every time I closed my eyes images from the night filled my head. I eventually gave up and switched on the light. On cue, my door creaked open and Rusty poked her head in.

"Want some company?"

"Love some."

She sat on the end of my bed for what seemed like hours while we talked through everything. We discussed Mullarcant and how someone could get away with such a thing. How people like Sandra Penny and Daren Oakes could allow themselves to be taken in. We talked about Beth and what I would say to her grandmother, and parents.

"I guess the truth is the only thing." I said. "But at least they'll hear it from me." I couldn't stop talking. It was as though I couldn't face the next day with things as they were. "I think I'll go back up to Banff, maybe put the degree on hold."

"Sounds like a viable option, but why don't you wait a few days and see how you feel then. I wouldn't make any snap decisions now."

"To be honest, I really don't think this is a snap decision. I don't want to be there any more. Not now, anyway. I couldn't imagine ever setting foot in that lab again."

"You can always change departments. Give it some time. I

think you owe yourself that." And then she finally mentioned the one thing we had both been avoiding all night. "And what about Zac?"

I fought back the tears. "What about him?"

"I know what he did was terribly, terribly wrong, Emily, but he was your closest friend."

"*Was* is the operative word here."

"Tell me something. How do you feel about Beth?"

"They're entirely different."

"Are they? Beth obviously knew something bad was going on, and yet she felt powerless to stop it. Don't you think it's possible Zac felt the same way?"

"I suppose."

"And thank goodness Zac didn't take the same route out that Beth did. But who knows, Emily, if this had gone on much longer, maybe he would have. Look at that poor Derrick fellow. He followed right in Beth's footsteps. Literally."

"And don't forget Christine Stevens."

"Oh, yes. But Hannah said she was involved with Ken."

"According to Ken she was seeing Mark Gunn."

"My my, that man certainly does seem to have a way with the ladies."

"Sure does, and Ken seems convinced his way is to kill them. He still believes Mark killed Christine and Beth."

"My heavens, do you think it's possible?"

"No. I don't. Mark was like a scared little boy. He told me about the video. In a weird way he was trying to protect me. And I think he really did have feelings for Beth, and he probably had feelings for Christine, and anyone else who's been stupid enough to give him the time of day."

"Don't beat yourself up, Emily. You thought he was sincere. Few people have defense against that. If it's any consolation, you can be sure that scared little boy will be a whole lot more frightened when he gets to his wife's home in Vancouver."

"I thought that's where he'd go."

"The police said he called his wife to say he was on his way."

"Good, I wish I could be there to see it."

"I wouldn't want you to waste your time. Better you spend it on your friends. Speaking of which, Zac needs your support."

I sighed. "Maybe I need his too."

"Perhaps you do."

"What's going to happen to him, Rust?" Just then Rusty and I cocked our ears. We heard a low, mechanical hum coming from somewhere below. "Sounds like the garage door," I said.

"No. It's the furnace," Rusty assured me. "It's still being balky. I'll have to get someone else out to look at it tomorrow."

We both listened again, but the hum had stopped.

"Good," Rusty said. "Maybe it's going to behave itself for the rest of the night. Anyway, the furnace is the least of our troubles. I don't know what's going to happen to Zac, dear," she continued. "He didn't actually participate in the experiments."

"No. But we *both* recruited the subjects for them."

"Unwittingly, Emily. Unwittingly."

"God, how can people be so cruel to one another?" I said. We sat in silence for a long time, until I finally came clean.

"Rusty, you know what's really eating at me?"

"No, dear, what's that?"

"I saw how easy it is to get pulled in. I went along with him too. I recruited participants and ran them through procedures I wouldn't put myself through. That was wrong. And I let myself be taken in by Mark just like Beth did. We're all just a bunch of sheep."

"Not all. You stopped it and that's the important thing. Don't be so hard on yourself. And don't lose faith in humanity. There are always enough good people around who will balance out the bad." With those words, she left and I put my head down and waited for sleep.

I listened to the pops and pings of the house, and then toyed with the idea of going back downstairs for a glass of warm milk. Just then my bedroom door creaked open and I watched a thin shard of light seep in and slide across the hardwood floor. I felt a little rush of relief knowing Rusty probably couldn't sleep, either. I sat up and flipped on the bedside light.

Mark Gunn was standing at the foot of my bed.

"Mark!" His name slipped out of my mouth like a final gasp. "What are you doing here?" I said, my voice hoarse and dry with fear.

He put his hands up like a man surrendering. "Emily, don't, don't scream or anything," he said in a whisper. "I'm sorry. I didn't know where else to go." He came to the head of the bed and knelt beside me. His face was the shade of sandstone, and he actually looked more frightened than I was feeling. His eyes were those of a man who had either been crying or drinking for days. He was close enough for me to smell his breath when he spoke and I didn't detect any booze. I took a deep breath and calmed myself.

"How did you get in?"

"The garage door. You left your car unlocked. I remembered you told me how you use your electric door-opener to get in."

I remembered too. "And you came through the inside door."

He nodded.

"Mark, it's all over now. Everything's out in the open," I said slowly as I reached for the phone. "Don't you think we should call the police? It'll be for the best."

"No." He yanked the receiver from my hand and tore the phone cord out of the wall.

Okay, wrong move.

"I just need to talk to you. And keep your voice down. Where's the woman you live with?" he demanded.

I lowered my voice. "At the far end of the hall." I pointed in the opposite direction of Rusty's room.

"Does anyone else live here?" I shook my head. Now I was afraid. Very afraid.

"I just need to talk. I won't hurt you, Emily."

"Okay, Mark, I'm listening." He took a deep breath. "I'm sorry, Emily. Damn it. I am so, so sorry. I never meant to hurt anyone. I could never do that." He was staring into my eyes and I knew I was staring at a very desperate man. Why hadn't I noticed this before?

"Emily, you understand, don't you?"

"Understand what, Mark?" I raised my voice in the hopes that Rusty would hear. Another bad move. Mark leapt at me, grabbed the back of my head with one hand, and covered my mouth with the other.

"Don't, Emily. Don't make me do this again. I can't do it again."

Again!

"I just need to talk. Can you let me do that?" I nodded. "I told you I won't hurt you. I promise. Do you believe me?" I nodded. "Okay, I'm going to take my hand away now. But if you scream or raise your voice again ...," he trailed off.

I nodded hastily to show I got the message. He let his hand fall from my mouth, but he kept his other one on the back of my neck, where his fingers toyed with my hair. He smoothed down the back of my head and then took my hands in his. My hands felt cold and sweaty.

"I loved her, Emily. I really did. But things just got so screwed up. It's because of him. He's the one. I was just ..."

"Following orders?"

"Yes. As ironic as that sounds. Yes. I was following his orders." Mark's fingers played with a knobby thing that was sewn into the pattern of my quilt. "But that's not what I came to tell you. I want to help you."

"Mark, please."

"Just listen, Emily. I think you owe me that much."

The only thing I owe you, buster, is a good swift kick in the chops. "Okay, Mark, I'm listening."

"I love you."

"You love a lot of people, don't you, Mark? Did you love Christine Stevens too?"

His head snapped to attention. "That was different."

"Different? In what way?"

"Than the way I feel about you. My God, Emily. You have no idea how difficult this is for me."

And you have no idea how difficult this is for me, I thought. I glanced at the door and back at Mark. He had a good seventy pounds on me, but I bet I had a pretty fair chance of out running him. If . . . if I could make it out the door.

"I want a second chance, Emily. I need you."

"For what, Mark? What can I possibly do for you? Mullarcant was arrested tonight."

He put his face in his hands and then ran them through his disheveled blond hair. "I know. Oh, God. I know. He told me to meet you at the hotel, but I headed for the airport instead. But when I was about to get on the plane I thought about you."

No you didn't, the only thing you thought about was whether the police would be looking for you. So you had to come up with a different plan.

"I drove up there—"

"I thought you didn't drive, Mark."

"I just don't like to. I have a car."

"Really. Go on. You drove up there and . . ."

"And I saw the police towing your car out of the way. I was so scared, Emily. I knew you were my only chance. I can't do this any more."

"Do what, Mark? What happened? Tell me the truth."

He lifted his head and wiped at his eyes. "If I tell you, will you give me another chance?"

"Maybe. I need time." Or a frontal lobotomy.

"But you didn't say no."

I couldn't believe how pathetic he looked at that moment. How did Beth or I ever find this man attractive? The thought of Beth made the image of the washroom come to mind. The long row of stalls. The last one next to the window. Beth had stopped me when I started to go down there. There was no toilet paper in the back stalls, she had said. Suddenly it all became terrifyingly clear.

"You were there, in the washroom, weren't you, Mark?"

"Yes," he whispered. "She showed up just after you went over to residence to find her. She wanted to talk to me. She said no one used that washroom."

"She told you then that she knew what was going on, didn't she?"

"Yes. Do you know about the study results she found?" I nodded. "After she found them, she wanted out. When she went to Mullarcant and demanded a letter of recommendation, he told her no way, and that her name would be on all subsequent reports dealing with this study."

"And that's why she was so upset in the lab that day. She knew something very bad was going on. She was probably going to warn Carmen to stay away from Mullarcant that night at the center, wasn't she?"

"I think so," Mark said. "When she found out Carmen was dead, she pieced it together. The next morning she went to Mullarcant."

"The day she died."

"Yes. She told him she was going to the police. And so he . . ."

"What?"

Mark lowered his head again. "He showed her another paper he had just finished. Her name was on it. When she said she didn't want anything more to do with him or the lab, and that she was going to the president and the police, he showed her the tape."

I retraced her steps. After she saw Mullarcant she must have gone to New Beginnings to see Ken. Then at noon she went to her grandmother's store to hide the study results. She didn't tell anyone where she hid them, not even her grandmother. So . . . so she must have been planning to come back for them, I reasoned. Which had to mean that her suicide had been a spur-of-the-moment decision, or—I didn't want to consider the "or" just yet. There were six or seven hours in Beth's day I couldn't account for. What happened between the time Beth left her grandmother's store and when she showed up at the party? What had happened to make her want to kill herself?

"Mullarcant called me and told me what he'd done," Mark was saying. "Beth tried to get hold of me all day. She sat outside my house for hours." Mystery solved.

"Why didn't you talk to her?"

"I couldn't face her. I didn't expect her to come to the party."

Coward.

"But when she did come and wanted to talk to me, I was over-joyed."

"Why, because you figured she believed it was Mullarcant who put you up to making the video?"

"Yes."

"But that wasn't the case, was it, Mark? You were the one who suggested it."

"No. That's not true. He wanted it more than I did. But I knew it was the only way." I felt sick just looking at him. And even sicker at the thought of him touching me and Beth. "In the washroom that night," he went on, "I tried to talk her out of going to the police. I told her Mullarcant would destroy her reputation with the videotape. But she said she didn't care if Mullarcant sent the tape to her father or to anyone else. She said people were dying and she was going to stop it. I tried to protect her. I told her she would ruin her career, my career, everyone's. The research would end. I told her how much I cared about her."

"And did she believe you?"

"Yes. Because it was the truth. She wanted me to come with her to the police. She even said she would tell them it was Mullarcant who bullied us all. And then—" He stopped.

"And then what?"

"You walked in."

I pictured Beth coming out of the last stall. Her nervousness, how anxious she was to see me leave. And me, standing there making small talk, oblivious to the fact that her life was about to end in less than ten minutes.

"Everything would have worked out, Emily, if you hadn't said that I was flirting with you. Damn." He hit the bed with his fist. "If only you hadn't come in there."

I saw Beth's face—the color draining away. "That's when she realized you were the one who suggested making the video. Isn't that right, Mark? That's when she knew you and Mullarcant made a habit of this kind of thing. Right?"

"Don't be mad at me, Emily. I only did it because I had to."

"Did you have to with Christine Stevens too? What did you use back then, Mark? Polaroids?" He didn't answer, he didn't have to, his guilty face was answer enough. "Never mind, what happened in the washroom after I went into a stall, Mark?"

"I heard you go in, so I came out and beckoned her to come back to me. I needed to explain."

"Explain why you were flirting with me? And while we're on the subject, why were you showing interest in me, when you were supposed to be so in love with Beth?"

He kept his eyes on his hands as they worked at the bed quilt. "Because Mullarcant told me to," he mumbled.

"He knew he was going to need a replacement for Beth?"

"He never said. He just told me to do it. But I really do like you, Emily. It wasn't hard."

I was losing my patience. "What happened after I went into the stall?"

"When I saw her face," Mark said, his voice robotic, "I knew she would never believe me. She was putting on lipstick. She wouldn't look at me. Like I wasn't there."

"That's when she must have put the key in my purse."

"She told me she had it and that she was taking it to the police," Mark said, his voice breaking to a whine.

"But after I told her what you were up to, Beth knew she couldn't trust you any more, so she slipped it in my purse, just to be safe. She was probably planning to borrow my purse again later to get it back. But of course she never got the chance, did she, Mark?"

"She was ignoring me. I beckoned her. I couldn't say anything because you were there. When she started back toward me, I turned on the water and the hand dryer so you wouldn't hear."

"So it was you. What didn't you want me to hear, Mark?" I held my breath, fearing my life expectancy might be getting considerably shorter.

"I wasn't going to hurt her, Emily. You have to believe me."

"Then what were you planning to do once she came back to you?"

"Tell her I loved her."

"And did you?"

"Yes."

"But she didn't believe you, did she?"

"She spit in my face."

"Oh." I couldn't imagine polite, quiet Beth doing such a thing, but if she had, I was damn proud of her.

Mark rocked back on his haunches, his eyes fixed on some spot that took him back to that terrible moment. I considered making a break for it. I moved the covers down to my knees, but when I stole a glance in Mark's direction, I noticed his jacket had fallen open to expose a mean, black-handled hunting knife tucked into his belt. I gingerly pulled the covers back up to my neck.

"Then I don't know what happened, Emily," he continued in a monotone. "It all went so fast. My hand was over her mouth. The back of her head was against my chest. I opened the window with my other hand. I scooped her up from behind, like a child. I was lifting her higher. Oh, God. And then . . . and then she was gone."

I was holding my breath. "Oh, Mark. You didn't." The words came out on a gush of air. From the moment I saw him standing at the end of my bed, I knew in my heart that he had done it. But as long as he hadn't actually said it, I still had hope.

"I didn't mean to, Emily. Please, you have to believe me. It was an accident. I lost my head."

"Did you lose your head with Christine Stevens too?" He was still staring off into space. "What happened with Christine, Mark? Did she find out Mullarcant was writing your thesis for you, and that he was using Ken's research?" He nodded. It was a limp, rubber nod. "Was she threatening to tell the president?" I was speaking to him as one might to a child or an insane person who couldn't grasp the meaning or significance of his actions.

"Yes," he said. "She was going to ruin everything. Everything I had worked so hard for."

"You wrote the note, didn't you?" Again the nod.

"And Derrick? Mark, did the same thing happen to him?"

"Yes. Mullarcant called me Tuesday night, late. Said Derrick wasn't doing very well and that he had taken off from Swallow Mountain after the procedure."

"So you weren't in Vancouver." He shook his head. "Did Derrick call you?"

"Yes."

"He trusted you, didn't he? He thought you weren't involved."

"Yes. Derrick told me what happened. And that he found some proof. He said he was going to take it to the police. He found it in Beth's office."

"Oh, so it was Derrick who ransacked Beth's office?"

"Yes."

"But you didn't know he'd been in there until you saw the office that day with me?"

"That's right. He had gone through Mullarcant's office. We didn't know he had been in Beth's too. We couldn't figure out how he got in." I thought guiltily about the key Zac and I kept "hidden" in the assignments box.

"Did it happen the same way it did with Beth?"

A tear rolled down his cheek. "I couldn't reason with him. He was out of his mind. I'm so damn sorry. I'm not like this, Emily. It's Mullarcant. He made me do all these terrible things. It's like our subjects. We're all just part of his grand experiment."

I needed to get out of there and fast. But I spied the black handle of the knife again. "Okay, Mark," I said and placed my hand on his shoulder. Now what was I going to say? That I grant him absolution? "I'm glad you told me this."

"I am too," he said his voice, weak and shaky." We can go away together once this is all cleared up. All you have to do is back me up. Say that I had nothing to do with any of this." He took my hand again. "We really could be happy. We can start over and I can show you the kind of person I really am."

"We are all painfully aware of the kind of person you are, Doctor Gunn." It was Rusty. She was in the doorway holding a cordless phone in one hand and a can of what looked like hairspray in the other. "I have just called the police and told them we

329

have an intruder. You will kindly leave this room and wait quietly downstairs." She said it with such authority I almost believed he would do as he was told. He got to his feet and started moving toward her. I remembered the knife.

"Rusty, he's got a knife," I screamed. Within a heartbeat, he had the weapon out and pressed against my throat. Rusty let out a shriek, and Mark yelled for her to drop what was in her hands and turn her back to us.

I closed my eyes and begged him not to hurt us. He grabbed my arm and lined me up behind Rusty and then led us down the stairs to the main floor. My mind was racing, but my body was capable only of moving when he told it to do so. When we were at the bottom, standing on the cold foyer floor, he rearranged us so that Rusty was in front of him and I in front of Rusty. Mark Gunn had some brains, after all. He knew that placing me in front would ensure I wouldn't try anything for fear of jeopardizing Rusty.

But the fact was, we were both in jeopardy, and I truly believed that the rest of my life and Rusty's amounted to little more than minutes. I couldn't imagine how we were going to get out of this alive. We both knew too much. The same thing was happening to us that had happened to Beth and Christine and Derrick.

"Mark," I said, hoping to stall him long enough for the police to arrive, "maybe we could work this out?"

"You don't lie very well, Emily," he said.

Mark told us to start walking toward the front doors. We moved across the darkened foyer to Rusty's angel sculpture. I said a silent prayer as I came under her wing. It was answered. Out of the corner of my eye I caught a glimpse of Ken. He was moving out of sight and around to the back of the angel in time with our steps. Rusty passed and didn't flinch. We were at the door and I was about to turn the handle when there came the familiar, sickening crack of Ken's trusty bat as it came down on Mark's skull.

I turned as if in slow motion to see Mark Gunn splayed facedown at the foot of our angel. There was blood coming from his ear. Rusty ran to the kitchen and phoned for an ambulance, and I sank to the floor as my legs gave out.

Ken stood over Mark. He was leaning on his bat, with one leg crossed over the other at a jaunty angle, looking for all the world like a star hitter for the Old Timer's Baseball league who had just hit another homer.

"Told you the son of a bitch killed Beth and Christine. And I knew he'd come back for you, kid."

"Thanks, Ken," I said, my voice shaky. "You saved my life."

"Told you I liked you, didn't I?"

"That you did." I narrowed my eyes at him. "How'd you get in?"

"Same way he did," Ken said, indicating to Mark. "You know, kid, you got a lot to learn. And there's a whole lot I'd like to teach you."

"I'm sure there is, Ken. I'm sure there is."

Chapter 30

THREE DAYS LATER, AND AFTER a good long rest, I was standing outside the Anderson apartments, trying to screw up enough courage to press the buzzer. I hadn't called beforehand because I didn't know what I would say over the phone. And as I stood with my finger poised over the button, I wondered what I would say then. I just pressed the buzzer.

He opened the door and stared at me through red-rimmed, sunken eyes.

"I just came to say good-bye. I'm leaving for Banff today," I said. My heart was pounding and the only other thing I could think to say was, "Look, I don't hate you, okay?"

"You should. I hate myself," he said in a flat voice.

"Can I come in?" He held open the door and I ducked under his arm. The place was a mess. Pizza boxes and beer cans, along with ripped-up papers and books, were strewn everywhere.

"Spring cleaning?" I said.

He didn't smile. "So why did you come?"

"I told you. To say good-bye. And to tell you I don't hate you."

"It'd be easier if you did."

"No, it wouldn't. So, got any of that pink tea for me?"

He gave me an exasperated look, and I saw a glimmer of the old Zac. "It's red. That's why it's called *Red Zinger*." He went into the kitchen to fill the kettle. I picked up the blue and yellow Smartie stools from the floor and righted them against the breakfast bar. I took a seat on my favorite yellow one and rested my elbows on the counter.

"Zac, I've been doing a lot of thinking the past couple of days."

He held up his hands to stop me. "I don't want to hear it, okay?"

"But I need you to hear it before I go. Zac, we were both in the same boat with him, and so was Beth." He looked at me doubtfully. "It's true. All that stuff he said about me was true. I went along with him just like everyone else. I was doing stuff I didn't want to be doing, but I did it anyway and that makes me the same."

"No, it doesn't," Zac said, pulling a face. "You didn't sell out on your best friend. I did."

"Zac, it's just a matter of degree. I put a mask on people's faces and filled their lungs with gas because I was told to."

"What else were you supposed to do?"

"Find another area to work in. Say no, whatever ... just not do it."

"Or maybe jump out a window?" he said. "Or better yet, get yourself thrown out of a window."

"All I'm saying is that I could have thought things through a little more. That's all. So what's going to happen to you now?"

"I don't know. Mullarcant's been charged with murder, as I'm sure you already know. Oakes and Sandra Penny have been charged with accessory. And Mark is still in the hospital. Your friend Ken has a mean swing."

"He does indeed. Is your noggin okay?"

"Oh yeah. I have a pretty thick head. And it looks like Mark's going to be okay too. Well, until they charge him with Beth's and Derrick's murder and Christine's. By the way, who was she?"

"Mullarcant's grad student, back in the late seventies. She was also Mark's girlfriend, one of them, at any rate."

"What was all the stuff Mullarcant was saying about Ken sleeping with her?"

"Mark just made it look like that." I filled him in on the details about how Mark had been Ken's student and how he ended up moving over to Mullarcant.

"I didn't know Mark did his graduate work at USA."

"Neither did I. Technically he didn't. Mullarcant did it for him, using Ken's research."

"Really? Was Ken drinking back then?"

"Oh yeah. But he apparently functioned well enough. That is, until the president let Mark off the hook for falsifying data and Mullarcant started lobbying to get rid of Ken."

"I'm surprised other faculty members didn't blow the whistle on Mullarcant when he stole Ken's research."

"Mullarcant and Ken had agreed to collaborate. But Ken was a drinker, don't forget. Who are they going to believe?"

"And since Christine was making whoopee with Mark, she knew what was going on," Zac said.

"Exactly, Christine knew Mullarcant was doing Mark's work, and she saw what was happening to Ken, so she threatened to blow the whistle."

"But Mark put a stop to that."

"Right, by taking a few dirty snap shots of her. Mullarcant, in turn, tried to blackmail her with the pictures just like he did later with Beth. When that didn't work, Mark threw her off the Admin building."

Zac let out a soft whistle. "Wow. The guy must have ice in his veins. And this is where the note comes in?"

"Yes. It was perfect timing. Mullarcant was trying to get Ken fired anyway. So after he does the dreadful deed, Mark types up a note on Christine's behalf, saying she can't live without Ken and blah, blah, blah. He presents the note to Mullarcant, who gleefully takes it to the president, who, in turn, does the Academic-Turn-a-Blind-Eye Two Step, and files the note away."

"So Mullarcant never knew what Mark had done?"

"You saw him yourself at Swallow Mountain. Be pretty hard to fake the surprise I saw in his face. But even if he had known, or suspected, I don't think he would have cared one way or the other."

"And Ken never knew about the note?"

"Nope."

"What about Marjorie from New Beginnings, was she working for Mullarcant?"

"Sort of. He was giving her money to select likely candidates for the study and to keep her mouth shut. I don't think she knew what was really going on. But what about you, Zac?"

"Oh, I don't know. They're still trying to decide what to do with me. I told them everything, Em. I admitted to all of it. But they keep trying to tell me I was a victim or something. And that's crap. I knew what I was doing. All I wanted was that fucking degree, so I could really be somebody. Well, I'm sure somebody now. I'm a fucking loser." He hung his head and kicked at a mangled textbook on the floor. "I don't know what happened, Em. It's like I was going along and everything was fine. And then the next thing I know, I find this despicable side to myself."

"Maybe we all have a despicable side, and it just takes the right or wrong situation to bring it out."

"Well, this sure was the ticket."

"But you know, Zac, I think it's equally true that most of us have a good side. And if we're lucky enough, we'll be in the right place at the right time for it to come out."

"Pity I wasn't able to seize the opportunity," he said bitterly.

"But you did, Zac. You did grab it. In the end, you did the right thing." He was about to protest. I put my hand up to stop him. "Ken told me what you did. Maybe it took you a bit longer, but the important thing is you tried to stop him and help us. Zac you were scared, I understand that. I was scared too." He stared at me for a long time until his face creased with emotion. I went into the kitchen and put my arms out to him. We hung on to each other and wept.

ON MY WAY HOME, I stopped by New Beginnings to drop off some kid's books, diapers, and clothes. The new director met me in the foyer and thanked me for everything I had done. Then I went to the hospital to check on Irene. She was doing fine and would be released the next day.

And Ken, she informed me, was at the Royal York, celebrating her recovery. I asked her to say good-bye and to thank him for me. I would have told him myself, but I wanted to remember him the way he had been at Swallow Mountain and at Rusty's. I didn't tell Irene this, but she seemed to understand. I thanked her, and told her I was going to miss them all and to send my regards to Mick. Before I left, I gave her Rusty's phone number and told her Rusty was waiting for her to call if she, Ken, and Mick wanted any help.

I packed up the rest of my things, and Rusty and I shared a tearful farewell with promises to visit soon. Then I set out on the highway. It was a bright Alberta day. The deep cerulean sky was cloudless, and the Rocky Mountains were so sharp and clear they looked too perfect to be real, as though someone had painted a backdrop and spread it across the horizon. It had snowed the night before, and the farmers' fields and the big round bales of hay were covered in a soft blanket of sugary-white down. Just after the Cochrane turn-off, I pulled off to the side of the road and walked to the guardrail. I breathed in the fresh, crisp air and took in the expanse of land that stretched beyond the foothills to the base of the Rockies, and I never felt freer in my life.

"... even when the destructive effects of their work become patently clear, and they are asked to carry out actions incompatible with fundamental standards of morality, relatively few people have the resources needed to resist authority."

—Stanley Milgram

Epilogue

Six months after I moved to Banff, I received this letter from Ken.

Hi Kid,

How are things going in Banff? Sorry I missed you when you left. Mick's doing okay but he's still going to be in for a while yet.

You'll never guess who got in touch with me, my daughter Donna. Can't remember if I told you about her or not. Anyway, she saw my picture in the paper when everything came out, and she asked me and Irene to move to Red Deer. Sort of a new start.

Irene's happy to be out of the city, and we're closer to Mick. I'm doing a bit of farming. Nothing too serious, just a weekend thing. The College here is hounding me to teach a couple of classes, but I'm not too comfortable in big groups. I'll see if I can talk them into letting me teach a seminar or something in the coffee shop.

I know what you're thinking, and the answer is no. I'm

not drinking so much these days. Smacking that bastard Gunn and seeing Mullarcant finally get what's been coming to him kind of gave me a lift.

Anyway, Irene says hi and so does Mick. Say hi to Rusty for us and tell her thanks again. Hope everything is going okay for you and you're staying out of trouble. Maybe we'll come up to the mountains for a visit sometime with the grand kids.

Regards,
Ken

author photo by Michelle Leoppky

Eileen Coughlan has had a varied past that includes a degree in psychology, a master's in communications, and a vast array of different jobs. Eileen was born in Fairview, Alberta, grew up in Edmonton and now lives in Calgary.